THE
NIGHTBLOOD
PRINCE

THE
NIGHTBLOOD
PRINCE

MOLLY X. CHANG

RANDOM HOUSE NEW YORK

Random House Books for Young Readers
An imprint of Random House Children's Books
A division of Penguin Random House LLC
1745 Broadway, New York, NY 10019
penguinrandomhouse.com
GetUnderlined.com

Editor: Tricia Lin
Cover Designers: Liz Dresner and Casey Moses
Interior Designer: Ken Crossland
Production Editor: Clare Perret
Managing Editor: Rebecca Vitkus
Production Manager: Natalia Dextre

Library of Congress Cataloging-in-Publication Data is available upon request.
ISBN 978-0-593-89736-2 (trade) — ISBN 978-0-593-89738-6 (ebook)

The text of this book is set in 12-point Garamond Premier.

Manufactured in China
10 9 8 7 6 5 4 3 2

The authorized representative in the EU for product safety and compliance is Penguin Random House Ireland, Morrison Chambers, 32 Nassau Street, Dublin D02 YH68, Ireland, https://eu-contact.penguin.ie.

To those who seek solace between ink and paper

and live a thousand lives as heroes and villains

and everything in between.

I write to help you escape, always.

PROLOGUE

I was born in the midnight crevice between two lunar years.

When fireworks shattered the star-woven sky, it drowned out my first cries. Sadly, not enough to disturb the divine fate uttered a thousand miles away behind palace walls.

A fallen goddess who bears the phoenix's mark is destined to rule a united An'Lu.

A curse disguised as a prophecy that ignited a want so violent inside our great emperor, it engulfed the land by sunrise.

He ordered the girl to be found and brought to him, and three days later, they found me under the roof of a seventh-ranked minister in a forgotten corner of the empire with the phoenix's mark bloodred between my brows.

"If anyone is to be the empress of a united continent, she can only be the Empress of Rong and rule from the arm of my son," the emperor announced to his court days later. His eyes were stained with tears as he cradled an infant close to his chest.

A baby boy born between the same lunar years as I was. The only surviving child of his beloved empress, who took her last breath when her son drew his first.

Rumors had it those gilded halls echoed with my scream when the emperor tied a blessed red string of fate between my and Prince Si-wang's stubby infant fingers.

"With her prophecy at Siwang's side," the emperor exulted, "my son will achieve what the ancestors before us could not: unite the continent and finally bring peace to these lands!"

The court roared in cheers and applause; no one dared to object to the emperor's fantasies of victory and glory.

Except me, whose cries refused to quiet.

PART ONE

The Empress
Promised by the Stars

1

I spent my life trapped behind crimson walls, inside this palace where I could dance along golden hallways and grand pavilions and do everything I wanted—except leave.

You are the future empress. You need to be protected, my father reminded me on the last day of each moon.

Since I wasn't allowed to leave the palace without written permission from the emperor, this was the only day of each month when my parents were allowed to spend rare hours with me.

We often wandered the peony gardens, took leisurely strolls along the koi ponds, and exchanged pleasantries at my pavilion on the rainy days when we could not find other distractions to fill our silence. I had so much to say. I yearned to hug them and laugh with them like a normal daughter, but not under the surveilling eyes of the palace ladies who were here to monitor my every move, not just wait at my beck and calls.

Their eyes were always watching, ears always listening.

When my parents asked me about my days, I forced smiles and

pretended I was happy. I in turn asked about their days as if I didn't have their lives told to me like soft-spun folklore by the servant girls whose favorite pastime was gossiping about the capital's families. Brief rays of sunshine against the vast gray of the palace life.

From my gilded cage, I listened with envy about how my sister was growing up and how my parents were aging. I listened with envy about my parents' nosy neighbors, the noble ladies with whom Mother played tiles, the ministers who disputed with Father, and the men who were asking for my older sister's hand.

For I didn't want to hear about that life. I wanted to live it.

But I was the future Empress of Rong before I was my parents' daughter.

Their words were always few and shallow and their smiles were tense, ever so polite. My parents bowed when they greeted me, and bowed when they said their farewells.

My parents didn't know how to talk to the future empress, who was torn from their arms before I was old enough to be off my mother's milk.

I did not know what to say, either. Especially to my father.

Seventeen years, and I could not remember a single moment spent with them when I had not felt like a stranger on the outside, looking in.

A child stolen, raised by servants who knew only to kneel and beg for forgiveness when I cried for my mother, father, and sister.

A girl whose only purpose was to marry a boy because the stargazer claimed I was destined to rule over a united Warring States. But if I was chosen by the gods and destined to rule, then why did visions of bloodshed and calamity haunt me every time I closed my eyes?

2

Premonition tingled at the edge of my senses.

A quick vision, a pulling instinct.

I foresaw the moment before I experienced it.

Magic.

I would have reached for my bow, if not for Father's warning.

The first kill is not yours to claim.

3

Nobody cheered when Prince Yexue's arrow claimed the first kill of the season.

The forest held its breath, waiting to see how Siwang would react.

Though Lan Yexue, too, was a prince, he was not a prince of Rong.

To put it kindly, Yexue was a ward sent here by his uncle, to be educated by our great empire.

To put it bluntly, he was a prisoner sent from one of our many tribute states, to be kept on a leash in case his uncle, the current Regent of Lan, dared to rebel.

A prince in name only, unworthy of claiming the first kill.

After two years in the Rong court, surviving under enemy roofs, Prince Yexue *should* have understood 人在屋檐下不得不低头. *When living under the mercy of another, one must bow one's head.*

"Is no one going to congratulate me?" Prince Yexue jumped from his horse to examine the prize, not an ounce of fear weighing down his tone.

How princely of him: ignoring what was expected of him to do what he wanted.

Jealousy rattled.

Prince Yexue of Lan was a boy of sculpted angles and porcelain skin. Thick brows, sharp jaw, and the kind of doe-brown eyes that made even the most proper of daughters lose their wits. To make it worse, he was also tall, towering over almost everyone with the exception of Siwang.

All that beauty, and the kind of arrogant, rebellious streak that only princes were allowed to have—no wonder he'd caused a frenzy when he arrived at the capital two years ago. Every maiden had swooned at the sight of him—and so had a handful of the imperial concubines and the city's noble sons. Rumor had it that half the court had tried to marry their besotted daughters off to him, despite his crumbling kingdom and uncertain fate.

Visitors from across the continent came to Yong'An, and the city had met plenty of beautiful faces before, though never one quite as haunting. Lan Yexue's heavenly face was almost enough to make the court overlook his odd name and forget those swirling rumors of dark magic that his family practiced, and how his ancestors were the once-cruel southern rulers who had almost driven Siwang's ancestors to extinction hundreds of years ago.

Empires rise and empires fall. Now Yexue's country was our tribute state, and their beautiful prince was our ward.

"You have a sharp eye." Tension eased slightly when Siwang finally cracked a smile.

"I've had practice," Prince Yexue replied, his voice cold as the frozen terrain surrounding. "Not everyone can be the pampered heir to the most powerful empire in the land with nothing to fear and nothing to want."

Caikun, the son of a first-ranked general and Siwang's personal guard, grimaced. His hand rested on his sword, his eyes on Siwang, waiting for a signal to strike.

Other lips twisted into half smiles, including mine. It wasn't every day that someone had the courage to make fun of our beloved crown prince, however foolish it was.

This hunting party of fur coats and leather riding boots and bows decorated with gold and silver and bedazzling jewels comprised some of our empire's most powerful heirs. The children of generals, first-ranked ministers, and the wealthy merchants whose coffers filled the imperial treasury and funded our never-ending campaigns to claim more land, more power.

All in the name of my prophecy.

The one thing these heirs had in common, besides status and wealth and gleaming gold spoons hanging from their mouths?

Their compulsion to worship the ground Siwang walked on as if their lives depended on it.

Because in a way, they did.

君要臣死臣不得不死. *If the emperor wanted a subject dead, the subject must die.*

Regardless of status, name, or who their fathers were, all their lives were delicate porcelain to Siwang, suspended on silk cords. If Siwang wished, he could make any or all of us fall to a death of ten thousand shattered pieces. Including me—even if he would never admit it, even if the entire court thought otherwise.

I was the empress-to-be, but an empress still had to bend to the will of a man.

"The imperial hunt doesn't officially start until tomorrow," I interjected before this could escalate. "This is an outing of leisure, and a chance for us to scout out the terrain before we hunt the bigger prizes tomorrow."

Though Siwang's jaw ticked with slight annoyance, the smile that followed was easy, charming, as princes were taught to be. "May the best man kill the first Beiying tiger tomorrow and bask in *true* glory."

Yexue's lips twitched, though it looked more like a sneer than a smirk. "May the best man," he echoed.

My gaze shifted to the fallen stag, a small thing not yet old enough to grow a full set of antlers or shed all its baby fur. The shot had gone straight through its eye to preserve the beautiful pelt. Crimson blood bloomed against the white snow, like winter roses. Like forlorn warnings.

Despite having sensed the stag before both princes, I hadn't reached for my arrows. Because Father would have scolded me if I had.

Girls were not here to win prizes. Our job was to exist in docile and delicate beauty, while princes like Siwang basked in glory and admiration. Or so everyone had told me.

These visions need to stay secret, I reminded myself for the ten thousandth time.

Magic had not existed on our continent for hundreds of years. If the emperor ever found out that I possessed visions of the future, he would deem it a sign that the prophecy was true and that these visions were bestowed upon me so that I could help Siwang in his wars.

For in his eyes, I existed only to serve the ambitions of his son.

If I was really a fallen goddess, destined to bestow my husband with glory, why did I dream only of bloodshed and a capital in flames, never glory?

I cast a long look at the snowy mountains. Somewhere deep within this terrain hid Beiying tigers with their coveted snow-white fur and midnight-blue stripes that glistened in the light. They were twice as big as regular tigers and three times as strong. Legend had it that they were beasts created by the gods themselves during one of the heavenly wars and left forgotten in the mortal realm.

They were the most dangerous animals to roam these lands—other than humans.

If I could track one down, soak my hands with its blood, and offer its pelt to the emperor, I might be able to reclaim my destiny once and for all.

Or die trying.

"Let's go!" Siwang called as he kicked his horse, Beifeng, into motion. "The day is still young, and I refuse to believe this is the only stag in this entire forest."

I was about to follow when I felt something burning at the edge of my senses. Not a vision. I looked up and caught Lan Yexue staring at me.

I did not flinch from his gaze, nor did I look away like some chaste maiden who had never felt the fever of a man's attention. Too many men looked at me, with and without the phoenix's mark. Especially after my monthly bleedings came, after my chest began to swell and my hips filled out.

I knew lust. Saw it in the faces of both men and boys. How their eyes lingered a little too long when Siwang wasn't around. How they licked their lips and hovered close like I was an object their hands itched to touch, or to take. Men like those made me want to cover every inch of my body and never step outside.

But if I did that, if I looked away and hid every time I caught someone staring, I would have to spend a lifetime hidden from sight, with only the the silk screens and lacquered walls of my pavilion for company.

Having men stare at me wasn't a surprising occurrence. What surprised me was that Prince Yexue did not look away when I caught him. And what sparked behind those eyes was something other than lust, something sharper.

Curiosity?

I kicked my horse into a trot before Siwang caught this temporary moment.

4

My earliest memories were of the questions I'd asked my father.

What use is power, without freedom? What good is the life of an empress if she is a prisoner chained by rules and tradition and others' opinions?

Questions my father didn't know how to answer.

Questions he said were dangerous beyond my years and told me never to repeat, not to Siwang and certainly not to anyone who might relay them to the emperor.

Fate chose you as the future empress of the Warring States, he'd whispered. *Your destiny was appointed by the gods themselves. Mortals cannot defy the will of the gods, Fei. If you try to outrun the path the gods have blessed you with, you will risk their love turning into wrath.*

If this was *my* life, *my* body, shouldn't *I* get a say in what happened to it, and how I wanted to live?

Why should gods and emperors be the ones to decide *my* fate?

Why should my voice sound the quietest in this crowded room of men, set on dictating every aspect of my existence?

Who gave them the right?

My hundreds of questions boiled and fumed like tiny sparks hungry to be set ablaze.

5

"Are you not going to praise me?" Siwang whispered when he came by my stall after we arrived back at the stables.

"For what? For tolerating someone else killing the first stag of the season?" I replied, making sure to be quiet so the other riders couldn't hear us. "It's not easy, being raised so far from his family and home."

Siwang's eyes softened. He knew my scars better than anyone.

His hand brushed my back, pulled me to him for a small hug. "When we are married, I will ask my father to let your family visit my palace anytime they want."

His palace.

Siwang's eyes gleamed as he said this, as if expecting my gratitude. He meant well, but he was still a prince.

I forced a smile, didn't tell him that I shouldn't have to ask for his permission in order to see my family. This was the way of men. As daughters, we were the property of our fathers. As wives, we were the property of our husbands. And one day, if we ever outlived our husbands, we would become the property of our sons.

Whether empress or peasant, we women were never our own.

"Look at the lovebirds," a young man with short-cropped hair and a scar across his right cheek said, laughing. An heir from one of our tribute states, someone insignificant because I didn't know his name. "How much longer are you making him wait, empress of all empresses? Weren't the two of you supposed to get married last year?"

Siwang positioned his body in front of me and gave what must have been a scowl, because the young man quickly bowed his head and murmured, "Apologies, Your Highness."

A motion of Siwang's head. The onlookers around the stable quickly disappeared.

He turned toward me. "Don't listen to them."

Another forced smile from me. "He's not the only one asking when we will get married. We are not children anymore, and will turn eighteen when the year ends."

The emperor would set a date for our wedding sooner or later. He was simply waiting for an auspicious occasion. If Siwang impressed the court by killing a Beiying tiger two years in a row, it would be the perfect opportunity to officially offer me to him like a prize.

"We will get married when *you* want us to get married."

"Not when your father wants us to be married?"

"I will handle him." Siwang's hand brushed my cheek, as if to reassure me.

Siwang had kept his promise and delayed our wedding year by year, waiting until I was ready. His father, however, was not so patient. The emperor wanted his son to claim the continent, and he wanted the prophecy to be sealed. Every day that I was not wed, our power-hungry neighbors eyed me and my prophecy as something that could be stolen.

A cold draft swept in through the stable doors, bringing with it a gusting of snow. "I have to go," I said. "I need to get changed before the feast tonight."

"I will walk you back to your tent."

"No. It's fine. I think I need some quiet after the chaos of today."

If Siwang was hurt by this, he didn't let it show. He nodded and stepped aside so I could leave the stall.

—❦—

On the long walk through camp, back to my tent, I passed men. Unfamiliar faces, dressed in lavish furs, likely nobles from one of Rong's tribute states.

Their eyes went wide when they saw me, or perhaps when they saw the phoenix's mark between my brows. A swirl of stark red, supposedly in the shape of a phoenix in flight, though I always thought it resembled more a sideways eye.

"The fallen goddess, promised to be the empress of all empresses . . . ," one whispered behind his hand, though not quietly enough.

"Or a country bumpkin, brought to the court as a child bride," another said, giggling.

"Amazing how one mark can change someone's life. 想不到一只山鸡都能飞上枝头变凤凰." *I can't believe even a mountain chicken can fly to a high branch and become a phoenix.*

I picked up my pace. I had heard insults like these my whole life. I didn't need to hear what would follow those words.

How do we know she's not some peasant with a strange birthmark?

Why would a goddess reincarnate as a peasant girl from the middle of nowhere?

I almost wished I had taken Siwang's offer to walk me back. At least when he was with me, nobody dared to look at me like this, or to be so careless with their whispers.

When Siwang was around, the girls hid their faces behind fans or handkerchiefs, always too busy looking modestly at the ground to notice me. And the men bowed their heads, as quiet as the girls.

In life, not everyone was created equal. I had known this for as long as I could remember. People were treated differently because of which region of the empire they hailed from, and which family they descended from. It wasn't until much later, in the imperial classrooms with Siwang and the other noble children, that I learned even children of the same father were not created equal.

Lijian was one of those sons: born of the mistress instead of the official wife, forever treated as an afterthought in his family and by our teachers, despite being the smartest person in every room. For this, people treated him like an outsider.

I guess that gave us something in common.

I liked talking to him. He was nice, funny, and he was patient enough to explain the poetry I didn't understand in the classroom.

But when Siwang caught Lijian and me sitting beside each other in the corner of the library three years ago, giggling about something I can no longer remember, sharing the red bean cakes he had the imperial chefs make for me each morning, it was the first time I realized Siwang had a dark side.

I had never seen him lose his temper like that.

Nobody from the capital had seen Lijian since. And perhaps nobody would again.

This wasn't the first time that Siwang had punished someone for getting too close to me. However, it was the first time he had banished someone from the capital.

Siwang was like the sun scholars said the continent revolved around. His kindness was light. When he shone upon you, everything was warm and dripping in gold. The moment that kindness turned away, the absence of him was a bitter darkness unlike anything else.

The court fought for his light. Father said I should curry his favor, too. For the more Siwang cared for me, the easier my life would be. . . . The easier everyone's life would be

But what if I didn't want his light? What if I wanted to be my own light?

—⚭—

When I pushed open the heavy sheepskin of my tent and saw my sister pacing inside with fevered strides, I nearly turned around and offered my body back to the winter wilderness like a sacrifice.

However, Fangyun caught me before I could spin on my heels.

"Fei." My name rang out in the cold air like a plea.

I turned, saw Fangyun's fingers clasped in knots. Fear gleamed in her eyes like freshly shed tears.

I let the sheepskin fall behind me, holding in a nervous exhale. I wished I had hidden my hunting manuals better when she visited me. "I have made up my mind; nothing you can say will change it."

"Not everything needs to be a fight," my sister hissed under her breath. I flinched, like I'd been struck. "You have a good life, Fei. You are betrothed to a *good* prince, who loves you. Sometimes—"

"You are supposed to be on my side, Fangyun."

While a chasm divided me from my parents, Fangyun was different. She was my sister, was granted special privileges to enter the palace and study alongside me and the noble kids. Though our time together was always too short, it was still more hours than I got with our parents. Even if we spent most of it sitting in silence, listening to the scholars lecture us about the poems of dead men.

"What's so bad about marrying Siwang?" Fangyun asked. When I didn't respond, she sighed and reached out so that her warm hands cradled my cold ones, bringing them close to her lips so she could blow warm air on them. "I told you to wear gloves when you go hunting. Your hands are freezing!"

Last night's nightmare flashed behind my eyes.

Fire.

Screams.

Yong'An in flames.

My sister, running, running, running. Her robes were torn and she was crying and—

I blinked it away.

"Fei, are you all right?"

You don't know the things I've seen, sister, I desperately wanted to tell her. *You don't know what I know.* "Just a little cold from the hunt."

My sister's demeanor immediately softened. "The Beiying tigers are *predators*. Great hunters have died for their pelts. What makes you think the pampered prince's bride who is raised in the palace by servants and protected by guards can accomplish the impossible? Even if you succeed, can you be sure the emperor will grant your wish?"

"君子一言驷马难追," I replied. *What is said cannot be unsaid, the words of an honorable man cannot be chased down by the fastest of horses.*

"If an emperor goes back on one promise, then all his promises will become worthless."

"But your prophecy is not a fast horse. It is the promise of uniting the continent for his son."

My lips thinned. She was right; I didn't know if the emperor would honor his promise. However, I could not sit idle and wait for death and destruction to sweep Yong'An. A prophecy was just words, strung together. If my fate was written in the stars, then I would fly up to heaven and rewrite it.

When Siwang had taught me combat, I could predict his every move through my visions, and if I moved accordingly, I could change the outcome, every time. A swipe of his feet that would knock me off balance in my visions would be met with nothing, because I knew to move out of the way. What if the stargazer's visions worked the same?

I could not turn back time and keep the prophecy from being spoken. However, I did have command over the present that controlled what would happen tomorrow. Time was a river that flowed endless. And with persistence, water could break stones. If I tried hard enough, I could change the future and save my city from ruin.

"The imperial hunt is too sacred, and the tradition of granting whoever catches the first Beiying tiger of the hunt a wish of their choice has been around for hundreds of years. The emperor can go back on his words; he cannot go back on tradition."

The imperial hunt was held in the days leading up to the winter solstice, to honor Rong's northern roots. It was a way to pay respect to the ancestors who had survived through hunting and gathering for hundreds of years when Rong was still a small tribute state to the larger, wealthier empires of the south.

As our society develops, and our empire prospers, we must not forget where we came from. The austere times when the only way to fill our bellies was by the mercy of the land or by killing with our bare hands . . . were words the emperor uttered at each hunt. So that both the Rong dynasty and its people would never forget how lucky we were, to live in a time of plenty, when agriculture and farming filled our bowls with rice and vegetables and all the meat we could pray for.

During the Century of Great Winter, the Rong dynasty's ancestral lands froze over and they were surrounded on all sides. Its people had to bow to the neighboring nations and assimilate to their ways to survive; they'd lost so much in that time.

Their culture.

Their names.

Their language.

So what little they had left of their ancestors, they clung to with both hands.

The hunt wasn't just a way to honor their ancestors' struggles, though. It was an important military exercise for the empire's top soldiers. This was a place for men to show off their martial skills, for warriors to 出人头地. *To stand out among their peers and rise above their stations overnight.*

If you could impress the emperor on the hunting ground, it didn't matter which family you descended from, which region you hailed from, whether you were of noble blood or a serf.

The emperor valued true talent above inconsequential things such as name and status and family. If one could prove their worth to the emperor, they'd be rewarded. And nothing impressed the emperor more than the king of these snowy mountains. The legendary Beiying tiger: the most coveted prize of every hunt. Many had died for its pelt, and as long as the world had desperate souls who wished for more, many would continue to die.

Last winter was the first time in almost three years that someone had killed a Beiying tiger at the hunt.

The hero who'd slain it? None other than the empire's favorite prince.

And Siwang, that fool, had wasted the wish on flattery. *I wish for the continued expansion and prosperity of Rong. So that one day our continent might finally know peace, as our ancestors had always dreamt.*

Words that had moved the emperor to tears.

Save the wish for something else, my son, the emperor replied. *Something more selfish, something you want not for our mighty empire, but for yourself. It doesn't matter what it is. Anything under heaven, I will give to you. Even if you ask for the blood of the gods, I will give it to you.*

I grimaced at the memory.

"Is it really worth it, Fei?" my sister continued to ask. "Do you know how rare it is for a man to adore his betrothed the way Siwang adores you?"

"To be loved and doted on by one's husband should be a basic necessity, not something to be admired," I shot back, then realized how condescending I sounded.

Most girls did not have the luxury of choice. All they had were their fathers' wishes, and the coins their husbands paid for them.

"So many girls would cut off their right hand to be Siwang's bride. And you're going to let it all go to waste, for what?"

So that everyone might live a long and happy life, I wanted to tell her Fangyun had not witnessed the horrors of my nightmares, had not watched everyone she had ever met die a hundred times, over and over again each time she closed her eyes.

I couldn't tell her the visions, so I gave her a half-truth. "I want a life beyond the palace walls, and to do more with my life than be a wife and a mother. If I must die for that kind of life, then I will."

"You're going to break Siwang's heart. When tributes arrive from our conquered regions, he always sends the best silks and the most lavish jewels to you. Do you remember how last year, he ordered ten men to take the fastest horses to ride from southern Lan back to Yong'An in just five days, so he could bestow you the freshest lychees for your birthday?"

"Those gifts mean nothing to him. He's the Crown Prince of Rong: he can have all the silk and fancy rocks his heart desires. Just because he gives me pretty things, it doesn't mean he loves me."

"Fei'er, you—"

"Siwang *assumes* I like silk and jewels." I cut her off before she could finish, because I knew what she was going to say. It was the same thing Mother and Father had said when I begged them to end the betrothal and let me come home. *Fei'er, you are so ungrateful.* "Did you know three stallions died for his little escapade, and for what? A few dozen pieces of fruit that tasted only a little sweeter?"

Fangyun went quiet, and I sighed. *It's not ladylike to lose one's temper.*

"The inner palace is not the paradise everyone believes it to be. You have not been smothered by its rules or heard the cries that ring through the night. Even the concubines of noble birth cannot escape an emperor's wrath. What makes you think a girl like me can survive?"

Lips parted, my sister looked like she wanted to push for more, then held herself back. If I wanted to tell her, she would not have to ask or pry these morsels of truth from me.

Siwang might be sweet to me now, but I had seen beautiful maidens come and go in his father's harem, watched them wander the gardens like ghosts, covered in pale balm and cosmetics to hide their bruises; always so beautifully made up and quiet . . . and *scared.*

Love and hate were two sides of the same coin. For men like Siwang, the only thing more dangerous than his hate was his love. To unsuspecting eyes, Siwang was a dream too beautiful and perfect to be true. Pristine in his silk robes the color of midnight, easily swallowing the crimson of all the blood that stained his hands.

"What if the thing Siwang loves isn't me, but the prophecy?" My loudest fear, uttered in the quietest whisper.

Anger drained from my sister's eyes as they misted with something akin to pity. "Marrying Siwang would bring honor to our house." She echoed the words Father had repeated a thousand times before, like a shackle wrapped tight around my ankles, weighing on me heavily each time I thought of running. "You have the dream of ten thousand maidens in the palm of your hand. As the Empress of Rong, you'll have ev—"

"Everything except the ability to leave." Something bubbled at the hollow of my throat, and I swallowed it. I would not cry. Not in front of Fangyun. "What use is all the wealth and luxury if my world is confined to a prison they decorate as a palace? If I have nothing to do but sit and read and embroider while I wait for Siwang to visit me? Which might happen once a week in the beginning, then maybe once a month, then once a year when he's filled his harem with beauties from every corner of the continent. Girls he chose for himself or who were pushed upon him by the ministers and tribute states who wish to see one of their own on the throne of Rong one day."

"This is the life girls have endured for centuries, sister, we—"

"What if I don't want to endure? The world is so much bigger than the palace or that gossipy, backstabbing city we call the capital, or even

Rong! Have you ever thought about all the things out there that we haven't seen or heard or tasted or felt? The kinds of delights scholars write poems about? All the beauty that inspires artists to pick up their brushes and create masterpieces between strokes? The kinds of delights that add color and flavor to your life, the kind of wonder that makes each day worth living . . . The kinds of things we'll never get to experience because men expect us to never leave our homes, so that we can be pretty and filial and chaste and all the ideals that keep us prisoners in our own bodies?"

My sister's eyes softened further. She came closer and put an arm around me.

We sat at the edge of my bed in silence. It didn't matter how many times Father had Fangyun recite his careful lectures; my sister understood why I had to do this.

She had no quarrel with my plan, or what I wanted. It was just . . .

"It's too dangerous, Fei'er."

It always came back to this. "I can do this."

"You could die."

"If I die, at least there would be no more wars fought in the name of my prophecy. Our neighbors would cease to attack our borders to claim me as their own symbol of power. Perhaps that would be a better future for all of us. Perhaps with my death, the continent—"

Fangyun pressed her finger to my lips, to keep me from uttering more of the unspeakable. "You will not die, my sister." She pulled something from her sleeve. "Take this with you. Give me some peace of mind, at least."

She handed me a jeweled dagger with a handle made of ivory and a sheath carved from gold. Extravagant swirls of feathers and flowers, gathering around a phoenix in flight. "This was your birthday gift, but since you insist on bargaining with Death, I shall give it to you now. I hope it can protect you when I cannot."

A riptide pushed at my eyes, relief prickling like needles. "Yun'er..."

"They will notice if you are not at the feast tonight."

"I will leave after I have shown my face."

"That's good." Fangyun turned away, blinking back her own tears. "Try not to die."

I laughed, and my eyes wandered to the silver-tipped battle bow, one of a pair that Siwang had made for us during the last hunt.

One for him, and one for me.

"I'll do my best."

6

"A toast, to victory!" A voice broke the buzzing chatter and crack-ling flames. Cheers followed. Sweet winter wine spilled from raised cups, trickling down the delicate hands of Rong's most revered heirs, all hubris and greed, coated over bitter resentment and centuries of blood debts between dynasties. Each boy was posturing, angling to be the most important person in the room after Siwang. And while the girls flashed hints of demure smiles behind their sleeves, I knew they were as ambitious as the boys.

The feasts held before the hunt were always small and intimate—as intimate as any feasts with a hundred guests and twice as many ser-vants could get, at least.

This year was busier than most. The emperor had invited guests from every tribute state to witness our empire's military talents. To re-mind them that if any of them dared to rebel, this was what they would go up against.

And while the emperor held court with the adults to discuss more delicate politics, it was Siwang's responsibility to entertain their children.

I had overheard the emperor tell Siwang: *They are the future of your empire, son. Get to know them, build relationships, most of all, seek out their weaknesses and let them know you are the alpha. You are power. You are the heir of the greatest empire this continent will ever see. Be human, be charming, but don't let any of them forget who you are.*

Fifty-something young adults, from teens to early twenties, sat organized in two rows of low tables positioned along the fire pits, where the empire's finest cooks sweated over sizzling meats and seasoned stews. Delicacies brought from every corner of the empire, expertly crafted concoctions of flavors served on golden plates.

How far the Rong dynasty had come since impoverished winters and being bullied by the southern warlords.

Without the supervision of parents, the air was light, the conversation abundant, and the laughter louder. However, this was not an innocent gathering. This was a game of power.

Siwang sat at the head of the formation, atop a dais that elevated him above the rest of us.

The girls threw longing looks, and so did the men. His favor was what they all sought. A prize more precious than even the Beiying tiger. And the closer someone sat to Siwang, the higher they were in this hierarchy.

"How do you like the food, Fei?" Siwang asked. While the room watched him, his eyes were on me, seated at the table to his immediate left.

I stopped pushing the thin cuts of cabbage and mutton around the plate and forced a sweet smile for him. My stomach was nauseated with nerves, and the only things that looked appetizing were the lamb skewers being smoked over the fires, sprinkled with cumin and chili flakes and drizzled with oil so that every bite would be juicy and flavorful. My favorite, which just happened to be one of the many things deemed too unladylike for noble girls to eat in public. And the meat didn't taste the same once they were torn from their skewers and served in bowls. The satisfaction was in ripping it from the skewer with my teeth.

"Congratulations to our empire!" someone cheered from farther down the tables in a naked attempt to get Siwang's attention. "Fulin is the last major stronghold of the northwest. All that's left between us and the barren ice lands are a few puny dynasties whose armies are no more than glorified farmers. Soon Rong will rule over the great north without contest! And Your Highness will be one step closer to fulfilling the prophecy as the emperor of all emperors!"

"The emperor of all emperors!" another voice cheered in response.

"The emperor of all emperors!"

"The emperor of all emperors!"

"The emperor of all emperors!"

That is not the prophecy, I wanted to remind them.

"To the greatest army in all of An'Lu!" Someone else raised his cup of wine, and more hollers followed.

I quietly raised my cup. It would be bad manners not to go along with a toast, though familiar irritations pricked under my skin.

What was there to be congratulated about? Another city besieged and burned, with its survivors shouldering hefty tax increases to fund the emperor's next conquest? Had any of these men been to the front lines, witnessed the cruelty of war with their own eyes, seen how corpses littered those streets?

These nightmares haunted me. Emaciated bodies curled small against rubble where their homes had once stood. I could still smell the burning of flesh as our soldiers launched fireballs over the city walls to destroy what remained of their homes and drive the already hungry and desperate into surrendering.

Did these pampered heirs know that for every inch of conquered land, countless orphans and widows paid the price? Wailing parents were forced to bury their children. 白发送黑发. *The white-haired burying the dark-haired.* The worst kind of punishment.

And the bigger our army grew, the more it would take to feed and pay them.

Did they know where that money came from?

Taxes. More and more taxes. Often on the already impoverished citizens of conquered cities.

Most of them might not know these things, but I did. For the stars and Fate forced me to watch it all, every night.

Behind Siwang, Rong's banner waved high against the northern wind. Originally, the banner had a gold dragon sewn over a swatch of red fabric. After the prophecy, the emperor added a bloodred phoenix to the banner that was visible only when it caught the light. To remind everyone that under the Mandate of Heaven, their prince was destined to become the emperor of all emperors, because he was betrothed to the girl who bore the phoenix's mark.

Rong waved this banner and waged wars in my name. But when was the last time my voice was heard in all of this? When was the last time someone asked me what *I* wanted?

"How lucky they are to have us as their new guardians," the conversation continued.

"The people of Fulin should be grateful that they are taken under *our* wing, and not one of the southern dynasties who treated us north-erners with prejudice and hate. . . ."

"My father said the southern dynasties used to treat us worse than they treat their dogs, before Rong rose up and liberated us. . . ."

"Speaking of southern bastards, where is the Lan prince?" a voice asked.

"He is not feeling well." The answer came not from Siwang but from the man who sat across the fire pits from me.

Wu Caikun sat at Siwang's right hand, just as his father currently sat at the emperor's right hand at the other feast. Caikun was perhaps Siwang's closest confidant and one of the only men in court who did everything to avoid me. For I had tried to kiss him a few years ago because I wanted to give away my first kiss before Siwang claimed it, and he had been absolutely terrified of me ever since. A part of me had briefly relished the idea of being feared, that smugness extinguished when I realized Caikun was scared only of Siwang finding out.

"Prince Siwang, did you uninvite him to the feast because he took your stag?" a man slurred.

"Not for a stag," someone corrected. "Perhaps Lan Yexue simply looked at Lady Fei for too long?"

The crowd laughed, and I grimaced.

"Lan Yexue did make Lady Fei smile today. And the last time another man made her smile, Siwang had to banish him and his whole family to some nowhere village in the far north."

I set my chopsticks down. The candles had burned halfway down and I had endured enough.

"Fei?"

I paused at Siwang's voice.

He handed a bowl to the eunuch closest to him and whispered

something that no one else could hear. The eunuch delivered the bowl to my table.

Cubes of lamb meat, torn from their skewers.

Siwang smiled at me, those hopeful eyes so gentle and soft. My chest ached. Fangyun was right: I would break his heart. If not tonight, then one day. For as long as bloodsheds haunted my dreams and my heart longed for freedom, I was doomed to leave him.

By choice or by the force of another man.

The fire in my belly quieted.

"Speaking of our princess, I hear Lady Lifeng killed those rabbits herself?" Another voice drifted from somewhere across the smoky fire pits. I had half a mind to tell them to go easy on the wine and sober up before someone said something they might regret. "I never realized our future empress had such heroic qualities."

"The women of my ancestors were just as good hunters as the men," Siwang interjected before I could. "They were the ones who fed the tribes when the men were busy fighting wars. And who are you to criticize my betrothed this way?"

"Everyone says Lady Lifeng's beauty is something to marvel at. It seems they neglected to mention that her archery skills are just as extraordinary," someone quickly added. The son of a conquered warlord. He didn't look at me when he spoke; his beaming smile and well-crafted compliment were not meant for me. They were for Siwang.

打狗还要看主人. *Even when striking a dog, you ought to consider who its master is.*

I forced another smile. This one tasted the bitterest of them all.

"It is truly the luck of a lifetime to be able to gaze upon Miss Lifeng, with all her talents and beauty, Your Highness," someone else added.

I wanted to laugh. What use was beauty? What use was any of this?

My gaze fell on the beautiful girls attending this feast, all dressed in intricately embroidered coats, draped in fur, and adorned with gold pendants cradling glimmering jewels. Some of them had drawn crimson marks of their own between their brows to imitate mine, and some had gone as far as adding tiny pearl beads to their foreheads to enhance their painted marks.

They coveted what I had, while all I wanted was a way to wipe away this mark like some day-old rouge and erase the prophecy from existence.

These visiting princesses and noble daughters were all here to catch glimpses of the noble sons, each seeking either the richest or the most powerful husband to advance their fathers' and brothers' paths in this world. Even those who had no interest in men.

Across the smoky fires, I watched as a man openly caressed the hand of a young servant girl with wide eyes and silky curls, while a woman with pinned-up hair who had to be his wife sat beside him in taut silence.

The servant girl quickly jumped away, and the man whispered something to the eunuch closest to him, then let out a leer so disgusting it made my stomach turn. His wife wordless and stoic through all of this. Forced to bear it all. He was her husband, and women without the protection of a powerful father or husband were treated as good as nothing in society.

No power.

No status.

I clenched my jaw so hard I hoped my beautiful white teeth would crack and shatter, become monstrous and sharp as a tiger's fangs, and strike fear in the heart of every man who dared to gaze at me with wanton eyes.

I leaned back and waved over the head eunuch. "Don't let that man anywhere near that servant girl. In fact, don't let any of these men near any of the girls."

He stared at me for a moment. "Such matters are not your concern, Lady Lifeng."

I shot him a sharp look. "If I am to be empress one day, the well-being of every inner court servant is my concern."

"Fei? Are you all right?" Siwang asked from his dais, brows knotted with worriment.

I forced my last smile of the night. "I'm feeling a little under the weather. Perhaps I caught a cold during the hunt today."

He quickly rose to his feet, stepped down from his dais, and came toward my table. The buzzing of conversations quieted, just a little. Once at my side, he knelt down on one knee so we were at eye level and placed a hand on my forehead. "You don't seem to have a fever. I will have the cook bring you some ginger soup and—"

"No!" I spoke too fast, too loudly. The chatter around us quieted further, and I felt the attention of the entire feast scorching me. "I am fine. I just need a long night of sleep. Please don't send anyone to interrupt me."

Without waiting for Siwang to reply, I quickly rose to my feet, bowed my head to the rest of the guests, and walked away.

7

The stables were dark and cold. I contemplated taking Beifeng, the fastest horse in the empire and Siwang's favorite. But someone would notice if the crown prince's prized stallion was missing, just as someone would notice if my horse went missing—though not as quickly as they would notice Siwang's missing steed. In the end, I climbed onto a thick-coated stallion at the far end of the stables, reserved for the guards and trained to withstand these wintry terrains.

In the distance, the camp was aglow with flickering fires and loud with voices. As the night deepened into drunken flushes, people began to sing and dance, and the music swelled. Which made this the perfect opportunity to sneak away.

I kicked the stallion into motion and adjusted the cloak over my head.

Yes, sneaking out before the hunt officially began counted as cheating, however the emperor never said we had to kill the tiger *during* the hunt.

To hell with principles; I couldn't afford to lose.

Over the past few months I'd raided the libraries for every piece of information I could find on these legendary tigers. One thing stood out: they were nocturnal animals that hunted exclusively at night. So my best chance of encountering one was under the grace of moonlight—also the most dangerous time to venture into the mountains.

As a child, I had begged Siwang to let me learn combat and archery with him not because I was interested, but because these were unladylike skills. And the more interest I feigned, the angrier it made the nannies and the high-ranked palace ladies who spent hours and hours teaching me etiquette and archaic rules.

I wanted their rage, and I wanted to fail every test they put me up to. I'd thought if I proved myself an unworthy empress, they would let me go home.

I never got to go home, though I hoped those lessons would pay off tonight.

As my stallion ascended the mountains, I tried to focus and prayed for Fate to grant me a single glimpse of the future, for I could use every advantage I could get. It did not work.

These visions were not mine to control. They were gifts from the gods, and mortals could not force the will of the gods.

While I hated the nightmares, I held each vision close to my chest. For they were the only power I had in this world. And perhaps the only thing that was mine.

As a child, the visions and the dreams were mere flashes of color and sounds, then became more vivid as I grew. Some nights, I still tried to convince myself that perhaps they were just detailed dreams, fueled by my overactive imagination in the boring monotony of the palace.

"Please." I murmured a prayer to my ancestors as I rode over

sleet-covered trails into the snow-crowned forest. "Let my foolish plan work. Let me end the suffering of this continent, and let me be free for the first time in my life." Then, to the stars and the gods, I wanted to say, *You'd better help me survive the night. If I'm dead, there will be no prophecy, no emperor of all emperors!* But all that came was "Please . . . don't abandon me tonight."

The mountains were so much louder in the night than during the day. Wild with nocturnal animals braver under the cover of darkness than in the light. I hadn't brought a torch, because I didn't want to be seen. The deeper I ventured, the more I regretted this.

I waited for Fate to guide me, but nothing happened.

No spark, no light. Just the chill of the winter air against my heaviest fur coat, and the sound of fresh snow crunching under my stallion's hooves.

"If those nightmares are punishment for what Rong is doing under my name, shouldn't you help me change my fate?" I grumbled into the darkness.

The darkness did not answer.

I searched the forest for a flash of white and black-blue stripes, which was impossible among the snow and brambles. If a Beiying tiger lurked among these trees, it could easily creep close and kill me before I had the slightest inkling.

Eventually, slender pines became ancient moss-covered trees with trunks thicker than my waist. Some of these trees had to be hundreds of years old. Majestic beings who had guarded these mountains long before Rong flew its banners over the land, and would continue to stand guard hundreds of years after Rong had fallen. After every creature who lived in this moment was dead, our bones yellowed and buried, replaced by another generation of empires and dynasties that vied to feed with violence their insatiable hunger for more power, more wealth, more excess of every kind.

In a hundred years, would there be another me, another prophecy? Another girl who hungers for choice, control, freedom? To live a life that was more than bearing heirs and waiting for the warmth of a husband?

By the time the forest thinned and I broke into a hidden valley of quiet streaming water, the moon was high and ten thousand stars dazzled in the silken indigo sky above.

I gazed up at the white cliffs and the precariously steep paths carved out by the local hunters. High clifftops were usually where Beiying tigers nested, peaceful places far from the lesser creatures that also frequented these woods.

However, all mortal creatures need to eat, and these tigers still had to hunt.

I took out the dagger Fangyun had given me. Legend had it that Beiying tigers could smell fresh blood from a mile away.

Wildlife is scarce this year. The tigers will be extra hungry. General Xu's passing words from when we first arrived at camp.

I unsheathed Fangyun's blade and pressed its edge against my forearm.

How much blood was enough to lure one to me? And how much blood could I spare? They didn't teach these sorts of things in my classes, and I couldn't find answers in the hunters' handbooks I'd browsed.

I dismounted from the stallion and surveyed the terrain.

For a trap to work, the location had to be perfect. I needed a space unobstructed by trees and hills so I could see my prey at the same time it saw me. Somewhere I could use to my advantage—

A twitch of midnight blue. A rustle in the bushes, the barely audible sound of labored breathing.

The vision of a thrown knife, slicing open my throat.

I barely had the time to dodge before a knife whizzed past and snipped off a strand of hair, missing my jugular by mere inches.

An enemy, though not a tiger.

Did the emperor's men realize I had snuck out?

No, they couldn't have caught up this quickly. And they certainly wouldn't dare throw a knife at me.

In one swift movement, I plucked an arrow from my quiver and was about to let it loose when a familiar voice made me pause.

"Stop!" A male voice.

Arrow still nocked and ready, I remained where I was. "Show yourself."

"I—"

"Show yourself!"

More rustling.

My breath hitched when the shrubs parted to reveal the last person I expected to see in these woods. There, among the snow-laced branches and pines, half crouched, was the Prince of Lan: Yexue.

Was he here to hunt the tiger as well?

I saw the reason he was half crouched. His hands were pressed against a crimson spot on his right leg, where an arrow was lodged.

White feather, black shaft, the arrow of the imperial guards, and it had gone straight through his thigh. Not a shot intended to kill, just to keep him from running.

A hostage was a hostage, regardless of their status or the polite titles the court gave them.

I lowered my weapon. "Rong's arrows have a code to them. These black-shafted ones contain a slow-releasing poison and a numbing agent that will make you lose feeling around the infected area. The two of them are relatively harmless by themselves, but mixed together? If someone doesn't clean that wound and apply an antidote soon, the circulation will stop, the flesh and nerves will begin to die, and you will lose that leg. If the poison spreads to the bloodstream, you will die a slow death."

"You think I don't know that?" Lan Yexue pulled another blade from his robes, teeth bared like a wolf ready to fight.

"Skies, how many knives do you have?"

"Come any closer, and I'll make you regret the day you were born." His voice was deep and raspy and would have been irritatingly pleasant if he hadn't been threatening my life.

I should have heeded his warning, jumped back onto my horse, and gotten on with what I had come here to do. 不要多管闲事 was an underrated mantra that more people should follow. *Don't meddle in the affairs of others, and mind your own business.*

But . . . He and I were both outcasts on the run, albeit in different ways. If I were the one wounded, I would want someone to help me.

I held his gaze with my chin tilted high. Siwang had taught me never to look away from a predator, never to let them know my fear. "May I ask what the Prince of Lan is doing so deep in these woods?"

"I could ask the same of the future Empress of Rong."

I deepened my smile, glaring daggers to match the one in his hand. "Sharp words from a man bleeding to death."

The prince's lips curled. "If you know what's good for you, you will cease your bragging, turn around, and run as fast as you can before I decide to kill you. My hands have been soiled enough tonight. What's one more to the tally?"

His words were an angry rumble of thunder against the dark night, yet his paling lips and sweat-beaded forehead told me there was no lightning behind those empty threats. He was just an injured wolf baring his fangs, trying to chase me away because he was scared I might kill him before he killed me.

"You are lucky you are not the prey I came here to hunt," I replied, then pulled out the small vial of *wan ling du* that I kept on me at all times. It was a concoction made from ten thousand poisons. One that could serve as both a weapon and an antidote in times of need. "以毒刻毒," I explained. "*Use poison to counter poison.* The imperial healers said all antidotes at their core are poison, and the only way to treat poison is with another form of poison. And this pot of *wan ling du* was specially formulated by them as an emergency treatment."

Wan ling du was very valuable. The only people who had it outside of the emperor were me, Siwang, and General Ma.

The dagger in Yexue's hand lowered, though his eyes continued to burn with ire. "And what do you want in exchange for this great antidote?"

"Nothing." I set down my bow and arrows and knelt beside him. At eye level, the venom in his eyes perished with a slow exhale, as if he was finally letting go of the breath he was holding.

He lowered his blade till it rested on the ground beside him, but didn't completely let go.

"*Men,*" I grumbled.

I pulled out a handkerchief from my winter coat, wrapped the small pill of poison with it, then crushed it so that it would apply easily to his wound.

"Why are you helping me?"

"Why indeed? Considering that you're the prince of an enemy nation, I hope I don't one day regret this. But I can't leave you here to die. Especially since . . ."

Since it is my fault that Rong conquered your homeland.

"I don't need your charity, Lifeng Fei."

"This isn't charity." *This is balm for my own guilt.* "Can you handle pain? I need to shave off the arrowhead and pull it out of your leg before I can apply the antidote."

His placed his blade in my hand. "Pain is an old friend."

"Good. Because I am no doctor. If you don't want the imperial guards to find you, I'd suggest you keep quiet." I snapped a piece of bark from the overhanging foliage. "Chew on this when you want to scream. If the imperial guards find us, we are both dead."

"Are you going to remove this bleeding arrow or not?"

I sneered. After two years as a hostage, Lan Yexue still saw himself as the prince of a mighty empire, not the son of a crumbling dynasty that ruled over a handful of failing cities, barely enough to call itself a kingdom anymore.

The Empire of Lan used to rule over half the continent; however, it had been in decline for centuries. Its last era of stability was when Yexue's great-grandfather reigned. And things had only gotten worse since his father fell sick and his uncle took over the duties of regent. If the rumors were true, Yexue's ailing father was not long for this world.

Was this why he wanted to go home? To see his father one last time, or to stop his uncle from taking the last thing that was his?

"This is a good place to stage an escape attempt," I said to fill the silence as I cautiously shaved off the arrowhead, careful not to leave any splinters. "If you make it deep enough into the mountains and find a cave to hide in, you might be able to wait out Rong's hunters. When the hunt officially starts, these mountains will be swallowed by chaos. That will be your best shot at escaping. Too bad—with this injured leg, you are not going anywhere for a while."

"Do you always talk this much?"

In one swift motion, I had him against the tree he was leaning on, with his own blade pressed against his throat. "If you want my help, you'd better show some gratitude. Otherwise, my face might just be the last face you'll ever see."

To my surprise, Prince Yexue didn't flinch or cry or retort with something just as vicious. His lips twitched. He was . . . amused?

"I want to help you," I told him. "But that doesn't mean I am here to take your endless insults like I owe you something."

"Very well, my lady." His smile was beautiful, contagious. The sort that took up most of his face, like a flower that had finally bloomed. There was a single dimple on each side of his face.

"Try not to scream. I'm going to pull the arrow out now; this is the worst part."

The Prince of Lan nodded. I put one hand on his thigh and the other on the arrow. I could feel the heat of his body burning through the fabric of his clothes, and my cheeks burned, too.

When I pulled, the arrow came away in one piece, and Yexue didn't so much as wince. He watched me with interest the entire time, as if pain really was the old friend he'd so boldly claimed it to be.

I tried not to linger on this. I didn't want to imagine what kind of trauma one would've had to experience to be so indifferent in the face of pain.

"Why are you helping me?" he asked again as I began applying the antidote to his wound, making sure to be careful with the dosage; this antidote was a poison itself, after all.

"都是天涯流落人," I replied after I was done. *We are both outcasts on the run.* "If I don't help you, who will?" I got up and retrieved the small bottle of bloodroot ointment that I'd originally prepared for myself in case of emergencies from my satchel. "A physician with proper medicine and training would have done a better job. However, the closest doctors all work for the Rong emperor and would rat you out if you sought their help. I'm the best option you have right now. Wherever you intend to go, take this with you."

He took the bottle, and a strong herbal smell burned my nostrils as he opened it. "Good stuff."

"Try not to die on your way home. If the Prince of Lan died under our supervision, it would only spark more conflict between our borders. I don't know about you, but I have seen enough bloodshed to last a lifetime."

Yexue arched a brow. "You are Prince Siwang's betrothed—when would a girl like you ever see bloodshed and war?"

I smiled. "When would a girl like me ever see bloodshed and war, indeed."

"May I ask, why is the future Empress of Rong on the run?"

"I'm not *on* the run. I'm just . . . running." I ripped a piece of fabric from his robe. It wasn't a proper bandage, however, it would do.

"You don't have to do that," he protested when I tore another piece off his robe. "The leg will heal by itself."

"That will take weeks. Wounds don't just magically heal by themselves overnight. If I don't bandage this for you, it will become infected and you might still die."

His lips parted, then closed, as if he wanted to say something then decided against it. "Are we running from the same people?"

"I guess."

The prince eyed the arrows strapped across my back. "Do you know how dangerous these mountains are at night? Have you not heard of the Beiying tigers?"

I laughed. "Why do you think I'm here?"

He cocked his head. There was that half smile again. "To impress the emperor?"

"Are you interrogating me?" I asked.

"Just trying to get to know the girl who's saved my life."

Knowledge and secrets were the most valuable currency. There was a reason they said the most powerful person in every room was not the richest, or the person who held the highest status, but the person who knew the most secrets. "From now on, if you want to ask a question, you will have to answer one of mine first."

"Ask away," he replied. "It's the least I can do to repay your mercy."

My fingers paused, surprised that he'd agreed so easily. "When did you escape?"

If the answer was in the last couple of hours, then the guards couldn't be far behind him. I should get on my way before we were both caught.

Sneaking out to hunt before the hunt officially began was something Siwang could defend by shrugging it off as me being competitive and childish.

Being seen with another man in the middle of the night?

That was another thing altogether. Memories of Lijian were still fresh. I didn't want that to happen to Yexue, because Siwang might not be satisfied with a simple exile this time.

"I left a little after we returned from the hunt, so almost three hours ago."

Long enough for the sentry to notice.

"My turn to ask questions. I assume you're here to hunt Beiying tigers to win the emperor's wish. What could the future Empress of Rong, the girl who has everything, want and not have?" His eyes were curious yet sharp, carefully observing me.

I bit the inside of my lip and ripped off another piece of his robe as a bandage. I had to make it tight, apply as much pressure as possible to stop the bleeding, which seemed to be slowing—there wasn't half as much blood seeping through the bandage as I'd expected.

I wasn't sure if it was a trick of the light, but I swore color was already returning to Yexue's sharp face.

"I'm waiting," he pressed.

"Freedom," I replied curtly. A half-truth.

"What do you mean?"

"My turn," I said quickly. "How far away are the imperial guards? Do you know?"

"Far," he told me.

"You sound sure of that."

"I am."

"How?"

The corners of his lips twitched the same way they had this morning. The almost-smile of someone who knew something I didn't. "A question for a question, Lady Lifeng. You aren't very good at following your own rules, are you?" he taunted, dark eyes glistening in the moonlight. "Since you are so kindly tending to my wounds, I'll answer this question for free. I am sure because those men are all dead now."

I jerked up, eyeing his immaculate white robe, not a stain of blood in sight except for the crimson patch at his leg. His sleeves, the part of clothing that got soiled first in a fight, were pristine.

"You can't have killed them."

"Why not?"

"Because." I gestured at his clothes. "If you had, you would be covered in blood."

"Maybe I'm just very good at killing people without getting my hands dirty," the prince replied, his dark eyes fixed on me.

A coldness slithered between my shoulder blades, something primal, urging me to run.

He is a demon. Words whispered behind cupped hands when Lan Yexue had first come to court two years ago.

I tried to laugh. He was lying. He had to be. "Oh, and how many men were there?" I asked, as if I were in on the joke.

"Twenty-seven."

I rolled my eyes. "That's not possible. You can't have killed twenty-seven men by yourself."

"I can take you to see their corpses if you don't mind venturing down the mountain again."

Did he think I was born yesterday? As stifling as the palace was, I didn't grow up under a rock. "If you want to lie, you should pick a realistic number. Like five, or—"

The familiar tingle prickled between my brows. Flashing fangs and talons, long like ivory blades, lunging from the shadows, in a motion to slash open Prince Yexue's throat like he was made of wax.

The blade! my better judgment screamed, but my body didn't listen.

"Run!" I cried, and pushed Yexue out of the way just as the tiger pounced from the trees.

I rolled back: a futile attempt to buy myself a few rapid heartbeats of time as I grappled for a weapon. My fingers grasped the hilt of the blade Fangyun had given me in the same moment that icy claws slashed down at me, tearing open my clothes and flesh. Pain exploded, and I heard a cry.

The sort of cry I had heard only in my nightmares, torn from the throats of humans thrown from city walls, plunged into infernos, or slashed open by some cruel soldier.

Focus.

The tiger raised its giant paw again to draw another lash across my body. This time, without the padding of my winter coat, the blow would be even deadlier than the last.

I pulled Fangyun's blade from its sheath. When the tiger brought down its claws, I thrust the blade into its eye.

A mighty roar, enough to make the trees shiver in fear.

I pushed the blade deeper and deeper, until my hand was hot with blood, until the tiger fell into a convulsing heap next to me.

I let out a wheezing exhale.

"Fei!" Prince Yexue cried, his hands grasping at my now ruined robe, trying to cover me for modesty's sake.

I laughed, or I wanted to. I couldn't breathe. There was no air in my lungs. Blood gushed out into the snow, fast like a fountain, leaving crimson stains on his silk robes.

He had lied. There was no way he could kill twenty-seven people without getting a drop of blood on his hands.

It had been maybe a handful of heartbeats since the tiger's claws raked over me, and already blood soaked my clothes an impossible shade of red. Even in my visions, I had never seen so much red.

Luckily, everything was so cold I barely felt the pain.

Your plan is not going to work. Fangyun's words echoed.

I wished she were here to tell me *I told you so.*

You were right, sister. The plan didn't work.

At least I took a Beiying tiger with me. At least I didn't die for nothing. With me gone, Rong would stop waging war in the name of my prophecy and Siwang's supposed destiny of becoming the emperor of all emperors.

Yexue stripped off his robe and pressed it to my wounds to stop the bleeding the way I had done for him mere minutes ago. 好人有好报, I guessed. *Good deeds really do come back around.*

Empires rise, empires fall. I just didn't expect it to happen so fast.

The gash in his leg was a lot easier to bandage than my mutilated body. If I were him, I wouldn't even know where to start.

"I'm . . . going . . . die."

"You are not going to die," he hissed.

Another almost-laugh, even fainter this time. Darkness began to blot my vision. *That's not up to you, my dear prince.*

As I closed my eyes, I felt his hand grab my face. "If I want you to live, not even Death himself can take you!"

I smiled and hoped that with me gone, Yong'An would not burn like it did in my dreams, and everyone I loved would live long and happy lives.

Darkness fell heavier and heavier.

Selfishly, I didn't want to go.

There was so much I hadn't seen or experienced yet.

I wanted more than this.

I wanted more than a life unlived.

I wanted . . .

"Do you want to live, Fei?"

Yes.

8

As I lay dying, I waited for darkness to consume me. Instead, I saw only bright memories.

Of him.

—ɱ—

Once, when I was younger and smaller, Siwang asked what I wanted for my birthday, and I said great golden wings to fly over the palace walls. So he gave me a robe with real golden feathers sewn into the sleeves and snuck me out into the city to light lanterns and watch New Year's fireworks.

The air was cold that night, but his hand was warm, holding mine.

—ɱ—

"What use is combat to an empress who will be protected by the emperor of all emperors?" Siwang's martial arts teacher had said when

Siwang asked if I could join his lessons. "She is beautiful to look at. There is nothing else you need from a wife."

When he said this, I bit my tongue so he would not see me cry, until I tasted copper.

When I asked Siwang to teach me in secret, my request was met with his hesitant frown. Yet when I pursed my lips and gazed up at him with teary eyes, Siwang melted like ice under the summer sun.

水滴石穿. *With time, water can wear down rocks.* And Siwang wasn't a rock. He was clay in my hand, so easily molded into whatever I wanted him to be. Just as Siwang eventually molded me into a semi-satisfactory student—with the help of the phoenix's mark, of course. If I ever covered the mark, my visions would fail to manifest, and I became as terrible of a shot as the sordid noble sons who preferred mischief over knowledge, leisure over practice.

Over time, constant practice eventually gave me a semblance of skill. Each time my arrow found its target without aid from the phoenix's mark felt like a victory. Each time I looked over my shoulder, he was there, cheering and flashing that proud, boyish grin. I used to feel so warm, bathed in his light.

—◊—

The palace walls were tall, so my winter days were darker than most.

When it snowed and the other kids failed to show up for class, I always cried. Because I knew they were on the other side of these walls playing, laughing, probably building snowmen and sledding down hills. Having fun without me. Doing all the things I wished I could do but would never be allowed to, given the endless palace rules.

Each time, Siwang took my hand and let me chase him around the imperial gardens and hit him with fistfuls of snow until his fur coats were white with ice. He let me boss him around for hours, rolling giant snowballs so that I would have the biggest snowman of all our classmates. He'd help me build it right outside our classroom and look for the shiniest pebbles for its eyes and drape his favorite coats around it.

I always proudly wrote my name under my creations. Every day, as the snow scattered in the wind and my name disappeared, Siwang wrote it again and again until it all melted under the early-spring sun.

So that everyone knew that the snowman who wore the crown prince's favorite winter coat was mine.

Never has a prince doted on a single girl so much, the court said.

—⚮—

When I got sick, Siwang would spend hours in the kitchen with the imperial cooks and learn how to make ginger and beef-bone broths for me.

When I cried, Siwang would hold my hand. He would tell me stories and bad jokes until I giggled.

Whatever I wanted, if Siwang had it, he would give it to me without question. If he didn't have it, he would move mountains to get it for me.

If I wanted to see a play, he would either sneak me out of the palace or have the entire performance set up in the palace for me to watch.

If I liked a song, he would learn to sing it for me whenever I wanted.

If I liked a book, he would recite every word to match me in verse.

—⚮—

Rong Siwang.

My only friend inside the palace.

The only thing that had made these seventeen years worth living.

My safe harbor.

The one person who would do anything for me.

The only good thing that had come out of this prophecy.

He loved me. I knew he loved me. I would be stupid not to see it.

But did he love Lifeng Fei the girl, or Lifeng Fei the empress of all empresses? And could this love withstand the test of time?

—⚊—

"How can you leave him, Fei? Do you not love him?" my sister asked, weeks ago.

Some days, I wondered if Father was right, that it would be futile trying to fight what was written in the stars.

But while I could love Rong Siwang the boy, I refused to love Rong Siwang the prince who wanted to rule the world.

The man whose greed might one day bring calamity to Yong'An and cause the deaths of everyone we had ever met.

9

I woke to flickering firelight illuminating darkened cave walls, where twisted shadows were etched high on all sides.

"You are awake." A soft voice spoke.

I blinked. My body hummed in a dull ache, heavy and numb, as if anchored by phantom chains. If it weren't for the steady *thud-thud-thud* inside my chest, the clear sound of blood pumping in my ears, and the winter air filling and emptying my lungs with every breath, I would have thought this the afterlife.

"Where am I?" I tried to move, tried to sit up, but even this small movement was too much.

"Stay still," Yexue warned, helping me into a sitting position. He propped my back against the ice-cold stone wall, and tucked his fur coat tighter against me. I noticed that the outer layer of his embroidered white robe was now wrapped over my shredded clothes, the sole confirmation that the bloody encounter with the tiger wasn't just a nightmare.

"I should be dead," I murmured, watching for his reaction.

While my clothes were ruined, my body was not. I touched my chest, and instead of deep gashes that should have killed me, I found soft flesh that was tender to the touch.

No mangling scars. Nothing.

"I saved you," Yexue replied, not quite looking at me as he moved toward the crackling fire at the center of the cave and fed it a handful of brambles.

"How?" My voice was harsher than it should have been. I bit my lip, immediately guilty. I should feel gratitude, not anger. Without him, I'd be a corpse abandoned by the creek waiting for wild animals to claim me.

But I had heard rumors about the Lan dynasty. How Lan Yexue's father practiced the forbidden kind of magic and worshipped gods who answered only after midnight. Some said his mother was a demon; some said she was a goddess who was beguiled by his father's beauty and fell in love despite heaven's laws against such feelings between gods and mortals. Rumors swirled like smoke, and often, smoke did not come without fire.

Nothing in life was free. Especially something as precious and sacred as the sort of magic that could bring someone back from certain death.

"Does it matter?" Yexue regarded me with those beautiful amber-lit eyes.

Porcelain skin, crescent-moon eyes, and a pair of seductive, pouting lips that would make even the fairest of maidens envious— Lan Yexue was ethereal in a way that didn't feel fair. If his mother really was a goddess who had fallen in love with a mortal, I wouldn't be surprised.

When he came back to me and touched my cheek with gentle

fingertips, I almost forgot how to breathe. This close to him, I could see subtle streaks of silver under his dark hair, slightly disheveled from today. I had never noticed this before. It was an odd feature against such a young face.

Yexue was the same age as me and Siwang, if I remembered correctly.

Something about the streaks made him look even more formidable. Like a tiger's stripes.

"You are still colder than normal, but your body is warming up. You should feel better in a few more hours."

I looked away before my thoughts could wander to places they shouldn't.

英雄难过美人关: *Even brave heroes struggle to survive the challenge of a beautiful face.* I'd killed a Beiying tiger with my bare hands. I would not let Lan Yexue's vexing good looks be my downfall.

"What do I owe you, Prince of Lan?"

Because I did owe him now. And it was the worst kind of debt: a life debt.

"Nothing. You saved me once when you gave me the antidote, then twice when you pushed me out of the tiger's way. If anything, I owe you."

"The price of simple kindness and bringing someone back from Death's arms are different."

"Are they?" The prince cocked his head, his eyes soft like melting honey when he regarded me. "Simple kindness means different things to different people. To me, a few drops of my blood is also simple kindness, perhaps less noteworthy than the generosity of saving the life of a man you do not need to save."

My stomach tightened into knots. "Blood?"

Yexue drew his blade, the same one I had severed his arrow with hours earlier.

I shrank back, my hand reaching for Fangyun's blade that was strapped to my waist, and found nothing. *The tiger.* A sting of guilt welled behind my eyes. I hoped both the blade and the tiger's pelt would still be there tomorrow. If someone tried to claim my kill as theirs . . . I wrinkled my nose. I would retrieve it at first light, even if I had to crawl there on my hands and knees.

"Relax," he told me as he made a deep cut across his palm. Dark blood pooled to the surface; then he thrust his bleeding hand toward my lips. "Drink it; it will make you feel better."

Had he hit his head when I pushed him? Why—

I drew a shallow breath when I saw it. Here, up close, I realized that Yexue's blood was not the scarlet of most people's, but a deep shade of crimson darker than even the grape wines from beyond the western sea. Not just this. There was also a *shine* under the firelight. Tiny specks of glowing blue shimmered like stardust as the blood pooled across his palm.

It was . . . beautiful.

"The cut will close soon," he urged me. Impatient, he grabbed me by the chin and pressed his hand over my lips. I was too weak to fight back. "If I were going to hurt you, I would have done it by now."

His blood poured into my mouth. I didn't taste the sharp copper I knew from when I bit my lips too hard. Instead, I tasted a strange sweetness, like winter melons mixed with the sharp, bitter tones of aged rice wine. Unlike the haziness that came with wine, I was hit with an undeniable alertness upon contact.

"How do you feel?" he asked when he removed his hand.

"Better." It was true. Strength returned to my limbs, warmth bloomed at my fingertips. I pushed myself to sit a little straighter.

"Told you so." He held his palm closer, letting me lap up the remaining blood clinging to his already healed flesh like a cat savoring the last drops of milk.

"Are you a god?" I asked when I was done. My body felt light, like it was floating, and I could simultaneously feel everything from the softness of the clothes on my body to the sharpness of the gravel under my hands. Whatever this was, it didn't feel human.

There was that half smile again. "Maybe someday I will be a god. Not yet, though."

"How?"

"You seem fond of that word," he replied. No real answer followed.

My attention fell to his left leg, the one that should still be injured. "I want my bloodroot ointment back if you don't need it."

He laughed. "I tried to tell you, but you didn't listen. I did need your help, however. That poison was preventing my body from healing by itself. If you hadn't offered me the antidote, I don't know if I would have survived." He paused, then added quietly a question I didn't expect: "Are you afraid of me?"

I watched him closely, observing the way he avoided eye contact and kept turning aside any and all questions about his unfathomable power. "Why would I be afraid of you?"

"Because magic is not a thing we mortals are allowed to possess. Not *good* mortals, at least."

I felt a pang in my chest. Recollections of me curled under my sheets, crying and wishing for a way to wash away the phoenix's mark and all the nightmares it brought, surged behind my eyes. *I am not a fallen goddess!* I'd cried. *I don't want to be an empress! Just let me go home!*

There was a reason I didn't want anyone to know what I could do. Not my sister. Not my parents. Not the nannies who had raised me.

Not even Siwang.

"Anyway." Yexue shifted away. "You might be safe from death, but your body won't fully heal for a while, so get some rest while you can."

It took all my control not to pull him back and ask him *How did you come across this power?* and whether he knew where it came from. Was his forbidden magic the fruit of some bargain with a vengeful god, or was it something that he was born with, like . . . like me?

Did his family know about his powers? If so, why had they sent him here as hostage, when his blood was so precious?

Most importantly: Did the Rong Emperor know about his magic?

No. If the emperor knew what Lan Yexue could do, he would not let Yexue roam freely.

I swallowed my questions before more curled to life. For even if I asked, Yexue would not answer.

I was just a girl he'd met in passing, destined to become the empress of an enemy nation. Perhaps one who would rule over him one day. If I hadn't saved his life first, he never would have saved mine. This was a trade, and we were now even.

"Thank you," I said, finally. "I promise that your secret is safe with me."

"I trust you." His eyes were focused on me again, concentrated and burning as he kept staring. As if I were a puzzle he wanted to solve, or a question he wanted to answer.

I turned away, my cheeks suddenly hot. "You know . . ." I steered the conversation to a safer direction. "When I ventured into these mountains tonight, I thought I was prepared for the probability that I might not walk out alive. I was wrong. Nobody realizes just how desperately and wholeheartedly one wants to live until those final moments."

Yexue leaned a little closer, so close I felt his tender heat permeating the frozen air. "May I ask you a question, Lifeng Fei?"

Dread crept down my spine. Reluctantly, I nodded.

"Why did you save me when you could have run? That tiger was lured there by *my* blood. *I* was its target. *I* should have been the one to get mauled by the beast."

"I don't know." It was the honest answer. Maybe it was instinct. Maybe it was a mistake. Everything had happened too fast. There wasn't time to think anything through. "Whatever the reason was, I'm glad I did it. Because both of us are alive."

"*You* could have died."

"I didn't."

The Prince of Lan looked away, and I swore I saw his cheeks bloom a softer shade. "I'm not someone worth saving."

I flinched. "Everyone is worth saving, Lan Yexue."

"I told you the truth back by the creek," he replied, his voice smaller and more hesitant.

"What truth?"

"I . . ." He stopped himself, brows furrowed ever so slightly, considering. "Nothing."

I tried to replay our conversation, but I was tired and my mind was hazy. I also knew men like him. If he wanted me to know something, he'd offer before it was asked of him. If he didn't, no amount of trickery or pleading would sway him. Princes who were raised on privilege and power. He and Siwang were cut from the same stubborn cloth.

"There's one thing I still don't understand: Why would the Crown Prince's bride-to-be want to annul her betrothal?"

Why indeed. "This isn't the time or the place to talk about that."

"We have a couple more hours until dawn, and you are too weak to go anywhere. We might as well make conversation while we are here," he said. "I am curious, that is all. In all respect, the Prince of Rong seems like a perfectly fine match."

I traced the pattern of his embroidered robe, still draped over me. A secret for a secret felt fair. Yet . . . "You are right. Siwang is perfect, on paper and in every other aspect. *Too* perfect, perhaps."

"And that is a bad thing?"

"It is not easy to hold on to the love of someone so perfect," I said, opting to give him half the truth. "Siwang is like the sun. When he bestows me his shine, I feel protected and invincible. However, I am not the only person who wants his light. When he becomes emperor, he won't be just mine anymore. I would have to share him with countless concubines. Yet if I dared to even look at another man, I would be marked as an unjust queen and my lover would be sent to the execution block. That doesn't feel fair."

"But when he becomes emperor, you will be empress. Isn't that what *every* girl wants in life?"

I chuckled. "If you think that's what every girl wants in life, then clearly you don't know many girls." He went quiet at this, eyes averted, and I could have sworn I saw him blush. "Some of us just want to love someone and have that someone love us back, treat us not as something to possess, but as his equal. A simple request if Siwang and I were simple people, of simple birth."

"You would rather live in a hut in the mountains with nothing to your name than share a husband with other women?"

"You are a man—a prince—you would never understand," I replied. "Can it really be love if your positions are always unequal? One person holding all the power, while the other holds nothing?" Yexue just stared at me. He looked stunned to hear this. "And just because Siwang is perfect now, it doesn't mean he will always be perfect. When he sits on the throne and bears the weight of an empire on his shoulders, he won't be *my* Siwang anymore. For that is the way of conquerors. Siwang the prince will be different from Siwang the emperor. This much I am sure of."

Silence crept up with a gust of wind, carrying flakes of snow from beyond the cave walls. The fire crackled; its light flickered like shivers against the darkness beyond.

"In order to make peace with our tribute states, our emperor has wedded many daughters and sisters and mothers of these conquered warlords and kings and emperors," I continued. "If they are lucky, they will bear him daughters who will be raised in the northern courts, kept like prisoners until it is time to marry them off to new warlords and kings and dynasties to forge alliances. Glorified bargaining chips, you can say. If they are unlucky, they will birth sons, who will be sent far away to be raised in wealth but also loneliness so that no one can threaten Siwang's claim to the throne. But because these concubines have given the emperor children, they will be spared from being buried alive with him when he crosses to the afterlife. The even more unlucky ones . . . ?"

I swallowed. "I remember when I was six, the emperor married the eldest daughter of the Chu clan to the south. Huge military family. They are rich with both metal and grains, and an important family in terms of trade. When the spoiled Lady Chu married into Rong, she knew the power her father held. She was also a maiden of barely twenty, marrying a man almost thrice her age.

"She hated the emperor and everyone within the palace. For petty reasons, she framed one of the emperor's favorites, Concubine Li, for stealing a family heirloom given to Lady Chu by her father. Though everyone knew that Concubine Li was innocent, the emperor still cut off her right hand and sent her to the Cold Palace, where all his discarded toys went to die. I had heard stories of the Cold Palace, a place where they didn't have enough food to eat nor enough firewood to keep warm. Concubine Li was one of the few people in the palace who was genuinely kind, and she was born the day after the Midautumn Festival. I snuck into the Cold Palace to give her mooncakes because I didn't want her to feel like the world had forgotten her birthday."

I looked up at Yexue to find him watching me intently. There was a tension between his brows. Again, I wished I knew him enough to read him. "What I saw inside those walls are things I wish I could wash from my memories. How those guards treated the women . . ." My stomach twisted as sounds of that night echoed once more. "They forced the women to kneel and beg for their food. Concubine Li once told me the palace is like a garden. Where the emperor graces it is always warm with sunlight. The Cold Palace is like its name: cold and forgotten. Because those women belong to the emperor, they cannot leave the palace, as it would be an insult to his honor for another man to touch them. And so those women will waste their lives inside the Cold Palace, in hopes of perhaps being remembered one day.

"I don't want my life to revolve around Siwang and the hope that he would remember me. No matter how kind he is now, nothing guarantees he would forever be this way. Sometimes when the emperor had guests, like that night, with many ministers and envoys arriving from faraway lands, he would let those visiting men into the Cold Palace and..."

Nausea boiled in the pit of my belly.

The screams.

Those men's leering laughs.

How those women had protested and fought.

Nobody did anything, even as those ladies were beaten by those vile men, simply because the emperor had allowed it.

"After that night, I helped how I could. I brought them the food that I saved and the winter coats that I stashed away and pretended to have lost."

Nobody in the palace had cared about those women, but I did. I *still* did.

Yexue didn't say anything for a long while. He just sat there, lips parted as if he had forgotten how to speak. He looked horrified, and I wondered if things like these happened in the Lan court, or if Rong was especially brutal.

Power corrupted. When men became accustomed to living above rules and consequences that the rest of us had to kneel for, the crueler their hearts became.

"That will never be you," Yexue said finally. "You are the empress of all empresses."

"And what happens after Siwang claims all the land and fulfills the prophecy—if it's even real? What if everyone is wrong and I do not have a great destiny, just a strange mark between my brows? What if Siwang loses everything, what if Rong is conquered by another who will one day set Yong'An aflame?" My words trembled as I said this. "Even if that doesn't happen, even if I want to believe that Siwang will be different from his father, I have seen his vicious side. I know he is capable of terrible things—even if he's never done such things to me. At the end of the day, Siwang is a prince. Men like him, like you, will always put their feelings before the feelings of others."

There was a darkness in Siwang. I had seen it when he banished Lijian from the capital. I saw it in rare flashes when his perfect mask slipped in moments of rage, before he expertly reined himself in. Deep in the palace, under the ownership of the most powerful man in the kingdom, what would he do to me if one day I pushed his benevolence too far?

Childhood memories and years of companionship tethered him to me. . . . Was that enough?

伴君如伴虎: *to accompany a king is like accompanying a tiger.*

Yexue straightened himself. "Siwang and his father won't let you walk away easily. Even if you bring them the first tiger of the season."

"I know. But if Rong is capable of uniting the continent, then they will do it with or without me."

I wasn't a divine token capable of changing destinies; I had watched Siwang die too many times in blistering dreams to believe my faithless prophecy was of any worth. Even if I had magic and the mark of a phoenix between my brows, I wasn't the fallen goddess the world wanted to believe I was.

"There is a second choice, Fei. You can just leave, and not look back."

I laughed. "You want me to run away, like you?"

"Run away like me . . . or maybe run away *with* me? I can get you out of Rong. I can take you to Lan and hide you where no one will find you. When the storm passes, you'll be free to do whatever you want, go wherever you want. You said you want freedom, Fei. I can give you that freedom."

"Are you out of your mind? If I ran away with you, the Rong emperor would hunt us until they reach the edge of the skies and the ends of earth; they would not stop until they found us. Rong would start wars to get me back."

"I'm not scared of him, or his empire," Yexue said. "If you are set on disobeying fate, I don't think the Emperor of Rong will let you live. I think if you don't marry his son, he will make sure you never marry anyone at all."

"Siwang won't let anything happen to me."

"人心隔肚皮: *our hearts are separated by skin and flesh.* How can you know that for sure?"

"It's a risk I will have to take. I can't run away with you and put both you and your people in danger."

"You have no idea what I'm capable of," he said, gazing down at his hands. "You are not the only one who wishes to defy fate. Have you ever met the stargazer who first spoke your prophecy?"

"When I was younger, yes. I don't remember her well, just that she was tall, had long dark hair like the night sky and wide-set amber eyes. She was pretty and gave me sweets."

Yexue laughed at this last part. "Child Fei had her priorities straight."

"She was kind, but the older I grew, the more . . . frightened she became of me."

"Do you know why?"

My worst instincts pricked. "I had no idea you were so interested in the stargazer."

He smiled. "Like I said, you are not the only one who wishes to defy fate. And I imagine you are not the only one who wants answers for being . . . *different*? I had looked for the stargazer when I arrived in the capital, but I never found her. Some say she retired to the countryside, while others say she either was exiled or ran away. Do you know where she has gone?"

"I don't." A lie. I lay down and turned away from him before he could say anything else. "Good night, I am tired now."

I heard the shuffle of clothes as Yexue moved to the other side of the fire. "Good night, Little Goddess."

10

Hooves thundered after me, riders chasing prey.

I've been caught was my first thought.

I won't go down without a fight was my second.

I reached for my arrows by instinct, bow already sliding from my back.

But when I turned, arrow nocked and bow drawn, fingers at the edge of a deadly shot, all the air vanished from my lungs, because I was not staring into the eyes of a predator or even prey. I was staring into the wide eyes of the one boy I could never hurt.

At my heels wasn't a small army of guards and soldiers, or captains with brandished swords here to capture and return me to that sweltering palace.

It was Siwang.

My stern, beautiful Siwang with his bronzed face and moon-carved eyes, lips exquisite and plush like blooming petals. His face of immaculate angles, as if molded by the creator goddess Nüwa herself. A haunting sight that always stopped me in my tracks.

When our eyes met, I expected his face to soften from vicious bloodlust to the tender benevolence I was used to.

It didn't.

A snap of the reins, and his stallion charged forth with all the might of a thoroughbred raised for the battlefield. Siwang drew his weapon. If the bow he'd used yesterday morning was reserved for stags and wolves, then this was something else entirely.

Carved to hunt a whole other species of beast.

Then the vision blurred at the edges without warning. One moment shifted into the next in rapid succession. . . .

Hoofprints in freshly fallen snow.

The bloodied corpse of a Beiying tiger abandoned at the riverside, the beautiful blade Fangyun had given me not a day earlier lodged deep in its eye. My surname, 历峰, carved into its gilded hilt.

Siwang's scowl, lips downturned at the edges.

A piece of my torn coat in his gloved hands, retrieved from the tiger's claws.

Dawn easing into the horizon, slow and creeping.

A launched arrow.

Blood splattered across fresh snow.

Yexue.

—❦—

I woke with a gasp to wintry blue daylight as the impending dawn chased the night away from behind heavy gray clouds that dusted fresh snow along the terrain.

My wet lashes were clumped with frost. Yexue was already awake, putting out the fire and tending to my horse. From the ashes, he pulled out two eggs, likely stolen from a nearby nest, and was about to give one to me when I uttered: "We have to go."

He smiled. A beautiful sight, with none of the caution and fear I had expected. Were all princes this fearless, or did his magical blood gave him a special recklessness? The egg was warm. I would have cradled it between my hands if we weren't running out of time.

I tried to push myself to my feet. My head spun at the sudden movement, and my legs felt like noodles, going soft under my own weight. Yexue was at my side before I knew it, letting me lean on him to stand upright.

"They are coming. We must go. *Now,*" I said.

There was no trace of fear on Yexue's porcelain face.

I waited for him to ask how I knew, and clutched tight to the secret I had hidden for so long.

Yexue had bared his own magic to me last night and saved my life. If I had to give away my own secret to get us out of these mountains alive, it would be fair.

Right?

Before the stargazer disappeared, she had told me there was a power inside me, something magnificent and dangerous.

Be careful, child, she had told me. *You are more powerful than you realize. But men do not like powerful women.*

"We'd best get moving, then," Yexue said finally. The look he gave me was one of understanding, not confusion. As if he already knew my secret. "Are you coming with me, or will you wait for your prince and leave your fate to the entitlement of men?"

"I . . ."

"If you want to run, this might your last chance, Little Goddess." I didn't like this nickname he had given me. "Come with me." His hand grasped mine and pulled me to him in a way that would have caused a scandal if anyone saw. "Siwang isn't going to let you leave. He'll keep you at his side and make you his empress even if he must force you. That's not the kind of life you want. That's not the life you *deserve*."

My heart writhed like a small fluttering bird, slamming against the confinement of her cage. "And how do you know what I deserve?"

"Because you are brave, and courageous, and good. Good people deserve to be free, Fei. If the stars won't give you all that you deserve, then let *me*."

"You don't know me, Lan Yexue."

"What I saw last night was enough. Come to Lan. There, I will make sure you can do whatever you want, be whoever you want. Forget about conventions and duty—it's about time we break some of these ancient rules. And if I must go to war to give you what you deserve, then so be it."

That vision of blood-splattered snow flashed again. Lijian's blackened eye and bruised cheeks when he announced that his family was moving away from the capital. "Rong is the most powerful empire on the continent. There is a reason why you were sent here as a ward in the first place. Why Rong has conquered half the continent in just two decades."

"Are you . . . worried about me?" Yexue chuckled and placed his hand on the top of my head and ruffled my hair, just a little. Like I was a child who had just said something cute. "You are not the only one who wants to defy your destiny, Lifeng Fei. I came to Yong'An for my own reasons."

I remembered his questions from last night. "You came to the capital to find the stargazer?"

Yexue shrugged, clearly unwilling to disclose anymore. "Think about what you *want* to do, Little Goddess. Not what you should do. I can take care of Rong. I can even get your family out of the capital. I've told you: I'm not scared. If anything, they should be the ones who fear me."

"Siwang isn't like the guards you escaped from. He's trained by the best martial artists on the continent. You won't beat him so easily."

A crooked smile. He really was so arrogant. "Do you want to bet?"

"You are not immortal, and you are not a god," I reminded him. "I watched you bleed yesterday. I don't want to watch you bleed again."

"Nothing has killed me yet."

"Hubris is a vice that has gotten many heroes killed in history." I pushed myself off the cave floor and stumbled toward where my horse was tied. "We need to leave, now."

"Is this your way of agreeing to let me risk my life for you?"

"Things might be worse for you if they find you riding alone, your robe stained with blood while I'm nowhere to be found. I can't go to Lan with you, but I can bargain with Siwang when he catches us."

Yexue broke into a victorious grin. "You would sacrifice yourself for me?"

I looked away. "Don't flatter yourself. If I'm going back to the palace anyway, I might as well save your life so that you owe me one more life."

—⚬—

He helped me onto my stallion, and I held on tight. We rode southwest to avoid the camp as snow fell slowly.

In my dream, Siwang would find the tiger's corpse just as the snow stopped falling.

I prayed that we'd be far from here by then.

As we moved through the icy terrain, I tried to keep alert, to listen for the thunder of distant hooves and induce another vision from Fate. But no matter how hard I squeezed my eyes, I saw only darkness, felt only the cold wind slashing my cheeks and the sturdy breathing of Yexue against my body as I clung on tight.

"What happened to my bow?" I asked, realizing it wasn't on the saddle.

"The pretty one with both ends dipped in silver? I left it at the riverbank."

"You *what?*"

"I had to either leave that bow or leave *you* on the riverbank." Yexue laughed. "How did the empress of all empresses come to be so versed in archery, anyway?"

I smiled. "Do you disapprove?"

"I'm just curious. I didn't expect that the emperor would let his docile daughter-in-law learn something so . . ." Yexue trailed off, as if trying to find a word other than *unladylike.*

"He didn't. But I wanted to learn, so Siwang taught me."

I felt Yexue tense at this. "Siwang?"

I smiled. "Whatever I want, Siwang always—"

An arrow whizzed past us.

Then another, and another, each one meticulously aimed so it missed us just closely enough to catch our attention.

Two dozen men in a dispersed formation moved through the icy trees at lightning speed, with Siwang leading the pack, a spray of snow misting in his wake.

Already, this wasn't how things had played out in my visions.

I clung to Yexue a little tighter. "We have to stop. The longer we delay the inevitable, the more impatient Siwang will get."

If I wanted Yexue to escape these mountains alive, I couldn't tempt Siwang's wrath. As was tradition with hostage princes, Rong was responsible for keeping Yexue alive and unharmed. Though nothing in the agreement said they couldn't punish Yexue as they saw fit.

Cut off a finger or two, or maybe his whole hand, depending on how daring Rong felt. And for a hostage prince to be caught with the future empress would make Rong *very* daring. If Siwang could exile Lijian for sharing sweets with me, what would he do to Yexue?

Over my shoulder, Siwang's usual elegant and princely mask had hardened into something stoic.

"We have to stop," I repeated. "I can get you out of this alive, but we must concede."

"You underestimate me, Little Goddess!" Yexue shouted over his shoulder, loud enough for Siwang to hear. The distance between our horses was shrinking by the second. Soon Siwang and his men would catch us, and there would be nowhere to run. "Close your eyes."

"Yexue, you are outnumbered! I don't care what magic you have, you cannot fight twenty-something men by yourself!"

"Watch me." Yexue pulled the horse to a sudden halt. The stallion reeled, front legs kicking high. Yexue grabbed my hands to keep me from falling. "It's okay, I've got you."

"Fei!" Siwang cried.

By the time the horse calmed, Siwang and his men had us surrounded.

"Close your eyes. I don't want you to see this," Yexue repeated before he leaped off and drew his sword from its sheath with a thunderous hiss.

"You are not going to win!" Judging from their armor, these men were not imperial guards; they were soldiers. Real, battle-hardened soldiers who had trained their whole lives to excel at one thing and one thing only: killing.

"You are just like your tyrant father, Lan Yexue," Siwang snarled as he brandished his own blade. "Always taking what does not belong to you."

Frustration slashed through fear at these words. As if I were something that belonged to him and not myself.

"Bold words for a man who's about to die." Yexue retorted, his blade relaxed at his side. "Close your eyes, Fei. I don't want you to see this," Yexue warned one last time, then lunged at the closest soldier, quicker than what should have been possible.

Blood splattered across fresh-fallen snow, just like in my visions.

"I usually try not to make a mess, but my robes are already stained." Yexue moved like a shadow, too fast for my eyes to follow. The only indications of his location were the marks of crimson that bloomed after him.

Blood. So much blood. And Yexue wasn't the one bleeding, like I had thought.

He was the *killer.*

They are monsters, Fangyun's court gossip echoed. *The Lan dynasty trade magic with Death himself.*

I had thought this slander, distorted lies that sprouted from prejudice and long-held grudges between our two nations. But where there was smoke, there had to be fire.

Lan Yexue moved with expert precision. Blood kept spilling until the scene looked like a painting of winter roses.

What have I done?

By the time Yexue came to a stop in the middle of the field and lowered his sword, Siwang was the lone figure standing among fallen comrades—*barely.* He was clutching a gash in his abdomen, unsteady on his feet.

Yexue ran a blood-soaked hand through his now disheveled hair, then turned to present me with a grin that said *I told you so.*

Tears burned my frozen cheeks.

"You should have closed your eyes," Yexue mused. His voice was casual, as if we were discussing something as trivial as the weather. He offered his blade to me. "Would you like to do the honor of ending his life?"

"You . . ." I tried to speak, but every word collapsed in my mouth like running sand. My heart was a rampant beast rattling against my chest, its deafening *thud-thud-thud* drowning out my everything.

"I told you I would free you from the Rong Empire and your marriage, didn't I?" Yexue flashed that wide smile again. Except it was no longer beautiful.

Behind him, Siwang fell to his knees as blood poured and poured through clenched fingers that desperately tried to apply pressure to the wound.

Crimson pooled at Siwang's feet.

My Siwang.

I thought of the boy who'd climb trees to get the highest berries for me, write out a copy of every homework assignment in case I ever forgot mine, spend hours rolling in snow even when he was sick, just to spend a little more time with me.

The boy who held my hand when I cried, who listened to all my tear-soaked thoughts, my wishes and dreams and worst fears—those that I could share with him, at least—and promised he'd move mountains to make every single dream of mine come true and burn my every fear to ashes and that I shouldn't worry. Because I had him.

The boy who had begged his father to postpone our wedding not because he wanted to, but because *I* wanted to.

Again and again, Siwang had proved his heart to me.

Again and again, I had pushed him away. Because I was afraid. Of his love. Of falling in love with him. Of my nightmares. And of the possibility that maybe I didn't deserve him, and would never deserve him.

In my dreams, I had watched Rong Siwang die hundreds of times, if not thousands. All because of me, because of this prophecy that everyone believed would bring greatness to Rong. What if instead of an auspicious fate, I was a curse that would doom him to losing everything?

Run, I wanted to tell him, *while Yexue has his back turned.*

Siwang didn't run. He wouldn't. He was raised to be a hero, to be the noble and honorable prince his father had demanded he be since he was a baby, swaddled in silk.

Honorable princes didn't run from battles. Didn't leave their betrothed in the hands of a cold-blooded killer.

"Would you like to finish him off?" Yexue repeated, still offering me his blade.

With a shaking hand, I took the blade from him.

Yexue's smile deepened. He opened his arms and reached up, as if to help me down from the horse.

I didn't let him touch me.

Instead, I drove the blade into the right side of his chest, then pushed him away. "A life for a life. You saved mine, so I will spare yours. Get on, Siwang!" I hissed as I kicked the horse into motion.

Even injured, Siwang leaped on effortlessly.

I snapped the reins and the horse bolted into a full sprint. I didn't know who was faster, this prized stallion or the monstrous abilities of Lan Yexue.

Thankfully, I didn't find out.

Yexue didn't try to chase us. As we raced through the pinewoods, I heard neither the sound of horses' hooves nor his impossibly fast steps.

Against my better judgment, I allowed myself one last glance over my shoulder to see Yexue standing right where I'd left him, the blade still plunged into his chest as blood soaked through his once-pristine white robes.

He watched me with the same amber eyes that had regarded me so tenderly mere hours earlier in the cave. Though they were too far away to read, I assumed they were no longer so kind.

Yet, as we rode away, I could have sworn I saw Yexue smile.

11

"Get me a physician!"

Siwang was no longer conscious by the time I rode through camp, frantically searching for someone to tend to his wounds.

I would have done it myself if not for fear of wasting time. I didn't want to give Yexue a chance to catch up or do a bad job and make things worse. Siwang was the crown prince, the root of the emperor's life, the flesh of his heart. If anything happened to Siwang, neither I nor my family would be able to bear the weight of his rage.

Siwang couldn't die.

"Help!" I cried, louder this time. The sun blazed above us, so stifling I could barely breathe. Sweat beaded across my skin. I didn't know if it was because of my hammering heart or Siwang's blood burning through the back of my clothes. "A doctor . . . !" I panted, slipping from the saddle. "Someone help the prince. Please! Please . . ."

"Lady Lifeng!" someone shouted through the murky darkness. "Lady Lifeng! Someone get the imperial physician! Quick!"

"Help him," I murmured as consciousness slipped from my grasp.

Please.
Save him. Just . . .
Save him.

—✺—

Siwang.

His name was the first thing I thought of when consciousness re-aligned with my body.

I opened my eyes. A blurred, distorted scene slowly came into focus. I was back in my tent, Fangyun kneeling at my bedside, her head resting beside my hip, her hand holding mine even as she slept. There were tearstains around the blanket under her face. An imperial physician napped in the corner, and a fire crackled at the center of the room.

"Siwang . . . Where is Siwang?" I rasped out.

"You are awake?" Fangyun jerked to alertness at the sound of my voice.

"How are you feeling, Lady Lifeng?" The physician bolted to his feet, hurrying over to check my pulse. "You've been unconscious for almost three days."

I blinked. "Three days?"

"You were running a fever when you got back. You also showed signs of blood loss, though we couldn't find a wound. We were afraid it was some sort of internal bleeding. Thank the gods that you are okay. Your father and Prince Siwang are incredibly worried."

I sat up straighter at the mention of his name. "Siwang is alive?"

"The prince is very much alive and well. He's lost a lot of blood, too, but he's strong. By the time the head physician finished treating his wound, the prince was lucid and asking for you."

Tears stung the back of my eyes. *Thank the gods.* "When can I see him?"

"I recommend that you stay here and avoid exerting yourself until we have made further observations. The prince is up and on his feet; he can come to you."

"He's come to see you every night," Fangyun quickly added. "The physicians had to drag him back to his tent because he refused to leave your side."

"I'll send word to let him know you're awake." With that, the physician exited the room and Fangyun perched herself at the edge of my bed.

Her hands grabbed mine. "What happened?" she whispered, head dipped low, close to my ear.

"It's a long story."

"Then you'd better be quick, because Siwang is going to be here any minute now. Did you kill the tiger? I heard you were with the Prince of Lan when they found you. There are rumors that you ran away with him. That's not true, right? He kidnapped you, didn't he? He tried to use you as a hostage and leveraged your life against Siwang, and that's how Siwang got injured, right?" My sister spoke not with curiosity but conviction. Her eyes were misty and pleading.

An alibi, and a lie. A version of events that was safe to retell. I frowned. "Siwang told you what happened?"

"The two of you need to get your stories to match before the emperor questions you."

I smiled. "No need. I'm going to tell the emperor the truth. And the truth is that nothing happened between me and Lan Yexue."

"Really?" Fangyun visibly let go of a held breath. "Thank the gods."

With as few words as possible and carefully avoiding any details of Lan Yexue's secret, I retold everything to my sister in a voice barely louder than a whisper. I was halfway through when Siwang burst into the tent, scarcely dressed, with a mismatched blue sash hastily tied around the waist of his black-and-red robes.

"Your Highness! You will catch a cold!" An army of guards and physicians ran in after him with fur coats in hand.

Cheeks flushed, breath labored, the Crown Prince of Rong looked like he was about to cry. Siwang pushed the servant aside when he tried to touch him.

I tried to get up and go to him, to touch his face and feel his warmth so that I knew this wasn't a dream, that he really was alive. But my legs crumbled under me.

"The doctor told you not to move." Fangyun pushed me back onto the bed.

I saw that Siwang's feet were bare and wet with melting snow. He had run across camp barefoot, through all the freezing ice and sleet . . . for me. Something inside ached again. I hated it when Siwang did things like this. I hated it when he made it difficult to hate him.

"Fei." He whispered my name like a prayer. His tears threatened to spill when he stumbled toward me, lips twitching like there was something gravely important he wanted to say.

The room cleared without anyone's being asked, including my sister.

"Fangyun." I tried to call her back, but she gave me a subtle shake of her head.

"Are you okay?" Siwang moved closer, sitting in the spot Fangyun had vacated.

"I feel fine." It wasn't a lie. Aside from the heaviness of my limbs and the slight lethargy, I felt normal. "A little tired, maybe. That's all."

"I'll ask the cooks to bring you some bone broth. You'll feel better after you've eaten something."

I nodded, awkwardly averting my gaze. "Thank you."

Siwang glanced at the entrance, then leaned close until his lips almost grazed the shell of my ear, and I felt his hot breath tingling against my icy skin. "You killed that Beiying tiger, right?"

My breath hitched. Then I gave a small nod.

"Do I want to know why?" Siwang was too smart not to understand why the future Empress of Rong would risk her life by venturing into the perilous mountains to hunt a predator at midnight.

"You already do, my prince."

Siwang pulled away. "I thought . . . I thought we'd agreed to at least try? I'll hold off my father's pressure for us to marry, and you'll give me a chance to earn your heart."

We did make this promise, a few years ago on our birthday when it became clear the emperor's patience was wearing thin. I was so scared that Father would finally yield and set a date for our wedding that I did the only thing I could to buy myself time: enlist Siwang's help.

It was a hollow promise, one I knew I wouldn't keep.

I turned away. I couldn't bear looking at Siwang's half-parted lips, almost quivering as he looked at me with misty eyes, brimming with tears, with heartbreak. He loved me, and all I ever did was betray him and push him away. I didn't deserve him. I had never deserved him.

My sister was right. Siwang was everything a girl should want from a match. If we were different people in a different life, I would hold on to him as tightly as he held me, and never let go.

"I don't want to be your empress, Siwang."

He flinched, and I could have sworn I heard something break

inside him like a snapping bone. "Is it Lan Yexue? Do you love him? Is that why?"

My breath caught at the mention of love. This was the first thing that came to his mind. Love. Not the prophecy, and not the title of emperor of all emperors. "No. I barely knew Yexue before our paths crossed in the mountains. He's been at court for, what, two years? You know I've been trying to get out of this betrothal for far longer than that."

"Then—"

"The two of us found each other by pure chance, nothing more," I assured him. "If I wanted to run away with Lan Yexue, then I wouldn't have stabbed him to save you."

His eyes lowered. I gave him a brief recounting of what had happened, again taking caution to leave out the part where I had almost died and Yexue had saved me with his blood.

"I had no idea that Yexue was capable of such monstrous things. When he started killing your men, I . . . I never thought I'd put you in danger, Siwang. You have to believe me."

Siwang's jaw was hard with restraint. "Lan Yexue is the least of your worries right now." A heavy exhale. He was no longer looking at me. His disappointment rippled the air, and I couldn't blame him. I had used him and broken our promise.

A promise that I barely remembered.

A promise he had kept close to his heart.

"My father would never let you break our betrothal. Not for tradition and certainly not for a mere tiger's pelt. You are playing with fire, Fei. If you choose this path, it won't end well for you."

"I've come too far and sacrificed too much not to see this foolish plan through," I murmured, resisting the urge to touch the place on my chest the tiger had torn open. "This is the path I've chosen, and I will walk it even if my feet bleed dry. If you love me, you will let me choose my own fate."

"You are wasting your time."

Without thinking, I grabbed both of his hands and squeezed tight. Siwang's breath hitched. "Help me convince your father. He might not break the betrothal for me or for the pelt of a Beiying tiger, but he will for *you*."

The light dimmed in Siwang's eyes. "You can't ask this of me."

"Siwang, please. *Help me*."

"Fei . . ."

"Any girl would be lucky to be your empress. Once this news breaks, every maiden in the empire will sell her soul for a chance of becoming your bride. You are the dream of—"

"I don't want them!" he snapped in a rare moment of untethered temper, so sudden I almost let go of his hands. But this time, he was the one who held tighter, who pulled me close. "I can make you happy, Fei. I know I can. If you just give me the chance, I can make you love me. Tell me what you want, and I'll do it. I'll change everything about me, about this country, about this *world* until it pleases you. . . . Until your heart matches mine in love, even if only a fraction."

"It's not that simple, Siwang."

"Try me."

I closed my eyes. "You might hold the power of an empire in the palm of your hand one day, but even you cannot change the expectations of society. The palace rules demand that I spend my entire life locked up behind its crimson walls. A life devoted to bearing your weight and birthing your heirs until I am wrought and empty, until I am a corpse ready for burial."

His lips thinned. "If you don't want that to be your life, I can take you out of the palace and spend days in the city. I can—"

"I don't want to spend another day inside that palace. There is a world beyond the palace, beyond Rong and its valleys and steeps. In the great north where our ancestors used to live, there was more. Icy mountains and whispers of dragons born from snow and frost. Beasts so mighty they can swallow Beiying tigers whole. There is a whole world out there beyond Yong'An. Cities and stories and beauties of every sort. Colors and scents and tastes and *everything*. I want all of it, Siwang. I want to *live*. I want more from my life than being an empress. I want and I want, but I can't have any of it because of that gods-forsaken prophecy. Because of . . ."

Because of the emperor's greed and Siwang's ambition and everything in between that made me a mere pawn in their quest for power. All the things that would one day lead to a massacre befalling Yong'An if we stayed on this path.

Two things could be true at the same time. I could want freedom and also want to protect him and Yong'An from calamity. It was fortunate that by leaving, I could accomplish both.

"As emperor, you would have hundreds of consorts and concubines and serving girls at your beck and call. And all I will have is loneliness. I don't want to share my husband. I don't want to see you only when *you* want to see me. How can I love you if one of us is the sun, the source of all power and warmth, and I am a mere flower in your gardens, hoping to bask in your light? How can I offer my heart to you, only for you to break it every night you choose to lie next to another?"

"But when I unite the Warring States, you'll be empress of the entire continent. I will give you everything you could possibly want."

"And how can you be so sure that you can give me what I want, when you don't know what I want? Maybe this is why we are wrong for each other. You've spent your whole life in the lap of luxury, used to being obeyed and desired and wanted. Everyone you've ever met will do anything to make your eyes linger just a moment longer, to exist within the halo of your radiance. Not because they love you, but because their lives depend on it. This is why you can never understand why I don't melt at your promises."

With every word, I watched Siwang's face drop a little more, his eyes watering and his lips quivering as if he were looking for words he couldn't find.

I felt like I had stabbed him and was now twisting the knife.

It is better this way. The sooner I broke his heart, the sooner he could begin to heal.

"Tiger's pelt or not, I will still ask the emperor to cancel our betrothal. Even if I have to die for it," I added after the pause.

"Your Highness?" A eunuch's voice cut in from outside. "The emperor has summoned both you and Lady Lifeng to his tent. He has important matters to discuss with the two of you."

Siwang winced.

"Tell him I'll be there shortly." I took a deep breath. "Now, Your Highness, if you could please give me some privacy, I need to change into appropriate attire before meeting with your father."

"Don't say anything once we see my father," Siwang warned as he turned to leave. "Let me do the talking."

12

*L*et me do the talking, he'd repeated over and over again on our way here. *Let me handle this.*

"You and the Prince of Lan spent the night in a cave *together*?" The emperor's voice was low and stern like rumbling thunder.

Chastity was a fragile thing, and the single hint of a rumor was all it took to ruin a girl's reputation. Great empires had crumbled because of lineage rumors. The emperor would never let a girl of questionable chastity become the Empress of Rong.

Maybe I didn't need the pelt of a Beiying tiger to change my destiny after all. Maybe all I needed was a rumor with a dangerous yet beautiful prince who was not Siwang.

The emperor's lips thinned with barely contained rage. I thought he might raise his hand and slap me, or draw a blade and grant me a swift end.

In the end, his eyes roamed past me. The emperor's wrath refocused on my still-kneeling father, who had remained silent.

I glanced at Siwang for help. His face had returned to its usual nonchalance. The emperor and Siwang were standing while Father and I were on our knees, waiting to be allowed to rise again. To my left was a gilded table with cups of still-warm tea and decadent cakes dusted in sugar.

My stomach grumbled, finally. From the moment I'd woken up until now, I had not had even a single drop of water, let alone anything to eat. It was a miracle my stomach lasted through the emperor's lengthy accusations without protest.

Siwang put a hand on his father's arm. "Let Fei have something to eat first. She must be hungry."

The emperor huffed. With a wave of his hand, a silent permission to rise was granted.

"Fei, Minister Lifeng." Siwang helped us up, making sure to hold me steady when my legs quaked under me, my head dizzy from the sudden movement. "Here." He guided me toward the table and pushed forward a plate of red bean cakes.

I took one bite, then another. They were sweet and soft, and my stomach rumbled for more, but I paced my bites. *Each bite must be small enough to swallow at a moment's notice in case your father or husband calls upon your attention.* Lessons taught by the palace ladies. I fought the urge to shove the entire thing into my mouth and chew with my mouth open out of spite.

This was not a time for rebellion.

"How many people know about this?" The emperor's attention shifted to Siwang.

"No one outside of this tent. Not anymore, at least. The only people who knew Fei was missing were the guards who went into the mountains with me."

The soldiers Yexue had killed.

The emperor nodded, pleased, then turned his attention to Father. "What about the maid who found Fei's room empty?"

No. Father tensed under the emperor's attention. "Your Majesty . . ."

"Have the maid and everyone she might have told killed before sunset. If anyone asks, when Siwang ventured into the mountains to capture Lan Yexue, Fei followed because she was scared he'd get hurt. She got lost and was cornered by the Prince of Lan. Luckily, Siwang saved Fei."

"No, please! They didn't do anything!" The words came so suddenly I almost didn't recognize the sound of my own voice.

"The palace ladies have already instructed the maid not to say anything, Your Majesty," Father interjected.

"Have them killed as well. Everyone who might know anything about that night needs to die," the emperor replied. "We must protect her reputation at all costs. A couple of lowly maids are nothing in the grand scheme of things. To be on the safe side, we should hold Siwang and Fei's wedding as soon as possible. 夜长梦多, *long nights are often fraught with dreams.* The longer we wait, the more problems we will run into."

"Father," Siwang protested. "We've talked about this. Fei and I are—"

"This is for your own good, son. If we wait any longer, we'd risk more incidents like this one. You cannot let the prophecy fall into another man's hand."

I hated it when the emperor spoke as if I weren't a real, breathing person with a beating heart and feelings and *ears.*

I took a deep breath, gathered the courage I'd been saving for the last seventeen, almost eighteen, years. It was now or never. If I wanted control over my own life, or even the slightest essence of freedom, I had to do this. Regardless of the cost. "Your Majesty, are you not curious about why I went into the mountains that night?"

The emperor's eyes sharpened when his attention fell back to me, as if irritated by the remembrance of my existence.

Just like the maid whose life he'd carelessly forfeited with just a few words, I was a mere pawn in his eyes. My only value was that string of words uttered seventeen years ago under a cursed constellation, and the phoenix's mark between my brows that had become a symbol for his military campaigns.

"I went into the mountains to hunt the Beiying tigers," I confessed after the pause.

The emperor forced a smile, feigned amusement. "Look at you, not yet Siwang's wife and already thinking of ways to honor me with your filiality. No wonder the gods chose you to be the empress of all empresses."

"*No.*" I choked. My heart hammered against my chest like a frantic dove, willing to break every bone in her body and paint herself bloody if it meant she could soar the cerulean skies one last time. "I didn't do it out of filiality, Your Majesty. I did it to break my betrothal to Siwang."

Originally, I'd planned to do this before all the high-ranked officials, hoping some of them would think of their own daughters and support me in my fight to seize my destiny. If I didn't make a scene, the emperor could easily sweep this under the rug, paint the request as a girl's cold feet. However, a private disobedience might be safer than a public disobedience right now.

The emperor would never let a girl speak to him so brashly in front of the court.

"You want to break your betrothal?" The emperor let out a low, chilling laugh. "You want to break your betrothal to Siwang . . . ?"

Without warning, he grabbed the ceremonial sword at Siwang's hip and drew the blade from its sheath with a screech.

"Father!" Siwang cried, reaching for the blade without thinking.

The emperor pushed him away, still laughing.

"Your Majesty!" Father fell back to his knees in an instant, repeatedly slamming his head against the ground, as if this could earn the emperor's mercy.

"You don't want to be Siwang's bride?"

"No, Your Majesty," I replied. Firm in my decision with all its consequences. I did not want to die, however if this was what it would take to change the future and save everyone I loved, then I would do it. "I do not."

"You don't want to be the Empress of Rong?"

"No, Your Majesty."

"Well." The emperor shrugged. "If the empress of the united Warring States isn't going to be the Empress of Rong, then I guess she won't be anyone's empress." The emperor raised the blade over his head.

"Your Majesty!" my father cried. "Please! It is my fault! I should have raised her better!"

I closed my eyes and waited for the blade to fall, resisting the urge to remind my father that he did not raise me. For the emperor took that from us. I was just an infant when he robbed me of my life the first time. What did it matter if he robbed it a second time?

"I wish for Fei to live!" Siwang cried. My eyes snapped open, and I saw that Siwang had thrown himself in front of me, using his own body as a shield against his father's wrath. "Last year when I killed the first Beiying tiger of the hunt, you told me I could have anything I wanted. This is what I want. For Fei to live."

Siwang.

The emperor laughed. A hollow, bitter sound.

Then, for the first time in my life, the emperor looked at me. *Really* looked at me, as if for the first time he saw not an asset but a person worthy of his true attention.

The moment didn't last long. The emperor's gaze shifted back to Siwang, and he shook his head. "You useless boy," he said through gritted teeth, then dropped the blade. It fell to the ground with a shuddering clang. "How many times have I warned you, Siwang? Never get attached to anyone. Never bestow anyone your real emotions. An emperor cannot afford to feel. Because as soon as we care about something or someone, it becomes our weakness."

Siwang reached back until his hand found mine. He squeezed tight—to comfort me or himself, I wasn't sure. "I don't want to lose her, Father."

"Then marry her."

"No!" I protested.

The emperor's gaze turned venomous in the blink of an eye. "This isn't the time or place for a woman to speak!"

"*No,*" I repeated through gritted teeth, louder this time. "I'm not marrying him."

"Lifeng Fei, you little—"

"Father," Siwang interrupted before his father could pick up the sword and finish me once and for all. "This is mine and Fei's marriage. Can we have a moment of privacy to talk this through?"

"What is there to talk about?" the emperor bellowed. "The two of you are getting married. End of discussion!"

"Your Majesty." My father spoke up with a trembling voice, head still bowed. "Since His Highness has asked, maybe we should give them a moment, let them smooth things out themselves? It is their marriage, after all."

"*Please,* Father."

The emperor stared at his son in disbelief, rage simmering beneath his suntanned face, so much that the graying hairs of his beard quaked ever so slightly.

After a strangled eternity, the emperor shook his head. He shot Siwang one last look before he exited the tent, Father following at his heels.

It wasn't until they were both gone that I let go of the breath I was holding.

"You okay?" Siwang asked, his voice soft.

"I'm fine."

With a heavy exhale, Siwang rose to his feet, putting some distance between us.

He poured himself a small cup of tea from the pot, then another for me. "Are you sure you want to do this, Fei?"

"I am."

Siwang nodded. "How long have you been planning this?"

"Six months." Another half-truth. I'd only begun planning *this* version of my escape for six months. But I had been planning for this moment for as long as I could remember. Perhaps since the moment our fathers sealed our betrothal, my little infant mind had been scheming for a way out. "There is something I've wanted to ask for a long time, but I don't know whether I should."

Siwang chuckled. "Things have already escalated to this point, what is left that you can't ask?"

"Did you know?"

"About your escape?" he replied. "I had an inkling."

"And you didn't do anything to stop me?" Maybe Fangyun was right: that one day I would regret pushing him away.

"该来的总是会来的. *What must come, will come eventually.* If I stopped you from pursuing this—no matter how foolish your plan is, and how much I don't want to lose you—you would find another way eventually. I know you, Fei. Once you've set your mind to something, not even ten bulls can pull you back from the path you chose."

I hated that he was right. Siwang knew me for all my good and bad, my capabilities and flaws. He knew me like a general knew a battlefield; a consequence of growing up side by side. I could never hide anything from him.

I took a sip of the tea and urged my heart to calm. "Thank you. For not stopping me."

"Don't thank me. If I were worthy of your gratitude, I would have asked my father to annul the betrothal and set you free a long time ago. You are not made for the palace life. I know this, yet . . ." He huffed a laugh, though it sounded more like a whimper. "For seventeen years, we grew up together. Before I was old enough to speak, to think, or to understand this world and all its complexities, I had memories of you. I can't remember any cherished moments without you. I can't imagine a *life* without you."

"Siwang . . ."

"I am not a good enough man to set you free. Neither am I prideful enough to not beg you to stay."

"Is this you, begging?" I whispered.

"If I knelt at your feet like a loyal servant and begged with all the love and devotion my mortal heart has to offer, would you stay?"

Our eyes met in this aching moment of stillness. Siwang's eyes cradled tears that both shone with hope and glistened with fear. His lips quivered; I had never seen my prince look so anguished and desperate. As if he really was a normal man, begging the woman he loved to stay.

I lowered my gaze. I couldn't bear seeing him like this.

"I have always loved you, Fei. I—" His voice cracked.

"Siwang, don't . . ." I closed my eyes, tears welling between my lashes. Whenever I thought of this moment, I'd never imagined it to be easy. Yet I'd never imagined it would be this hard.

"I thought that with time, I could win your heart and make you happy, just as you've made me happy for so many years," he continued. With every hitch of Siwang's breath, every devastated sniffle of his words, I felt like I was being cut open, over and over again. I would rather the mighty claws of the Beiying tiger over this torment. "I guess I was wrong. I'm not the man Fate planned for you."

My chest was so tight that I could no longer breathe. "It's not your fault, Siwang."

"I know this isn't what you want to hear," he continued. "But if I don't tell you how I feel now, I might never get the chance to. Even if you're inclined to believe this is a ploy to keep you at my side for the sake of the prophecy. Even if you choose to paint my love as obligation or ambition. That is your choice. Just as loving you is mine."

I squeezed my eyes tighter, trying to keep the tears at bay. Each word felt like the lash of an iron-tipped whip, shredding my heart into bloodied ribbons. "I'm sorry, I never wanted to hurt you."

"Why won't you stay?" His voice was coarse and fragile, like a man on the verge of tears. I squeezed my eyes tighter. As if by not looking at him, I could pretend this moment wasn't real.

"It's not you, Siwang." I gave him the words I knew he needed to hear. Siwang expected too much of himself. As the crown prince, he had been burdened with the weight of an empire's expectations. "If we were in different circumstances, if you were a normal man and there were no prophecy, I would have loved you—every broken piece of you with every broken piece of me." I sighed, slowly opening my eyes again but still not looking at him. "Maybe to some people, the title of empress is enough to forgive the other things. To me, an empress is just a title. Revered as the most powerful woman in the land, when in reality she still bows to the whims of a man. Everything I will have as empress will be an extension of you. You can give me power, just as you can take it away. 伴君如伴虎, *to accompany a ruler is to accompany a tiger.* You might love me now, but one day you might hate me enough to want me dead."

"I would *never.*"

"We don't know what the future holds." Vivid flashes of my nightmares pushed at my consciousness. I would not let such a fate befall Siwang, nor Yong'An.

Still, I wondered: Would Siwang still love me if the situation were reversed and he were the one cursed with glimpses of a blood-soaked future? Would he choose to banish me to save his people? Whom did Siwang love more—me, or his empire? A question I had never given much thought to.

Hopefully, I would never find out.

"But this is the way. Not just in Rong, but across the continent."

"What if I want my life to be more than just marriage and bearing children? The world is so much bigger than the palace, than Yong'An, than Rong. I want to experience all of it, firsthand, not hear about it from poems, or imagine it from the inks of a priceless painting that could never capture the real thing. I want everything in vivid colors and clarity." Slowly, I reached my hand across the table and took his hand into mine, squeezing it tight as my eyes focused on his. *I want you to live a long and happy life.* "Have you ever wanted something so much that you can't breathe? That you don't feel life is worth living without it?"

The knot between his brows tightened. "We don't always get what we want."

His words had an edge to them. I let go of his hand and returned to my ladylike position across the table, hands folded in my lap, spine straight, and shoulders back the way Mother had taught me.

In the Warring States, mothers raised sons to be brave and courageous, daughters to be delicate and agreeable. Sweet and docile, we were to be. Timid as we were fair. Obeying and submitting. Cursed to bow to the orders of our fathers, then kneel to the commands of our husbands. Living life more like property than people.

If Siwang wanted to, he could keep me in this betrothal by force. He was the prince of the most powerful empire in the land, and I was just a girl. There was nothing I could do to stop him. As the man, as the prince, he had all the power, and the only things I had were my threadbare hopes.

And my belief that he loved me enough to make the right decisions.

"Forget about me, Siwang," I whispered into the frigid air. "One day, you will have so many lovers that you won't be able to count them all. A few years from now, when you are the emperor, I bet you won't even remember my name. You don't need me in your life."

"You really think I'd forget your name?"

No, I don't. I didn't tell him this.

Let him think I was heartless and oblivious to his feelings, so that he could remain oblivious to mine.

Siwang rose to his feet and marched toward the entrance of the tent. His stoic, princely mask fell over his features once more.

"Please tell my father and Minister Lifeng that they may come back into the tent now," he told the men standing guard. Then he turned to me. "Are you sure this is what you want?"

"I . . ." It took me a moment to understand what he was asking. "I am sure."

"Very well. This is the last thing I can offer you, Fei. Whatever happens next is up to Fate."

There was a chill in the tent when the emperor reentered, with Father a few steps behind him, his head still bowed.

13

"Cancel the betrothal," Siwang told his father.

Disappointment shadowed the emperor's face, but Siwang didn't cower. He kept his head high and his eyes locked with his father's.

"You useless boy. Did I not just remind you that a real emperor can never love anyone?"

"You loved Mother, didn't you?" Siwang pushed, and the emperor winced at the mention of his late empress. "If Mother had asked you to set her free, you would have chosen the same. If Fei doesn't want to marry me, then I'm not going to force her. I'm the future Emperor of Rong. I won't marry a girl if she doesn't want to marry me, not when there are plenty who would give everything for this honor."

"What about the prophecy, son? Are you going to let another man become the emperor of emperors?"

"That won't happen!" I blurted out. Luckily, this was a hurdle I'd prepared for. "I . . . I promise you that if I don't marry Siwang, then I won't marry anyone. *Ever.*"

The emperor huffed at my declaration as if it were the words of a child. "You promise? What use is a promise? Promises are made to be broken, you foolish little girl."

"Then I will swear on it! I will swear on the bones of my ancestors. I will swear on the sun and the moon and all the stars who blessed me, and my own life! As long as I live, I will not marry anyone besides Rong Siwang."

Father's eyes went wide, his lips parted with an objection that never became sound.

To promise on my own life was one thing. To promise it on the bones of our ancestors was another. If I ever broke this promise, it would be blasphemy, and I'd be banished to the eighteenth level of hell after death.

When the tension between the emperor's brows eased, I knew it had worked.

The emperor stared at his son with all the rage of a ruler and all the love of a father.

In the end, he closed his eyes and shook his head in defeat. "死罪可免活罪难逃. *You can be exempted from the punishment of death, but you will still be punished.* You have tarnished the Rong name with your defiance, and that cannot go without punishment."

"Punish me instead!" Siwang interjected. "I knew Fei's plan and I didn't stop her. I am as much to blame for all of this as she is."

The emperor shot Siwang a look of disdain. "Lifeng Fei, I hereby banish you and your family from Yong'An. You and your family will return to the Su'He region, where you were born. There you will think over your mistakes. You may return to Yong'An only if you change your mind and choose to marry my son. Do you understand?"

My heart sank. I looked at Father, whose head remained so low that I couldn't see his reaction.

I'm sorry, I desperately wanted to tell him. *I never meant for this to implicate you.*

It was too late to change things now. This was the path I had chosen, so now I must walk it. Of course my recklessness would ensnare my family one way or another. It was naive of me to have hoped the emperor would spare them from bearing the weight of my actions.

I closed my eyes, knelt for the emperor for the last time, and bowed to receive this decree. "I . . . I understand."

14

It snowed on the day my family was set to leave Yong'An. Feathery white flakes fell from the sky like specks of sugar.

I'd always loved the snow, and how it illuminated the gloomy winter days. I loved it the most on the days when our imperial teachers would allow the other kids to stay in the palace a little longer after our classes to play. It meant I got to see Fangyun for a few more hours, got to sit with her and hear her whisper news of Mother and Father and the world outside the palace. Gossip and rumors always delighted me, despite the nannies constantly telling me that the empress of all empresses should be above all this. I treasured these flickers of joy amid the monotonous gray of a life imprisoned.

Occasionally, if the emperor was free and in a fine mood, he'd come to judge our snowmen and award prizes for the best ones.

Years ago, before the pressure of being crown prince robbed Siwang of his childhood innocence, he spent two days in the gardens building an ice statue of an intricately scaled koi.

A symbol of fortune and luck. The emperor was so overjoyed by his son's creation that he rewarded him with a precious luminescent pearl. Which Siwang crafted into a hairpin, set in a crown of serpentine vines, and gave to me on my next birthday.

I had no idea where that hairpin was now. Like most of my things, I'd left it behind. The palace was the only life I had ever known, however that life had never felt like mine. It was temporary, and it was a cage. I didn't need shiny memorabilia to remember my time behind those red walls, because the one thing I did want to remember, I couldn't take with me. So I might as well bury him with the past.

When my carriage exited those iron gates and I watched the golden roofs of the heavenly pavilions grow smaller and smaller until they were specks in the distance, I knew this would be the last time I saw these lavish halls that had been my whole world for almost eighteen years.

After today, I would never see Yong'An again. Never see Siwang again.

Leaving was bittersweet. Sweet because I had gotten what I had prayed for. Bitter because regardless of how much I hated it, that palace was the only home I had ever known.

I'd never liked goodbyes, so I didn't say them. Not to the nannies who'd raised me, not to the servant girls who'd become the closest things I had to friends outside of Siwang and my sister.

No goodbyes. Not even to Siwang, whom I had avoided up until my departure. I was afraid that the moment I saw him, everything would sink in, and that he would be the straw that broke my back.

I couldn't risk tears. This was a seed I'd sown with my own hands, and there was no turning back now.

"Take that to the front yard," Fangyun instructed the servants extricating our belongings from the family manor.

My sister was diligently picking up pieces of the life I'd shattered.

Only two years my senior, Fangyun had always felt so much older and more mature than I was. Some days, I wished Fate had placed the phoenix's mark between my sister's brows instead of mine.

She wouldn't have crumbled under the pressure. She would have thrived and been the empress that Rong deserved, that Siwang deserved.

Our house was loud with chaos, soldiers stomping, hastily packing up my family's belongings to be returned to the emperor. Mother was crying while Father sat in a corner, praying.

Neither Mother nor Father had said a single word to me since I'd come home. I wondered if they would ever forgive me for ruining their lives here in the capital.

You are doing it for them, I tried to remind myself. If I didn't remove myself from this path, the capital would go up in flames, and they would burn with it.

"Be careful with that statue—it's solid jade. If you drop it, the emperor will have your head," Grand Eunuch Su instructed, watching everything carefully, ticking things off the list in his hand.

This house, along with most things inside, had been bestowed by the emperor, gifts he was now taking back.

A small act of pettiness, though in the grand scheme of things, it was nothing.

I had broken the heart of the emperor's favorite son and stolen his fabled fate to become *emperor of all emperors.* I wouldn't be surprised if worse punishments had crossed his mind, and the only reason I was still alive was because Siwang had to physically hold his father back.

A life in exile was too easy a sentence—we all knew this. Hence, we had to leave the city as soon as possible, before the emperor changed his mind.

"Let me help," I said to Fangyun. *Please, let me do something for this family.*

"It's okay, Fei. I have everything under—"

She was interrupted by the sudden sound of horses' hooves rushing into the courtyard. It was Siwang, followed by a slew of his uniformed guards.

My sister grabbed my hand immediately, pushed me behind her as if to shield me. Her hand squeezed mine so tightly that tears welled behind my eyes.

"What is he doing here?" she asked.

"I don't know."

"Fangyun." Siwang greeted her with a nod before his eyes landed on me. Then, more softly, "Fei."

My sister and I curtsied, as the law required. In the palace, I rarely followed this rule, but things were different now.

With an outward motion of Siwang's hand, his guards came forward to help the men load our things onto the cart. "This isn't a job for noble ladies."

"We are no longer ladies," I replied, but didn't object. *And we weren't doing any of the hard labor.*

An inward motion of Siwang's hand, and someone quickly stepped forward and offered him a long wooden box. Siwang opened it. Inside was the silver-tipped bow he had given me all those years ago. The same one that had been left behind on the riverbank that day.

"For protection" was all he said.

I smiled. "Beautiful things like this belong in the palace, not small villages in Su'He."

A bow grand as this one would be admired in the palace. But in small villages like the one where we were set to go, it would be a curse, the sort of priceless treasure that might lead to my entire family getting slaughtered by thieves.

Siwang nodded, as if he had expected this. Then from his sleeve, he drew a smaller ivory box.

"Take this, at least. It's powder and makeup, to cover up your phoenix's mark. The world outside the palace might not know your face, but they've heard of the prophecy and the mark. Keep it hidden, protect it. When these powders run out, send letters. Address them to *Siwang,* just Siwang, no titles and no surname, and sign them with *Fei,* just Fei. So that I'll know they're from you. I will have people deliver more powder to you, no matter where you are. Whatever you want in life, all you have to do is ask, and I will give you it."

I bit the inside of my lips. Was this a vessel of kindness, or a way for Siwang to keep track of me?

"Don't reject me, Fei. Let me do this for you, at least."

When receiving gifts from men, it is best to receive them gracefully even if you do not want them. Something a nanny had told me long ago. So I smiled. "Thank you."

"You . . . you don't have to write only when the powder runs out," he said, half stumbling over his words. "You can send letters to me anytime. . . . Tell me about your travels. Where you are and who you meet and . . . I . . ." He lowered his gaze. There was a tinge of redness to his eyes.

"I'll write," I promised him. "I'll tell you about the world outside."

"Tell me everything. Write to me so that I can experience everything with you . . . if only in spirit." He looked around. "Can I have a moment alone with you?"

I froze. "We have to leave soon."

"It won't take long. I just . . . I just want to talk to you. One last time."

"I'll give you two some space," Fangyun replied for me. She gave Siwang one last bow, then made her way toward the parlor where our mother's cries could be heard.

I led him through a red half-moon gate toward the garden, away from the busy eyes and careful ears of the courtyard. "We don't have much time."

"Are you trying to get rid of me?" There was an edge to his voice. Hurt? "Today is your last day in Yong'An. If I hadn't come, would you have left without saying goodbye?"

I kept my head low because I couldn't bear to tell him that yes, I would have. Not because I didn't want to see him, but because I wasn't sure my heart was strong enough.

I didn't want to look into his eyes and realize that this was the last time I'd ever gaze upon his golden face, hear his laugh, behold his smile . . . Almost eighteen years of just me and him inside that vast palace. So many memories.

He was the closest friend I'd ever had. And by leaving, I would forfeit my right to watch him grow and age. But with me gone, hopefully the calamity from my visions would never come true, and he would live a long life as a fierce emperor, revered and beloved by his people.

I blinked away the mist in my eyes. Now that he was here, I realized how much I didn't want to leave him.

How much I wished to keep him at my side despite everything.

Icy flakes continued to fall from the sky, dusting us in white.

"Fei'er." My heart leaped at the way he said my name. The softness of it, coated in the affection I didn't deserve.

Perhaps more than his darkness, I had always feared this gentler side of him. I had feared it before, and I feared it now. The way it threatened to thaw my heart, dissolve the resolution I'd sacrificed too much not to keep.

The Siwang I wanted to see was the ruthless prince whose ambition could swallow mountains. I wanted him to be the emperor his father expected. Selfish and cruel, a man willing to do anything and everything to get what he wanted. However, if Siwang were such a man, he would never let me go. If he were such a man, I wouldn't love him so . . .

I wanted Rong Siwang to be a villain, easy to hate, easy to leave. Not a kind man who loved me more than I deserved, who would rather break his own heart than see me unhappy.

For a held breath, I thought he would reach out and kiss me, ask me to stay.

He didn't.

"Talk to me," he whispered. "Say something. *Please.*"

"I have nothing to say to you."

"Aren't you going to miss me?"

"No." A lie. The crueler I was to him, the easier it would be for him to forget me, the shorter his suffering would be.

I owed him too much. This small mercy was the last thing I could offer him.

"What do you feel right now?" he asked.

My eyes darted toward the courtyard, where I could no longer see Fangyun's shadow. "I'm worried about my family. My parents have grown accustomed to life in the capital, as the parents of the future empress. My sister was barely two years old when we left the small village where I was born. She's never known a life not bathed in luxury. I'm scared she won't be able to adapt."

I'm scared I'm *not going to adapt,* I thought silently. *That I've made the biggest mistake of my life, running away from you.*

"That's not what I meant, Fei."

"I know."

He took a step closer. His long, elegant fingers brushed a stray strand of hair from my face. "Even if you don't want to marry me, you don't have to leave. If you'll bow your head and apologize, I can beg my father for mercy, let you and your family stay. . . . I will take care of you for the rest of our lives, Fei."

Take care. Not *love.* I noticed this subtle choice of words.

"Your father won't take back this decree. Everyone has a limit, and we've pushed the emperor beyond his. It is a miracle that I am walking away from the capital in one piece."

Siwang's other hand reached forward, as if to touch me; then he stopped himself. Something flickered in those eyes. Hate, or heartbreak? His hand trembled in the space between us, suspended in motion, so afraid of my rejection.

Then Siwang look a deep breath and stepped back, straightened his posture.

"Would you stay if I promise to change things?" A murmur, no louder than a breath. "What if I promise to marry only you? I'm willing to be yours and yours alone, Fei. If you choose me, then I will also choose you. There won't be any consorts or concubines. I will love only you. Forever."

My heart jerked in my chest. *Yes,* a voice deep inside me replied. *Yes, I would stay.*

But this wasn't just about us. Freedom was only one half of truth, and I couldn't tell him the other half, because if I did and his father found out that I had magic, he would never let go. He would use me and my visions against the world and treat me like a weapon in his warfare.

So I forced myself to laugh. "Do you want to be the emperor of emperors that much? When will you realize that the prophecy is just nonsense? I'm not some magical rite to unite the continent."

In fact, I might bring about the downfall of everything you and your family have built.

Something blazed in Siwang's eyes. "Stop painting my intentions as things they are not! That's not why I'm proposing this, Fei, and you know it."

The outer courtyard was quieter now. They had finished loading the carts.

It was time to leave.

"I've made my decision and paid the price. I'm not going to go back on everything over an empty promise. If you want to win my heart, then let me *choose* to marry you. I want to be your equal, Siwang. And if I'm never given the power to choose, we'll never be equals."

His eyes turned hard at this. "Some things are more beautiful in theory than they are in real life. And sometimes, we get what we want just to discover that it is not what we imagined. What if by pushing me away, you are willingly giving up the love you are looking for?"

"I don't want my last memory of you to be an argument, Siwang."

His eyes shifted, blinking something away. "Remember to keep your identity a secret and your phoenix's mark covered. My father will not stop his campaigns to conquer more lands in your name. News of your departure will not leave these walls. Even if people ask, we will deny it."

"In the end, the prophecy is the only thing that cannot be sacrificed." I forced a smile. "Why don't you tell the world that I am sick, and after a year or so, announce that the empress of all empresses has died?"

Siwang's eyes went wide. "Why? Are you unwell? Is there something you are keeping from me? Are you—"

"I think it is best that we erase the prophecy from the world. I fear that it will one day put a target on Rong's back."

He laughed. "Rong can handle anyone who wishes to attack us."

Not everyone. Not forever. Sooner or later, Rong would fall like every empire that had come before.

I hoped that by leaving, I was doing enough. I had not slept well in the days since leaving the palace. If there were nightmares, I didn't remember them.

A good omen, perhaps.

Silence fell over us. Neither of us wanted to be the first to say goodbye, it seemed.

Siwang still wasn't looking at me. Something glistened in his eyes, something I was pretending not to see.

He didn't want me to see him cry, either, which gave me the perfect opportunity to take him in for the last time. Against the snow-lit glow, I realized just how much I hated him.

I hated how beautiful he was.

I hated how his words had the power to make my heart sing no matter how much I wished otherwise.

I hated the way he smiled at me, as if I were the only person in this world.

I hated the way he looked at me. As if he loved me.

Most of all, I hated how much I wanted to cry at this moment.

How fears welled behind my eyes, urging me to stop, to give in and lean in and kiss him and let go of all my foolish and stubborn wants.

I wanted a life of freedom. I wanted to stop the wars and for those I loved to live long lives despite my nightmares telling me otherwise.

But I also wanted Siwang.

I couldn't have everything.

I closed my eyes, willed the tears not to fall. "I'm sorry," I whispered before I did something I never thought I'd have the courage to do.

This was my last day in the city. This could very well be the last time I ever saw Siwang.

I wanted this moment, just once. Even if I would regret it afterward.

I inched forward on my tiptoes and gently pressed my lips against Siwang's. Just a second. Just a taste. Just so I knew how it felt. Just so I wouldn't spend the rest of my life wondering *what if.*

"Goodbye, my prince."

15

Our new home was a small cottage with a thatched roof and mud walls, a stout thing at the edge of the village, perched atop a steep hill that would not be easy on my parents' aging limbs.

"At least we have some privacy," my mother said.

The inside wasn't much better. Dust and cobwebs and a strange, sour stench that made my stomach turn.

My father was the first to set foot inside the house, making sure to clean up all the cobwebs around the door before we entered. I wondered what he felt now that their life in the capital was gone.

I didn't know whether to smile or cry.

That night, when I closed my eyes, I hoped for dreams of Siwang old and gray and wise on his throne. I hoped for dreams of my parents living out their long lives in peace and serenity. I hoped for dreams of Yong'An bustling and its people content.

I should have known better than to hope.

16

The nightmares continued that first night, then the second, then the third.

Yong'An in flames, children being slaughtered. My sister's screams, my parents' lifeless bodies. And Siwang...

My dear, beloved Siwang.

Drenched in blood, dressed in the dragon robes of an emperor, kneeling in the grand hall as a faceless man in pristine white robes swung down a dark blade.

They're just dreams, I tried to tell myself. *They are not real.*

But then...

17

War broke out three weeks after we left the capital.

Apparently, Lan Yexue had made it back home just as his uncle died of a mysterious illness. And now that he was home, he was set on revenge. Rong had humiliated the young prince during his time as hostage. And such transgressions would not be tolerated by men as prideful as the newly anointed prince regent . . . Or so the gossiping aunties at the morning market said.

The men of the village laughed at how this foolish prince of a crumbling empire thought himself strong enough to conquer the mighty Rong.

All I could think about was Lan Yexue's blood that gleamed like the midnight sky. The same blood that had brought me back to life. And his impossible strength and speed that were beyond the scope of mortality.

Then the nightmares grew worse.

More vivid.

More violent.

The screams, louder than ever.

I began to feel the hot splatters of Siwang's blood as the faceless men slashed his throat over and over in that familiar throne room.

To make it worse: each time I jolted awake in sweat, half a scream in my throat, I was often greeted by another sort of heartbreak. I heard Mother and Father arguing in the night. As war began, it was only a matter of time before the price of food soared beyond our means.

"We need money," Mother told Father. "We need food and firewood, and we need to stock up on rice and grains before the war reaches the farmlands and the emperor starts conscripting soldiers again."

"You worry too much. Lan is just a small nation with a small army and small coffers. They stand no chance against Rong."

"Lu-*ma* who sells noodles in the market said—"

"Who is Lu-*ma* to know? I am a first-rank minister. I have met the generals who patrol the borders, seen their armies with my own eyes. Lan doesn't stand a chance."

"You *were* a first-rank minister, husband."

More than once, I caught Fangyun standing next to their room, weeping.

—◆◆—

I packed my bags the next day, and left a note because I couldn't bear the thought of a real goodbye:

I'm going hunting. I am sorry money is tight. Let me make this right.

I had not put my family through all this turmoil to stay put in a run-down cottage.

There were questions to be answered, and a prophecy to be broken.

Back in the cave, when Lan Yexue had asked whether I knew where to find the stargazer who had sealed my fate, I had said I didn't—and it wasn't a complete lie.

I didn't know where the stargazer was, but I had ideas.

In the palace, every secret had a price, and it didn't take much more than a few gold bangles to find out all there was to know about the stargazer and her family.

PART TWO

Empires Rise,
Empires Fall

18

Everybody expected the war to be over before the ice melted and spring spun green leaves and delicate bulbs from the lingering frost.

It wasn't.

TWELVE
MONTHS
LATER

19

Some nights, I dreamt of him.

Through the ravenous dark, he whispered to me. A lulling melody of haunting incandescence.

Some nights, I saw him in a candlelit study, hunched over maps.

Other nights, I saw him on the battlefield, surrounded by red-eyed demons baring bloodied fangs.

But tonight was different.

Tonight, I was not a shadowy wraith following him through his life.

Tonight, Lan Yexue turned, and his eyes met mine, and he uttered a single, spine-chilling word.

"Run."

20

Seasons came and seasons went.

I never wrote the letters to Siwang. When the pearly white powders ran out, I smeared rouge so the phoenix's mark looked like any other birthmark. Sometimes, when I was short on money to buy the pigments, I simply wore a headband to cover it.

For some reason, by covering the mark I lost my abilities to glimpse the future. So I did it sparingly when I could.

I hid well in plain sight, disguised as a man traveling alone.

A year passed in the blink of an eye. Before I knew it, snow softened to water the earth and spring was upon us again. The air grew warmer and sweeter with every passing day.

—※—

I woke in the cold bunk of the only inn in Duhuan, a city to the west of the empire, closer to the Lan border than I liked. I was surrounded by the stench of men and the damp scent of mold—two things I'd rarely experienced during my time inside the palace.

Sleep was futile in places like these, where bodies were packed like livestock for winter. Especially when nights quite literally *rumbled* with the snores of men.

I stared at the ceiling for one heartbeat, then two, and hopped up from the bed. My eyes were still heavy, but I couldn't stay in this pigsty a moment longer. I also didn't want to fall back asleep and witness more bloodshed on the front lines.

My fault. That constant voice surfaced again. *Everything is my fault.*

Siwang had been right after all. Sometimes we got what we wanted, only to find out it wasn't how we'd imagined it. Leaving the palace was just like that: what I'd wanted, though not how I'd imagined it.

I peeked outside the papered windows and onto the dark streets. Some vendors were already setting up their carts for the morning.

The innkeeper was still asleep when I stepped outside. "One scallion pancake," I told the old lady setting up her stall across the street.

"Three coins."

"*Three* coins?"

"We all have to make a living, young man. Flour is expensive, and the price of eggs is going up, too. It won't be long until I have to charge you five or six coins for a scallion pancake."

I took in the old lady's empty eyes and wrinkled hands. The early morning was freezing cold, yet someone her age was already out to sell food. I couldn't help but think of my mother and sister, who had also resorted to selling food at the market. I wondered if they, too, were waking up at dawn just to spend the day letting hot oil splatters scald their hands for coins they'd never had to count in the capital.

It is not too late to change your mind. I heard Siwang's voice in my ears, lulling me home.

"Three coins it is." I gave her the money and took a seat on a low wooden stool while she mixed the batter and heated the oil.

I took out the address again. Trying to track down the stargazer was more difficult than I had anticipated. Almost a year later, and I was still coming up on dead ends, trying to find new leads that might indicate where she was. She hid like a woman who did not want to be found, and I wasn't sure how I should feel about this. For one to hide, there must be a hunter not too far behind.

Thankfully, not everyone in her life was so good at hiding their trails.

"What is a northern girl like you doing so far west?" the old lady murmured once she handed the pancake to me.

My head jerked up.

She laughed. "Relax, your disguise is good. I used to be young once, used to travel disguised as a boy because it was easier. I'm just saying it is not safe for a girl to be this far from home in times like these."

"The war is pretty well contained to the south side of the empire," I reminded her. "The west should be fine for a while."

"Nowhere is safe in the times of tyrants, my dear. There are some things you will understand when you get to my age."

"We are going to be okay," I said out of habit, even though I didn't believe it—even though I had seen the future and knew it to be a lie. One had to hope. "Speaking of why I'm here, can you tell me where this is?"

I handed her the piece of paper. When my original lead for finding the stargazer's family came to the cold end of an untended grave, I bribed this from a neighbor.

The neighbor said she had not seen the stargazer, whose birth name was Yinxing, since she was a child—the younger of two daughters, sold to the palace at five years old to be trained in the art of foresight. She had told me that six months ago, right around the time that Yinxing's father had died, a strange woman had shown up. She wore a long, dark veil, so the neighbor couldn't get a good look at her face, but her stature and voice and mannerisms reminded the neighbor of Yinxing's mother, who had run away years ago.

"You are here looking for family?" the old lady asked as she handed the piece of paper back to me.

"The *mother* of a friend."

"Zhang Jing is not a friendly woman," she whispered, voice low like it was a secret, or a warning. "She lives on the outskirts of the village and keeps to herself. She has a garden and chickens and only comes into the village for red meat during times of festivities."

"Have you seen her recently, or do you know if she still lives by herself?"

"Like I said, she doesn't come into the village often, and has no friends or family that I know of."

"Her husband died six months ago. Do you know—"

"You are asking a lot of questions for someone who—"

I reached into my pouch and handed her ten more coins, and the old lady stopped midsentence. She pocketed the coins, looked around as if someone on this empty street might be listening to a random traveler and a gossiping aunty. "What do you know of her family, especially her daughter?" I pressed.

The old lady took the seat across from me and sighed. "I know her family was poor. The butcher is kind to her, and he said that her husband is—*was*—a gambler and she was . . . well, she was a woman with few options. She had two daughters once upon a time, and had to sell both to cover her drunk husband's gambling debts. One to the palace to be trained as a seer, and the other . . . well."

I swallowed the lump in my throat, forever grateful that in some ways I was lucky the Emperor of Rong had found me first and promised me to his son, who grew up to be a good man. If someone else had found me first, someone who was not as kind . . . I shuddered to think how my life would have turned out. "Has either of her daughters ever visited her?"

The old lady shook her head. "I know nothing. However her place isn't far from here. West of the village. When the sun comes up, walk in the opposite direction and you will find her."

—◊◊◊—

I didn't wait for the sun to rise. The village wasn't very big, and I found the small cottage to the west soon enough.

The cottage was small, behind a short fence covered in vines. The door to the garden was unlocked, so I stepped inside. Everything was quiet, and the house was dark.

I looked around for the chickens the old lady had mentioned. I saw their pen though I heard nothing inside. The garden was overgrown with dead plants. Snow covered everything, with no signs of footprints coming in or out.

My stomach twisted tight. There was a familiar odor that grew stronger and stronger as I approached the door and contemplated whether it was too early to knock, only to realize . . . the door was already unlocked. There was a slight gap where snow had blown inside and built up.

Run, my better instincts told me. *Run, and don't look back. . . .*

I tried to push the door open, however something was blocking it from the other side. Something heavy and limp and—

I screamed.

A corpse, long dead and half rotten, fell into view.

I quickly covered my mouth. I recognized that stench now, one I had known only from my dreams.

From the state of the corpse, the stargazer's mother had been gone for a while.

And there were words written in dried blood on the pale walls: 天命不可违. THE WILL OF HEAVEN WILL NOT BE DEFIED.

Bile burned the back of my throat. I couldn't afford another dead end. I should go inside, look for a clue telling who had done this to her. For my last lead would require me to venture more south than I wanted to go: behind the battlefields and into Lan's borders.

My stomach retched again, and I stumbled back. I had seen enough.

I ran back to the village just as the sky began to brighten. I should find the butcher. He knew the stargazer's mother well. But I didn't know where the butcher was and could find only the old lady, who sat by her now set-up stall.

"Sh-she's . . . ," I stuttered. "She's . . ."

The world fell away.

A flash of colors.

A vision.

Red-eyed soldiers wearing the deep blue uniform of Lan, running against a darkening twilight sky that was impossible to distinguish as morning or night.

Screams. The same earsplitting screams that filled my nightmares.

"Run!" I screamed. "They are coming tonight!"

The stray villagers on the street turned toward me. "Who?" someone asked.

"Lan's army!" I shouted for the people in the market to hear. The sun was coming up. They were going to attack either now or tonight. "You have to run! We don't have time. We—"

"Shut up!" someone shouted from inside the inn. "We are trying to sleep!"

"No, you have to believe me! Lan is going to attack soon. They are coming!" I grabbed the old lady. "Please, you have to believe me!"

She took me in, and her eyes lingered on my forehead, where the phoenix's mark was barely covered by rouge.

"I am not leaving my stall."

"We are going to die!"

"These bones are not made for running! If they want to kill me, they will! If the Lans plan on attacking, then I am going home! I will not fight! I will surrender, because I am not leaving!"

She handed me one of the scallion pancakes she had already made, and the coins I had given her earlier. "Take this. I will make more food," she said, her voice unsteady and her eyes misty. "When Lan's army comes, they will see that I am useful and make good food. They will let me live. You go now, child. Take care."

I watched her. She didn't look like the sort of woman who would change her mind, and I wasn't a saint. I couldn't save everyone I came across. Especially those who didn't believe me.

"Let the village know—"

"This is my home, girl. I have watched half the people in this village grow up and get married and grow old. Do you know how many flags we have seen in that time? Regardless of who rules over us, this is our home. We will not fight if the enemy comes. And if they want to kill us, then we will die where we were born. We are nobodies in this world, and when asked to choose between tyrants, we will always choose whoever is winning."

"Lan is not winning." *Lan can't win.* Because if Lan won, what would happen to Siwang?

"I will pass the message on to those who might want to flee if Lan's army does come. Now go, girl. Go home. It is almost the New Year; don't you want to see your family?"

So I did as she told me.

I clutched the pancake and ran as fast as I could through the market, until I reached the end of the village and the quiet, icy forest where snow piled up to my thighs. I ran as fast as I could. I slipped and got back up and then slipped again and still I didn't stop. Even as a trail of red bloomed in my wake.

And I imagine you are not the only one who wants answers for being . . . different? Prince Yexue had uttered in that amber-lit cave. *I had looked for the stargazer when I arrived in the capital, but I never found her. . . .*

I headed east.

I headed home.

21

Every night, I was forced to watch those I loved die.

That night, I dreamt of my father's throat slit over a military map of the continent, his blood soaking through the parchment as Lan's army swallowed the land.

22

Home was almost a week's journey on horseback. I waited for more visions of bloodshed, but none came. I waited for news of Lan's attack on Duhuan but heard nothing.

Perhaps the old lady was right. Perhaps by surrendering, they had spared bloodshed. Or had Lan's soldiers killed everyone so that there were no survivors left to tell the story?

The thought nauseated me.

Demons, Lan Yexue raised an army of demons, stolen from the eighteenth level of hell, people on the road said.

How I wished I had let Lan Yexue die a quiet death a year ago.

—⁂—

Before I entered my village, I rebandaged the wound on my leg to make sure the gauze was tight and that no blood seeped through. A small injury from my many falls in Duhuan.

My parents already hated the idea of me traveling the lands alone in times like these, though the game I hunted helped defray the rising costs caused by the war.

After everything my stubbornness had cost us, they didn't want to take me from one cage to lock me in another. Still, if Mother saw that I was injured, she would never let me leave the house again.

Since our exile, my family had enough to worry about.

The problem with small villages where everyone knew everyone was that when unfamiliar faces appeared, they were often treated warily. We had tried our best to settle in. Father now taught at the school, though it didn't pay much. Mother sold her embroidery and food in the market with Fangyun to make up for the shortfall.

Despite neighbors who greeted us with polite smiles, we felt like outcasts. Life here was a far cry from our lives in the capital, where everyone from court officials to famed merchants groveled for my family's attention, all hoping to have the future empress as an ally.

When I thought of Father's weathered face, Mother's failing eyes, and Fangyun's hands, now hardened by manual labor, my heart ached.

I got what I wanted, but at what cost?

—⁂—

The village market was nothing compared with the festive bustle of Yong'An, or even some of the bigger cities I'd visited in the past year. This didn't mean it wasn't full of personality, the kind that only small villages had.

At this hour, Father was in class teaching the village children poetry and numbers. Mother was probably home, embroidering. I wasn't ready to meet their stern gazes and hear their lectures about how I should have sent more letters, should have come home more often.

I went to find my sister first. The one person who was always happy to see me, no matter how often I disappointed her.

The village had changed in minuscule ways in the time I had been away.

Qing-*ma*'s baby had grown into a toddler, with chubby cheeks and wobbly feet, beaming dimpled smiles at every passerby as his mother hawked small, stale winter fruits. Zhangxi, a beautiful girl a year younger than me, was now married to the cowherd, her belly rounding, cheeks flushed with a motherly glow. Her husband was a sturdy man, big-handed, small-eyed, preferred animals to humans, but doted on Zhangxi with love. His face bloomed in awe whenever she was near. Everybody in the village had known they would end up together. A love match destined by the stars, a blessing so few girls could afford. Even in small villages like this one.

I wondered how Si—

I caught myself before I could let myself think of him again. My eyes quickly focused on the nearest thing. Lu-*ma*'s back was beginning to hunch as she carried out bowls of noodles from her shop to eager customers. She made the best beef noodles I had ever tasted, comparable even to the imperial chefs'. Her face had weathered and wrinkled in the months since her son had gone to war and returned without one of his legs and three of his fingers. However, now that her son was home, her smile had returned, enough to light up even the dreariest of days. "Li Fei! You are back!"

I smiled, too. "I am."

"Did you bring me any decent kills this time?"

"I'm staying for a few days. I will go into the forest and hunt soon. What do you want?"

"Venison or wild boar would be great. I'll give you free noodles if you give me a good deal."

"Don't I always?" I pretended to roll my eyes. "Have you seen Fangyun today?"

"She's at her stall. I was just about to bring her a bowl of noodles. Poor girl, standing outside all day in the cold. Why don't you take it to her? You know how my legs are; it will take me half an hour to walk from one side of the market to the other."

"Just for her? Don't I get a bowl?"

"I will give you one big bowl of noodles with two sets of chopsticks *and* a bowl of wontons if you bring me some wild boar meat."

"You drive a hard bargain, Lu-*ma*." I took the bowls from her, my gloved fingers curling around their warmth. "I'll see you later."

"Don't forget to bring back my bowls!"

I found Fangyun at the edge of the village, just as the delicious aroma of her scallion pancakes hit my nose. A smell I had always loved, but now it just reminded me of that old lady in Duhuan, and the stench of—

I flinched at the memories and quickly pushed them down. *There is nothing you could have done,* I told myself as my heart thudded like a drum. Someone was hunting the stargazer. I hoped she could outrun whoever this predator was.

"Fei?" Fangyun's voice pulled me back to reality.

My sister stood alone in her stall, my mother nowhere to be seen. Fangyun was mixing a bowl of batter in her arms, a basket of steamed buns at her side. She was better at making sweet treats, like red bean cake, lotus seed cake, and *tangyuan,* but such ingredients were hard to find in times like these.

Her once-delicate face was sliced red by the winter winds, her skin dry and peeling at the cheeks, just like mine. Her eyes were also duller than I remembered. She looked older, too.

When she saw me, she flashed a smile that made me feel like I was home. Because home was not a place. Home was the people who loved you, the people who waited for you, the people whose eyes lit up when they saw you. Home was my sister and mother, and though he scowled at me more than he smiled, it was also my father. Home was Siwang—

I shook the thought away.

"You have flour on your face." I kept my head down, blinking away my tears as I set the bowls on a table by her stall.

With me gone, Fangyun had to shoulder more responsibility than she should, taking care of both Mother and Father without complaint. If I hadn't been so selfish, she would be married to a minister or a wealthy merchant by now, belly round like Zhangxi's, dressed in silk and dripping in gold.

Guilt gnawed at me again. I absentmindedly touched the pouch of gold at my hip, my earnings from hunting. I had precipitated my family's downfall. It was only fair that I make it up to them.

"Heavens, why didn't you write letters like you promised?" Fangyun pulled me into a hug before I could say another word, then buried her face in my shoulder.

A muffled whimper at my ear. I felt her warm tears trickling down my neck, so I hugged her tighter, arms intertwined, pressing her to me so that she knew I'd missed her, too. So much. And in this moment, with my sister's breathing and her milk-sweet scent enveloping me, everything felt warmer.

Even the washed-out winter colors felt a little brighter.

"Thank the gods I set those bowls down before I interrupted you," I joked.

Fangyun shoved me away. For a second, I thought she was going to hit me. "Do you know how worried we were?"

I laughed. "I'm sorry, I forgot." A half-truth.

"Don't be sorry to me! Be sorry to Ma! And Ba! They have been worried sick! Do you know how white her hair is now because of you? Even Father's hair is beginning to gray!"

"Fangyun, I'm sorry."

"What were we thinking, letting you leave? Do you know how dangerous things are right now? There is a war going on, Fei! You've heard the stories of the Lan dynasty's demons, right?"

I had. Everyone on the continent had heard of the war between Lan and Rong, and the ghost stories that drifted from the battlefield.

Twelve months was all it had taken for Yexue to transform the Lan Empire from a crumbling nation at Rong's mercy to a semblance of its former glory, capable of rivaling the once-feared Rong Empire.

"How did Lan Yexue end up as Rong's hostage for two whole years if he was capable of raising demons from hell?" I joked, more for her than myself. Yexue had already brought Rong to its knees. If the world found out about the magic he was capable of, it would bring our people's morale to an all-time low.

When the war began, the emperor had promised that Rong's sons would be home before summer. However almost a whole year had passed; our situation looked worse by the day. Lan continued to claim town after town, city after city, pushing our soldiers and villagers northward toward the capital.

Already I had heard too many stories of frontline deserters who would rather face the wrath of Rong than to stand face to face with Lan's army.

"Demons don't exist!" someone from the table next to us hissed.

I thought he was talking to us, until the man who sat across from him groaned. "My uncle knows someone who saw them with his own eyes! The Prince of Lan raises them from the dead! They are impossibly fast, stronger than ten bulls, and feed on the blood of mortals! At this rate, if Rong's armies don't turn the table soon, they will reach Yong'An by summer."

"What about us? Do you think they will attack small villages like us?"

The louder of the two men went quiet. "I don't know." He set down the bun he was picking at.

"I don't believe in demons."

"I don't want to believe in demons, either. . . ."

"Why don't we ask Lu Bao? He just came back from the front lines!"

The second man grimaced. "What's the point, even if he can tell us whether the rumors are true? What can we do? People say the Prince Regent of Lan made a deal with demons to punish the Rong emperor for the humiliation he'd suffered as a ward. But this war isn't hurting the emperor; it's hurting men like us."

"I've heard that this war isn't about his time as a ward; it's about the empress of all empresses," the other man whispered, his eyes wide as if he were sharing some unfathomable rumor. Too bad it was the same rumor half the empire had already heard. "They say no one has seen the empress of all empresses for almost a year. Apparently she is sick, but the people in the palace think she has run away, and the prince regent is waging the war to find her."

"Selfish harlot. All this for a stupid woman? I've told you: that empress of all empresses is a bad omen. How many nations have tried to invade us because of her? Now all the freshly claimed borderlands are rebelling because they think the crown prince will no longer become the emperor of all emperors."

My sister pulled my arm. "Don't listen to them."

I smiled. "I've heard worse."

"Are the rumors true?" my sister quietly asked.

"That I'm a selfish harlot?" I teased, and she scowled at me. "The stuff about demons sounds like propaganda from Lan to scare us into surrender or from Rong to scare us into fighting harder—I can't be certain. However I can confirm that Yexue is . . . *different.*"

Fangyun's face dropped at this, her eyes no longer looking at me. She then changed the subject: "Have you seen any beautiful scenery in the past few months?"

I shrugged. "It doesn't matter what I've seen. What matters is what I've brought home." I handed her my pouch of gold coins, then patted the bag over my shoulders. "A snow fox's pelt, to make Mother a scarf, and leather to make shoes for Father. I've made enough money these past few months that we don't have to worry about food anymore. You don't have to come here every day and—"

My sister's hand covered mine. "I don't care about the money, Fei. I just want you to be alive and safe. If this is the reason you keep disappearing for months at the time, then don't. We—"

"I know."

"Don't leave again, sister. I'm scared that the war is going to reach our doorsteps soon. When it does, I don't want to spend every day wondering where you are and whether you are safe."

"I know." I gently put my hand over hers. "Come on, the food is getting cold."

23

Fangyun and I sipped from the same bowl of noodles, something I had never done in the palace. It was strange, knowing this was the sort of closeness we should have experienced our entire lives. If not for the prophecy. If not for the emperor.

"I'm sorry," I murmured.

"You keep saying that," Fangyun grumbled through a mouthful of noodles, something she wouldn't be caught dead doing back at the capital. "What are you sorry for this time?"

I nodded at Zhangxi, who was walking past with her husband. "If it weren't for me, that could be you by now. A noble husband, a kid on the way. Warm home and full belly." Fangyun sneered. A splutter of soup rolled down her chin, and I stifled my own laughter. I reached over and helped wipe it off her face. "Never mind, I take what I said back. If you keep talking with your mouth full, no amount of dowry would have helped you secure a good marriage."

My sister rolled her eyes. "You have nothing to be sorry for. The ending would have been the same either way. Marriage, motherhood, death. What does it matter if my husband is rich or poor if I don't love him? You were the one who showed me that there is more to life than doing what's expected of us. And now, far from the capital, we are both experiencing *more*. We are the choices we made, Fei. If I'd wanted to stay in the capital, believe me, I would have found a way. You are not the only one who wanted to leave that stifling city with all its rules and never-ending schemes."

She wrapped her arm around my shoulders and pulled me close. "I didn't lose anything because of you, Fei. Instead, I've gained things more valuable than money and status. I get to be myself out here. I get to do what I want, when I want. Do you think I could have talked with a mouth full of food back at the capital? If I laughed too loud, walked too fast, or talked too much, I would have been the gossip on every noble lady's tongue the next morning. No one wants to live that sort of life. You didn't want to live it, and I don't want to live it, either. After your antics, Father wouldn't marry either of us off to a husband who doesn't love us. And if giving up that old life in Yong'An is the price I have to pay for true freedom, then I'll pay it willingly twice over. Do you know that in the capital, I couldn't even leave the house without a chaperone? Now I can gossip with the other market ladies about the war and the emperor and how bad a job he is doing."

"If you put it that way, then perhaps this exile is the best thing that's ever happened to us. Because if you ever dared to criticize the emperor in the capital, you would have had your head chopped off."

I was about to get up and take the empty bowls back to Lu-*ma*'s stall when someone limped to stand beside our table.

Lu Bao, Lu-*ma*'s son.

My chest tightened.

"My mother sent me to collect the bowls before the shop gets busy."

"Oh, I was just about to—"

"No worries. I like the practice." Lu Bao laughed and gestured at his wooden leg. "Still need to get used to it."

"Thank you," my sister and I said at the same time. We handed him our empty bowls, and he gave each of us a polite smile.

After Lu Bao was gone, my sister reached across the table and brushed away the tears I didn't know I had shed.

"The Warring States have not seen peace in the last thousand years," Fangyun said. "There are always skirmishes and territorial disputes between dynasties. This is simply the first time in our lives that casualties are so close to home. Lan Yexue did not start this war because of you. He started it because of his own greed."

You are destined to be the empress of all empresses.

"I thought that by leaving the palace, I would stop the nightmares from coming true. It seems I have only made things worse."

"What nightmares?"

I scolded myself. "I . . . Just these nightmares that my prophecy would bring calamity to Rong."

"You are just a girl, Fei'er. You have no power over any of this. And who is to say destinies even exist?"

Was I just a girl? The prophecy had called me a fallen goddess. The phoenix's mark brought me glimpses of the future, things no mortal should be able to see.

What if the prophecy was right? What if I could help the people of this land, and by hiding from my destiny I was prolonging their sufferings?

"Don't you wish you could join the army and fight? I wish they'd let women enlist," my sister mused.

"I don't," I said quietly. "I wish the emperor would spare these young men and fight Lan Yexue himself. Just the two of them. The winner gets all."

My sister laughed. Then, in a quieter voice, she said, "Is it true, that you saved Lan Yexue in the mountains?"

My heart jerked in my chest, and I looked up to see not blame but curiosity in her eyes.

Again, I saw flashes of blood in the snow. Lan Yexue's eyes wet with hurt after I had plunged his own blade into his chest. "Yes. And it was the worst mistake of my life." *I should have aimed for his wretched heart.*

"It is not your responsibility to teach men how to live with bruised egos," my sister said. I waited for judgment to show in her tone: it never did. "What have you done in the past months besides hunting? And don't give me the same lies you tell Mother and Father. It is winter; what scenery is there to see when everything is covered in ice and snow? I know you hate the cold."

I'm trying to undo my prophecy, I wanted to tell her, yet feared she wouldn't understand. Or worse, finally see me for what I was: Not a good omen but a curse upon the land. The reason young men like Lu Bao were forced onto the battlefields, to fight for the pride of an emperor who would never know their names.

Before I could, a thunderous tempest of horses' hooves made everyone in the market go silent. Soon, a parade of red-bannered soldiers rode through the streets, stirring up a maelstrom of slush and mud.

I recognized the rider at the front before I recognized the imperial banner.

Caikun. Armored and stoic, a golden scroll in hand.

"By the Mandate of Heaven and in the name of the emperor, I hereby announce that all able-bodied men over the age of eighteen will be conscripted into the army in our fight against the demons of Lan. . . ."

Just like that, my heart dropped, and the whole world crumbled to dust around me.

Father.

24

The cottage was nothing like I remembered. With each visit, it felt more and more like a home. Far from nosy neighbors, this was a quiet piece of the world that belonged only to our family.

By the time Fangyun and I raced home, the envoys had already been. Father's conscription letter sat at the center of the table. The house smelled of familiar sweetness. A ceramic pot sat over the crackling fire.

Sweet-and-sour pork. Father's favorite.

"Father!" Fangyun was the first to rush into the room and fall at Father's knees while I lingered in the doorway, unsure. "Please don't go, Father!"

"My daughter, I have to. It is the law," he replied without looking up. "I am of able body, and the only man from this house. If I don't go, who will?"

"You've already given half your life to the empire," I grumbled. Father's eyes shot up at the sound of my voice. His entire face tensed when he saw me. "Twenty-three years as a minister, and fifteen more years as the emperor's advisor. You've given enough, *Baba.*"

"Fei?" Father's voice trembled when he said my name.

My chest ached, a lump of grief and happiness clotted in my throat. "I . . . I'm home, F—"

Before I could finish, he grabbed the yellowed broom leaning against the table and immediately chased me into the snowy yard with it.

"Six months! You didn't come home for six months! Your mother and I thought you were dead!"

"Father, I'm sorry!"

"Did you know you still had a home to come back to? Why didn't you write? That was our agreement! You would write every week and let us know you were safe! You said you would come back every two moons! Y—"

Father's voice broke. Hand clutching chest, he sank to his knees, heaving for breath.

"Father!" Fangyun and I rushed to his side. Fangyun rubbed his back and I helped him into a crouching position, just like the doctor had told us.

Don't let him get angry or stressed. Things I always failed at.

When I was around, I always did things that made him angry. And when I wasn't around, it only made him angrier. Nothing I did was ever right when it came to my parents.

"I'm sorry. I know I should have come home sooner. But if I came home before midwinter, you would never have let me go out to hunt again until spring."

"Hunt?" Father rasped, his voice barely louder than a breath, his face still red and angry. "Why would a girl want to hunt? That's the job of men, Fei!" His voice cracked again, a sob bubbling in his throat. I watched, helpless, as tears welled in my father's eyes, his brows knotted in anger, frustration, regret. "I never should have let you go. I should have made you stay home, where it's safe! There is a war going on, Fei! What if something happened to you!"

"女儿不孝, 不能在父母身边陪伴." *It is unfilial of me, unable to be at Mother and Father's side.* I lowered myself to my knees, then handed him my pouch of gold and the pelt of snow fox. "I know money is tight, Father. I'm no scholar like you, no good at embroidery like Mother. I couldn't even help Fangyun with the stall. This is the only thing I'm good at."

I closed my eyes and pushed away memories of the better days. Regret sank its fangs again.

Father sighed, covered my hand with his. "Silly girl. Nothing is more important than you coming home, safe and well. Let me worry about money." He patted my knee. "Come, help me up. Your mother is going to be so happy when she sees you."

25

We ate dinner by candlelight. The four of us around a single table, something that had not happened for too long. The room was warm with crackling firewood and the aroma of pork and rice.

"Here, Fei," Mother said as she placed the biggest piece of meat into my bowl. "You must not have eaten well while you were away. You've lost so much weight. Why travel and hunt when you can be here with Ma, and eat my good food?"

I blinked back the tears. "Thank you, Mama," I said, then fell back into silence. Leaving the palace didn't change my inability to converse with my parents. Perhaps it was the years we'd spent apart; the chasm between us seemed as wide as ever. I didn't know what to say to them, and they didn't know what to say to me.

We had finished dinner by the time I found the courage to bring up the ghost in the room, the conscription scroll that Father had tucked away.

"I can't let you go, Father."

"It's the law, child," he repeated.

"You've given enough of yourself to Rong," Fangyun protested with me, her voice louder and harsher than I had ever heard. Raised to act like a lady even in the tensest of situations, this might be the closest my sister had ever gotten to losing her temper.

"What about your heart, husband?" Mother whispered. "You can't fight. You can barely chase Fei around the yard without collapsing."

"Even if I can't fight, I still have to go. An emperor's wish is the law."

That is the stupidest thing I have ever heard, I wanted to snap at Father. An emperor was still a man. And he had no right to steal my father from his life and family and home like this.

Mother lowered her gaze so we couldn't see the disappointment pooling around her eyes, and how her thinning lips quivered. There was more she wanted to say, but she knew Father better than anyone, knew how stubborn he was. Once he'd made his mind up, there was no way to convince him otherwise. Something my father and I had in common.

"All of this is my fault," I murmured.

Mother's hand touched mine. "Don't say that, Fei."

Father's lips shuddered into a scowl. "Stop with that nonsense, Fei'er."

"If I hadn't asked the emperor to annul my betrothal, you'd be the father of the crown princess by now. No one would ask you to enlist for this stupid war."

"We left Yong'An not because of you, Fei'er. We left because that life wasn't meant for us, and we were destined not to keep it." Mother's eyes were so kind when they gazed at me that I might have believed her if I did not remember her cries on the day we left. Her sobs haunted me, until this very day.

"If I'd just accepted my fate, done what was expected of me, we—"

"Do you know why I named you Fei?" Father's question reeled my thoughts to a halt.

"Because it's . . . pretty?"

"No. The emperor wanted the empress of all empresses to have an extraordinary name, with an extraordinary meaning. So 非 is what I came up with. A word that means *not,* a word that defies every word that comes before it." He put a hand on my shoulder. "You are everything I had hoped you would be and more. What you did that day at the imperial hunt is proof of that. Going against tradition, seizing control of your destiny instead of letting it rule you. How can I hate you for being so brave? I'd rather have a daughter who is brave than someone who is beautiful yet cowardly. *Always.*"

"Am I brave, or just reckless?"

Father took my hands and Fangyun's. "My greatest pride in life has never been status or wealth, or even my scholarly knowledge. My greatest pride lies in the daughters who will outlive me. Fangyun, Fei, as long as the two of you are alive, safe, and happy, I have nothing to lose and nothing to mourn. Do you understand, girls?"

He pulled the two of us and Mother into his arms.

"I will fight in this war. Not because the emperor asked me to, but because I want to protect those I love the most: the three of you. Whether I live or die on that battlefield, it will be worth it. As long as the three of you can live peaceful, happy lives after the war."

"*Baba . . .*" I cried. I had watched my father die enough times in my nightmares to know that I would move heaven and earth to keep him safe, even if it was just one more day. "Please, Father. Don't go."

"I have to, my love. I have to."

26

A blade, whetted and sharp, safe in its sheath. The conscription letter at his bedside. A bag of fresh clothes and dried meats, packed next to his thick winter coat. Father was set to leave for the army in the morning. Originally, he'd planned to leave earlier because the camp was far away, so the journey would be arduous for his legs. But Mother had begged him to stay longer so that we could have one last New Year as a family.

At midnight, I would turn nineteen. A year ago, the emperor had suggested that Siwang and I get married on our nineteenth birthday.

So much had changed since then.

In the past days, I did the only thing I was good at: hunt. I walked the snowy forest every day so that Father got to sleep full-bellied every night. Beef stewed in fermented cabbage, pheasant roasted in cherry oak, a whole wild hog leg cooked with the eggplant and potatoes that Lu-*ma* gave me in exchange for the other leg.

We didn't let the unused meat go to waste, either selling it to the villagers who were desperate for even a single bite after a long winter, or smoking it to keep for the following wintery months.

In this village far from the bustling markets of walled cities, fresh meat made even the coldest of neighbors open their arms to us.

On the last day of the year, we ate braised ribs and toasted my nineteenth birthday with the rice wine I got from Luyao, the cowherd. Luyao also gave me a bag of jujube seeds, which I ground into powder and poured into the cabbage-and-boar filling of our dumplings.

It was not only tradition to eat dumplings on New Year's, but a tradition to eat them before a big departure. 上马饺子下马面. *Begin the journey with dumplings, and end it with noodles.* In case anything happened on the journey, at least our last meal would have been a good one.

I also poured a little of the jujube powder into the rice wine. Then I filled my bowl with leftover braised pork and rice instead of wine and dumplings.

Even Mother, who'd drunk only one small cup, was falling asleep at the table before the midnight hour.

Once all three of them were lulled to sleep by the jujube seed, I helped them to their beds before taking our ancestral blade and the conscription scroll from Father's bedside, then left a letter of apology in their place.

I was the reason we were here, the reason Lan Yexue was still alive. Perhaps even the reason he had waged this war. If anyone should go to battle, it was me.

"Take care of Mother and Father when I'm gone," I whispered to Fangyun, before placing a kiss on her cheek the way she used to kiss me goodbye.

I left the house just as a strike of lightning flashed across the sky, along with the fireworks that marked midnight.

27

I arrived at camp just two days before deadline. Most recruits must have stayed home for one last New Year's meal, because camp was quieter than I'd imagined.

That, or there were more deserters than enlistments—voluntary and forced.

The camp was a stronghold of towers and long fields of tents and barracks, enclosed by enormous fences that reminded me of a cage. My stomach turned.

Absentmindedly, I touched my old hunting bow, bought from the village butcher a year ago, right before I set out to find the stargazer. I nodded greetings to the soldiers standing guard when I approached the imposing gates and offered up my conscription scroll.

"Li Hude?" the soldier asked.

历峰, Lifeng, was a double-charactered surname, too uncommon to be kept after our exile. It was also not our real surname, but one given to us by the emperor. A signifier of his faith in my prophecy. Li was my family's ancestral name, the name we reclaimed after we left the capital.

"Li Fei," I replied. "His son."

The soldier smiled and patted me on the back. "A lot of sons are signing up in place of their fathers. Our country will remember your courage."

"Thank you." I touched the silk headband that covered my phoenix's mark. Half to make sure it was secure, and half for comfort.

Though I had practice disguising myself as a man during my travels, I had never lived with so many men in close quarters for more than a night or two. Women were not allowed in the army. To be found would mean a certain death.

I wasn't ready to forfeit my life just yet. Though as I walked through camp, I feared I might have bitten off more than I could chew.

Training hadn't even begun, yet most of the men were already covered in dirt. And oh, *skies,* the smell.

If you want to live among clean servant girls and polite eunuchs who only flash gentle smiles and speak with respectful tones, then you should have stayed in that gilded cage, I had to remind myself over and over again on the road.

Palace etiquette was drilled into my head, and it was difficult, adapting to how normal people lived. For not everyone had to grow up bearing the unfathomable weight of an entire empire's expectations.

I was assigned to the Fourth Company of the Third Battalion. By the time I found our campsite, there was just one corner bed left in the bunks. I quickly claimed it by setting my bag down. The tent was abuzz with sounds. Some men were sitting around the table at the center of the room playing cards and dice, some were introducing themselves, while others were making themselves at home. Next to me, someone was shaving his dirty and overgrown toenails with a knife, leaving clippings all over the bed.

I nearly gagged.

Hygiene! I heard the furious voices of palace nannies.

Whenever I saw men spit in the open or heard them cough too loudly, I would hear the scoldings I would have received if I did anything similar. So did I hate these men and their behaviors, or did I hate my childhood of being held to impossible standards?

I lowered my gaze so I wouldn't have to look at any of them and began storing my things under the bed when a familiar voice froze me dead in my steps.

"Fei?"

I turned to find the square face of Luyao, the cowherd from my village, seated at a low table with three other men, holding cards. I cursed under my breath. Out of all my preparations, I'd failed to predict that I'd run into someone from the village. There were so many training camps, so many companies to be separated into. It was just my luck that Fate put us in the same tent in the same camp.

"What are you doing here?" he asked in a low voice.

"The same as you," I whispered. "Enlisting in the army."

His eyes darted around and he stepped closer. Then he added in a whisper, "Girls aren't allowed in the army."

"Who's the kid?" one of the other men asked from the table. Everyone was looking at Luyao, waiting for him to introduce me, and he just waved them away. "Da'sha, you can take my turn!"

I hastily pushed a roll of coins into Luyao's hand. "Keep this a secret. If anyone finds out, my whole family will be implicated."

"If you know how dangerous it is, why did you enlist in the first place?" he whispered.

"Because if I didn't, my father would have to. You know him; he teaches your little brother in school. His gets out of breath by walking up the hill by our home. He'd never survive a war."

Luyao's face softened. He pushed back the coins. "I'm not going to tell anyone. But the military isn't a place for girls. My father fought in these wars, and so have my brothers. Forget about the front lines; these training camps are brutal by themselves. A girl like you won't survive for long."

I almost smiled. "I think you are forgetting who caught that pheasant for you, Zhangxi, and your soon-to-arrive baby."

"A good archer does not a good soldier make."

"Then help me," I whispered. "Please. Think of it as doing good deeds for your unborn child. Zhangxi would want you to help me if she were here."

Luyao's lips twitched at the mention of his wife and unborn child. "Fine, but only because Zhangxi has been craving roasted pheasant all winter, so you did me a big favor."

I smiled.

"First thing." He gestured at my bag behind me. "Keep your bag under your bunk and keep your bed clean. The superiors will check, and you don't want to be scolded by them. The rules of the military are cast in iron, and they will not be broken for anyone. If you step out of line, you *will* be punished, no matter how scrawny you look."

I glanced around. "Does anyone else know that they should keep their beds clean?"

Luyao grimaced. "They will soon enough. And take your bow and arrows to the armory, in case someone tries to steal them when you're not looking."

"Luyao?" his friend called again.

Luyao turned back to the table. "He's just some boy from my village. I didn't think he would enlist in place of his father. Look at him, a breeze can blow him over."

The men laughed. "Never underestimate the short ones!" one interjected.

"Odds that he won't make it through the first battle?"

Another man laughed. "He won't make it through the first month."

My lips twitched. All the more reason to survive, then. "I'll take the bet," I said, making sure to speak from my chest and forcibly pressing each word down so they sounded lower and manlier. It was exhausting, and my throat always ached at the end of the day when I spoke like this.

Skies, this was going to be a long couple of months.

I walked up to them and dropped the roll of coins on the table. "I bet that not only will I survive the first battle; I will survive the longest out of us."

The men looked at me dead-faced; then smiles began to crack. "I like you."

"Fei," I offered.

"Yangdong," said the biggest of the men.

"A'du," offered another.

"Da'sha!"

28

The armory was next to the stables. When I passed, a familiar shadow caught my attention.

Midnight-dark mane, finely groomed like a sheet of glimmering silk as if someone had cut a piece of the night sky and molded it in the form of a horse. There was a single splash of white between his eyes, kind of like my phoenix's mark—something the noble sons used to joke about.

"Beifeng?" What was he doing here?

The horse must have recognized me as well, because he dipped his head forward, as if asking to be petted.

I approached with slow, cautious steps. In case he didn't remember me the same way I remembered him from when I was a different girl, in a different place, dreaming of sprouting wings.

Some wistful longing pulled me toward him. Beifeng was Siwang's favorite steed, and—

Before I could touch him, a rough hand caught mine.

"大胆!" the voice snapped. *How dare you!*

Memories fled, dropping me back into the present. I was no longer Lifeng Fei. The empress of all empresses died the day I annulled my betrothal to Siwang. I was now Li Fei, an insignificant soldier, a girl pretending to be a boy to protect her father. A peasant like me had no right to be near a royal steed, let alone touch it.

"This is the Crown Prince's steed; can't you read the mark on its stall?"

That voice . . .

Caikun, who wore the last year around him like a warm, golden halo. He was so much taller than I remembered. Jaw sharper, eyes darker, yet those pillowed lips had remained the same throughout the withering months. The very same lips I'd once dared to kiss me when we were both five years old, crouching between stone statues in the imperial garden.

He looked me over, and I was met not with recognition but a soft pity. "How old are you, boy?"

"I just turned nineteen," I said, keeping my head low so that he couldn't get a good look at my face. After that kiss, Caikun had refused to look at me. He always looked the other way whenever I was near. Perhaps my childhood recklessness would save me from being caught?

Caikun frowned. "Are you sure you are old enough to enlist?"

As a girl, I was once among the tallest of the palace kids. Until my thirteenth summer, when Caikun and Siwang and almost every boy who'd studied in the imperial lecture halls sprouted like trees.

Now I was forced to arch my neck for the boy with whom I'd once stood shoulder to shoulder.

"I'm scrawny for my age," I said, beating Caikun to his own conclusion.

"You don't look a day over fifteen."

"Fifteen is just old enough to enlist," I corrected him. Newly implemented. The original age was eighteen. Since the war with Lan erupted, many things had changed.

"Third Battalion, Fourth Company?" His eyes fell on the military tag at my waist, and he sighed. "I told them to send me men, not boys who can barely lift a sword. Being able to do farmwork doesn't count as being a man. You won't last a day on the battlefield."

"It was this, or let my ailing father come to war," I retorted.

"You think you're protecting your father by putting your neck on the chopping block like this? You are not protecting anyone. You've condemned yourself to die by playing hero in a war that has never shown mercy to anyone, no matter how young they are and how bright their future may seem."

"I would rather condemn myself to die than my father," I countered. "He's old, his legs are weak, and his heart won't be able to take the training, let alone go to war. At least if I can learn, I can try. I'm willing to die in this war if it means my father gets to live out his full life."

It was not my job to save the world, but it was my job to save my father.

Caikun shook his head. "You think yourself so noble and filial by coming here, don't you? Let me guess, you stole his conscription notice and came here without telling him? Do you know how you'll break his heart if anything happens to you? You've never witnessed a father losing his son, have never seen what grief does to a man, have you?"

I thought of Caikun's older brothers, the tales told in teahouses of how the eldest of General Wu's three sons had lost a leg in the first six months of the war, and Caikun's second-eldest brother had been declared missing on the battlefield last spring.

"Yes, I have no idea what it's like to lose a family member. But I can imagine what it's like to watch the father who had raised me for nineteen years walk into hellfire and burn when I have the power to do something. If anyone has to burn, I'll burn in his stead."

"You think you have what it takes to survive?"

"I don't know. But I will do everything to protect my family, which is why I am here. To fight. To protect them."

Finally, Caikun's lips inched into a slow, genuine smile. Before he could say anything else, Beifeng started nudging at my neck, still waiting for his petting.

"He seems to like you," Caikun murmured. "Beifeng doesn't usually like strangers."

With the exception of Siwang, I was the only other person Beifeng allowed to ride him. Something the emperor took as an auspicious sign. A rare "heavenly" horse. Beifeng was a tribute from one of the smaller western kingdoms. Centuries ago, the southern warlords used to wage entire military campaigns to the far west in order to obtain these precious horses.

A treasure that a select few were allowed to touch, which contributed to Beifeng's hostile temperament toward strangers.

"I'm good with animals," I lied.

"Really? Being a stable hand is one of the most coveted positions, and one of the safest. If Beifeng likes you this much, maybe I'll see to it that you are moved to stables. I'm tired of watching young boys die."

"Please don't," I begged before I could stop myself. "I want to fight. If Lan keeps pushing north, my family's village will be in danger. I know what happens when soldiers raze small villages like mine."

Caikun frowned, but didn't argue. "Don't say I didn't warn you. The battlefield has no mercy. Not you, not me, not even the emperor himself can deny Death when it is his time."

"I understand."

With a final pat on my shoulder, he said, "Maybe the Fourth Company of the Third Battalion won't be so bad after all. I hope you live to see your father again."

"Thank you, Commander."

He looked at me for a second and tilted his head as if remembering something.

Shit.

"What is your name?"

I couldn't say Fei. "My name is Little Li."

"Have we met before?"

I laughed. "I've seen you before, but you have never seen me. You delivered the conscription scrolls to my village."

"You look . . . familiar."

Another deep laugh. "I guess I just have one of those faces."

29

"I think this is everyone," Caikun announced when I returned to the barracks. "As some of you may know, my name is Wu Caikun. My father is the chief general of the First Army, and I will be your commander. I believe it's fair to warn everyone beforehand that I was raised among soldiers. By nature, I set a high standard for my men. I expect every one of you to become the best soldiers you can possibly embody before our inevitable advancement to the front lines."

He counted heads with his eyes. "There's a saying in the army: military laws are above even the country's laws. Hence, I expect every single one of you to familiarize yourself with the fifty-eight laws of the army. With every law broken, intentional or accidental, you will be punished with ten laps around the camp, regardless of weather. Understood?"

"Understood!" some of the men responded in unison.

"To start us off, rule number seventeen is that our beds and the barracks must be kept clean and free of clutter at all times." He gestured at the bunk beside him, littered with my bag and the scattered pieces of clothes I'd used to solidify my claim to that precious corner bed. "Whose bed is this?"

Skies. On the first day?

Gingerly, I raised my hand.

Upon seeing me, Caikun's lips curved into a crooked half smile. "Ten laps around camp, Horse Whisperer!"

He then turned to another bed, three down from mine, cluttered with peanut shells and stray cards from an earlier game. "Whose bed is this? Ten laps around camp!"

I sighed, pulled my coat tighter around me, and braved the cold once more. Behind me, I could still hear Caikun giving out laps like red envelopes on New Year.

On my way out of the tent, I passed Luyao. "Call me Little Li from now on," I whispered.

"What?"

"Don't let anyone know my name is Fei."

30

B e it rain or snow, or rare days of blissful sunshine, the camp woke at dawn to run laps before gathering in the courtyard for morning roll call and breakfast. Then we fetched water from the nearby stream, followed by either archery lessons, combat lessons, or practice drills and battle formations.

I excelled at absolutely nothing. Not with my phoenix's mark covered. Perhaps if I had Fate's guidance to help me cheat my way through these lessons, I would have been promoted in no time. At least that was what I liked to believe.

As much as I wanted to exceed and enjoy the satisfaction of showing off my Fate-aided archery skills, I couldn't risk Caikun seeing my phoenix's mark. It was better to keep my head low and be a soldier unremarkable as unremarkable came. The more forgettable I was, the less likely it was that my identity would be exposed.

In the evenings, if we were still on our feet and breathing, Caikun did something no other commander did. He took us to the mountains and identified plants for us, taught us survival skills for both icy winters and scalding summers. It wasn't uncommon for soldiers to go missing during battles. Some by pure accident, and some not so much.

Though most of us had enlisted willingly, many had not. And some were like me, here out of choice but only to protect someone we loved. Caikun claimed the survival lessons were in case any of us got stranded in the wild or the army ran out of supplies. But some days, it felt as if by showing us how to survive in the wilderness, Caikun was giving us a chance to run, if we wanted to.

He kept us on our toes with his infinite list of military rules, under which the smallest of mistakes warranted laps around camp—or worse, fetching water from the mountaintop wells. My peers complained that we had the worst luck, as no other commander was this strict. Caikun operated less like a commander training farm boys and more like a general preparing for battle.

An unsettling thought lumped in my throat each time it surfaced. At nights, I often looked around the barracks and wondered how many of these young men would see their families again.

—⚬—

Weeks passed in the blink of an eye.

The sun had set, and the camp gathered around fires as we waited for our food. Some were trading stories, and others were playing card games to make the monotonous days feel bearable.

A crumpled piece of paper entered my vision. "Can you help me write a letter to my daughter?" asked a tall man with large, callused hands and a menacing face. "I promised her that I—"

"Of course." I stood up to grab my ink brush and inkstone from the tent, where our comrades were lying about, reminiscing about home and laughing about childhood memories. The air after arduous days always felt easy, languishing, and short-lived.

Most of these men came from the countryside, forgotten by the capital unless it was harvest season, born and raised for the rice fields that fed the empire. These men knew many things—things that kept the empire alive—but words and calligraphy were not things their villages prioritized.

"What would you like to tell her?" I asked when I sat down at the table where Luyao and his friends were playing cards. Everyone shuffled to make room for me. This was not the first time I had helped someone send letters home.

"That I am happy, and she should behave and take care of her little brother and grandparents. She shouldn't worry. The food is good here, and so are the people." The men around the table cheered at this. "I will come home as soon as I can."

It was always the same sentiments of happiness and reassurance. 报喜不报忧, *only share the happy details, not grim ones.*

Though our camp whispered Caikun's name in bitter tones, I hoped eventually they would realize that Caikun only wanted what was best for us. He wanted us to go home to our loved ones.

I hoped he would be successful, that more of these men got to see their families again than those who wouldn't.

When I was done with the letter, I handed it to the stranger, and he thanked me with a smile.

From across the table, Luyao watched me, eyeing the brush and inkstone. He wanted me to write more letters home for him but knew my inkstone was running low. Once it was gone, the letter-writing would end, for I had no idea how to get a replacement.

Perhaps I could ask Caikun to show mercy, or steal one from the barracks where the high-ranking officers lived? Couriers came and went every day with letters and information from the front lines. With Fate's help, it would be easy to slip one into my sleeves without anyone noticing.

"When is the baby due?" I asked him. "I still have ink; I can help you write letters to Zhangxi."

Luyao smiled and shook his head, though I knew nothing would please him more. "It's not just your inkstone, Little Li. Think of the couriers who have to deliver these letters in these times."

He was right. It couldn't be easy or safe to travel thousands of miles to deliver letters with a war going on. "There are so many aspects of life that we take for granted in times of prosperity."

"You sound like a capital rat," A'du said, and it was not a compliment. "Times of prosperity are just lies told to us peasants to keep us from rebelling. I alone have seen three different flags fly over my borderland town. My father has seen seven."

"Who is the best ruler?" I asked in jest, and A'du grimaced.

"Good emperor, bad emperor, all tyrants are the same. There is no good ruler, only those who are more benevolent than others."

I thought of my prophecy. If it ever came true, would the gods finally bring peace to the continent? Or would I become just another bad ruler that my citizens saw as the least of all evils?

I sat at the edge of the table while everyone else traded stories. Everything from village gossip to the monstrous rumors uttered of Lan's demons.

Luyao always spoke of Zhangxi. Every night, he stared up at the sky and whispered loving words, in hopes that the moon and the stars would relay his love to her and their unborn child.

Another boy—younger than I was, barely fifteen—spoke of his family every night. Of his elderly father, his blind mother, and his little sister, whose smile was vibrant and sweet as the peaches they gathered from summer forests. He hadn't enlisted by choice. Forced here by the richest merchant of the village to replace his silver-spooned son in order to pay off his father's debts.

Others had similar stories, having been paid by wealthier men to enlist in place of their sons in order to keep their siblings fed or buy their parents medicine.

With them, I cried.

With them, I laughed.

However, the conversations always ambled from reminiscent memories to fears of the inevitable. The same fables of war, which sounded more like ghost stories to scare misbehaving kids.

Lan Yexue's soldiers walked into a downpour of arrows and came out alive.

They say his men move fast like lightning and are stronger than bulls.

Those are not men. They are demons, with glowing red eyes. My uncle saw them! They have fangs in place of teeth!

None of this is true! someone would proclaim every night. *These are just haunted men repainting their worst memories with demons that don't exist!*

I wasn't so sure. If Lan Yexue could move like lightning and fling grown men around as if they were rag dolls, who was to say his soldiers could not do the same?

The way Yexue meticulously pushed Rong's army back with languorous slowness felt personal. Like a predator toying with his prey, or a strategist, waiting.

Was this really revenge for the degradation he'd suffered at Rong's court? Or was Lan Yexue planning something more?

Memories fluttered: my dagger in his chest; his eyes that bled with pain as he watched me ride away with Siwang.

How I wished I had gone for his heart when I had the chance.

—∞—

Day by day, night by night, these strange faces slowly became familiar.

Men whose laughter I began to recognize, whose families I felt as if I had already met. Men whose quiet sobs lulled everyone to sleep in the dark. The ones who laughed the hardest also cried the loudest.

Every night, after the fires whimpered into smoke and exhaustion forced my eyes to close, I watched these newfound friends die in my never-ending nightmares.

Lan Yexue's haunting, bloodstained smile against falling snow.

You can run, but you can't hide, my goddess.

31

On the thirty-fifth day of the year, exactly one month since I'd arrived at camp, our monotonous schedule shattered like dropped porcelain.

Instead of waking up at dawn to run laps around camp, Caikun gave us permission to sleep an extra hour—on the condition that we were washed and uniformed and gathered in the courtyard at the seventh hour. Any tardiness would be punished by laps, barefoot in the freezing snow.

Caikun always followed through on his promises, so nobody dared to disobey.

We weren't the only ones who gathered the courtyard, however. The entire Third Army was here. Each battalion had its own separate schedule determined by our commanders, and we were almost never at the same place at the same time, except for dinners around the fire. There wasn't enough room in the courtyards and the archery field for all of us to train at the same time, so we went in alternate slots.

Are we going off to war? This was my first thought, because we were nowhere near ready. If they sent us to the front lines now it would be like sending lambs to the slaughter.

I absentmindedly touched the headband covering my phoenix's mark, tempted to pull it a little lower for a glimpse of what might happen. Patience was a virtue I'd only half learned, given Fate's blessings.

Thankfully, before curiosity fully dug its talons into me, the drums began to sound. Caikun said learning to decipher the tempo of drums was on our agenda: an ancient method of passing messages in the chaos of war.

I shifted my weight from foot to foot, unease growing tight in my belly.

Then a young man stepped onto the platform at the center of the courtyard. Dark brows, pillowed lips that were almost offensively beautiful, and those familiar, sharp eyes, capable of turning at a pin drop's notice. Kind one second, cruel the next.

My heart writhed. Despite the distress of the past year, Siwang looked well. Better, even. He was taller than I remembered, his shoulders wider and body sturdier. Gone was the lingering baby fat around his cheeks.

The prince standing before me was no longer a boy, but a man.

A soldier.

"Good morning," he addressed the camp, hands behind his back and head tilted high.

There was a new gravitas to the way he spoke, something that hadn't been there before. A deepening of the voice, like a quiet rumble of thunder that commanded attention with every uttered word.

Siwang sounded just like his father.

"For those of you who don't know, I am Rong Siwang. The Crown Prince of Rong, and the commanding general of the Third Army."

Shit. Out of all the armies he could be in charge of, why did—

From the elevated platform, Siwang's eyes caught mine as if he'd heard my thoughts. Those pale eyes pierced all my armor with just one look, and I flinched back. I tried to lower my gaze, but not before Siwang's lips twitched, ever so slightly.

Did he recognize me? Surely not. I had spent every waking second of the past moon under Caikun's watch. Despite the initial comment on the first day, there was no further indication that he knew I was a girl, let alone remembered I was Lifeng Fei. And in the long months when I had traveled as a man, the only people who saw through my disguise had been other women.

"On behalf of the people of Rong, I'd like to thank each and every one of you for your service," Siwang continued without missing a beat.

He can't spot me in a crowd this easily, I told myself. A year was long enough to heal a heart. Even if it wasn't, the political stress of going from a conqueror to the conquered would surely take up all Siwang's attention. By now, I was likely a forgotten face gathering dust in some forgotten corner of his mind.

Still, I lowered my head and strategically positioned myself behind my comrades. My family's life depended on my identity remaining a secret. I had to be discreet.

Typical Fei. I could hear my father now. *Reckless and thoughtless. She never thinks of the consequences.*

A side effect of growing up in the imperial palace as the prince's bride. I rarely had to think far enough to consider the repercussions of my actions because Siwang was always there to protect me.

No more.

"Now, why don't some of you come up and show me what you have learned?" Siwang rolled up his sleeves and descended from the platform. "You there, with the blue headband." He pointed toward my direction, and everything stopped. "Come and demonstrate what my commanders have taught you."

Instantly, a flock of eyes turned toward me.

Siwang's lips tilted into a crooked smile.

It took all my courage not to make a run for it.

"Your Highness." I bowed as Siwang made his way toward me, the crowd dispersing for him like oceans parting for a dragon.

Once Siwang and I stood face to face, fellow soldiers quickly gathered in a circle around us. Sly smiles and eager eyes: they were itching to see whether the crown prince would get his ass handed to him, or if I'd be the one to walk away from this fight bloodied and bruised.

A spectacle, either way. A break from our mundane drills.

My insides shriveled. Siwang had been trained by the best combat teachers the empire—hell, the *continent*—had to offer since birth. I was not his match. I knew this. Our teachers knew this. *He* knew this. *Which means he doesn't recognize me, right?*

"How do you suppose I should demonstrate my lessons to you, Your Highness?" I continued to keep my head low, feigning innocence, shuffling back to put space between us while he circled me like a predator.

"By sparring, of course. And no need to refer to me by my title; we are all men here, brothers in arms. To Death, we are all souls trapped in mortal flesh. There's no difference between prince and soldiers on the battlefield. Everyone," he called more loudly for the crowd to heed, "my name is Siwang, and you should all refer to me as such."

The crowd exploded in hollers and cheers. He was endearing himself to the men who would charge into battle and sell their lives for him. However by doing so, he was also establishing bad military discipline. Military ranks existed for a reason, and the chain of command had to be clear. I looked around the camp at the senior officers to see their reactions.

They were all stone-faced. Except Caikun, who was frowning.

There was no reason a prince should lower himself like this.

Suddenly, I no longer feared whether Siwang recognized me. I feared the state of the front lines.

When Siwang returned his attention to me, his lips curled into a soft smile, one I remembered all too well.

I lowered my head farther, my hands formed tiny fists at my sides.

"*Your Highness*..." I insisted on the title that I had never used with him, because if I called him Siwang, he would recognize my voice. "I'm just a farm boy from a small village. I'm unworthy of being your opponent. You should pick another. Someone taller, stronger, more experienced. Maybe another highborn who matches you in training. Or—"

Siwang stepped forward and touched my shoulder. I jumped back. He was so close. If I lifted my head now, he'd see my face clearly.

My startled reflex earned a restrained chuckle from the prince's lips.

"There's nothing unworthy about a farm boy. Every single one of us eats rice here, right? Who plants those seeds and reaps the grains? We are all soldiers here to protect our home and loved ones. When we put on our armor, we are equals. We are brothers. I will treat every one of you as if you are my family, and I hope you'd all do the same for me."

Again, the crowd cheered.

Siwang failed to mention that the emperor had forced every single one of his half brothers into exile to protect Siwang's claim to the throne. Being his brother didn't confer the splendor one might have expected.

"Shall we?" Siwang shrugged off his heavy fur coat to reveal a gray cotton uniform, the same as mine.

Even in drabs, Siwang was beautiful. When he moved, the uniform hugged his perfectly defined chest and biceps. If I didn't notice before how much taller and broader he'd grown, I did now.

Despite the same clothes, Siwang looked nothing like the men around us. His grace and aura were not attributes these lusterless uniforms could hide. Just as it was not something fanciful clothes could replicate, though the wealthy young men of Yong'An had tried.

Power and grace were things that had long settled deep in Siwang's bones, morphed into the way he spoke, stood, and moved.

"Let us begin," I murmured.

We each took three steps back. Siwang was the first to bow, and I quickly followed suit.

"May the best man win," he said.

My heart beat a dangerous tempo in my ears. Siwang wouldn't kill a new soldier just to establish dominance, right? Or was this the reason he'd chosen me, because I was small and an easy target?

Siwang lunged, led by his right foot.

This was not the first time we had sparred. Even without Fate's help, I knew he would aim for my abdomen, either get me on the ground or immobile. So I took a wide step to the left at the last minute to avoid him. If he lost his balance, it would be great, but Siwang was too good. So he would likely re-collect, then lunge again. If he did, then I would have to dodge again. Could I hit the Crown Prince of Rong? What would happen if—

Siwang anticipated my wide step. *Of course.* He was Rong Siwang. Trained to perfection and expected to exceed all expectations. He swiftly shifted his weight from left to right and grabbed me by the arm, his shoulder lodging in my belly.

I was thrown onto my back before I knew it.

"Best out of three?" Siwang offered his hand to help me to my feet. I didn't take it.

I pushed myself up and took a step back. "I'm as unremarkable as they come, Your Highness. Ask anyone here and they will tell you so. I am weak and I am lazy." This earned a few snickers from the soldiers who didn't know me. "If you wish to see a better example of our commanders' efforts to polish rough stones into marble, please, pick any of my peers. They'll show you just how capable they are."

"I volunteer." Relief washed over me when Luyao stepped up. He shot me a pitiful look. "Little Li is just a boy. If you wish to fight a real opponent, fight me."

Tears welled behind my eyes. If we survived this war, I would hunt all the boars for him and Zhangxi. Their child would be the roundest, fattest, chubbiest baby the village had ever seen. That child would never go hungry. I would make sure of it.

Siwang's eyes darted between me and Luyao. "The two of you know each other?"

"We are from the same village."

"The same village, huh?" Siwang's voice suddenly went cold. Without waiting for my response, he grabbed my hand by force and hoisted me to my feet. The motion nearly sent my body crashing into his before I found my balance and stepped back. I tried to pull my hand from his.

His grip held tighter, just for a moment, before a smile broke out on those lips. He turned to Luyao. "Let's fight."

I scurried to the back of the crowd the moment Siwang let me go, and tried not to think about how the feel of his skin sent every nerve in my body exploding like fireworks.

32

Luyao was no match for Siwang. With a single swing of his fist, Siwang all but knocked Luyao out within the first breath of the match.

More men volunteered for the chance to fight, ravenous for the honor of beating the Crown Prince of Rong in combat. The same excitement I had seen ten thousand times before—in the emperor's court and during the imperial hunt.

None had ever succeeded before, and none succeeded today, not even as exhaustion slowed Siwang's stealthy feet.

The sun climbed higher into the sky. By the time sweat beaded on Siwang's forehead, and the raised hands of brave challengers fell in masses, it was almost noon.

Half a smile at his lips, our beloved prince gazed at this battalion of astonished men, whose trust and respect he had just earned like conquered land. He straightened his back, as if ready to go for another round, though I noticed the way his chest rose and fell rapidly beneath his porcelain facade.

Then, almost in unison, the soldiers bowed for their prince and general.

His half smile blossomed into a full smile, pride gleaming like the golden sunlight he radiated.

Just like that, he'd won the hearts of thousands of men.

All in a morning's work.

Siwang laughed. "I want to tell everyone that you can take the rest of the day off, but I've already borrowed enough time. If I stole more, your commanders might riot. Why don't we take the rest of the morning off, at least?"

Siwang looked to the commanders, who stood in a line before the gathered crowd like guards, ready to step in if anyone posed a real threat.

They exchanged glances, then nodded in unison.

Again, the crowd cheered. Nobody seemed to notice that the morning was almost over, so he wasn't giving us much of anything. Yet, the excitement was palpable.

"Thank you, for your time, and for showing me just how magnificent Rong's soldiers are. Every single one of you is Rong's pride. Don't you ever forget that."

I let out the breath I was holding when Siwang disappeared among his waiting guards and the crowd began to disperse.

Luyao met my eyes from across the courtyard. If he had not intervened, would Siwang have found me out? I wasn't sure what would hurt more. For my identity as a girl to be found out and to be sentenced to death on the count of treason, or to be completely forgotten by Siwang in just one year?

"Luyao." I called out his name. "Thank—"

A slender eunuch in dark blue robes caught my arms.

"The prince wishes to see you in his tent."

Shit. "I . . ."

"*Now.*"

—⚮—

Siwang's tent was north of the camp, far from the barracks, surrounded by smaller tents that housed his advisors and hand-selected warriors who went wherever he went, men whose entire lives were dedicated to keeping him safe.

In the distance, lunch was being served. Congee with beans, slender shreds of pork sparingly dispersed atop it like a dainty garnish, and sides of fermented cabbage for the soldiers to share. A lot of the recruits were from the north, where fermented vegetables were a must with every meal.

It wasn't much, but it kept our bellies full, which was more than most had, especially those at the borders.

There was a reason many of those who voluntarily enlisted were from poorer families: they came only for the prospect of a hot meal, knowing they might pay with their life when it was time to meet Lan's army. If the only other option was starving to death under winter's breath, then was there ever a choice? In the army, they had the prospect of growth. Promotions, though rare for boys of no name and no means, were possible.

Something was better than nothing.

My stomach growled. If I didn't go back soon, there wouldn't be any shreds of pork left; the congee would just be water and a few floating grains of rice. It would be foolish to even dream of seeing any fermented vegetables left at the table.

The prince's guards gave me suspicious glances when I approached the tent, but lifted the flap for me to enter.

Inside, Siwang was holding court with six men: three of them in silk winter robes, two men in armor, and Caikun, standing just a few steps behind Siwang, was in his commander's uniform.

I didn't recognize any of the other men, but to hold court with Siwang meant they were important in some way. My feet whispered against the soft rug. The men stopped what they were doing and looked at me. Narrowed eyes and confused glances, probably wondering the same as the guards outside.

What was a scrawny, green recruit like me doing here?

Even Caikun seemed surprised when he saw me, a slow frown forming between his brows.

I lowered my head and hoped they could not see my face, that they would not recognize me.

"He's with me," Siwang said casually, dismissing my presence with a wave of his hand. "Continue, General Wang."

Siwang had changed back to his black dragon robes, fine silk hugging his wide shoulders and tall frame even better than the tattered linen robes he'd worn earlier. He'd taken the time to comb out his hair, previously disheveled from the fights. Now it sat in an elegant topknot on his head, held in place by a small crown of gold and a slender hairpin.

I looked away before he could catch me staring.

"Everything said in this tent is confidential, and nobody is going to say anything. Right, *Little Li*?" Siwang turned his attention to me.

I shuddered at the way he said my nickname, one that only my comrades called me. "Right, Your Highness."

"Continue, General Wang," Siwang repeated.

"Well, um, as I was saying, the soldiers are improving. Some are better than others. The Second and Third Companies of the Fifth Battalion are battlefield-ready."

"And the others?"

Silence. Hesitation. An answer that didn't need to be spoken out loud.

Siwang sighed. "Keep training them. We are losing men quicker than ever. Send the most qualified soldiers to the front lines within the moon, and toughen your training on the others. The front lines are waiting."

"But Your Highness, Lan's soldiers are killing our men quicker than we can train them. This isn't sustainable. We—"

The general paused midsentence, as if suddenly remembering my existence. He shot Siwang a troubled look.

"Do your best, General Wang. I will try to come up with a solution. We are going to beat Lan's armies. I know we will."

By the somber looks around the room, I wasn't sure Siwang's advisors were as optimistic.

"But Your Highness—"

"This is enough for today; leave us."

"Your—"

"*Leave us,*" Siwang repeated, rubbing the bridge of his nose with thumb and forefinger, something he used to do under stress. A headache was setting in. Before, I would have gone to his side and rubbed his temples for him. Now I was just his foot soldier. Someone like me was not allowed to touch the Crown Prince without his permission.

The men must have realized Siwang was irritated, and relented. If they kept nagging Siwang like a bunch of aunties, they would only anger him further.

Siwang was just and calm in the worst of situations, though he did have a temper worthy of an emperor.

Throughout history, countless eunuchs, ministers, and generals had lost their heads by saying the wrong thing at the wrong time. Cautionary tales.

Steadily, the advisors filed out, one by one. Until Caikun, Siwang, and I were the last three standing.

"You too, Caikun."

I stole a glance up at Caikun, whose icy gaze made every muscle in my body go tense.

I'd lost my fight earlier. Was he ashamed of me? Or was this a warning?

Just as Siwang had been raised to rule and to lead, Caikun had been raised to protect Siwang with his life, to study beside him, support him, and be everything the prince needed him to be. A best friend and a guardian.

Relax, you saw how quickly he beat me earlier, I wanted to say. *The person you need to worry about is me.*

With a reluctant bow, Caikun exited the tent.

In his absence, the full weight of Siwang's gaze descended on me like the judgment blade of an executioner, precariously balanced at the nape of my neck.

The Crown Prince of Rong, and the chief general of the Third Army: if he wanted me dead, I would not live.

Siwang exhaled, a soft sound that dispersed the tension, if only a little. "Drop the act, Fei."

Words I'd been dreading since his eyes caught mine in the courtyard.

He'd recognized me. Of course he had. He was Siwang. It was fatuous, thinking I could bypass those eyes.

When I finally met his eyes, Siwang's lips were curled at the edges, his eyes clear and benevolent—for now. This meant nothing; I was not safe. More than once, I had witnessed those eyes change fast as a summer's storm.

I slipped the headband from between my brows.

He might hold the power, however I had the advantage of fore-sight. Though it was unlikely, if I was smart and fast on my feet, then maybe—just maybe—I could outscheme my beloved playmate and beat the prince at his own game. Whatever that game might be.

Siwang's eyes lingered on me. Lips woven into a conspiring smile, he perched at the desk's edge. "When I saw your name on the enlist-ment sheet in place of your father's, I thought I was dreaming again."

Something in my belly turned sour. "You knew my father was con-scripted, and you didn't do anything to stop it?"

Did he not remember how Father had struggled to walk up the steps of Heaven's Hall on rainy days, how the imperial doctors con-sulted him on his ailing heart, constantly telling him to rest and not to get angry?

"I was the one who put him on the list."

Something cold coiled in me, freezing my every muscle, every thought, every heartbeat. I wanted to grab that blade at his hip, slash that ravishing neck of his, and watch him choke on his own blood.

In the end, the only thing I could manage was silence. A stray tear gathered in the corner of my eye.

"Relax, Fei. I did not intend for him to serve as a soldier and fight the war. I wanted him to be my advisor."

"My father no longer serves the crown," I replied. "You have no right to take him from his home, his family, without his consent."

"As long as he lives within Rong's borders, he must serve me as I wish," Siwang replied, his voice deep and words heavy like a warning. I was treading dangerous waters. "Your father might not be of the court anymore, but he's still one of my best teachers: someone whose morals I respect, whose knowledge I revere, whose opinion I trust. *And,* with his year spent far from the politics of Yong'An, he has no allegiances in court anymore. No one can use him to sway my choices. Things have changed since you left. I have as many enemies as I have supporters now."

"You always have as many enemies as you have supporters," I murmured.

"Things have gotten worse since Lan waged this war that is draining all our resources. There are cowards in court who want Father to surrender."

I didn't want to say it, but I wondered if those men had a point. "Siwang, I've heard that as enlistment grows, the numbers of men who farm our lands and keep food in our bowls are dwindling. If we don't have enough men to plant crops when spring comes, it can affect this year's harvest, and the rice prices will rise again," I said, which made Siwang raise his brows. "You are not the only one who paid attention in class. I care about Rong the same as you. Hungry peasants will lead to angry rebellions if things don't improve. And I have met many hungry peasants in the past year."

"Are you telling me we should surrender?"

"I think you should stop forcing men to enlist, or—"

"*No.* We need the soldiers."

"*Let me finish.* As I was saying: stop forcing men to enlist, or command the women to work in their place and take over their roles. Some villages are already doing this, but there is still prejudice in many rural villages. Their elders forbid the women from doing men's work."

Siwang pursed his lips. "I can pass this to Father."

"You'd better do it quick. Spring is coming, and those crops need to be planted." I sighed. "So tell me, how are things on the front lines?"

"That's classified information."

"If you didn't trust me, you wouldn't let me listen in on your meeting. You said you want my father because you want his advice, however I don't think that's true. I think you want someone who isn't embroiled in court politics to talk to. Someone you know will not betray you for one of your half brothers and their families."

Siwang smiled. "What if you are right? Will you let me send men to escort your father here to sit at my side and listen to my problems?"

"You will not bring my father here or anywhere that is dangerous," I snapped, remembering my most recent nightmare of his limp body, and the blood that soaked a military map that was too similar to the one in this tent. "Talk to me instead. You know me as well as the back of your hand. I don't care for court politics, and I will not betray you."

"You haven't changed one bit, Lifeng Fei."

Li Fei, I wanted to correct him. Lifeng Fei died the day I ended our betrothal.

"Lan Yexue wants Rong to become his tribute state." Siwang exhaled, rubbing his temples.

His body visibly deflated. That rigid posture crumbled before my eyes, and immediately, Siwang went from looking princely to looking exhausted. It was so easy to forget how young he still was. A nineteen-year-old trying his best to be the man his father, his court, his empire wanted him to be. The weight on his shoulders was immense; could he really bear it all?

"What does your father want?"

"He wants me to make the decision, as it is my empire to inherit."

"Then what do you want?"

Siwang looked away. "This war has gone on for too long, Fei. I can no longer see the forest for the trees. Every defeat, big or small, feels like the end of the rope. . . ." He met my eyes. "I'm scared, Fei."

My heart ached, hearing this. I had never known Siwang to admit defeat. Even when the entire court was against him because they didn't think he was worthy, he had never shared his sadness with me. "How long have you been bottling this up?"

"Too long."

"I guess since my father isn't here to listen to your problems, I'll have to do it in his place?"

Siwang's silken laugh melted my bones like wax. He picked up the inky calligraphy brush at his desk and jutted it at me like a weapon. "Don't make it sound like such a chore," he teased. "Do you want me to tell everyone at camp how you're actually a girl who broke at least half a dozen military laws by coming here?"

I sneered at the calligraphy brush, then shook my head.

"Good." Siwang winked, a smile threatening to dance across his golden face. "Defy me again and watch me draw some ugly turtles on your face like we did as kids."

"You know, I never understood what was so dishonorable about having a turtle on my face."

"Does this mean you want me to draw one, so you can find out?" He rose from the desk, chuckling.

Immediately, I ducked out of his way, skittering away from him until I had the fire pit between us for safe distance.

"Come here," he taunted, our laughter filling the space. I hoped the fabric of the tent was thick, because what would his guards think if they could hear us giggling like children? "If you couldn't outrun me as kids, you cannot outrun me now!"

He lunged for me, his longer legs giving him an unfair advantage. I didn't bother to move this time.

I yelped when he pulled me into his arms and smeared a giant line of ink across my nose.

When our laughter died down, I realized just how close we were. My body pressed against his, my heart like a blooming peony straining against my chest, velvet petals fluttering in my throat between shallow breaths. His lips were too close to mine. His hand too hot on my back, sending my body tingling like something slumbering finally coming back to life.

Though I'd tried everything to pretend otherwise, I had missed this, missed *him*. How easy and carefree things were when it was just the two of us, far from watchful eyes and courtly rules.

"Fei, I—"

My stomach rumbled. A fire lit up across my cheeks, and Siwang smiled.

He let me go. "I suspect you haven't eaten lunch yet?"

I ignored the ache in my chest when he walked to the entrance of the tent and said something to the guards outside.

A minute or two later, two servants entered bearing two ceramic bowls. Lamb and potato stew, I knew without having to look. They also brought a side dish of fermented vegetables and two bowls of rice. Not watery congee, but real *rice*.

My mouth watered. I hadn't had anything this good since I left home.

"You didn't think I'd let you go hungry, did you? Sit, we will catch up over food." He guided me toward the silk cushions around a low table, then proceeded to pour jasmine tea into small teacups. "I try to be frugal with my meals and eat the same as my men. But I want to treat you to something nice for our reunion. I assume lamb stew is still your favorite?"

Warm broth poured down my throat, fragrant and delicious. Ginger, star anise, garlic, salt, and the tender chunks of lamb that were falling off the bone, cooked to perfection. I closed my eyes and relished the taste.

"You used to bring this stew to me whenever I was sick," I said.

"Yes. Stew for when you are sick, and *tang hulus* for when you're upset or angry with me."

"My forgiveness is a master that can be bought only with candied hawthorn berries. Nothing else." I repeated the words I used to tease him with.

Memories of childhoods long past fell like dusted sugar around us. Deliciously sweet. Just like his eyes as he watched me, so intently and with so much unspoken longing. "I've missed you, Fei."

I lowered my gaze as a warm flush crept up my cheeks. Such simple words, yet capable of making my flesh burn and my bones sing: a haunting symphony of memories and nostalgia, mixed with something else.

In the palace, I had heard stories of how the concubines would paint their bodies with shimmer and wear immodest dresses, then wander the gardens frequented by the emperor even on the coldest of nights in hope of being seen by him. And that their soft flesh and wanton eyes could coax his hands into touching them.

It seemed that all anyone wanted in the inner palace was for the emperor to touch them, to kiss them, to part their legs and bear his weight and let him give them the pleasures that apparently only he could give them.

As a child, I was always curious about what happened at night between two people, wondered what sort of pleasure could be so consuming. How could the touch of a single man devour those beautiful concubines to a point where they devoted their days to scheme ways to seduce the emperor and make him touch them?

As Siwang's betrothed, the only person who could touch me was him. And if he ever touched me, then it would mean I would be forever trapped in that palace.

But this wasn't the palace, and I was no longer his betrothed. Since leaving the palace, I had heard more rumors of the pleasures that conspired at night. Some of the cheapest lodgings in a village were often rented out by brothels, where I may or may not have heard some things that made my toes curl.

I've missed you, too. Four words at the tip of my tongue, yet I couldn't bring myself to say them.

Instead, I asked, "How bad is it?" The question snipped the humming melodies in my bones, and from the way Siwang's face fell, it did the same to his. "I've heard the stories of Lan Yexue's army."

"Everybody on the continent has heard the stories by now."

"Should I be scared that your father sent you, his favorite son, to train recruits? This might not be the front lines, but it is close."

If the First Army, kept for war, and the Second Army, kept for border protection, lost their strongholds, we—the Third Army—would be the reinforcements and the last hope. As the chief general of the Third Army, it was Siwang's duty to lead us into battlegrounds if the moment ever called for it.

A bunch of ragtag farmers and boys too young to be sent to war, facing enemies as vicious as Lan? The thought was profoundly unsettling.

"This isn't a fun little exercise for you to exert your military skills, is it?"

I waited for Siwang to smile and tell me I was being ridiculous.

He didn't. "Nothing I say can leave the room."

It's a little late for that. "Do you trust me?" I asked.

"With my life."

Something in me fluttered. Just a little.

33

"Are we losing the war?"

"Not *yet*," Siwang replied, voice low. As if he spoke the words quietly, it would not ring true. "However, as the men of our First and Second Armies keep dying, things might change, fast. . . ."

"Isn't that the only thing we can count on in times of war? People dying?"

"Not us. Not normally, at least. Rong's soldiers are the best on the continent, and we haven't lost a war in decades. I can't lose this war, Fei. I won't let our people return to the life of our ancestors. Ants at the southerners' feet. Their so-called savages, to be trampled and abused as they wish. If we are not conquerors and emperors, then we are nothing."

Rong's soldiers *were* the best on the continent.

My eyes dropped to his fist, curled on the table. I wanted to cover his hand with mine, let my flesh warm his, and tell him everything would be okay.

I didn't.

Fate might have blessed me, but I couldn't see the futures she didn't want to show me. And Siwang didn't want syrupy lies. He had put my father's name on the conscription list because he wanted someone honest at his side.

I would listen to Siwang's worries, I would not pour salt over his wounds, and I would not lie.

"I begged my father to send me here," Siwang continued, his voice smaller than before. "So that I could do *something* as my people continue to die by the hundreds and the thousands. As this land that is soaked with our ancestors' blood, laden with their bones, is stolen from under our feet. Inch by inch, mile by mile, city by city. All of it is my fault, because I let Lan Yexue escape. I am the crown prince, the heir of heaven's mandate. I have a responsibility to stop this madness before it consumes Rong."

You are not the reason Lan Yexue escaped, I wanted to tell him. I was the one who had tended his wounds, saved him from the Beiying tiger's jaws, warned him that Siwang and his men were close, and when I had the chance to end him, I did not.

If anyone was responsible for this carnage, it was me.

"Are these lands really worth the bloodshed?" I asked.

"This is the land our ancestors gave their lives to claim. Of course it is worth it. To relinquish our land is to dishonor everything that's come before us."

My lips thinned; a protest rose into my mouth.

Empires rose, and empires fell. Life bloomed, then life withered. Nothing was eternal. Not even the greatest dynasties the continent had ever seen. The Huang, the Qin, the southern Chu. All had tried to unite the Warring States. And all had failed.

One day, Rong would decline, just like all the great empires that had come before it.

This was the cycle of life. We would be replaced, erased, and perhaps forgotten by future generations until we were nothing but the ruins and dust of a crumbling legacy.

"This chaos, a war here and a war there, when will it end? Today Lan wants a city. Tomorrow Wei wants a village. One enemy falls and two rise in its place. All men who amass power are greedy. Will the people of these borderlands ever know peace?"

Will the bloodshed ever end?

"They will know peace when I become the emperor of all emperors. One day, Rong will become so powerful that no one will dare to rebel or wage war. When I rule over a united An'Lu, the continent will finally be free of wars, and know only prosperity."

I exhaled. Absentmindedly, I toyed with the spoon on the table, not knowing what to say.

"You don't believe me?"

"I don't think uniting An'Lu is going to be as easy as you imagine it to be."

"If it were easy, someone would have done it by now." He leaned a little closer, his golden eyes glistening with want. "I'm going to do it, Fei. No matter the cost, I will unite the continent. Or die trying."

"Don't say that," I protested.

"There is another reason why we can't let Lan win," Siwang continued.

I thought of Yexue's glittering crimson blood, its sweetness as it filled my mouth. "Your pride?" A moment of lingering childhood courage, which I regretted as soon as it was out of my mouth.

Thankfully, Siwang gave me a half laugh. Tolerant, though the warning was there. "Were you angry when I put your father's name on the conscription list?"

"Angry?" The word felt too small, too gentle to describe how I had felt.

I wasn't angry. I was furious. Hands at my bow, ready to kill anyone who dared to force my father to fight in a war he had no stake in kind of furious.

I was tempted to tell Siwang that this war wasn't just killing soldiers, but also parents through heartbreak, and children through poverty. Widows sold their bodies on the streets for bread to feed their weeping babies. I had seen too much on my travels. The cost of war would always be greater than the justifications.

A year ago, I would not have hesitated to tell Siwang this.

"If we lose," Siwang said, every word slow and deliberate, "worse fates will fall upon everyone in the empire. This war is only the beginning. The real bloodshed will come afterward, once Lan has Rong at its feet. Then they can do whatever they want, to whomever they want. Forget about conscripting your father into the army; he can slaughter your entire family in their own beds, or feed them to his demons . . . and that will be his right to do as Lan's prince regent."

"The stories are true?"

He nodded. "There are creatures who are not human in Lan Yexue's army. *Blood-drinking demons.* The kind that should exist only in nightmares. Father's scholars from beyond the great western sea call them *vampires.* Undead creatures who roam the night in search of human blood. We have other words for them from the various dynasties. Jiangshi. Xixuegui. The Undead. The names vary with regions and lore."

"How much do we know about them?"

"Between our lore and the western scholars, we can piece together things here and there, though not enough."

I thought of the red-eyed monsters from my vision weeks ago. "Where do they come from? Were they born like this or were they made?"

"Or invited here from the depths of hell," Siwang offered. "We don't know for sure. The scholars have different stories. Some say they are creations of ancient gods. Others say they are demons who escaped hell. All we know is that they are dangerous, and they are the reason behind Lan's continuous victories. And that Yexue is capable of commanding them."

"Can we kill them?"

Siwang hesitated. A beat longer than was comfortable. Dread twisted in my belly as I watched his face change, ever so slightly. "They are weakened by sunlight."

"And they drink blood?"

"We think they need it to survive."

I remembered how the demons in my dreams always had impossibly sharp teeth, and they killed not with blades, but by ripping open the throats of prey. "How many does he have?"

"At least one or two battalions' worth. And because those demons need blood to survive, I have heard that Lan Yexue lets them feed on the civilians of the cities he has conquered."

I shuddered to think what would happen if our people fell to the jaws of these monsters. If my family . . . "Do we have a chance of winning this war?"

"Yes," Siwang replied without hesitation. A small boost of confidence for me.

"How?"

He leaned across the table and gently touched the tip of my nose with the nail of his forefinger. "天机不可泄露." *The machinations of heaven cannot be shared.*

I rolled my eyes.

And with that, he kissed me.

34

The vampires came in the dark of the night, followed by ear-splintering screams and the stench of fresh blood.

"Run!" Mother cried, pushing Fangyun and me through the window just as the door was kicked open. A large man with bloodred eyes crept into view. I could see Father's limp, bloodless body in the background, impossibly pale, his eyes empty. "Run!" she cried one last time, and I obeyed.

Hand in hand, Fangyun and I ran into the forest. Snowy terrain stretched as far as our eyes could see. Pine needles and sharp stones bit at our bare feet; we didn't stop.

Help. We have to get help.

Manic laughter echoed behind us. Footsteps. The vampires were coming. They—

From the shadows, a beast pounced on my sister.

"Fei!" She cried my name just as he wrapped both hands around her throat, and—

Snap.

"Fangyun!"

Slow steps. The beast walked out from the shadows, until finally, I saw his beautiful, porcelain face.

Lan Yexue.

I stumbled back. His eyes were red, and in place of teeth, he had fangs like the tiger that almost killed us a year ago.

"It's been a long time, Fei," he purred.

I tried to run, but he was faster. I tried to fight, but he was stronger.

Before long, he had his hand around my throat, a wicked smile on his lips.

"Miss me?"

I jerked awake just as his fangs came down on my throat.

35

When Siwang came to watch us practice, I kept my head low.

In the evenings, I ate with him.

I never mentioned the kiss, and neither did he. Instead, we talked about more important things, like war and strategy. He bounced ideas off me, told me the dire situation of the front lines, and I told him about my year in exile. About the people I had met on my travels, and the everyday struggles of a normal civilian, far from the palace—this interested him more than anything else.

Days passed.

After our evening combat practice, I was tasked with cleaning up. So I gathered all the wooden swords and took them to the armory. On my way back to the barracks, I spotted Siwang in the stables.

Foolishly, I approached without invitation, and his guards stopped me at first sight.

Siwang smiled, waved the guards away. "That's Little Li. He is all right."

Guards were not in positions to question princes, so they stepped aside.

By now, people were used to seeing me talking to Siwang, and rumors were spreading like wildfire: that the prince had found a new lover in a foot soldier. This gave me a newfound fame around camp. People stared and whispered everywhere I went. I felt like Lifeng Fei again, and I wasn't sure how I felt about this.

We are not lovers, I had tried to tell my comrades whenever they asked.

Then what are you?

I didn't know how to explain things without exposing the truth: that we had grown up together and he was my best friend. Though he did kiss me a few days ago, neither of us ever brought it up, so was it really a kiss?

A year ago, I would have fought these rumors tooth and nail, declared that I felt nothing for him. But the more time we spent together, the more I longed for more.

"You were at camp when I arrived. I remember seeing Beifeng on my first day here." I leaned against Beifeng's stall doors as Siwang tended to the horse.

"I was."

"And you didn't say anything, because . . . ?"

Siwang shrugged, turning the full heat of his gaze on me. Degree by degree, my skin grew warmer. "I wanted to bide my time, see why you came, how you were doing."

"Did you recognize me immediately?"

"How could I not? I think about you every day. After you left the palace, I pictured your face every night before I went to sleep, and hoped I might see you again in my dreams."

I should tell him that I had done the same, that I'd missed him the way he'd missed me. However that would be a lie, and Siwang's heart was not something I should toy with, not anymore.

I turned to Beifeng instead, picked up a carrot from the bucket and fed him. "You're not going to tell anyone my secret, right?"

"As long as you don't tell anyone the classified military information I divulged."

"I wonder how much Lan Yexue would pay for such information." My lips twitched. "You shouldn't tell people Rong's military secrets so easily, you know."

"I trust you."

My heart did its cursed flutter again, but I couldn't tell if this feeling was good or bad. There was a sour taste on my tongue, a seeping dread that I didn't deserve Siwang's unconditional trust.

Did he ever stop to think that I might take advantage of his feelings? I looked away. Perhaps we shouldn't be spending so much time together after all, regardless of how much I enjoyed it. "I'm honored by the credence you give to my character."

A silence befell us. Siwang's attention shifted to the silver brush in his hand as he ran it through Beifeng's mane. "Was everything . . . worth it? Did I make the right choice by letting you go?"

I thought of my sister's eloquent smiles, my parents' tender warmth when they looked at each other in the cottage's flickering candlelight. All the things I couldn't see when I was Lifeng Fei, the girl betrothed to a prince, trapped inside a gilded cage.

But I also thought of my mother's squinting eyes, my father's slouched back, and the blisters that marred Fangyun's hands.

"In some ways, yes. Though in other ways, no. . . . I am happy. Happier than I was inside the palace. I only wish this happiness didn't cost my family their life in the capital. I was the one who wanted to leave, yet they are paying the price. They never complained, and never blamed me. But I blame myself."

Siwang didn't say anything else. I couldn't read his expression once his princely mask fell into place. This mask used to be something he wore around the court officials, never around me.

Another reminder that things had changed. We had changed.

The next day, Beifeng was gone from his stall, Siwang from his tent, and Caikun from the morning roll call.

The camp suddenly felt empty.

"The prince returned to the palace," I overheard one of the commanders say. He didn't say why, and I didn't ask. Anyone important enough to know the whereabouts of the crown prince would never tell a nobody like me.

Rong Siwang was allowed to do what he wanted, when he wanted.

He didn't have to explain himself to me.

Not anymore.

36

Days passed in slow blinks; spring breathed life back into the frozen plains. Snow thawed to water, whimpering green sprouts broke from the derelict ground, and life blossomed under the warming sun.

Gradually, color bled back into the land.

Even with Siwang gone, the camp continued to whisper whenever my back was turned.

"I didn't know the crown prince liked men."

"That's what the guards claim. He ate with the prince and they . . . you know!"

"I saw them talking by the stables!"

"Maybe this is why his betrothed ran away?"

"Did she really run away?"

"That's what the Lans claim!"

"I heard the Prince of Lan is in love with Siwang's betrothed, and that's why he started this war!"

"A war, over a woman?"

"I heard Siwang's betrothed is destined to be the empress of all empresses! If he claims her, then he is the rightful ruler of the continent!"

"All these gold-spoon babies care about is power."

"What do you care about?"

"Getting drunk!"

Whoever said men didn't gossip like aunties clearly had never set
foot within a military camp.

I let them talk. Anything to take their minds off our arduous training and the fate that awaited us at the front lines.

It helped that—secretly—I didn't mind how I went from the scrawny
loser at the bottom of the pecking order to someone the other recruits
revered. When it was time to do our laundry, the camp practically
fought to wash my clothes for me. When it was time to eat, they fought
again to give me the juiciest pieces of pickled cabbage.

Life as Siwang's betrothed had been a thing of luxury. It seemed life
as his rumored lover was just as good. For Rong Siwang was the sun
and it was lovely to bask in his light—a feeling I both loved and hated.

For if Siwang could bestow me his light, he could also take it away.

I didn't want to forever reflect his light. I wanted to be the one
emitting this light.

—m—

In my head, I kept going back to that kiss in the tent. Did he kiss
me because he'd missed me? If he had, then why would he leave without saying goodbye? Was he trying to break my heart because I had
broken our betrothal? Or was he trying to seduce me so he could claim
the prophecy?

Rong had begun to lose battles only after I left. And I didn't want to believe that Siwang would do this for the prophecy. His joy had been beautiful and convincing in that dimly lit tent, after his lips brushed mine, yet . . .

My delirious thoughts ran in furious circles morning, noon, and night. I hated that the longer he was away, the more I thought of him.

"Focus!" Luyao hissed, and took this opportunity to swipe his staff under my feet, sending me crashing to the ground.

"Ow!" I cried. While most of the recruits went easy on me because of the rumors, Luyao treated me the same as ever.

"Pick up the pace, Little Li! Your pretty face won't save you on the battlefield!" Caikun snapped from somewhere behind me. Though he and Siwang had disappeared on the same day, when Caikun returned to camp, Siwang had not been with him.

"I'm sorry, Commander Wu!"

Caikun scowled as he paced the length of the courtyard, only half paying attention to us.

I couldn't tell if something had happened. Caikun looked like he was on edge, but the entire camp had been on edge since the snow had begun to melt.

Spring meant warmer weather, and it also meant death. Now that the soldiers of both sides were no longer distracted by the mortal need to survive the cold, the war would inevitably pick up its pace.

However, from what Siwang had told me, the cold didn't bother Lan and its vampires as it did us. The warmer weather could be a blessing because the vampires didn't like daylight. As the days grew longer, the vampires would have to spend more time in hiding. This meant Rong would have to fight only the human soldiers, who were much easier to deal with.

We can still turn this war around, Siwang had said, though I wasn't so sure.

Winter or summer, men would continue to die. And at some point, we would be ushered to the front lines.

At some point, these friends I had made around campfires would begin to die like they did in my nightmares.

37

Five days later, I saw Beifeng back in his stall.

Midmorning that same day, right before our combat training, a slender man in a eunuch's uniform pulled me aside. He must have been a new addition to Siwang's staff, because I didn't recognize him and he didn't seem to recognize me. At least, if he did, he didn't let it show. I couldn't help but wonder whether my disguise was good enough to bypass so many eyes. Or did these men simply follow Siwang's orders? "The prince wants to see you."

An order, not a request. Was this who I was to Siwang now? Someone at his beck and call, summoned when he pleased and abandoned when he grew bored?

"I have to train."

The eunuch's eyes went dark. He leaned a little closer, a sharp smile at his lips. "The prince wants to see you, Little Li. Whether you prefer to walk or be dragged there by your shiny locks, it's the same to me. The prince does not enjoy waiting, and I do not enjoy seeing my prince upset."

I sighed and bowed my head in submission. I was smart enough to choose my battles, and this was not a worthy battle.

"Come with me."

I looked across the courtyard. The commanders had intensified our training after Caikun's return. As if they were fighting against time to turn this group of misfit recruits into a company worthy of the battle-field. Every second felt precious as gold dust slipping through our fingers.

From the other side, Caikun watched me and the eunuch with an expression that could be described only as melancholy. I half expected him to come tell the eunuch that I couldn't afford to miss practice.

He didn't. Instead, he turned away and yelled for everyone to find their sparring partners.

The eunuch led me north of the camp, into a sectioned-off area of the forest, where a small courtyard hid between trees.

Siwang was there, waiting. "From what I remember, you used to beat up the heirs in our scholarly classes on a daily basis," he mused as I approached.

"Only if they were rude to the girls, or chose to harass the servants."

"You used to be a good fighter."

I flinched. "I am *still* a good fighter."

"Not from what I've seen." Siwang's lips curled into something re-sembling a smile. "And not from what I've heard from Caikun."

"Do you want a rematch?"

He shrugged; indifference smoothed over his features, but I caught that tiny spark in his eyes. "Take off the headband," he ordered, voice stern as the Crown Prince and not Siwang.

I heeded his command. Partially because he had asked, partially because I wanted to. When the headband slipped off, I felt like I could breathe again. The air felt different with my phoenix's mark uncovered. *I* felt different.

Everything was brighter, sharper, as if I woke from a drowsy dream.

"Never take your eyes off your opponent," Siwang said.

Like last time, he was the first to attack. Unlike last time, with my mark uncovered, I knew when he was going to lunge, and where.

I slipped through his grasp like a fish that didn't want to be caught, then dodged his quick pivoting leg as it swept across the ground. An unexpected move that should have knocked me out had I not seen it coming.

Even without Fate's guidance, I knew Siwang's habits. All attack, no defense. Stealthy and strong, he liked to finish his opponents quickly, so he always went for the killer move.

I dodged his attacks until I finally felt an opportunity. I twisted and swung my leg high. The heel of my shoe slammed him square in the jaw and knocked him to the ground.

"You lost," I announced.

"Where was this two months ago?" Siwang laughed. "I guess Caikun's training is working."

"I didn't want to embarrass you in front of your men," I lied. "I make a living hunting wild animals for rich merchants. If I wasn't a good fighter before, then I have become a good fighter out of necessity."

Siwang sneered. He didn't move, didn't bother getting up. He simply looked up at me from his spot on the ground. "Then how come Caikun says you're as unremarkable as unremarkable comes? It's as if you are a better fighter without your headband."

My body went tight. *He knows. He knows about the visions and the magic and—*

Siwang laughed. "Keep the headband off if it makes you uncomfortable."

"What if someone sees the phoenix's mark and makes the connection between me and your betrothed? Girls are not allowed on military grounds, remember?"

"What are they going to do? You have me, Fei. I will protect you." Siwang extended his hand.

"I can protect myself," I murmured, then pulled him to his feet.

"If you are a hunter, then I suppose that makes you a good archer?"

"If my father hadn't trained me to believe it's improper to beat you at these so-called *manly* sports, I would have overshadowed you our entire childhood. Instead of the crown prince's betrothed, the people would know me as the goddess of archery, Fei."

Siwang's laugh was a deep rumble. One that crinkled his eyes and made everything shine a little bit brighter. "You honestly think you're better than me?" He rose to his full height and took a step closer.

This time, I didn't cower. I lifted my head high to meet the heat of his gaze. "I know I am."

"Well," he continued, "in that case, why don't we engage in another friendly competition?"

I glanced at the target that was already set up. His silver-tipped bow was waiting on its stand. He had always intended for us to compete in archery.

A dizzying dread crept up on me. Was this a test? Did he suspect that I had magic? But if I backed out now, he would be even more suspicious. "Fine," I murmured, "and the winner gets that bow."

Siwang followed my eyes. "That bow is one of a pair; do you remember?"

"I do remember."

"Do you regret abandoning the bow when you left the palace?" Siwang's hand grazed mine, and my breath caught in my throat. We were no longer talking about the bow.

Siwang watched me, those dark eyes hauntingly beautiful as ever.

"Your Highness!" Caikun shouted as he approached us with furious steps.

I spun around and quickly slipped my headband back on.

From the corner of my eye, I saw Siwang frown and make an outward motion with his right hand, as if dismissing Caikun. But he must have noticed Caikun's eyes brimming with tears, and he paused mid-motion.

For a single heartbeat, the world was deafeningly silent. Then a sob broke from Caikun's lips, and I knew.

The world would not be same from this moment forward.

"It's the First Army. . . ." Caikun's voice cracked. "It's my father. He and his men are trapped inside Changchun. He needs reinforcements *now*."

38

I didn't see Siwang the next day, or the day after that. I volunteered to return equipment to the armory after every lesson and walked past Beifeng's stable at every opportunity in hopes of seeing him.

But it seemed that in life, the more you wanted something, the more it refused to be yours. How the tables had turned. As a child, I'd hated that Siwang was always around, trailing at my heels, bright-eyed like a puppy.

Now I was the one who wanted to see him, constantly.

How embarrassing.

Caikun, along with a handful of senior commanders and military advisors, was absent as well; these were the people who had Siwang's ear, whose opinions were required to make big decisions in war.

Panic simmered in the camp like oil sizzling in a hot pan. I didn't tell anyone what I'd overheard that day on the practice field. Still, they sensed the tension in the air, smelled the brewing storm, felt Death breathing down our necks.

I looked around at my friends and acquaintances and the other faces that had become familiar with every sunrise and sunset. Caikun had trained us to the best of his ability. However, four months would never be enough time to turn boys into men, or civilians into soldiers. We were not qualified to be the reinforcements the First Army needed.

Still, I wanted to go and help.

Four months ago in Duhuan, I had run in the face of danger. Now I wasn't sure if I could do the same. Not when so many men had so bravely marched into battle to protect those they loved. If they could do it, then so could I.

My visions could be changed. The bloodshed of my visions was still preventable—if I tried hard enough, anything was possible.

An empress was the mother of the land, and mothers protected. Was this what the prophecy had suggested all along? That I must protect those I loved, fight for those who couldn't fight for themselves?

By the time I gathered the courage to seek out Siwang, three days had passed.

My heart was pounding when I approached his tent. I bowed to the soldiers stationed outside, half expecting them to shoo me away for daring to venture this close to the prince's quarters without invitation and during this time of crisis.

They didn't.

"The prince has been waiting for you," one said to me, and stepped aside.

The day was gloomy. Pale clouds covered the sun, leaving everything tinted in teary gray. The tent was dimmer than last time, the candles unlit.

He sat at the same table where we'd shared our meals, a teacup in hand. I smelled the wine on him.

"I was waiting for you to come to see me, of your free will." He let out a soft sound, a cross between a laugh and an exhale. "You were taking so long, I feared we wouldn't get to say goodbye before I left."

"You were avoiding me because you wanted me to come to you?"

He shrugged. "I'm always the one chasing after you. For once in my life, I want you to chase me."

I stared at him for a moment, unsure of what to say. "We are not kids anymore, Siwang. I have been worried sick. If you wanted to see me, you should have . . ." I sighed. This wasn't worth it. Neither of us wanted to argue with the other. "You're leaving?" I added after a moment of silence.

"Tomorrow."

My heart sank. It was so soon. "If I hadn't come, would you really have left without saying goodbye?"

"Just as you tried to leave me without saying goodbye?" Siwang snapped. Something he had never done with me, and as soon as the sharp words were out, he seemed to deflate. "I'm sorry."

"Are you punishing me for what happened a year ago?" When he didn't answer, I asked another question, perhaps the first question I should have asked: "Are you leaving for the palace, or the front lines?"

"Do I look like someone who cowers in the face of danger?"

"You are your father's 心头肉, *the flesh of his heart, the center of his world.* He will want his heir and favorite son to be safe, not on a battlefield infested with monsters."

"Are you talking about my father, or yourself? If you don't want me to go to the front lines, then tell me, Fei. Don't go around in circles and waste what little time we have left."

My lips parted. However, no words came out.

He waved me closer. "Sit down."

I did as he asked, knelt by the table as he flipped over another porcelain cup, poured a suggestion of wine, and offered it to me. There was something so captivating about the way Siwang's long, elegant fingers held that tiny piece of porcelain. The way his head tilted back with each drink, delicate strands of inky hair framing his face like he was a painting.

Siwang wasn't one to indulge in alcohol. He loved control too much to relinquish it for something as trivial as wine. I remembered the state dinners with envoys and high officials—his wine pitcher was always filled with water.

He drank alcohol only when the stately visitors pushed wine onto me and he would step in and drink for me.

Perhaps this was why he drank from teacups instead of the bronze *jue* most men of nobility used. Or bowls, as many of the hunters I'd encountered on the road did.

There was something so ineffably Siwang about this moment; if this had happened at a winehouse in Yong'An, every man in the city would have grabbed the nearest teacup and started imitating in hope of re-creating his effortless grace.

He was so unfairly perfect. Right up to my departure from the palace, my etiquette teachers had slapped my hand for the way I sat and walked and ate, constantly comparing me with Siwang and all his charms.

The same went for the scholars, who had taught us poetry and history and novels and proverbs, which Siwang could recite in perfect rhythm after one read. Whereas it often took me two or three times to remember the words, and when I tried to recite it was never as lyrical.

Siwang was perfect. Everyone who'd helped raise us would agree. And I was just . . . well.

Why would a goddess reincarnate as a peasant girl from the middle of nowhere? The slander they used to say behind my back echoed, because they were right. If I really was a goddess reincarnated, then why was I so . . . ordinary? Why was I so unworthy of this impossibly perfect prince?

Compared with Siwang, I was never good enough.

I took the cup in my hands but didn't sip from it. Rice wine gave me a headache, and I didn't like the way it made me feel. A blurring numbness that made my hands and feet seem fragile and my heart heavy. The wine also had a way of interfering with my visions, either blocking them entirely or propelling them into an intense mirage of nightmares, impossible to outrun.

If Siwang noticed that I didn't touch my drink, he didn't comment. He kept tilting his cup back, then pouring himself more. His face was already red, but his eyes were still sharp as ever.

Tipsy, but not yet drunk.

"The First Army has lost both Xiahui and Guilan. They are now trapped in the city of Changchun with limited food and water, surrounded by enemy soldiers."

He didn't have to say what would happen if we lost Changchun, our last stronghold for miles.

Only seven major walled cities separated Lan's army from my village now. From everything I'd seen, this war wasn't going to end itself.

"I'm ready," I said. "I know most of the men in my company aren't ready, but *I* am, Siwang. Take me with you. Let me fight."

He laughed. "You are not coming with me. It's too dangerous."

"I'm one of your best soldiers!" A lie. I was not good. I was barely average. But I had magic. My glimpses of the future, however brief, however rare, were an asset in this war where Rong needed every advantage we could get.

"You are just a fool who thinks too much of herself. You have not seen the men my father had trained, and how fast those vampires killed them. Tore them apart like rag dolls. Even if you *were* a seasoned warrior, I wouldn't let you risk your life like that."

"But you are fine with all these men risking *their* lives? Men with parents and lovers and families who depend on them?"

He set the teacup down, not loudly, not aggressively, though with enough force to make me pause. "It's not the same."

"Because of that asinine prophecy?"

"Because . . ." He paused and looked away, hesitation humming in the air between us. A quiet secret at the tip of his tongue. "I won't risk losing you a second time, Fei. This is my final answer. You will stay here. And if a day ever comes that this camp is no longer safe, then you have my permission to flee. Go home, take your family somewhere north and far from the bloodshed."

My breath snarled like a ribbon in my chest. "It's bad, isn't it?"

Siwang didn't answer. He had come to the last dregs of his wine now. He swirled the liquid in his cup, somber as I'd ever seen him.

"They say that Lan Yexue started this war because of me." I searched Siwang's face for a reaction. "Let me end this."

"Over my dead body will that monster touch you."

"The people of Rong cannot take any more bloodshed. If we can't plant crops soon, then there will be no food come autumn. Our people cannot take a famine as well as a war."

"I have written to my father, and he has agreed to let the women join the farming forces and—"

"Siwang, if you are going to rule, then you need to make these decisions for the greater good. If you cannot stop Yexue, then why not let me try—"

Siwang slammed his hand on the table. When he looked up, I saw that his eyes were brimming with tears. "I don't care for the greater good; I never have. I will sacrifice myself before I sacrifice you." His voice cracked, just a little, and my heart cracked with it.

My breath caught in my throat. Siwang was a man who cared for his duties above all else. Never in my life would I expect him to say something like this. A warm silence fell between us, and I desperately wanted to reach across the table and hold his hands, pull his body against mine and hold him. I wanted to tell him that everything was going to be okay, though I didn't believe it. "Can we still turn this war around?"

"I don't know."

"What *do* you know?"

"This." With that, Siwang leaned forward and kissed me.

Really kissed me. It wasn't the gentle touch of lips that it had been before. This time, there was hunger, and neither of us was afraid to pull the other in. His arm wrapped around my waist, our bodies so close I could feel the heat of him through our clothes, and his hard muscles underneath.

One violent swipe of his hand, and the porcelain tea set shattered on the floor. He pressed me down onto the table, and I pulled him in closer. His hand slipped through the folds of my robe and I pushed my body against him, desperate to feel more of him. I burned hotter with each heart-pounding inch left between his hands and my flesh, already going soft for him, craving the roughness of his fingers, craving him.

Siwang pulled himself back. "I'm sorry," he whispered. "I lost control of myself. I—"

"I want you," I whispered against his ear, slowly crawling into his lap and guiding his hands toward my thighs. If this was the touch that the concubines went feral for, then I understood now. "If not now, we might never get this chance again."

"Fei, you shouldn't. You don't have to, I mean." Even as he said this, his fingers were sliding up my legs, his lips kissing me with more fever than before.

My body was as hungry as his, and I was sick of suppressing this want. No matter what happened tomorrow, and tomorrow's tomorrow, I didn't want to regret a thing. For it suddenly occurred to me: after tonight, I might never see him again.

"Fei, we can't . . . I want to do this right." Though he said this, he did not push me away. He only held me tighter, his lips claiming mine between breaths.

"As long as it is with you, it is right." I pulled myself away so I could look at him, so he could see that I meant these words. "I want it to be with you."

I moaned and my whole body quivered when his fingers finally touched me where I wanted him to. My breath hitched as I felt his fingers enter me, so much bigger than mine, so much stronger. He moved slowly at first, then quicker.

Harder, I wanted to beg him. My hand wandered lower like the concubines said to do when pleasing a husband. When my fingertips reached between his thighs and brushed him, the mighty Siwang mewed like a kitten, the softest sound I had ever heard him make.

"Fei," he whimpered, pulling me closer, lips trailing my jaw, neck. Kissing, biting, sucking. "I love you."

There it was.

The unspoken confession from earlier. The words I'd almost heard him utter before self-control got the better of him. Always controlled. Always composed. So much had changed between us, yet so much was the same.

I kissed him harder. With every aching want inside me, I kissed him. He was the temptation I had resisted for too long. But just because Lifeng Fei and Crown Prince Rong Siwang could never be happy together, it didn't mean we couldn't have this moment.

"I love you," he whispered again.

I love you, too, I wanted to say. Especially now, as I invited him closer, guiding him toward all of me.

"I love you, Fei!" he cried as he entered me, and I flinched. It hurt, but I wanted him so much I didn't care. I needed him more than I had ever needed anything. I was desperate for more.

Siwang moved slowly, cautiously, as if I were a delicate vase he didn't want to break. I smiled at the thought of me, breakable.

I grabbed his waist and pulled him in, until I felt like my world was consumed by him.

I wanted him to remember me.

If anything happened, I wanted him to die not with the echoes of me leaving him under snowfall, but with this memory of our embrace.

Siwang's touch was soft, his lips sweet and heady like the plum wines we used to steal from his father's feasts, two giggling kids running through the gilded halls. His eyes were always on me, even back then, and he did whatever I told him to.

My prince.

My Siwang.

His teeth brushed my neck as we moved, our raspy breaths the most beautiful symphony I had ever heard. Back arched, my hand tangled in his silky hair to keep him close, I felt myself growing hotter, lighter, higher.

—ɯ—

The warm candlelight in Siwang's tent flickered as the world turned darker, darker, darker, until I was standing in the middle of a bloodied battlefield, stained crimson. Half-dead men and severed limbs were scattered at my feet. Swords and axes and arrows flew from all directions.

And at the center of the chaos was Siwang, on his knees, a bloodied gash in his torso and another one in his leg.

"Siwang!" I tried to run, pumping my legs furiously to close the distance between us. But no matter how hard I forced myself to move, he was always beyond reach. Blood pooled around him, crimson as winter roses.

Before him stood a young man swathed in silvery white, too pristine to belong on the battlefield. He raised his sword, and—

"No!" I gasped awake to the interior of Siwang's tent, a white tiger's pelt draped over my body.

It was a vision. Magic lingered like a hum on my skin, Fate's touch ringing in my ears.

"You can't go to Changchun," I said as I reached across the bed for Siwang.

Only to find it empty, except for a piece of paper.

Stay safe. Wait for me, the note read. *I love you.*

He was gone.

I leaped to my feet and quickly gathered my robes. By the time I ran outside, half the camp was either gone or in the process of packing.

"What's happening?" I asked the man guarding the tent.

He bowed as soon as he saw me, as if I were someone important.

I guessed that to him, I was, considering I had climbed into bed with the crown prince last night. I blushed. "The prince and the commanders got word that the situation at the front is becoming dire. They had to leave overnight with the First Battalion. The Second and Third will follow in the coming days." He spoke with the rigid fluidity of a well-practiced speech, which meant there was more that he wasn't telling me. Siwang wouldn't leave in the middle of the night without a good reason.

"What kind of emergency?"

The man opened his mouth, then closed it. He had not rehearsed this part half as well. I pulled out my dagger and slammed him against the pole of the tent. "Tell me."

"I don't know! I'm just a guard!"

"What do you know, then?"

"The . . . the prince told me to tell you to wait for him if you asked anything."

Wait for him? Who was I? A docile wife, expected to sew and embroider while she waited for her beloved to come back from the war?

I let him go. "Very well."

I could send a messenger to warn Siwang, but what if the message couldn't reach him in time? In the dream, I had no idea where they were. I didn't see Changchun in the background. They could have been ambushed for all I knew.

They'd left last night. If I left within the hour, I'd still have a chance of catching them before they reached Changchun.

"Can I borrow a horse from the stables?" I asked the guard, not knowing if he had the power to grant my request. Horses were valuable in the army, and we didn't have many to spare.

"The prince left his steed, Beifeng, for you."

I paused. Beifeng was the fastest horse in the land; this boded well for me. "Did he tell you anything else?"

"No."

I had never been to Changchun; I knew only that it was south of here. "Get me a map, fast. Prince Siwang's life depends on it."

I slipped back into the tent and picked up the silver-tipped bow Siwang had also left behind.

39

I moved as fast as I could through the unfamiliar terrain. But the land between the camp and Changchun was sandy and barren, criss-crossed with too many intervening paths and footprints leading from all corners of the empire. Navigating them would be difficult even for those who regularly used these roads.

I thought it would be easy, following an army, but these men moved in units. They traveled on different roads in case of ambush. Which was a great idea, usually, but not right now. I had no idea which direction Siwang had gone. All I could do was head for Changchun and hope for the best. However, between frequent checks of the map and getting myself lost on the wrong roads, even my fastest wasn't enough. Especially since my visions gave me only glimpses of what would happen, not directions to get there.

Eventually, I did come across small groups of people carrying heavy bags, some pushing carts full of the elderly, children, and amassed belongings. Too heavy for a trip between villages to visit family.

I had seen people like them during my travels over the past year.

Wind-beaten folks forced to leave behind all that was dear to them, all they had ever known, to flee for their lives. Like too many had done since Lan's rise.

In war, there were three types of people: those who ran, those who fought, and those who stayed to die.

I remembered Siwang's warnings about Lan's vampires, who needed blood to survive. I hoped these people could find refuge farther north, where they might live to see more dawns and watch their children grow.

Day by day, as I passed the sun-bronzed faces of the escapees, who became more and more frantic, their steps hurried and fearful, I knew I was getting closer to Changchun.

When I started seeing bloodied soldiers peppered throughout the crowd, clad in the faded reds of our uniform, stripped of their armor, heads low to avoid attention, I knew the battlefield was not far.

Deserters. Men who did not want to fight, or merely feared the prospect of dying—as they had every right to.

War was fought in the name of empires and conquerors. Nobody would remember these nameless foot soldiers in a hundred years. No honor, no glory. The men at camp liked to shame the deserters, but until one experienced this kind of trauma, we had no right to judge.

I kicked Beifeng into a sprint.

I could still atone for my mistake, showing Lan Yexue mercy when I should have driven my blade through his heart and ended his tyranny before it could begin. But by protecting Siwang, and helping him win this war however I could, it was still possible to prevent my nightmares from coming true.

Fate had given me my powers for a reason. If I could wield them and foresee the future, we might have a chance at achieving the impossible.

If not by defeating Lan once and for all, then at least by reminding them that Rong was not an empire they could conquer so easily.

I took in the hollowed faces of those who were paying the price of this war.

They were the people these supposed "heaven mandated" emperors and armies should be fighting for. Not to conquer, but to protect. Instead, they waged wars for pride and greed, and passed these human lives from one rapacious hand to another. Lan might claim these lands from Rong today, but someday someone would claim these lands from Lan. As was the way of life.

Empires rise, empires fall.

However, the ones whose hunched backs built these empires were always the first to suffer. The collateral damage, seeking refuge in any city that would take them, praying for the amity that might never come and a bounteous son of heaven who might not exist.

When would these borderlands know peace?

If I condemned myself to a life behind palace walls, would that buy the continent a few decades of peace?

. . . Or could there be another way to fulfill the prophecy and become empress of all empresses?

I pushed the thought away before it could take root.

To become an empress, I had to first rescue my prince from certain death.

40

When the stench of rotting bodies hit the back of my throat, I
gagged.

I saw the dying before I saw the battlefield.

A scene torn from my nightmares.

A path soaked in blood, covered in corpses and the injured. Even
Beifeng, who had no doubt seen more than his fair share of violence,
flinched upon the harrowing sight. His hooves hesitated at the scattered limbs and chunks of torn flesh.

I caught glimpses of some familiar faces. Men with whom I had
eaten and laughed with around campfires, whose families I had met
through their well-worn stories.

Something inside me shuddered, and my better instincts begged
me to turn back. To run from this place as fast as I could.

I kicked Beifeng into motion, followed the crimson trail despite my
wrenching stomach. It was too late to save these men, but it wasn't too
late for Siwang.

I shifted the bow from my back, arrows already in hand.

Siwang. His name was the only thing that could drown out the terror in my bones.

Siwang.

Siwang.

I thought of his name like a chant, hoped Fate's magic would lead me to him.

Dread clutched me tight until I heard the screams. In the distance, I saw blurry shadows of men who moved faster than what should be possible—though not as fast as Yexue. Red-eyed soldiers in blood-stained twilight-blue uniforms—the color of the Lan dynasty—circled what should have been a mighty battalion of elite soldiers, now dwindled to just dozens of men, being picked apart one by one.

Still, the Rong soldiers remained united in formation, forming a wall around Siwang, ready to protect their prince until their dying breath.

I snapped the reins to prompt Beifeng into a full charge, nocked an arrow onto my bow, and waited for Fate's magic to guide me. But I saw nothing, *felt* nothing. There was no hand of Fate guiding me. I touched my forehead. Nothing was covering my mark.

No. I willed a vision to come, but there was nothing. Another cruel reminder that I couldn't do anything right. My only skill was not even mine to control. *Fine, I will do this the old-fashioned way.* I fired the first shot, but the vampires' instincts were sharp and their bodies were fast. My target dashed out of the way before the arrow was anywhere near it. I wasn't even close, however I wasn't shooting to kill. I wanted their attention, and to buy Siwang time to run.

"Oh, look, another fool!" one of the vampires cackled, and I was stunned by how human he sounded.

"Run, Siwang!" I cried.

One of the vampires charged at me, moving so fast his body became an indistinguishable blur, and knocked me off Beifeng. Hands came for my throat, and I let out a scream when I saw his face.

As monstrous as the demons of my nightmares. Bone-white skin and eyes that were burning red, dark veins like an intricate embroidery covering his face. And his teeth?

They were not the teeth of a human.

"Fei!" someone cried in the background. "Don't hurt her! I'll go with you! I'll do whatever you want! Just don't hurt her!"

Run, you idiot! I would have screamed if I didn't have a demon's claw around my throat. When the vampire's fangs fell on my throat, I had only one thought in mind: *I've come too far to die like this.*

Without thinking, I stabbed the silver tip of Siwang's bow into the vampire's eye, and the monster let out an earsplitting scream.

I tasted ash in my mouth, smelled the scent of burning flesh.

"Fei!"

Siwang.

When another vampire charged at me, I barely had time to react. I tried to stab him with the bow the way I'd done the last time, but he was too fast.

A sword plunged into my chest.

"Stop!" A voice broke the chaos. Deep and rumbling, like thunder cutting through a storm.

Overwhelmed by the disarray, I had failed to notice the man standing at the edge of the battle, clad in silvery white, a color too pure to exist among the gruesome hues of blood and death.

While everyone else was crusted by blood, he alone was pristine.

Ethereal was the first word that came to mind.

"We meet again." The wind carried his voice to me.

As I fell to the ground, gasping for air, I saw him smile.

The dimples flashed.

Lan Yexue. The captive prince who was no longer a captive.

Please, don't let me die, I thought as a blaze of fireworks lit up the twilight sky and something akin to fear flashed across the monsters' faces.

They weren't invincible.

Fire.

They are weakened by sunlight, Siwang had said.

We can still win this war. . . .

41

F^{*ire* . . .}
    "Can you save her?" A furious tone, yet muffled and quiet, as if someone were screaming from under water.

Light.

"I . . ."

They are not invincible. . . .

"Can you?" Louder this time. "Can you save her?"

"The first vampire didn't tear open any of her major arteries, however the second one punctured her lungs with the blade. She's also lost so much blood. . . ."

"Save her! I don't care what it takes; you have to save her!"

"My prince, it's a miracle that she's still alive. I . . ."

"If you can't, then I'll have you buried with her! She is my bride; do you hear me? If you, a doctor, can't save the crown prince's bride, then what use do I have for you?"

Silence.

Siwang...

"You really shouldn't be here." I heard a new voice through the waters.

"I'll be fine." A second voice, familiar this time. I couldn't remember where I knew it from.

"Your Highness—"

"*Shh.* I don't have long. Go and keep watch for me."

"But—"

"*Go.*"

The rustle of clothes.

Fire...

Soft laughter. Closer this time. "You should stop getting injured around me, you know that? I hate it when I see you in pain."

Siwang...

"I also find it exceptionally rude that you're calling the name of another man, while I'm risking my life sneaking into enemy territory to save you, *again.*"

They are not invincible....

I felt something warm touch my lips. A liquid sweet as honey, mixed with the sharp, bitter tones of rice wine.

My mind flashed back to snowy mountains and cave walls painted gold by flickering firelight.

"*Lan Yexue.*" My eyes fluttered open.

"I've missed you, too. Drink up, don't die on me now."

Dusk parted to reveal the sharp planes of the prince regent's face, mere inches from mine. So close my heart leaped in my chest, skipping a beat upon the sight of those familiar dark eyes drinking me in the same way they did a year ago in that amber-lit cave.

Except this time, the curiosity was replaced by a sliver of wonder. His lips twitched at the corners, a phantom smile as he moved closer and closer, until his lips were mere inches from mine. "You remember me."

My eyes darted around the room, quickly taking in my surroundings, searching for something to defend myself with. A splash of red caught my eye in the background.

Rong's colors.

This was our tent. He really was breaching enemy territory.

"Are you here to kill me?" I choked.

Yexue's blood had pulled me back from the brink of death, but a dark spear of pain stabbed me each time I drew breath.

"Sneaking onto enemy grounds just to kill an already dying woman? Lifeng Fei, do you think so little of me?"

I thought back to the battlefield, the broken bodies of my comrades.

I thought of him in his snowy-white robe against all that red. His demons with their monstrous fangs.

I thought of the fireside stories told by soldiers who had lost everything because of him. Their recollections of the vampires were so terrifying I'd once thought they couldn't possibly be true—until I had witnessed the horror with my own eyes.

And those demons served one master: the Prince of Lan.

"Yes," I whispered. "I do."

He leaned closer so that his nose was almost touching mine. I could tear off a chunk of his face if I wanted.

Under the sheets, my hand searched for the dagger I always strapped to my thigh and found nothing. The physician must have removed it.

"Be careful what you say, my goddess. You don't want to make me your enemy. Especially since I can kill you as easily as I can save you." Yexue pulled away, bit into his palm, and offered it to me, the same way he had all those moons ago. "Keep drinking if you want to live."

"Why are you doing this?" I had stabbed and abandoned him in the forest a year ago. Why would he want to save my life after that?

He laughed. "Did you think I came all the way here to watch you die? *Drink.* Before the cut closes."

"What's in it for you?"

The prince shrugged, and I couldn't help but notice how close he was, how intimate this moment felt. He was cradling my body in his arms, my face resting against his chest, and his arm wrapped around me, holding me upright. "Maybe I'm just a merciful man. Maybe I don't want to lose the only other person who knows what it's like to be plagued with an ungodly magic. Maybe I want to claim your prophecy and become the emperor of all emperors. Or *maybe* I just want to repay a debt? After this, I think the two of us will be even, and I no longer owe you anything."

"I never should have saved you in those mountains."

Yexue broke into a smile, clearly amused. "You can tell yourself that, my fallen goddess. Now drink."

"*No.* I don't want your blood. I don't want anything to do with a monster like you!"

"*Drink,* if you want to live," Yexue whispered. An order, and I did as he said.

Blood poured in. Though I refused to satisfy his wish, the moment I tasted its sweet nectar, I couldn't stop. I felt that sensation again. With every drop, my body sang for him. As the euphoria began to take me under, I felt my wounds begin to tingle and burn as my body healed itself just like last time.

"I'm sorry you were dragged into this war. However, I am happy to see you again, my fallen goddess." Yexue leaned closer and placed a kiss on my forehead as my eyes began to close. "But you need to leave, Fei. I don't want you to get caught in the cross fire of this pointless war."

I lapped up every last drop of his sweet, heavenly blood. "If this war is so pointless, why don't you stop attacking us?"

"I see your prince still has a habit of keeping secrets from you." A soft laugh before his thumb brushed my forehead. "Seven days. I will give you seven days to remove yourself from this war. I don't want to watch you get hurt again—because I may not be around to save you the next time you flirt with Death."

42

"It's a miracle," the imperial physician murmured to himself the next morning when he saw that I was alive and well. His face came alight like that of a man in rapture.

Then he fell to his knees and wept.

I smiled. "Morning."

"It's a miracle!" the physician cried again, running to throw open the tent flap. Two men stood guard beyond it. Were they also here last night? How did Yexue get past them? How did no one notice the enemy prince who had snuck into our camp?

"Send word to the prince! Tell him he doesn't need to bury me alive!"

I laughed.

Within minutes, I was surrounded by physicians checking me over while they murmured that this was impossible. The injury on my neck had completely healed, with not even a silvering pink scar left as evidence. The stab wound in my chest had closed, too, though the skin there was still soft and tender, pinkish in hue.

"How?" the head physician tried to ask.

I didn't know how to answer. Thankfully Siwang entered at just the right time.

Slow steps. He wasn't as excited to see me as I'd expected. Instead, he seemed somber, as if he'd known this would happen.

"The stars must be protecting her," Siwang said quietly, not looking at me, something he did only when he was hiding things from me.

"Your Highness." The physicians bowed.

"Can we have some privacy?" Siwang asked. A command phrased in the manner of a request. "Oh, and I don't have to remind anyone that what happens in this room, stays in this room, right? Lady Lifeng's identity must stay secret."

The physicians nodded in unison, then exited.

The small tent suddenly felt empty with just the two of us. The familiar cadence of a morning camp hummed in the background. Soldiers laughing, the clatter of bowls and spoons, and murmured gossip. The yawns and rushing feet of those who were up early to train. I had missed this during the lonely days on the road.

"How are you feeling?" Siwang asked at the same time that I said, "Lan Yexue was here last night, though you already know this, don't you?"

Siwang sat at my bed's edge. "I do."

"You had a chance to kill him and win this war; you should have taken it."

Siwang laughed. "I never thought you'd be this bloodthirsty."

"If Lan Yexue dies, then—"

"Currently, he is the only one who can control those vampires. What if he dies and those monsters end up running rampant?"

"Those demons won't die with him?" I asked.

"I don't know. There's so much about those monsters that we don't know." Siwang exhaled, then rolled up his right sleeve until I saw the long cut around his bicep. "And who said I didn't try to kill him? I remember how fast he was during our fight in the mountains a year ago. I thought I was prepared. . . . I was wrong."

"Oh." I slumped back down on my bed.

"Do you think less of me?"

"For what?"

"For ambushing the man who came here to save you."

He was not here to save me. He was just here to repay what he owed me, and now that the life debt had been paid, we were even. "This is war, we are losing, so you did what you had to do. Speaking of the war, I think I know how to turn things around."

Siwang arched a brow. "How?"

"The vampires are not invincible. You said they are weakened by sunlight, but I think they are also scared of fire. Anything that is bright and hot. When—"

"I know."

I blinked. "You do?"

"Did you think it was all a coincidence, how our reinforcements just happened to launch fireworks in the middle of spring?" Siwang mused, a smile teasing his lips.

"*Oh.*" My heart sank. Suddenly, I realized just how naive I was, thinking I'd discovered something so crucial. Rong's armies were already spearheaded by some of the best minds and most experienced generals the continent had ever seen. If winning against the vampires were so easy, we wouldn't be here. "How embarrassing. I thought I'd found the key to winning this war."

"You did find the key to winning this war." Siwang leaned a little closer. "Do you remember your silver-tipped bow? Usually when we try to kill the vampires, unless we sever their heads or cut their hearts straight from their chests, they always heal. But when you stabbed one with the silver of the bow, he perished, crumbling to ash."

"He did?" I could hardly remember. Everything had happened so fast. I remembered only the taste of ash in my mouth, how the monster disappeared from sight before another charged at me. "You think they are vulnerable to silver as well as fire?"

"They might be. I've sent word to the capital, and they're using all the silver they can get their hands to make weapons. If the vampires are truly vulnerable to silver, then you might have single-handedly changed the fate of Rong."

I stared at him, speechless. *I did something right . . . for once.* "Can we turn things around?"

"If vampires *are* vulnerable to silver, then yes, we can."

The knot in my chest loosened. Victory meant peace, and peace meant safe families, villages unburned. If we won, maybe those escapees would get to go home. Parents would cease sending their sons off to battle knowing they might never come home.

Please, I thought to the stars and the gods above. *Let this war be over soon.*

"Fei, if you want to stay at the front lines, I need you to promise you won't do anything foolish from now on. If you stay at the camp, you have to do as I say."

"I didn't come here to hide."

"I know you didn't. But I can't lose you again. Not after I just got you back. Between your life and mine, I'd choose yours every time. The only way I can do my duty and lead this army is if I know you are at camp, safe and sound."

His eyes brimmed with tears, and I couldn't help but lean in and kiss them away until I felt him smile.

43

The imperial physicians kept close attention on me in the following days, their eyes curious yet cautious. Nobody asked questions about how this miracle had occurred. Siwang's orders, I assumed.

Two days passed before I could stand without feeling dizzy.

"You can have A'Zhe and Ke as guards. They are two of my best men," Siwang told me in the morning. He was having breakfast in my tent again. Watery porridge and fermented cabbage, the same as the soldiers. Except we didn't have to fight twenty or thirty men for the tiny bowl of fermented cabbage here.

"To do what, follow a foot soldier around like guards? Don't you think that will look suspicious?"

"You are a hero, if—"

"These are the front lines, Siwang. My identity needs to remain a secret; you've said it yourself. No one will know that I am a girl if we don't tell anyone. But if you insist on special treatment, you might as well shout it from the rooftops."

Siwang's lips thinned, like he wanted to say something.

Oh. "You are not worried about the other soldiers finding out who I am?"

"Lan Yexue knows you are here now," he said quietly, pushing the fermented cabbage around in his bowl. Siwang tried his best to eat the same as his soldiers, but I could tell that he hated it. After a lifetime of enjoying carefully prepared delicacies, men like Siwang would never get used to food like this.

Something misted behind my eyes. What would happen if Rong did fall? Could Siwang live the life of a normal man, after having been prepared to rule since birth?

If he lived at all, that was.

"If Lan Yexue wanted to take me, he would have. He said he was here to repay a life debt because I had saved him a year ago in the north mountains."

"I hate that I can't protect you from him," Siwang whispered, still not looking at me.

I wanted to remind him that I could protect myself. "I don't think Yexue expects you to. He actually asked me to leave the front lines and stay as far away from the war as possible."

Siwang visibly tensed. "If that is what Lan Yexue wants, then I think you should do as he asked."

Nightmares flashed again. Siwang on his knees, an obsidian blade slicing open his throat. Was that Yexue's blade? Was Yexue the man who would one day end Siwang's life?

"*No.* I'm not running away again. I will stand with you." *I will not let Rong fall and I will not let you die.*

"Have you never heard of the saying *'Heroes die, cowards live'*?"

"I am no coward," I repeated, my eyes on my silver-tipped bow in the corner of the room. "When will our silver weapons arrive?"

"Tomorrow."

"Good." I didn't make him false promises—*Everything is going to be okay*—though I did want him to know I was here, and that I cared about him.

My fingers touched his, but Siwang pulled away. "I have to go. There's work to be done."

—⁂—

Siwang was locked away in yet another meeting with his high council when the weapons arrived the next morning, delivered straight from the capital, guarded by the Fourth Company of the Third Battalion. The men whom I had trained among, whose voices were familiar as my own breathing after our countless nights by the fire.

"Is it true that General Wu is trapped in the city?" The voice of Da'sha—the youngest yet the tallest of us—rang out like a bell, piercing the frenzy of the camp.

"I heard they ran out of food days ago. Lan's army has the city surrounded. If we don't get to them soon, it's only a matter of time before we lose Changchun."

"I heard he's going to send us to attack."

"That's not possible. He won't send soldiers as green as us out front. Lan's army will—" Luyao stopped midsentence. His face lit up like the sky at midautumn. "Little Li?"

"You seem surprised to see me," I said. "Did you think I was dead?"

"Little Li!" Another voice followed.

"You are alive!"

"You didn't run away!"

"Do I look like a deserter?" I teased, and before I could finish, I was surrounded by my comrades, pulling me into hugs that rumbled with laughter.

"Is it true?" someone asked. I couldn't see whom with all the bodies that surrounded me.

"Is what true?" I laughed.

"That you are a hero now, that you saved the crown prince from Lan's demons!"

"Do you have any idea how worried we were when you disappeared?"

"We thought something had happened!"

"We thought you'd deserted!" Da'sha exclaimed.

I gasped at this, and playfully punched him. "You were being serious? What do you take me for?"

"The smallest and weakest soldier of the weakest company in Rong's army?"

"Weakest soldier? You're thinking about yourself. I can take you in combat any day. In fact, if I remember correctly, I *have*. Several times."

"Little Li's right; if anyone is the weakest soldier, it's you, Da'sha!" someone chimed in, and everyone laughed.

"Are you hurt?" Luyao asked, putting a hand on my shoulder.

"I'm fine now."

A brief shadow of concern pressed between his brows, but he knew better than to ask too many questions in front of so many people. "I'm glad you're alive."

"I promised I would hunt all the meat for you and Zhangxi and your child come winter, didn't I? I am not the sort of man who doesn't keep his promise."

"Are Lan's soldiers as vicious as the stories?" Da'sha cut in, his eyes eager. He checked me over for bandages and wounds. "You look fine. If you can take them on in a fight, then so can we."

I should have lied and said yes just to give them some hope, but . . .

I glanced at the cart of silver behind them, and the mournful camp around us. In just a year, Rong's mighty army had dwindled to a husk of its former self. The fate of our empire balanced at knife's point. Our survival hung suspended like a question between frosted breaths.

There was a reason my comrades were here, despite their lackluster training and lackluster skills.

Siwang was too proud to admit that things were turning dire. Somewhere in the capital, the emperor was growing desperate.

"May the gods bless us" was all I could say.

44

Whispers rumbled through the camp. The stench of fear always spread fast among soldiers.

It was near twilight when Siwang's meeting finally ended. Heavy footsteps departed the war room to the north of camp. I searched the men's despondent faces for clues, or any form of hope to cling to.

And found nothing.

—⁓—

I went to find Siwang at nightfall. His guards were used to me by now and let me enter and leave as I pleased.

My prince was slumped against his fur-covered seat, staring at the swirling incense placed on a stand before a golden statue depicting a menacing god of war. An offering.

Siwang was not superstitious.

There were dark circles under his eyes, and a lingering trace of redness. Had he been crying?

"You can't win a war on an empty stomach," I told him, and set down the lamb-bone broth I'd asked the cooks to make for him.

He always forgot his body's mortal needs for things like food, water, and even sleep when other things occupied his mind. I wouldn't have been surprised if this was his first meal of the day.

Everybody in that war room had their own agendas, their own points of view. Some would press Siwang subtly, while others would push their visions like fists at his throat. Everybody wanted to make decisions through him, forgetting that Siwang was just one man—barely. He was just nineteen. Too young to carry the burden of a nation.

Yet here he was.

When he failed to respond, I silently dipped one of the silver needles into the broth for him, to check for poison. When the silver came away untarnished, I scooped the broth into a bowl, set it at his side, and rose to leave.

"Don't go," he whispered. "Don't go, Fei."

He asked, so I didn't. I pulled up a chair to sit beside him, then placed the bowl in his hands. Strong and callused, his hands no longer felt like the soft silk I remembered from the palace.

Up close, I saw that his eyes were as red as I'd imagined, and tears still clung to his lashes.

Something twisted in my chest. I wished there were something I could do for him. A way to command Fate and force her to show me a way to win this war for Siwang—something I had tried, more than once. Every night, I prayed for her to divulge some heavenly secret to me. And every night, I dreamt the same nightmares and bloodshed. Always the same blood-soaked ending.

I was no strategist or scholar. I could offer him nothing except my shoulder to lean on and my ears for his worries.

女子无才便是德—*having no talent is a virtue for a woman.* A saying repeated too many times by the scholars who were supposed to teach me, the father who was supposed to love and believe in me, and especially the emperor, who saw my yearning to learn as a threat against his son. It was only after excessive begging that I had been allowed to study with the rest of the noble children.

Though, as with all girls, our education was limited.

War and strategy were subjects I was banned from. This didn't stop me from hunting them down in the imperial library. I devoured as much power as I could from their pages despite knowing that the simple act of reading these books would not equate to being taught by the greatest minds of our time, as Siwang was.

Now I wished I had been more stubborn, made Siwang teach me these things even if the world forbade him to.

I knew my power over him; I would have been able to convince him if I had tried. Perhaps in another lifetime, I would. And in that lifetime Siwang would have a girl who could help carry his burdens with intellect instead of silence.

I wished I was capable of more. Just as I wished the world believed I was capable of more.

But I wasn't. So I placed my hand over his and squeezed tight.

"What did you argue about today?" I tried to keep my tone light, humorous. He didn't laugh. So I added, "I heard you're preparing an attack for tomorrow."

Siwang let his head fall back, eyelids fluttering closed. "If we don't win tomorrow, if silver fails to make a dent in Lan Yexue's monsters, it might be the end of Rong as we know it."

I didn't want to think about the bleak future that awaited our continent if we couldn't put an end to Lan Yexue's reign.

My eyes fell on the unfurled map in the center of the room, and the formations of enemies that stood between us and the city of Changchun, where Caikun's father and thousands of civilians were trapped.

"Pray to the gods that the attack goes well tomorrow," Siwang whispered.

"What is tomorrow's plan?" I asked.

"Lan's army is a mix of vampires and humans, with the vampires patrolling the night and the humans patrolling the day." Siwang relented after a beat of silence. "We will attack before the vampires retreat to their tents, close enough to dawn so that even if we don't succeed, the sunlight will aid us. When it's just human to human, we have a much better chance. If things go well, we will send in more men with silver weapons."

I knew the real plan had to be more complicated than this, but I didn't want to force more military secrets from his lips.

Siwang had already said more than he should have.

—⚊⚊—

I couldn't sleep that night. How could I, when so much hung in the balance?

I counted the sunsets. *Seven days. I will give you seven days to remove yourself from this war.*

Seven days had passed since Yexue had snuck into my tent. According to the senior soldiers, this was the longest ceasefire between our two sides.

I see your prince still has a habit of keeping secrets from you.

What did he mean by this? Was this ceasefire for me, or was he waiting for something else? Biding his time, planning for—

A loud, spine-chilling scream pierced the night. Outside the tent, orange flames surged brighter than the bleeding dawn.

I jumped to my feet, wrapped my robe around me, and claimed my blade from the bedside.

Blood. I smelled blood as I ran for the door, my heart pounding in my ears.

调虎离山. *Lure the tiger away from the mountain before attacking.* With our best men sneaking behind the enemy lines with most of our silver weapons, the camp was left vulnerable to an attack.

We'd been tricked. There had to be a spy among us.

I pushed open the tent flap just as a cacophony of cries erupted. My phoenix's mark burned at my forehead, and I caught blurred glimpses from an overload of visions, trying to warn me of the dangers that could come from all directions.

Run, my better instincts told me, as they had all those months ago when I witnessed that village being raided by vampires.

I drew my sword just as someone covered my mouth and forced me back into the shadows.

"Shh," a voice cooed, soft and nectar-sweet, fingers firm yet gentle around my throat.

Yexue.

He pressed me against a wooden beam of the tent to keep me from struggling. "I'm not going to hurt you," he whispered, removing his hand from my mouth.

"You think I was born yesterday?" I tried to free myself from his hold, but Yexue grabbed both of my hands and tried to pin them above my head just as I changed course and opted to stomp on his foot instead, hard enough to break it.

Lan Yexue didn't even flinch. *Stupid magic.*

His lips twitched, and he leaned even closer. "I'm not your enemy, Fei. I've never been your enemy."

I thought of his blood, which had brought me back from the brink of death more than once now, and then Siwang, kneeling in his throne room, the white-robed figure with his obsidian blade. . . . Yexue might not be my enemy, but he could be Siwang's killer. Which was worse.

"Need I remind you that you wouldn't even be here if I didn't save your life back in the mountains!"

"If we are talking about blood debts, then your beloved Prince Siwang is *twice* the killer I'll ever be."

"Siwang is nothing like you."

"If you think that, then you don't know your prince at all, Fei."

"Really? Well, how about—" I headbutted him, and it felt like smacking my head against a stone wall. At least it was enough to stun him for a moment, enough for me to pull my blade from its sheath. And drive it straight into Lan Yexue's long and elegant neck.

Lan Yexue didn't even try to move. When the blade met his throat, instead of piercing his skin, it cracked and shattered. His flesh, so soft when he touched me, was now hard enough to splinter iron.

How was this possible? What had he become in the past year?

"What are you?" I breathed.

"You think you are the only one who wants me dead? If I were so easily killed, I would have died a long time ago."

"You weren't like this a year ago. You weren't invincible. You bled. I *watched* you bleed." Three days ago, he'd bled for me when he cut open his palm. I'd tasted the sweetness of his blood.

"Things change," he replied. "People change."

"How?"

"I'll answer under one condition." He offered me his hand. "Come to Lan, and everything will be explained. You are too smart not to know that Siwang is keeping something from you. Aren't you curious?"

Half of me wanted to shove him away and run for my silver-tipped bow. But the other . . .

I peered outside, where the dying cries of men made my stomach turn.

"I will go with you under one condition," I said. "End this war."

"Oh, he really doesn't tell you anything, does he? I am not the one prolonging this war. If you want peace, you need to ask that cruel prince of yours."

"What do you mean?"

He extended his hand once more. "Come with me, and I will explain everything."

"Will you stop this war?"

He laughed. "Like I said, that is not up to me. But if you come with me, I can promise that my men will retreat immediately. We did not come here to take innocent lives. We came here to teach Rong Siwang a lesson. And hopefully, this time he will learn." Lan Yexue wiggled his fingers. "My arm is getting tired, Little Goddess."

I could still hear the screams outside, which sounded exactly like something from my nightmares. "If I come with you, you promise that you will retreat?"

"You have my word."

I placed my hand in his, and he flashed that beautiful, dimpled smile.

"You should have run when you had the chance, Little Goddess. Because I'm not going to let you go a third time."

PART THREE

The Nightblood Prince

45

M isty spring breath cascaded down from the mountains, its movement as elegant as a dancer's arching limbs, bitter cold by the time it fluttered the hem of my silk robes. The kind that seeped through clothes and flesh, deep into your bones.

The manor Yexue had brought me to was built against a vast mountain, jade green with bamboo forests and mossy streams.

I didn't know where we were, only that we were far from the front lines. I could no longer hear the thundering rhythms of war. When I opened the windows, lulling sounds of markets and leisurely footsteps, the hawking of street vendors and the creak of slow-moving carriages, greeted me from beyond the courtyard.

A city, though not bustling enough to be Lan's capital.

The manor had plenty of staff: cooks and gardeners and servant girls who dressed me in silk robes and adorned my neck with jewels that reminded me of my days as Siwang's betrothed. There were even nannies who brushed my hair and powdered my face, though these nannies did not scold me over perceived slights, and the rules here were not as strict as at the palace.

In fact, the only rule was that I stayed within the confinement of the courtyard. Anything I wanted, they would bring to me.

Was this what Yexue wanted, to groom me back into that girl who had run away?

He'd disappeared as soon we arrived, so I couldn't even confront him about it. Days passed with no news. And whatever answer he had promised was nowhere to be found.

"Where is your prince?" I asked the staff morning, noon, and night. "Can you tell me what is happening at the front lines? Is Lan still fighting with Rong? The prince, Rong Siwang, have you heard any news of him?"

No one gave me a real answer. It was always some version of *The prince regent has duties elsewhere,* and *We do not hear news of the front lines.*

Even my nightmares kept me in the dark. For the first time in a long while, my dreams were quieter. There were still screams and fire, but everything was muffled. No matter how hard I tried, I could not remember them when I woke.

I'd never thought there would come a day when I would miss the vivid bloodshed.

Fine. If no one was going to give me answers, I would take matters into my own hands.

—◊◊—

The guards here worked in rotation and paced the hallways with eagle eyes. But they couldn't watch every corner of the manor at all hours.

Just as no emperor, no king, no man, regardless of his status and power, was omnipresent.

Finding Yexue's bedroom and the adjacent study was easy. Getting inside, however, was much harder. Located in the opposite wing of the manor, they were the only rooms that were locked. When I asked to see the rooms, the nannies shook their heads in unison.

I had learned how to pick locks during my months on the road; the trick was not to listen for the click, but *feel* it through the vibration of the metal.

I studied the rotation of the guards carefully and took note of the hallway around Yexue's rooms, creating a mental list of places to hide and various escape routes just in case.

Ten minutes to get inside before the next guard turns the corner, I reminded myself as I crouched beside the door and cupped the lock in my hand. I wedged in the thinnest pin from my hair, then twisted, hoping to feel something click. But this had to be a particularly quiet lock, because I neither heard nor felt anything.

"Come on, you stupid lock!" I muttered, turning and turning, pressing my ear as close to the lock as possible. Until, finally, a *click*.

I was biting down the urge to cheer when I heard someone chuckle from behind me.

"You could have asked me for the key."

I jerked to my feet and immediately recognized the pristine, silver-embellished white robe.

Lan Yexue stared down at me with an amused smile. "You are not breaking into my study, are you?"

"No," I lied.

"Are you trying to steal military secrets?" He cocked his head, and I had half a mind to stab him with my hairpin and make a run for it. But memories of my last act of rebellion were still fresh, how my blade had bounced off him as if I had struck a statue of stone.

"... No."

"Then what are you doing?" Those amber eyes watched me with interest. I wagered he was just waiting for me to trip over my words so he could mock me.

"Um." *Shit.* "I ... didn't know where you were and thought perhaps someone had locked you inside this room?"

His smile deepened. "Oh, my savior! I knew you had a soft spot for me after all." He offered me his hand, and I realized I was still half kneeling against the door. This made for a precarious position. "If you don't want to get up, you are welcome to stay on your knees, Little Goddess."

I didn't take his hand, and rose on my own accord. "Well, now that I know you are safe and sound, I will leave you to it." I tried to sidestep out of his way, but Yexue moved his arm out to block me.

"After all that work, are you not going to come in and see what kind of military secrets I am keeping from you? Because I clearly need to change my locks, and the next one might not be so easily picked." He pushed open the door and gestured for me to enter.

Inside was an airy space with high carved ceilings and large windows that overlooked a small water garden bathed in a slant of golden light. A large desk occupied the center of the room, and there were rows and rows of bookshelves stacked high in all directions, full of aged scrolls and yellowed books, organized into neat piles. I peered at the wooden tags that seemed to organize everything into categories and realized they were sorted by empires and dynasties.

A large hand came over my eyes before I could glean anything else. "Stealing from me already?" Yexue chuckled.

My face went red while my feet remained frozen at the threshold. The wolf was inviting me into his den; this was the sort of trap parents warned children about. Nothing good could come of this.

However, I was already in his territory, my life in his hands. What else did I have to lose?

"I'm not going to eat you," Yexue added, teasingly pulling the door closed. "If you don't want to hear—"

"You claimed Siwang was keeping secrets from me." I sidestepped him and barged into the room, taking a seat at the large desk before he could change his mind. "I came here for a reason, and I'm not letting you go back on your promise."

I had hoped there would be a mess of scattered papers I could glean intel from, but the desk was empty. Everything about this space was organized.

"You look surprised," Yexue mused as he followed me in, leaving the door open behind us, as if to reassure me. "Is this not what you expected?"

"I expected your quarters to be more chaotic," I said.

He faked a gasp and clutched his heart. "Are you insulting me?"

I rolled my eyes. "You don't come here often?" I ran my finger along the desk and came away with a thin layer of dust. This place might be organized, however it was not clean.

"I have been a bit preoccupied, with that little war between Rong and Lan," he said, and my ears perked up.

You mean Lan and half the continent? I almost corrected him, because in addition to his war with Rong, Yexue had invaded many of his neighbors. Unfortunately, he seemed to be winning every fight he'd picked so far. "You said you would stop attacking. We agreed that if I left the front lines with you, you would end this war."

"*I* would end this war?" He huffed a laugh. "I told you already, I've seen enough death to last a lifetime. I don't want to watch more foolish men charge into battle for lies like glory and honor. I don't want to watch another city burn, another child die, hear the ghostly wail of another parent forced to bury their baby . . ."

Yexue's voice cracked. He looked away quickly, though not before I caught the tears that glistened at the corners of his eyes.

These words felt genuine. But . . . "But you are the Prince Regent of Lan. If you want this war to end, it will be as easy as a snap of your fingers."

Lan Yexue laughed. He walked around the circular table to stand on the opposite side. "Come here."

From a secret compartment under the table, he pulled out a stash of papers. I quickly got to my feet and caught sight of what I could only presume was special paper made for royal mandates, and a row of jade-and-gold-encased seals—my breath caught in my throat. Forget about military information; if I could steal one of Yexue's imperial seals and somehow send it to Siwang to fake mandates with, that might be more useful than every grain route and army location.

"These are the rejected peace treaties," Yexue said, and handed me the small stack of paper, which I almost dropped, so distracted by his imperial seals. "I've been sending these to Siwang since last summer. I only ever wanted to reclaim the land that was rightfully my ancestors'. No more. No less. I offered peace on the condition that Rong agree to become Lan's tribute state—which is fair. As Rong forced Lan to be their tribute state for so many years. Siwang seems to take these offers of peace as a sign of weakness, however. Each time, he responds not with compromises and envoys to discuss the terms, but aggressive attacks, which forces me to retaliate by pushing farther and farther into his territories."

I had heard plenty of tyrants try to justify their greed this way. "If you had given Siwang a way to end this war back in the summer, he would have taken it in a heartbeat. Even if he didn't back then, he would have come to the table and agreed to negotiate by now." I flipped through the pages and tried to look for the egregious demands Yexue had to be hiding.

"Like I've said, he's very good at keeping secrets from you." Yexue offered me his hand. "I am not the villain of this story. And if you don't believe my words, why don't you see things for yourself?"

46

While a mountain of lush bamboo and trickling streams sat east of the manor, a city sat at its west. Built at the mountain's base, it was a gleam of terra-cotta and bronze. Houses made of stone, wood, and glazed bamboo stretched out into bustling streets. Teahouses and winehouses were vibrant with music and voices, with fluttering banners and red lanterns dancing in the breeze. At the main market, merchants peddled their goods while children begged their parents for sugarcoated treats.

"Welcome to Longyan," Yexue announced as we wandered through the streets that reminded me me of Yong'An.

In this lively and beautiful city, joy shone bright on its people's faces. A far cry from the way I'd imagined life under Lan's rule.

However, hand in hand with splendor, the city was also laden with memories of violence. Along each street lingered the devastation of war, with crumbled buildings and flame-scorched walls peppering the city like festering mold.

Fire. The very thing Yexue's monstrous creations were scared of.

"Siwang did this?"

"Like I've said, each time I try to end this war, he takes it as a chance to reclaim the land that he perceives as his."

I grimaced. It always came back to this. Men and their pride and their self-righteous explanations as to why they had a better claim to a piece of land than other men, always forgetting that there were already people who called these lands home.

The seed of every conflict was never ancestral rights or justice; it was always greed.

I don't believe you, I wanted to tell him. I had grown up beside Siwang and knew him like the back of my hand. He was a good leader, and he would not let his people die when peace was an option. . . . Right?

I said nothing, and as we walked, I noticed a pleased smile tugged at Yexue's lips, the pride gleaming in his eyes. The citizens of this city smiled when Yexue passed and tilted their heads in greeting like sprouts reaching for the warm spring sun. Shopkeepers called to us and offered samples of dumplings and cakes and pieces of smoked meat. Children giggled and gasped when they saw him; the admiration in their eyes was not something that could be faked.

"Prince Yexue! Buy a red string for the pretty girl and the two of you will find each other in every lifetime!" an elderly lady hollered from her stand.

I was surprised she had the nerve to summon the prince regent like this, and was even more surprised when Yexue did as she asked and pulled me toward the little cart of braided red strings.

"One for the pretty girl and one for the handsome boy." She beamed as she handed each of us a red string. "That will be five coins each."

I gasped. Five coins? In times like these? It was enough to feed a whole family for three days.

Yexue laughed and handed her the money, then offered me his hand. "Tie it for me."

An order.

"You don't strike me as someone so superstitious," I grumbled, but did as he asked.

"I believe what I want to believe in." Once I was done, Yexue took the red string from my hand. "May I?"

I held my hand out, expecting him to tie it around my wrist like I had done for him. Instead, he tied one end to the third finger of my left hand and the other to his finger. "Those from beyond the western seas say this finger holds a vein that is linked directly to our hearts," he said casually. Then he grabbed my hand and pulled me toward him. "Caught you."

Blood rushed to my cheeks; I was suddenly too aware of his imposing stature and broad shoulders, the cold of his touch and the hardness of his body. "People are watching."

"Let them." He gripped my hand tighter and continued to guide me through the city as the people all but knelt for him like he was some kind of god. "I'm not the man you see on the battlefield," he continued as we ascended the stone steps that led up the city walls. "I'm good to my people. I offer every city the chance to surrender, and I don't abandon them in ruins in favor of the next conquest. I take the time to mend the infrastructure of every city I capture. I want every person who lives under my rule to be happy, their bellies full and their homes warm."

From atop the city walls, I looked out at the bustling streets and jubilant citizens, then at the soldiers stationed on the streets at regular intervals, still on alert.

Yexue's eyes followed my mine. "These people look happy, don't they? They will thrive under my reign; I'll make sure of it."

"And if they don't want to be ruled by you?" From the buzzing streets, it appeared that many had knelt for Yexue and surrendered in the name of peace. But did they really have a choice?

Yexue could rebuild on the ashes of these claimed lands all he wanted, but the damage was already done. Each conquered city was a shredded painting: no matter how hard he tried to piece it back together, it would never be whole again.

"When I was a child, my father told me that good emperors are the good men who rule by respect, not fear. But if the end result is the same, does it matter how we got there?"

I whirled to him. "In other words, your main objective is still more land, more resources, more power."

He shrugged. "In history, no kind man has ever amassed the sort of power and respect it takes to build an empire, regardless of how hard they pretend. A dragon will die without a head, and society will crumble without a leader who upholds law and order. I want to be a good emperor, but a good emperor does not necessarily mean a kind emperor."

"Every emperor is a tyrant, deep down," I grumbled, and Yexue chuckled. He watched me with that same amusement and curiosity he had a year ago in the northern mountains.

"Do you include your beloved Prince of Rong in that list of tyrants?"

I straightened. *Yes, I do,* was the answer I kept to myself. However, I didn't want to give him the satisfaction of being compared with Siwang.

"Do you know that he sent men into my cities disguised as refugees, fire powder hidden in their clothes?" he added after a beat of silence. "With cries for Rong, they threw firebombs at children before setting themselves alight. That is the real reason we are still tangled in this gods-forsaken conflict. Not because of my greed, but because of Rong Siwang's pride."

"You are lying," I said without thinking. I refused to believe we were talking about the same righteous Siwang I had known my whole life. But my eyes drifted down to the scorched streets below us. "Your soldiers are *monsters.* How do you explain that?"

"Is that what your prince has told you?"

Not my prince. "I've seen them with my own eyes. I watched them raid a village and—"

"Not everything that appears monstrous *is* monstrous, my goddess. Yes, while some of my soldiers are humans, some are . . . *not.* But neither am I, technically. And neither are you."

I stilled. On the horizon, the sun was beginning to set, painting the skies in brilliant hues. Below us, children's laughter could be heard as parents herded them home. "Say what you mean, Lan Yexue."

Yexue leaned against the wall, watching me admire his city. "Have you ever wondered why I risked my life to heal you when I knew Siwang would have an ambush ready?"

The prophecy was my first thought. But if that was the reason, he would have taken me that night instead of telling me to run.

Yexue's fingertips grazed mine. He watched me with bated breath, waiting to see how I would react.

I didn't pull away. When he had touched me a year ago in that cave, his skin had been warm. Now it was so cold that it sent shivers up my body.

"We are the same, Fei," he said. "Born with magic in our veins, and prophecies marking our fates."

"Prophecies?" *Plural.*

"You didn't think you were the only one whose fate was written in the stars, did you?" His smile faltered, the light in those eyes dimmed, just a little. "The empress of all empresses. Your prophecy was echoed by many across the continent, not just by those who worshipped different gods but also those who worshipped the land and the sky."

"It's all nonsense," I interjected.

"If you truly thought it nonsense, you wouldn't have spent the past year searching for the stargazer who first uttered your prophecy."

My eyes shot up to meet his. "You were *stalking* me?"

Yexue smirked. "You think too highly of yourself, Fei. I have eyes everywhere, and you simply happen to constantly fall within my line of sight."

My hands balled into fists. "If your men aren't the monsters people say they are, then why did you attack that village where the stargazer's mother was hiding?"

He raised an eyebrow. "I never attacked Duhuan. When my men found out someone had murdered the stargazer's mother, they rounded the villagers up to find out what had happened. That was it."

"Really?"

"Swear on my cold, cold heart."

"Did you find anything?"

"Nothing of use. Even if I did, do you expect me to just hand it over? Knowledge is power. Do you think I will go soft and just tell you?"

I glared at him. "Don't think I don't know how much you love to gloat. If you knew something, you wouldn't be able to keep it a secret longer than a few hours before you start taunting me."

Yexue laughed at this, his head tilted back, eyes gleaming—the kind of laugh that lit up his whole face. Not for the first time, his beauty sparked something inside me.

But the light left his eyes as quickly as it had come. When he spoke again, his voice was quiet, fragile like I had never heard it. "While your prophecy foresaw such greatness that burdened you with men who wish to possess you, mine was something crueler. Something that befits not a man or a prince, but the sort of monstrosity that would make our continent shudder. Thankfully, my mother slit the throat of the prophet as soon as they uttered it."

My breath snared on something sharp.

"To this day, I don't know what exactly was said," Yexue continued. "But it drove my mother to end her own life because she couldn't stand the monster she'd shepherded into this world. I guess I'm lucky that my father was a coward, too soft to do what should have been done. He had tried his hardest to love me, but love is fragile, not nearly enough to overshadow something as primal as fear. That prophecy is the reason my uncle sent me to Rong as a prisoner after my father became ill." His gaze fell on me again. "When I left, my uncle told me that if I knew what was good for me, I'd die in Rong. And when I couldn't find the stargazer or any of the answers I was looking for . . . that became what I wanted, too. Because if I couldn't change my prophecy, the world would be a better place without me."

In the dying amber light, Lan Yexue was a sculpture of ivory. His pale skin seemed to glow. In his eyes, as they gazed upon me, I saw a reverence rapt as the devotion that holy believers reserved for gods.

His eyes were haunting. Something inside me rattled harder like a chord struck, refusing to be silenced even as I pushed it down.

Once, years ago, when I was a child barely taller than a tea table,

I had snuck into the stargazer's tower and watched her stand among moving platforms of metal and wood, decorated with ornaments that were supposed to represent the stars in the sky. The spellbound focus she had then was the same that Yexue held for me in this moment.

My cheeks burned, and I tore my eyes from his to stare at the city beneath us, at its people and the lanterns that were slowly beginning to glow. I looked at anything and everything that was not Lan Yexue.

His cold fingers caressed my chin, ever so delicately. "I never intended to make it out of those mountains, Fei," he continued. "I thought if I were to die, I would die by my own hand, when I wanted and how I wanted. But . . . then I met a girl who saw me as a life that deserved to be saved, not an abomination who had no right to exist." He laughed. "Even if she did drive a dagger through my chest, she had also risked her life to protect me."

I turned to face him then. "That day in the mountains, you were planning to . . ." I couldn't finish the thought; my heart was beating so hard in my chest I thought it might break as more words welled up to my lips.

No sound came from them.

What kind of life had Lan Yexue lived, to make him want to leave this world so young? And what was the prophecy that was bestowed upon him, to make his own family fear him so?

"Fei . . ." My name from his lips was a chilling brush of satin against the nape of my neck.

I didn't think when I saved you from the tiger, I wanted to tell him. Whatever he felt for me, I could not reciprocate. I wasn't worthy of the way he looked at me, with the vehemence of the very stars that marred our destinies.

"Once, I believed destiny was a thing dictated by gods, written in the stars. But that was before I met you. The girl who didn't care about prophecies and what the world expected of her? The girl who was brave enough to venture into the winter mountains and hunt the mighty Beiying tiger for a mere chance at freedom? Before you, I had never thought it possible to defy my destiny. Now it is all I think about. To defy the gods who think themselves worthy of dictating my life." Gingerly, his fingers touched my hairline, brushing away the stray strands that danced with the evening breeze. "Whatever happened to the girl I met in the mountains? The girl who knew what she wanted and would stop at nothing to get it?"

"Perhaps she's changed."

"Because she finally fell in love with her prince?" There was an edge to Yexue's tone.

"Because she grew up and learned responsibility," I replied. "If you are looking for the girl who was reckless enough to send her entire family into exile, then I am not her anymore. I have learned that being selfish has consequences. Perhaps you should, too."

"I liked the selfish you," he whispered.

"That makes one of us."

"Tell me what you want, Fei. And don't say peace."

His question caught me off guard. "I do want peace," I whispered. "*But . . .* I also want to know the truth. Of destinies, and what it means."

He broke into a wide, double-dimpled grin, as if he had been waiting for this moment. "Then we will find you answers. 解铃还须系铃人. *To untie the bell, we must find the person who had tied it in the first place.* Mine is no longer of this world, but I believe I know how we might find yours."

I stumbled back. "You know where the stargazer is?"

"No, I don't. But I do have one last lead—same as your last lead, perhaps. The location of her favorite student. Xiangxi is not far from here. We will be there in a day or so if we pick the right horses."

"We are going together? What about your city?"

"I have excellent generals and captains. They can still do their jobs while I take care of more pressing matters."

"Such as reclaiming your destiny?"

Yexue smiled. "Such as corrupting you."

I shouldn't have laughed, but I did. And beneath that laughter was an echo of something he had said earlier: *A dragon will die without a head.*

An empire without its leader would crumble faster than spring's scattered seeds of hope.

47

I stared at the ceiling as dusk turned to night.

The day's events flashed in vivid succession. The burned buildings. The children who revered Yexue like he was a god. The city that radiated life.

Recovery in progress. Those children had a right to grow up innocent of the violence of war, as those parents had the right to watch their babies grow up without fearing that one day the emperor might force them to become soldiers.

However, one thing didn't escape me: Yexue's demons were nowhere to be seen. The only people I saw were the ones who showered him with admiration, love, and nothing else.

I had grown up around eunuchs and palace ladies who shuddered at the mention of the emperor; I knew fear like the back of my hand and would have recognized it in the civilians today.

With cries for Rong, they threw firebombs at children before setting themselves alight. That is the real reason we are still tangled in this

gods-forsaken conflict. Not because of my greed, but because of Rong Si-
wang's pride.

There was a desk in my room. Papers and brushes and a gorgeously chiseled inkstone.

I trickled water onto the stone and then slowly ground it into ink. With it, I penned a letter, detailing Yexue's plan to travel to Xiangxi, the state of the city, and anything that I thought might be useful.

But as I wrote, one thought kept coming back: *Would Siwang lie to me?*

If there really was a peace treaty on the table, why would he not sign it? I didn't want to believe Yexue, however he had no reason to lie. Not about this, at least.

I looked at the red string Yexue had tied around my wrist like a bracelet before we parted, a fragile shackle that matched his. Regardless of everything else, he had a soft spot for me. I could use this to my advantage and help Siwang from behind the enemy lines.

When I was done, I tied the letter with the headband I'd worn on the night I left, so that Siwang would know it was me.

Peace treaties were one way to end the war. The other was by slaying the dragon at its head.

Now all I had to do was find a way of getting this letter to Siwang, and hope I was not helping the wrong prince.

—⁓—

We left the city just after dawn. Yexue promised we would reach Xiangxi by sunset provided that we made only one stop on the way.

To my surprise, it wasn't just us. By the time we got to the stables, five men in plain winter coats were saddled and waiting. Most of them were burly men whose ages ranged from a few years to a decade older than us and looked like they'd happily kill me if they suspected I was coaxing secrets from their prince. Seasoned warriors with swords and spears and bows and arrows strapped to their backs, covering both long-range and short-range forms of attack. There was also a boy who couldn't have been older than fifteen. He held his head high like the rest of the guards. I almost asked Yexue why there was a boy coming with us, then decided against it.

If I was to gather information for Siwang, I had to parcel out my questions sparingly, save them for things that actually mattered.

None of the guards looked at me, so I doubted they would answer my question if I asked.

As we kicked our horses into motion, I had only one thing on my mind: if I wanted this letter to reach Siwang, this might be my only chance. Inside the city, Yexue was a god who would not be disobeyed. My every move was no doubt watched and reported back to him. The open road, however, was another story. There had to be people willing to help me, who were not influenced by Lan's might.

But Yexue's stallions were the best of the best and were clearly trained to run fast regardless of the wishes of their riders. I held on tight, even when my thighs burned and my back felt like it was going to break from endless galloping through the barren terrain while cold air slashed at our faces. I clung tight to my collar to keep the wind from escaping into my clothes. That was how riders catch fevers high enough to kill. At least the snow had mostly melted; in its place was hard, red-stained dirt that might never see flowers bloom again. We passed strangers on the road, but only in brief flashes as we clung to these furious horses who would not slow for anything.

It was almost noon when we stopped in the middle of nowhere, at a small tea shop that was not much more than a hut strung from bamboo and a few low tables. It was the first functioning establishment we had come across, and I was surprised when an elderly lady came to greet us.

"We don't see many visitors these days," the old lady said when we dismounted from our horses.

"Five jasmine, one oolong, and . . ." Yexue turned to me, and it took me a minute to realize he was asking what kind of tea I wanted.

I laughed. While everyone else in these conquered lands starved and took whatever food or water they could get their hands on, Yexue was here making demands. "What kind of tea do you have?" I asked her.

"We have tea, green tea," she replied in a quiet voice, her head bowed low. Though we were dressed in plain civilian clothing, Yexue's princely attitude was not so easily disguised; neither did he try to hide it. The imposing build of his guards was also impossible to ignore. It took money to keep men like these fed during times of calamity.

"We will take green tea," I said.

"I do have some jasmine," she said quickly. "My son loves jasmine, and no one has drunk any since he . . ."

She couldn't finish the sentence. *Enlisted* or *died* was the only possible ending. From the sadness in her eyes, it didn't matter which it was. If it was the former, I hoped he came home soon. If it was the latter, then . . . perhaps no one would ever drink her jasmine tea again.

I looked to Yexue, whose face was somber. "Green tea is fine, thank you," he said, and placed a handful of gold coins on the table. "For your hospitality."

The lady's eyes went wide. "No, that is—"

"Take it." I placed the coins in her hand. For everything Yexue had done to these borderlands, it was no more than she deserved.

She flashed me a gracious smile, one that reached wide and pinched the tears that misted her eyes.

I thought of my own mother. With what I assumed was this woman's only son gone, life would not be easy. Mothers like her were too common in these lands.

I flinched when Yexue placed a hand on my back and gestured me toward one of the tables. "You must be tired."

"Sorry," I murmured, and turned to the elderly lady. "Is there a washroom?"

She nodded and pointed toward a small shed a little farther away.

I didn't look back at Yexue for permission before I walked toward it. We had been traveling all day and were in the middle of nowhere. It wasn't like I could outrun him even if I tried. And I had no reason to, not when we currently shared the same goal: finding the stargazer and seeking more information on our prophecies.

By the time I returned, Yexue and his guards were seated, drinking tea and picking at the buns that they had brought themselves. The old lady was sitting by the fire again, warming her hands.

I walked quietly, ducked behind the tea stall to avoid being seen, and pressed the stash of gold hairpins and rings and necklaces that I had stolen from my room into her hands. *Can you get a letter to the Rong camp?* I mouthed.

The lady shrank back like a frightened animal. She glanced at where Yexue was sitting, eyes wide and shifting as if panicking between choices. To help me or to snitch on me. I waited with held breath, had already come to terms with the risk of seeking a stranger's help. Thankfully, she nodded in the end.

I let go of the breath I was holding and gave her the letter. Addressed to just *Siwang,* and signed with just *Fei.* The way he had told me to do it when I left the capital a year ago.

It was better late than never.

"The fate of Rong depends on this. Get it there as fast as possible, and once we win this war, I promise you will be rewarded like the hero you are," I whispered, then rose and returned to the table.

The old lady's eyes watered even more at this.

She did not move from her place by the fire, for Yexue and his men did not ask for another round of tea. We ate and we rested, and then we climbed back onto our horses. I let Yexue help me up into the saddle, letting my hand linger on his for a moment longer than was appropriate.

I would not waste my position here. When I first proposed it, Siwang had turned down the idea of me offering myself to Yexue to gather information from behind enemy lines. But I had to do something, and if this was the only way I could help, then I would sacrifice myself and my body for Rong.

—⁓—

We did not arrive in Xiangxi at sunset, but after midnight.

"It seems that even the great Lan Yexue is wrong sometimes," I murmured when we stopped in front of a quiet inn close to the center of the city. After nightfall and with lanterns few and far between, it was hard to tell how much damage Yexue had inflicted on the city when he captured it. Most of the buildings seemed to be standing, so they had to have surrendered.

"Even geniuses make mistakes," Yexue shot back, and came to help me dismount from my horse.

Again, I let him treat me like a damsel, purposely letting my weight press against his hard body as he settled me onto the ground. I stumbled when he let go, my legs almost giving out under me, and he caught his breath like a nervous kid. "Are you okay?"

"Yes," I lied. After an entire day of arduous riding, my thighs were numb to the point that I could barely feel them.

The ground beneath me seemed to shift, and I was suddenly nauseous.

Yexue laughed and handed me a piece of scallion pancake from his saddlebag. "The cooks are probably asleep—this is the best you are going to get until morning."

I reluctantly accepted the food from him and took a bite. It was slightly stale, but the moment I ate it and my stomach was less empty, I felt better.

One of the guards went in first and handed a pouch of coins to the innkeeper. "Seven rooms," he said.

"We only have one room left for the night, apologies."

"One room?" I gasped.

"We will take it," said Yexue. "The guards will sleep downstairs in the hall, and you and I can share the room."

"Are there two beds, at least?" I asked the innkeeper, who shook his head. I wanted to throw up right there and then.

Yexue laughed. "You don't expect me to sleep downstairs, do you?"

"I . . ." Rooming with him would help with the plan, but . . . "So what if I do?"

"Then *you* sleep downstairs. If you don't want to share the bed, then don't."

"I will take the bed if neither of you want it," said the youngest of the guards.

"Can I have some pillows and blankets for my men, please?" Yexue asked the innkeeper.

"Of course."

I looked around the space. It wouldn't be the worst place I had spent the night, but the hall was cold and there were only low tables and cushions. My back was on fire from riding all day. "Fine, we will share."

And . . . a chance to stay in close quarters with an exhausted Lan Yexue was a chance to pry more military secrets from him.

Yexue flashed a smile. "One room it is, then."

—⁂—

The room was bigger than I had anticipated. A small bed in the corner and a bamboo tea table at the center, surrounded by two chairs that looked a little unsteady from use, and a desk to the far side of the wall. The entire room wouldn't take more than five steps to cross, however after a long day on horseback, just having stable ground under my feet was a blessing.

When I stepped inside, Yexue remained close to the threshold, leaning against the rickety doorframe with half-lidded eyes that trailed my movement. Suddenly I wasn't so tired anymore.

Lan Yexue looked like he wanted to devour me.

With a face as beautiful as his, if Yexue had been another man and I had been another woman, I might have let him.

But he was the Prince Regent of Lan. He was the enemy. And I was already in love with Siwang.

Still, my heart beat a little too fast, and I could feel warmth creeping onto my cheeks. I looked away, though cautious not to turn my back on someone like him.

"Stop looking at me like that," I said. This wouldn't be the first time that the two of us had spent the night together, yet the privacy of a closed room felt more intimate compared with the cave of last time.

"Just taking in the view," said Yexue.

"Me?"

"Ah, no. Don't think so highly of yourself. I'm taking in the room where you are going to seduce me." He made an exaggerated inspection of the room. "A little dusty, that bed looks a little small for both of us, and it doesn't look very sturdy. Fear not, if we break it I will reward the innkeeper handsomely."

I sneered. "*Me, seduce you?*"

"That's what you said in your letter, isn't it? *I am alive and well, and I will not waste my time here behind enemy lines. I will gather military secrets for you however I can. I know you don't want me to be involved in this war, but in calamity there is no innocence, and no sacrifice too great in the need to protect those we love. If seducing Lan Yexue is what I must do to save you, then I will.*"

I felt sick.

The smile fell from Yexue's lips. He rose to his full height and stepped into the room finally, closing the door behind him. My hand reached for the dagger that wasn't there. Suddenly, this room felt suffocatingly small. "Women like you, raised in safe, manicured gardens, will never understand the evil that exists in this world. Did you not for a second wonder why an old lady was tending a tea shop in the middle of nowhere? And did you honestly think it prudent to give that letter to the first person you saw on this trip?" Yexue sighed. He didn't look angry, just . . . disappointed.

I stared at him; I didn't know what to say and wanted to curse Fate for not warning me that the shopkeeper was not trustworthy.

Perhaps this was the problem. I was too dependent on the power the gods gave me, too dependent on the protection of the palace and my old status as the future empress of all empresses. Bathed in Siwang's light, my life was so easy. Everything always worked out because Siwang made sure it did. . . . Without him, what was I? Without my magic, what was I?

You can't do anything right, Fei. That familiar voice crept up again.

"Why did you do it?" Yexue's voice pulled me back into the moment. "When I said you should do what you wanted, this was not what I meant."

He took a step forward, and the butterflies in me hardened to fear, heavy in the pit of my stomach. "I don't trust you."

The prince stopped midstep, eyes wide as if what had left my lips were knives, not words. His face twisted, a suppressed wince. The shadows of anger dispersed, just like that. "Congratulations, I am seduced. Your wish is my command when it comes to anything else, just not when it comes to Rong Siwang."

He took one step forward, then another.

I tried to back away, but there was only so much space between these four walls, and before I knew it, he had me backed against the small writing desk.

His hands came to rest on either side of me.

I tried to shift backward and put more space between our bodies, but Yexue was leaning in, one of his long legs gently pressed against my knees.

My heart was thudding in my ears now, and no matter how quickly I drew my breaths, I didn't seem to have enough. I couldn't tell if my pulse was quick from fear, or . . .

"Fifteen moons," he whispered. "What would you say if I said I have thought about you every night of the past fifteen moons? Not the empress of all empresses, but the girl who was brave enough to defy fate, and kind enough to save the heir of a crumbling dynasty. Did you know the gods created us on the same night, Fei?"

"You were also born at New Year's Eve?"

"In the midnight hours between two lunar years," he whispered, his hand reaching out, those doe eyes so soft as he watched me, so different from the man I had known from campfire stories.

However, looks could be deceiving. As his hand touched my face, I took advantage of the moment and seized the dagger strapped to his waist, and pressed it to his neck.

Yexue smiled. "Do you always have to ruin the moment by holding a knife to my throat?"

"I don't think it's fair that you have a knife and I don't."

This time, Yexue let out a low chuckle. "Fine, you can have my knife. Do you need anything else? The clothes I'm wearing, the mortal body I'm inhabiting? It's all yours; just say the word, Fei."

Gently, his hand let go of my face and trailed up to the hand holding the dagger, and I remembered how fast he was. This was a man who moved as fast as shadows, was strong enough to tear men apart with his bare hands. He would have stopped me if he'd wanted to, easily.

He could also snap my neck right here and now if he wanted to.

"Daggers like this one can't hurt me anymore," he murmured, so softly. "Not if I don't want it to."

The last time I'd tried to stab him, the blade had quite literally bounced off him as if I had struck a statue of stone. But as his fingertips brushed mine, I could tell that he was made of soft flesh just as I was.

I pressed the blade harder against his throat, and he simply smiled, as if he truly didn't care. Still, he leaned back, just a little, giving me some space.

"If peace between Rong and Lan is your goal, then this is not the way to win me over. In fact, this little scheme makes me want Rong Siwang on his knees in the very throne room where I knelt for his father so many times before."

My heart leaped in my chest, remembering all the nightmares of Siwang in the throne room, and the blade that swung down. Was this the moment I was seeing? Was Yexue destined to kill Siwang?

I pressed the blade harder against his throat, watching the flesh dent from pressure. If I tried to cut him, would he let me? More importantly, would he bleed like a mortal, or would this blade shatter upon impact like he was some divine god? "If I tried to kill Siwang, would you—"

"I will kill you," I said before he could finish. "If you so much as touch Siwang, I will kill you with my bare hands."

Those doe eyes suddenly went cold. I fought the urge to shrink back farther against the wall.

"I hope you know that the more you try to protect your precious little prince, the more I want to hurt him. If I sucked him dry until every last drop of him was within me, would you care for me the same way you care for him?"

Yexue didn't wait for an answer before he pulled away again, just a little. Still close enough that he had me trapped between his body and the desk. Still close enough to make my blood sing and make my entire being feel like it was on fire.

"Tell me you don't feel it," he whispered after a moment. "Tell me you don't think of me every night when you close your eyes, look for my shadow in every crowd, waiting for the day when our paths cross again."

"I don't." It was the truth. Every time I thought of him, it was with rage or regret that I hadn't finished him when I'd had the chance.

There was only one person I searched for in every crowd, and that man was not Yexue.

"Really?" Gently, he guided my free hand to his chest, until my fingers were hovering over the small patch of pale skin exposed by the loosened collar of his robe.

I let him guide me into the hems and touched his bare chest, and the low gasp he let out made something inside me clench. My fingers moved down, until I touched the spot where I had stabbed him.

There was a small bump of scar.

He is not invincible, I reminded myself. Lan Yexue was capable of pain, for I had inflicted it myself once upon a time. *So why did my knife shatter the last time . . . ?*

"My wounds always heal," he said softly. "Except the one you gave me in that forest. It is the only thing that has ever scarred on my body. Something tethers us together, Fei. The fallen goddess and the monster . . . Perhaps you are my salvation. Perhaps you are the answer to all my worst fears. Because if the fallen goddess can love me, then I can be redeemed, right?"

I pulled my hand away. "I don't think prophecies work like that."

"Don't lie to me." The leg that was pressed between my knees nudged forward until my legs parted for him.

"I can hear your heartbeat. You want me, as much as I want you. I can love you better than Siwang ever could." When he leaned in and his lips brushed my cheek, my jaw, my neck, I held back the whimper in my throat.

I pushed him back. Just a little, my hand still touching his chest, fingers tugging against the hem of his robe, as if contemplating whether to pull him back in. As if I were holding on to something that I shouldn't. "Do you want me, or do you just want to take something that you think belongs to Siwang?"

He laughed. "You don't belong to him. You don't belong to anyone, and don't ever let the world make you think that. One day when you stop loving him, you can always leave, no matter what the world tells you. I hate you for choosing him and not me, over and over again, but I want you because you might be the single person in this world who is my equal and understands what it's like, to feel suffocated by a destiny you did not choose."

I pressed my hand more firmly against his chest to keep him from coming any closer, for I feared what I might do when his lips finally touched mine. "We can't always have what we want, Yexue."

"*I can,*" he whispered. "If not tonight, then tomorrow night. If not tomorrow night, then the night after that. Eventually, you will give in to this pull between us. I plan on living a long, *long* life, and I plan on making sure you do as well."

"You are so . . ."

"Romantic?"

"Embarrassing." It was better to end this now than to let whatever this was fester.

He winked. "You said you want to seduce me for military secrets. Well, you are fortunate that I am a *selfless* man. Who am I to deny you what you desire the most in this world?"

"I really regret putting that in the letter now."

"Be careful what you wish for, Fei." He came closer again, his strong hands toying with the collar of my robe.

I stopped breathing. I should stop him, but . . . I couldn't, and I didn't want to. I refused to admit it, but he was right.

As his fingers trailed up my thigh, it was enough to send my entire body tingling like fireworks. I couldn't help but think, what if I pulled him in, what if I let him kiss me until I was faint. His eyes really were so beautiful. And his lips . . .

"Say the word, and I'm yours, Fei. I will get on my knees for you. I will beg if I must. I will move mountains, drain the oceans, set the sky on fire if that's what it takes for you to look at me with a fraction of the desire with which you look at him." His fingertips touched my chin.

We were so close now, and my heart was beating so fast. All I wanted in this moment was to lean in and taste the Prince of Lan for myself.

I didn't do that. Instead, I pushed myself off the desk, and Yexue backed away. As he stepped back, the consuming heat on my skin began to quiet.

"It's been a long day; we should go to sleep." I went to the bed and threw him a half-shaped pillow that was just a sack and a couple of bird feathers. "You can sleep on the floor."

"You are making *me* sleep on the floor?"

"Do you expect *me* to sleep on the floor?"

"We can share."

I grabbed the other pillow. "*Fine.* I will sleep on the floor."

"You're not going to crawl into my bed and seduce me for military secrets in the middle of the night?"

"黄鼠狼给鸡拜年, 没安好心." *Never trust a weasel who tries to get cozy with a chicken, his attentions aren't pure.*

"害怕我把你给吃了?" *Scared I'm going to eat you?*

I didn't respond.

Yexue sighed. "My plan has worked: I now have the bed all to myself!"

—⁂—

He didn't let me sleep on the floor, in the end. He offered the bed to me and went to sleep downstairs with his guards.

48

I was flying, high in the sky as dawn bled fast across the land until everything was scorched into a shade of bloodstained gold. Rong's soldiers in their crimson uniforms were changing shifts when blurs of deep blue materialized on the horizon. Lan's soldiers in their uniforms of indigo, dark as midnight, crossed no-man's-land—human soldiers, not vampire soldiers. Blades drawn.

Behind them were cannons and archers. The formation of an army ready for battle.

But they did not charge as I had expected. They hovered on the horizon.

A golden scripture passed from trembling hand to trembling hand until it landed on Siwang's desk. He opened it, glanced inside, and huffed. He grabbed his sword, and the furious tempo of war drums rang through camp.

My stomach twisted as the comrades I had trained with, the comrades who were not ready for battle, picked up their swords.

The sun rose higher, and higher.

Two armies, one red and one blue, meeting from opposite sides of a crimson-stained field that should be green and blooming with wildflowers this time of year. Instead, it was trampled by horses' hooves and wheel marks.

When Siwang looked across the field and saw human soldiers, he smiled and rode forward alone, leaving his army behind.

He and Yexue stopped a hundred yards apart. Close enough to hear each other, far enough that they had time to run if one army suddenly advanced.

"I knew you had spies in my camp, but I didn't think you'd be this stupid," Siwang mused aloud.

"Let her go," said Yexue, his voice stern and cold. The tone of a man whose patience was on its last thread.

"Or what? Or you will attack?" Siwang cast a glance behind Yexue. "You are nothing without your hellish creatures." He raised his hands, and the army behind him shifted into their battle formation.

Yexue's lips tightened into a scowl. "I don't want to kill you. She would never forgive me if I did. This is your last chance. We can end this the easy way, or the hard way. But be warned: if we do it the hard way, I will take *everything* from you. Your name, your honor, your empire, and all that rotten pride. The only thing I'll leave you with will be a pitiful life in chains, as a dog at my feet. Is that what you want?"

Siwang laughed at this. "I am not going to be the one who loses everything." Then, at a wave of his hand, his men charged.

Yexue grimaced but drew his sword when Siwang drew his. "You should have listened to her," Yexue whispered, and I braced for the vision to shift into a clash of swords, the spray of blood, and that never-ending symphony of bone-splintering screams, a sound that haunted me long after I woke from the nightmares.

It never came, because before the two armies could clash, Yexue threw his sword across the field, and it pierced straight through Siwang's throat. So fast that no one had the chance to scream before Siwang's headless body fell off his horse with a stomach-turning *thud*.

"No!" I jerked awake, panting and covered in sweat.

Outside the inn, golden hues of dawn poured over the land. Magic tingled on my skin.

That was one of the most vivid dreams I'd ever had.

I didn't know what ultimatum they were talking about, but if the treaty was real, then Siwang had to sign it, as soon as possible.

I grabbed my robes and slipped on shoes before I charged out of the room.

By the time I came downstairs, I realized there was something missing—the guests of this supposedly fully booked inn.

The only people downstairs were three of Yexue's five guards, who were sipping congees and laughing about something.

Yexue was nowhere in sight.

"That bastard."

I ran upstairs and kicked open every door and, as expected, all the rooms were empty until I came across one that wasn't and found a half-dressed Yexue inside, in the middle of tying his robe.

"Here to seduce me again?"

"You didn't sleep downstairs?"

"Of course I didn't. I am also not the ward you met in Yong'An anymore. Did you honestly expect me to sleep in that drafty hall? If this inn had actually been full, I would have made the innkeeper kick everyone out."

"You told the innkeeper to lie about this place being full and there being only one room left?"

"Of course."

"Why?"

"What can I say, I am simply a too-kind and generous man. You wanted to seduce me, and I wanted to give you the opportunity. If you want this inn to be full so that we will be forced to share one room and one bed again for real, I can make that happen, too." He was laughing, but after the dream I'd just had, I was in no mood to laugh.

"Get dressed. I want to find the stargazer's disciple, then get out of here and away from you as soon as possible."

"I found her months ago. She is with the general who governs this city."

"What?"

"You are not the only person looking for answers, Fei." He gave me a look that said I should have expected this from him. And in all honesty, I *should* have expected this. Lan Yexue did not seem like the sort of man who did things halfway.

"Then why did you insist on coming to get the information yourself? You could just have sent a letter."

He shrugged. "The same reason this prince regent would rather sleep in a dusty inn than a beautiful manor for the night. The things I do to 搏红颜一笑." *The things I do to make the beautiful girl smile.*

"I am not smiling."

"Well, I tried. Would Siwang travel so far just to spend some quality time and make memories with you?"

I didn't tell him that Siwang didn't need to do all of this. He wasn't this pathetic.

I turned around and walked out. "Let's get going. I assume there is breakfast at the general's manor?"

—⚏—

The general's manor was a small house with a walled courtyard and a constant patrol of guards, sitting at the east of the city.

"This is his temporary residence," Yexue explained. "The previous governor of the city burned his house down when the people surrendered."

"The people surrendered, but not the governor?"

"Greedy men like to hold on to power when they can, regardless of the good of the people. And from what the people of this city have told us, their governor was not a good man. If he hadn't ended his life on his own terms, he would have spent the rest of his life in prison, paying for the crimes he had committed against his people."

This shouldn't have surprised me. Regardless of the banners they flew, regardless of how righteous they saw themselves, power corrupted everyone who possessed it.

The guards bowed when they saw Yexue dismounting his horse and opened the double red doors of the manor before we reached the front steps. The guards we had come with followed us in, but trailing at a distance.

The interior was organized. If Yexue hadn't already told me the occupier was a general, I would have guessed. Despite the decorations and the swallow-tailed roofs with their intricate carvings, the manor looked more like an army's training field than a respectable home. Rows and rows of weapons were lined up neatly along the walls, and the center of the courtyard was cleared to make space for sparring.

For all its beautiful structure, the manor was not well kept. The paint was peeling from the brown beams, which could have been red a long time ago, and the stone tiles beneath our feet looked like they had not been washed in years.

"Is this the biggest house you could steal?"

"It was the biggest *empty* house. Unlike your prince, I do not have the habit of stealing homes and kicking their inhabitants out." Yexue grimaced. "Once the war is over, I will make sure these borderlands never suffer again. I will bring them the peace and stability that they deserve."

"You and Siwang both say that."

"Unlike your prince, I mean what I say and I don't go back on my promises."

I bit back the urge to remind Yexue that every man on the continent believed they would be the just ruler this land needed, but everyone who had tried to unite these Warring States had failed.

How long would Lan remain as a revered power, and how long until they eventually crumbled like all the mighty empires before?

The empress of all empresses . . . Could I change things, put us on a new path where the people could finally see peace?

As we walked through the manor, a young man in plain black robes came to greet us. He was tall but lean, with the posture of a soldier. "Your Highness."

"Peizhi." Yexue greeted him with a nod. "Is your father still at the training camp?"

"He is. Your visit is so sudden, he—"

"No need to call him back; we will leave tonight at the latest. Where is the seer?"

"Right this way, Your Highness."

The young man, Peizhi, brought us to what seemed to be the library of the house. At the center of the room was a young woman kneeling at a table covered with plain white paper, with her eyes closed. Except there was something peculiar about how her eyelids seemed to sink into her—

I gasped.

"The Rong emperor tried to kill her with poison," Yexue explained in a quiet voice as we entered the room. "When they discarded her body, they took her eyes and cut off her tongue as a precaution. But Ping's teacher knew this would happen when she left the palace, and gave her an antidote that would cure ten thousand poisons, the same one you had used to save me. She was able to escape the capital with her life, but there's no way to replace what the emperor took from her. She can still hear you, so if you have questions, ask away."

Yexue gestured at the seat across from Ping. I sat down across from her. From here, I could see that she was still young. Late twenties, perhaps, and beautiful. "You are the disciple of the stargazer who foretold my fate?"

Ping nodded.

"Where is your teacher?"

She fled, Ping wrote on the paper placed before her.

"Do you know where?"

She shook her head.

"The prophecy, do you know . . . is it real?"

She wrote: *I was a child, but I was with my teacher the night she foresaw your fate, and I have never seen her so shaken by the stars as she was that night.*

"Why did she leave the palace? Did she know something that the emperor didn't want her to know? Did he try to 杀人灭口, *kill the person and silence the lips*? Is this why he tried to kill you as well?"

Ping's brush hovered over the paper until a drop of ink splattered onto the stark white, staining the words before it. I was suddenly struck with guilt at how many questions I was asking her.

"You can tell her, Ping," said Peizhi. "She won't hurt you. No one will ever hurt you again."

Yes, she wrote. *The emperor tried to kill my teacher.*

My world came to a stop. "Why? And is she still alive?"

I don't know, she wrote.

It took me a moment to realize that this was her answer to both questions.

Again, she hesitated before she dipped the pen back into the ink and wrote: *My master told me once, a long time ago, that you are our best hope of a better tomorrow. Of peace. Your fate is the answer to everything. It will either bring the ruin of the continent, or save it.*

My breath caught at that last part. "But they say I am the empress of all empresses; I am to wed whoever unites the continent. The prophecy never said anything about me *saving* anything."

Ping was still for a moment, as if collecting her thoughts.

"If I become the empress of all empresses and marry the emperor who will unite the continent, will that finally bring peace?"

If Teacher was right, then I believe yes, it will.

"Did your teacher ever say anything about who that person might be?"

Your true love, she wrote.

I laughed. "How am I going to know that?"

Follow your heart.

"I don't trust my heart." Considering how dangerously close Yexue and I got last night, I didn't trust myself to make any decisions.

If you choose wrongly, then I guess we will all die. I should say that I hope I don't live to see that day, but I already can't see anything anymore, so I guess it doesn't matter. Ping smiled as she wrote the last part.

Despite the tragedy she had endured, she still had a sense of humor. I liked her.

I believe it would do everyone a great deal of good if you would stop running from your fate, she wrote. Then, a second later, she added:

I have heard about how you ran away from your betrothal to Prince Si-wang. It seems he is not your true love. Why don't you give Prince Yexue a chance?

I glanced over at Yexue, grinning at this. "Did he pay you to write that?"

Yes. A whole chest of gold and a manor at the heart of the city.

"A manor?" I gasped.

He is very generous; you should give him a chance, Ping wrote, her lips pinched as if holding back giggles.

"You weren't supposed to tell her that," Yexue groaned.

Peizhi only told me to say good things about you, not lie for you.

Yexue rolled his eyes, and Peizhi was looking at the ground. "Tell her to lie next time, Peizhi."

Peizhi nodded. "Yes, Your Highness."

Ping was biting her lips to hide her grin. Even I couldn't help but smile. "Did your master know about Yexue's prophecy?"

From the corner of my eye, I noticed how Yexue stood a little taller at this question. *Be careful,* I reminded myself, conscious that Ping was living within Lan's borders and she couldn't afford to upset the prince regent. Her every word could be influenced by Yexue's wishes.

"It's okay," Peizhi reassured her.

Yes, she did.

"Do you know if our prophecies are intertwined?" Yexue asked.

She never said. I remember only that she argued with the emperor the day it was announced that Lan had sent you as a ward, and she disappeared not long before you arrived at the capital.

I looked over at Yexue. "What if she ran away because of you?"

"Don't blame me. I have never met her," Yexue replied. "And Ping has said that she ran away because of the *emperor.* Read carefully, Fei. Weren't you taught by the best scholars Rong had to offer?"

"The scholars were always too focused on Siwang to pay me any attention," I shot back. "Ping, can you read the stars like your teacher?" If Yexue and I couldn't find the stargazer to decipher our fates, maybe Ping could help?

I can, but losing my eyes has made that difficult. Peizhi helps me. He describes them, and has built a table of moving blocks that follow the pattern of the stars through these tiny dots. But it is not the same. Even if I figure out a way to read the stars as I did, I was only ever a disciple. If you want real answers, you will need to find my teacher.

"I'm trying to find her, but she has left us almost no trace to follow." I glanced at Yexue. "Did the prophecy ever say anything about what would happen if I don't marry anyone?"

Ping shrugged. *The continent continues to fight?*

"And if I don't find my true love?"

Ping pursed her lips. Again, she wrote: *The continent continues to fight?*

"And if I marry the wrong man?"

She giggled before she wrote again: *The continent continues to fight?*

Surprisingly, I giggled, too. "What if I just married every warlord on the continent?"

"Then I will have to kill everyone and become the last warlord standing," Yexue put in.

He's persistent, Ping wrote. Then: *Peizhi told me that Prince Yexue likes you.*

"Likes me or my prophecy?"

She shrugged. *I would love to look into it for you. Perhaps one day, when I relearn my abilities without having to see the stars with my own eyes. In the meantime, why don't you try to see the future for yourself?* Ping smiled and touched the spot between her brows.

I was struck by a sudden coldness. "Who else knows?"

Teacher told only me. She specifically instructed that the emperor could not know about your abilities.

I could not imagine what would have happened if the emperor had learned that I possessed the magic of Fate, and that I could see the future, even if it was brief glimpses. "Thank you."

I never told anyone about your gift, Ping added. *But I did confirm it to Yexue when he guessed it.*

"Nothing is going to happen to you under my watch, Fei," said Yexue. "You don't have to worry."

But I don't want to live my life under your protection. That familiar hunger crept back in, though this time not for Yexue's lips or his skin, but for his power and his status. There had to be more ways for girls to obtain power in this world than through marriage.

I didn't want to be the water that reflected his light. I wanted to be the light itself.

The prophecy said I was the one destined for greatness, not my lover and not my husband. *Me.*

And what would happen if I killed the love of my life? I bit my tongue. "What else do you know about my magic and why it stems from the mark?"

Your magic is an extension of you, but you are not your magic, Ping wrote. *I wish I could answer your questions about your prophecy and your phoenix's mark. However, the will of the gods is not for mortals to know. All we can do is guess and steal glimpses from the stars. Or in your case, steal from Fate herself.*

49

We stayed for breakfast, which was a bowl of hearty egg drop soup and a basket of beef-topped scallion pancakes, and fried dough. We sat in the sort of grand hall I was too familiar with, for I had sat in too many of these for too many feasts. High ceilings and sleek red beams, two rows of low tables carved from a cherry-scented wood. Yexue sat at the head of the hall, with Peizhi at his right hand. I sat at Yexue's left, and Ping had originally moved toward the table next to Peizhi before I gently touched her hand and asked, "Can you sit next to me? I have more questions to ask."

Ping had hesitated for a moment before obliging.

I'd hoped that Yexue and Peizhi would walk off and discuss military matters too important for my eager ears, so that Ping and I could get a moment of privacy.

They didn't. Yexue and Peizhi conversed in quiet, casual tones. Unlike a prince and a general and more like friends.

"How is Uncle Du?" Yexue asked after taking a brief sip of his tea.

I noticed that almost everything on Yexue's table had gone untouched, except the tea that he was drinking.

"My father is the usual. Training the new recruits and getting angry that the soldiers these days are nothing like the soldiers he raised when he was my age. But I think he's just angry that you won't let him lead armies anymore."

"It's for his own good," Yexue said.

"And the emperor?" Peizhi asked. My ears perked up at this.

"The usual," echoed Yexue.

If they weren't going to go off and catch up in private, I wished they would speak more about the front lines, or better, the vampires I was desperate to know more about.

They didn't.

Every once in a while, Peizhi's vigilant eyes found me, full of caution, like a soldier monitoring the movements of a thief.

Ping had a pad of paper and brush with her. She indulged my questions about how her visions worked and answered everything in detail:

Teacher's visions are more vivid, and mine are mild like strange dreams, she wrote. *I find it hard to decipher dreams from visions sometimes. But Teacher said that I will improve with practice and one day take her place—*

Her pen stopped there, and there was a quiver to her lips.

"Ping?" Peizhi was quick to step in. "Are you okay?"

Ping just smiled and made a motion with her hand that I didn't understand before turning back toward me and writing: *Stargazing is not entirely of magic and can be taught from teacher to student. Teacher used to say I was the most talented of all her disciples, and I, too, thought I would one day join her as an imperial stargazer and serve Rong for decades to come.* A teardrop fell on the parchment, then another.

My heart sank. I felt like I should say something, but what was there to say other than that the emperor was a monster for what he had done to her? The stargazer had been smart to leave before the emperor turned his wrath on her. I wished Ping had escaped the palace sooner.

It struck me that I would likely have ended up with the same fate as Ping if Siwang hadn't begged for my life.

"If I find someone who is willing to teach me, will I be able to control my visions and learn to read them like you and your teacher?" I asked.

Yes, she wrote. *I have never taught anyone, but I can relay everything Teacher taught me. However, I'd suggest you try to find my teacher, for she will know so much more than I do.*

I looked up and found Peizhi's concerned eyes again. Judging by how protective he was of Ping, I doubted he would let her come to Rong to teach me. I wouldn't want her anywhere near Rong, either. Though I grew up in the palace, I could count on one hand the amount of times the emperor had spoken to me directly. I didn't know what kind of man he was other than stern warnings from Father to never provoke his wrath. The emperor was a kind father to Siwang, but that did not a good man make. And Ping was right. If I wanted real answers, I had to find the stargazer.

A bowl of congee later, Peizhi bowed for Yexue, then the two hugged and parted ways. "I will see you soon, brother," Yexue said to Peizhi.

"I will see you soon, Your Highness."

The riders who had accompanied us here were already outside

waiting on their horses. But the normal attire they had worn earlier this morning had been replaced by light armor. The horses Yexue and I had ridden had also been replaced by a carriage with six horses.

"The difference between horse and carriage is half a day at best," he proclaimed, stretching his arms above his head in an exaggerated manner like a cat preparing for a long nap. "I don't know about you, but I am exhausted after yesterday. I am not like my soldiers, I was not trained to ride continuously for days on end."

I should have protested, but my back felt like it was on fire after yesterday. He was right: neither of us was trained to endure this kind of arduous riding. Even during my yearlong search for the stargazer, I had never ridden a horse nonstop for so many hours. "Thank you," I murmured, then stepped forward to climb into the carriage.

Yexue shoved an arm forward to stop me. "Who said you can ride in the carriage with me?"

I stared at him, dumbfounded. "You are the one who keeps calling me a garden rose!" Pride be damned, now that the carriage was a viable travel option, I was not going to let myself be bounced around on horseback for another day.

Yexue broke into a smile, then held out his empty hand. "If you want to ride in the carriage with me, you need to do something for me."

Peizhi came up and put a heavy scroll into Yexue's hand, which Yexue then handed to me.

I grimaced. Throughout history, bargains with tyrants never had happy endings. "What is it?"

"Have Siwang sign this," he said. "You can read it in the carriage."

I rolled my eyes as I climbed into the carriage with him. I didn't tell him that I would have Siwang sign the treaty either way. Even if it was unfair. For it was that, or die by Lan Yexue's sword.

Fate be damned, I would not let anything happen to Siwang.

The carriage's silk-lined interior was beautiful, but I was most excited about the cushioned seats. It felt good to sit down with something supporting my back instead of being tossed about on a saddle. "Have you ever thought about joining the theater?"

To my surprise, Yexue laughed and made an exaggerated stretch, his long legs taking up half the carriage, and he was making a show of bumping them against mine, giggling as he did. "Are you saying that I am dramatic?"

"I'm saying you are the drama," I murmured, and Yexue laughed harder. It was nice, hearing him laugh.

The carriage began to roll, and I opened the window to see Ping and Peizhi waving us goodbye.

"I will bring you back another time," Yexue said.

I almost smiled. I would like to see Ping again, but what were the odds of that happening if Ping was here behind Lan's border and I was on Rong's side?

I closed the window and noticed how heavy the sliding panel was. Instead of curtains, there was a strange type of mesh made from interlinked metal chains.

There was something odd about the carriage. When I pressed my hand against the walls, I noticed it did not vibrate the way wood did. The material of this carriage was denser.

Metal.

"Has something happened?" I asked. This could be the only carriage that was available, but if Yexue wanted to get back to his city as soon as possible, why wouldn't he choose a lighter, wooden carriage?

My question was met with silence. Yexue closed his eyes, so I knew not to press for more. "If you have any other questions for Ping, you can write to her, and I'll make sure the message is delivered."

"In other words, the message will be read by Peizhi, who will read it to Ping?"

"Anything Ping knows, Peizhi will also know at some point."

"You could have sent her a letter of questions and saved us this whole trip."

"Having someone ride back and forth with letters would take twice as long. It is easier for you to get your answers here, in person, where you don't have to wait days for responses. And be honest: Would you have believed me if these letters had arrived from someone claiming to be the stargazer's disciple?" he asked.

No, I wouldn't have.

"I know you think of me a certain way, Fei. I had secretly hoped that by showing you more of my cities, meeting more of my people, that you would see the truth with your own eyes and realize that I am not the monster Siwang paints me to be."

I bit my lip. "Your people do look happy."

"What's that, I didn't quite hear you, can you say it again?" Yexue teased, and I fought the urge to kick him.

"Thank you," I grumbled, turning my attention to the city we were passing. I still clutched the scroll Yexue had given me. I wasn't ready to open it yet.

"What's that, I didn't quite—*Ouch!*"

I kicked him for real this time.

Though traces of the siege could still be seen in the burn marks and crumbled buildings, Xiangxi was already in the process of being rebuilt. Despite everything, the people here looked genuinely happy

as they hopped from market stall to market stall, selecting vegetables
and cuts of meat.

"You have absolutely squandered your chance, despite my *extremely*
selfless cooperation," Yexue grumbled, making an exaggerated act of
rubbing his ankle, when all I did was tap him with my toes. "Next time
you want to seduce me, I will expect earth-shattering poetry and a dramatic declaration of love. I am not a man who travels thousands of
miles for just anyone, you know."

"Are you only interested in girls who hold a knife to your throat?"

"Unfortunately for me, yes, I am only interested in girls who are
interested in killing me. Unfortunately for you, I seem to have a short-
age of those. It is a pity—the girl whom I am trying to offer my beating
heart to would rather stab that heart than cherish it. No wonder the
emperors of the past often referred to themselves as 孤家寡人: *lonely
souls who must choose solitary paths.* For love is a concept so far off when
the one I admire . . ."

"Oh, skies." *How many more hours of this?*

"Yes, do pray to skies and beg them to help you get back in my good
graces."

I huffed. "I never realized you talked this much when we were in
Yong'An."

"你在嫌弃我吗?" *Are you judging me?*

Yes. I wanted to tease him back, but didn't want to open this door
of friendliness. Regardless of how kind he appeared to be, a tiger was
still a tiger.

However, I did prefer this Yexue to his serious side. "I never realized you had a sense of humor."

"Did you expect me to brood constantly, like some sad prince who only wants to recite obscure poetry, or a tyrant whose heart is stone cold and devoid of kindness?" he said, laughing, and my lips twitched before I pressed them down.

"In Yong'An, you constantly looked like you were in a bad mood."

"That's because I was," he replied, his voice suddenly heavier. "I'm not like you, Fei. In Yong'An I was a ward, living under the roof of bitter hosts. Yes, I had the power to run away, but where would I go? I was a kid, and my father was dying and my uncle had told me to die in Rong and never come home. When my dream of finding the imperial stargazer and having her rid me of my prophecy failed to materialize, I didn't know what I should do next. During my time there, between waking up and going to sleep, I thought of one thing and one thing only: whether it was worth trying to survive." The humor faded from his voice. "You might not know this from your days as the empress-to-be, but the world is not fair, and it is not kind. Yong'An is a dog-eat-dog place, and the only way to survive it was by pretending that I was the most dangerous dog of them all, one that would never whimper or flinch, no matter how hard you kicked it. You had a family who cared about you and a prince who adored you. I, on the other hand, had nothing. Just a mother who hated me, a father who feared me, an uncle who wanted me dead, and a monstrous ability that I didn't know how to use at the time."

My stomach twisted, remembering the words he had spoken on the city walls. How he had walked into the mountains two years ago with the intention of dying.

Yexue turned away. "None of it matters anymore. Sooner or later, I will make everyone who ever hurt me pay."

The horses began to pick up their pace. The carriage was too dark, so I slid the window open just a little, enough to let in some air and light. Though the gap was barely wider than a finger, I could see that we had left the city, and another group of riders had joined the guards.

Something had happened, and Yexue was keeping it from me.

"Speaking of Yong'An, why did the Rong emperor insist on collecting you as his ward? Why do he and Siwang hate you so much?"

A beat of silence. Yexue leaned back against the seat and stared up at the ceiling, his expression somber. That brief ray of light I had enjoyed so much was gone now.

"We can talk about other things. It's a long ride back," he said.

In other words: end of conversation.

I leaned back against the seat, my body mirroring him. "I feel bad for Ping. What the emperor did is beastly."

From the corner of my eye, I saw Yexue visibly tense, and the carriage felt colder. "Is this the first time you realized the Rong emperor is an evil man?"

No, it was not. "Is it possible that we are the reason the Rong emperor tried to kill her and her teacher?"

Yexue was quiet for a moment. "If I told you it was because of our prophecies, would you feel guilty?"

"Yes."

Yexue stared at the ceiling for a moment, his eyes drifting to a close. He seemed as exhausted as I was.

"I'm going to tell you something Siwang will never tell you: wicked people do wicked things. You are not responsible for another person's bad actions, even if they do bad things because of you."

My chest hollowed at his words. The carriage jolted over a sharp curb, and our hands brushed, just a little. I was suddenly too aware of how small this carriage was, how close our two bodies were. Our arms were mere inches apart, and our hands . . . Another jolt, and Yexue's fingertips touched mine again.

I pulled my hand away and shifted in my seat until I am pressed against the far corner, putting as much distance between us as possible. "What about you?"

He chuckled, grinning when he replied, "I wish I could say that I am different, that I want to be better, yet I fear I may be as rotten as the rest of them. The point is that even if you didn't exist, even if the Lan and Rong and Wang and Zhao and every dynasty who rules this land did not exist, there would be other dynasties. Because this is the way of men. We want power, and the only way we know is through war. Prophecy or not, this land will not know peace until someone strong enough unites it once and for all."

My mouth was dry; I didn't know what to say. All my life, people told me was that I was the reason Rong had to conquer our neighbors so that they would not one day grow greedy and covet the empress of all empresses. When the emperor waged wars, he had waged them in my name, in the name of my prophecy. "They say that I am blessed by Fate and the stars and all the gods. But why do I feel so powerless? Every decision made in my name is made by men more powerful than I am. They say they do it to protect me, but no one ever asks what I want."

I didn't know I was crying until Yexue reached over and brushed a tear from my cheek. "What do you want, Fei?"

To be free. Of everything. I pushed his hand away and dried my tears with the hem of my sleeve. I let go of the breath I was holding and un-furled the scroll. I couldn't run from the truth forever.

The terms were simple. Lan wanted to keep all the land they had al-ready conquered and for Rong to relinquish their rights to these lands. They also asked for Rong to become a tribute state of Lan, and for

Rong to offer up a fraction of their annual tax revenue in addition to a yearly quota of domestic production. All material things, nothing that crossed the line of citizens offered up as indentured servants, like some empires demanded from their tribute states.

The terms were unfavorable toward Rong, but such was to be expected. I had no doubt that the Emperor of Rong had drawn up worse peace treaties during his years as conqueror.

风水轮流转, *the fortune comes and the fortune goes.*

"Siwang would be a fool not to sign this. Is he the one turning the treaty down, or is his father?"

"Have you ever heard of a peace treaty being on the table? If Siwang had passed it to the Rong court, rumors would have spread. You know how these things work."

I did. "Why would Siwang keep this to himself?"

"Ask him yourself." Yexue glanced past me, at the narrow opening of the window. "I will send my best guards with you to Rong's camp."

"I don't need them. Siwang wouldn't hurt me. Besides, if I returned to camp with your men escorting me, Siwang wouldn't trust me. War changes men; he is paranoid, and if—"

"The guards are mandatory. You might be foolish enough to believe you are safe with Siwang, but—"

I arched a brow. "What are you trying to say?"

"That maybe you don't know that prince of yours as well as you think, and you—"

A spark at the edge of my vision.

A narrow valley, surrounded by trees on both sides.

Arrows, descending like rain around our metal carriage, piercing straight through the legs of a horse—

"Stop the carriage! We are going to be ambushed!" I screamed, moments before the cart came to a screeching halt and someone from outside cried, "Get down!"

Yexue immediately pushed me to the floor, closing the window as he covered me with his body.

This was why he had left in such haste, and why he had changed from horses to a metal carriage. He knew someone had been tracking us, planning an attack.

"Stay down."

I closed my eyes, tried to will another vision into existence and do something, *anything,* to help.

"Don't be scared," Yexue whispered as the sound of clashing swords erupted outside. He brushed a thumb between my brows; he must have mistaken my concentration for fear.

I tried to push him off. "Give me your sword."

Yexue smiled, handed me his dagger, then placed a hand on my shoulder before I could rush outside and join the fight. "My men are trained, Fei. You are just a green soldier with a few months of practice. That is nothing in a fight against *killers.* Frankly, it is ridiculous that Siwang even let you or any of the idiots you trained with get this close to the front lines."

Siwang is desperate. My attention once again fell on the peace treaty. Could it be true? Could it—

Another spark.

A man, dressed in black, coming behind the youngest and smallest of Yexue's guards.

The glint of a blade. The *swish* as it sliced through air and found the young man's throat.

I leaped out of the carriage. It took me a heartbeat to find the young man in the chaos. Just as the assassin came up behind him.

I threw my knife, letting Fate's glimmer guide it, and it sliced through the assassin's hand before he could sever the head of the young guard.

I smiled. I almost couldn't believe it. I had saved someone's life.

"Fei, be careful!" Yexue jumped out of the carriage, his hand grabbing mine, and I half expected him to pull me back inside. Thankfully, he did not.

I had spent my entire life hiding while men fought and bled to protect me.

No more. It was time I started protecting myself, perhaps even protecting those who—

A scream pierced the air, and it sounded just like it had in my vision.

I turned to see the same young man I thought I had saved. The very knife I had thrown to stop the assassin was now plunged into his abdomen.

"*Ruichan!*" Yexue cried, panic flaring in his eyes for the first time.

"Go," I choked. "I can protect myself."

Yexue thrust the hilt of his knife at me and lunged into the battle. He was as fast as I remembered, moving with the grace of a dancer, leaping through the air, leaving a path of crimson behind him like he had a year ago in the mountains. Faster and stronger than any mortal had the right to be.

He said his magic was a curse, yet all I felt was envy.

How I wished to be burdened with his curse, his power, and the control he had over his magic.

Soon, dead men lay cradled by puddles of blood, their throats slit. War was cruel and swords had no eyes. From their uniforms, it seemed the attackers were not of Rong.

By the time Yexue had snapped the neck of the last assassin, his men were crying around the dying boy I had tried to save. Even from a distance, he looked too young to be called a man.

"I know you said you wanted to join your brother as a vampire, but this isn't the way, Ruichan," I heard Yexue say as he knelt beside the dying boy, who spluttered a sound that was more blood than laugh.

The men moved to give Yexue better access to him, and as they parted, I saw the huge wound in his stomach, blood pouring fast, slipping through the fingers of frantic hands that were trying to apply pressure and keep everything inside.

Yexue scooped a handful of blood from the dying boy and poured it into his mouth. Then he bit open his hand, to give the boy his blood, moments before he went limp.

"Take care of him," Yexue said before he returned to the carriage. Some of the men followed him, but two stayed behind with the lifeless body of the boy.

There were tears in Yexue's eyes when he returned to the carriage. I could smell the blood that covered his hands. I gasped when I saw the crimson of his eyes, the same shade as my phoenix's mark, as the blood that poured from every man he had just killed. Yexue quickly pressed his lids closed and turned away from me when he sat back down, tucking his body against the other side of the carriage, as if trying to hide himself from me.

We sat in silence as the carriage began to move again.

I peeked out the window to see Yexue's men digging.

"Did you not heal him?"

Tears were trickling down his cheek. "I did heal him."

"Then why are they burying him?"

"Military secrets."

"This is how you make vampires," I murmured, an observation, not a question. Those red-eyed demons weren't demons from hell. They were people, just like that boy. . . .

"If I say yes, will you report it back to your prince and use it against me?"

I picked up the forgotten peace treaty from the floor of the carriage. "I will make sure Siwang signs this. You don't want to watch more innocent lives end, and neither do I."

"Good," Yexue whispered. "Let your prince know that if he doesn't surrender while he still has the chance, I might have to become the monster he wants the world to think I am."

I swallowed the lump in my throat, this morning's dream still fresh in my mind. "I believe you."

50

Yexue and I went our separate ways just as dawn peeked over the horizon. I traded the carriage for a fast horse and three of Yexue's guards, on which he insisted. I didn't want to argue. They would follow me only until I reached Rong's camp, at least. If Yexue required that they follow any further, then they might bring more trouble than protection.

We raced down trampled roads marred by blood. Crimson slush showered the hems of my robes with each thunderous thump of the stallions' hooves. In the days since I had been taken, Yexue's army had once again pushed Rong farther north.

Night after night, they slaughtered our people with harrowing attacks that rarely left anyone alive, Siwang had told me.

I clung tight to the reins and resisted the urge to touch the treaty strapped to my back. I would not let my nightmares come true. If Siwang didn't sign the treaty now, I feared Yexue would change his mind and decide he was not satisfied with these morsels of Rong, not when he could have *all* of it.

Gradually, the terrain turned mountainous, snowy peaks rising into view. We rode past Changchun, the walled city now open in surrender to the Lan army: another prize in Yexue's string of victories.

As we approached Rong's territory, Yexue's men halted their horses so I could continue alone.

The patrolling Rong soldiers recognized me when I approached camp. From their wide eyes, they had not expected to see me again.

Half a moon had passed since Yexue stole me in the night. Everyone probably assumed I'd either been killed or deserted them. Despite their hesitation, the soldiers waved me through without much questioning. I kicked the horse into a gallop.

Camp was no longer the lively place I remembered. A heavy somberness hung in the air, chatter quieted in favor of the grunts of training boys and the cries of wounded men.

My heart sank when I saw them. New recruits with round faces and lean bodies. Teenage boys who were too young to be here.

Something inside me twisted.

Some of the men turned to look at me as I rode through camp.

"Little Li, you are alive!"

"Little Li! Gods, where have you been?"

"Little Li . . ."

I kept my eyes high. I had come here for one reason and one reason alone: to convince Siwang to sign this stupid—

I stopped. Because in the distance, I saw Caikun, clad in the bone-white garments of a man in mourning.

No.

I should have known when I passed Changchun earlier. If we had lost the city, his father must no longer be with us. General Wu would never let Changchun fall to Lan.

I had met Caikun's father only once or twice. Brief glimpses from across the long imperial hall whenever the emperor held feasts for his esteemed general. He'd been a good friend to my father, one of the few men in the capital he spoke to with true heart. General Wu had loved his country more than anything else. A man who'd given his whole life to Rong, and raised all his sons to do the same.

I touched the treaty inside my robes.

Siwang. I had to find Siwang.

"Fei!" When Luyao called to me, I didn't answer.

I kicked the horse into motion and raced for Siwang's tent.

51

I knew something was wrong when Siwang's guards greeted me with tight frowns and stern faces. When I jumped from my horse and approached the tent, their spears dropped in a cross formation to bar me from entering.

I clenched my jaw. If Yexue's words had been lies, then Siwang would have run to me the moment he heard I was safe and alive, not barricaded himself behind his soldiers and their blades.

"Let me in," I snapped. It took all my self-control not to grab the nearest guard and shove him out of the way, military rules be damned.

The men exchanged apprehensive glances. Thin lips and cautious eyes. The air was heavy with trepidation, like a fabric strained at the seams.

"He would want to know I'm alive," I told them.

"Wait here," the tallest guard said finally.

With a deep breath, he dipped into the tent. A composure of slow vigilance.

There was always a mindful diligence to the way Siwang's men approached him. But Siwang wasn't one to let his emotions influence the way he treated those around him. The loss of Changchun must have hit him hard.

Half a minute later—too long—the guard finally slipped out.

When the guard returned his attention to me, I prepared myself, hand ready to rip the headband from my mark. The stars knew I couldn't win in a fair fight against these battle-trained soldiers. But I might if Fate helped me cheat.

In the end, none of us brandished our weapons. The guard gave a subtle nod of his head. "You can go in."

I braced myself, then entered.

Watery daylight peered through the tent. Without any lit candles, every color inside was subdued to a subtle gray hue.

Siwang sat at his desk, his back to me. There was a calmness in his silhouette.

This was far from the reunion I'd painted for us in vivid, imagined colors. I'd thought there would be tears in his eyes when he heard I was alive.

Perhaps Yexue was right. Perhaps Siwang didn't care so much for me after all. Perhaps my palace fears were true, that despite everything, I was just another pawn to him.

"Siwang." I whispered his name, hoped the sound of my voice would bring him back to me.

When he finally turned, my breath caught in my throat, and a dull ache weighed heavy in my chest. Relief shone in Siwang's shining eyes, tinged red in the sallow light. He had been crying, for a long time, it seemed.

Then he flashed the slightest of smiles. Not enough to ripple his stoic features, but enough to make my own eyes sting.

"Fei." He said my name quietly. "You are back." There was no emotion in his words. no joy, only emptiness. "Did he—"

"Yexue didn't hurt me," I replied before he could finish. "He was . . . kind, actually."

Siwang merely nodded. "开门见山吧." *Open the door and reveal the mountain. Let's get to the point.* "Yexue didn't send you back out of the goodness of his heart, did he?"

I took the treaty from its folder and placed it on the table across from him.

"So you are choosing him?"

"There is nothing to choose, Siwang. You are right. You *have* lost the ability to see the forest for the trees. We are going to lose this war, and the sooner we agree to peace, the sooner we can send those innocent men and boys too young to even be here *home*."

A sob threatened to rise from my throat, causing my voice to crack.

The Siwang I knew, as flawed as he was, was a good man. I refused to believe he'd watch his people suffer in the name of pride.

"We won't know if we don't try," he whispered. "Even monsters can be killed. With fire. With *silver*. We can kill them. I have a plan." His eyes burned with a fervor I didn't recognize. "We are so close to turning the tides, Fei. Lan Yexue attacked that night for a reason. He was trying to scare us into submission because he knew we had found his weakness. Silver is fatal to his beasts, and if we—"

"It's not worth it."

Siwang shook his head. "It will be. When we are victorious, every death and sacrifice will be worth it. Rong is not a tiny northern tribe bowing to the southerners anymore. We obey no laws and listen to no man who is not our own."

Sentiments I had heard before, from the scriptures of the fallen dynasties. *Those who do not know history are doomed to repeat it.* Siwang had read the same books I had; if I remembered this, then so did he. Yet . . .

"War is not about land or power. It's about protecting those who cannot protect themselves. Our ancestors would not want to see blood-bath after bloodbath over piles of dirt and dust when peace is *offered* to you. If you don't sign this treaty, men will keep dying. Is that what you want?"

If you don't sign the treaty, you will die, Siwang. I tried to reach for his hand from across the table, but he pulled away.

"We have *not* lost the war yet," Siwang snarled. His eyes were blades, sharp enough to cut when he looked at me. This wasn't the Siwang I knew. He felt like a whole other man.

"We have already lost. You just don't want to admit it." I closed my eyes, my breath shaky. "I am on your side, Siwang. And because I am on your side, I can't let you do this."

I pushed the treaty toward him, and he turned away. Stubborn, like a child. A side of him I had rarely seen.

"What did Lan Yexue say to you? Did he show you the cities that he conquered, full of people who sing his praises because that's the only way they are allowed to live? Did he boast about how happy those people were, under his rule? How benevolent a regent he is?"

"His citizens looked happy," I said, and it was the truth. I'd believed Yexue when he said he wasn't the sort of conqueror who abandoned cities after he got his hands on them, as so many emperors did.

Siwang's laugh was harsh. "Oh, I'm sure they *looked* happy. A wonderful charade of smiles and sunshine, until night falls. I don't know how many vampires are in his battalion, but I assume it's not a small number. All those mouths . . . hungry for blood. Lan Yexue has to feed them somehow, right? Fei, Yexue can weave a veil over your eyes, but not mine. I know what he's done to the people who refused to kneel for him." Siwang reached forward until his fingertips gently brushed over mine. "Fei, surrendering sounds lovely from your lips, but do you know the true cost of kneeling for him?"

I thought of the young soldier who had died, then the vampires I had seen on the battlefield. They looked terrifying from a distance, but when they spoke, they sounded human. "His vampires are not demons from hell. I think they are humans, who are . . . not quite human anymore. But that doesn't make them monsters—"

A half sneer made me stop midsentence, Siwang was shaking his head. "I should have known a girl would never understand the price of war."

My heart broke. There and then.

Words I'd been hearing all my life from men, other men, but never thought I'd hear from Siwang. "Well, this girl understands that we are outnumbered. This woman understands that a good emperor would never send his men out there to die for the sake of pride. Even if an emperor wins wars and conquers all the lands the four oceans have to offer, if he doesn't love his people, put them first, then there's nothing separating him from a tyrant. Sign the treaty, Siwang. Save what's left of your empire."

I pushed the treaty toward him again, and as I did, my finger brushed the scroll sitting at his right hand. The one he'd been reading before I entered the room.

Immediately, a blaze of vision burned across my eyes.

Fire. A whole city burning into the night, like the bloodiest of nightmares.

People screaming.

Men, women, and children, burning as they leaped from the city walls.

Fire swallowing everything it touched.

Humans and vampires, the flames did not discriminate.

Burning.

Burning.

Changchun.

I pulled my hand back, gasping.

No.

"You are going to burn down Changchun with everyone inside it." I remembered the scorch marks in the other cities. This was not the first time he had tried to do this.

Siwang's eyes went wide, and all his attention immediately fell on the scroll next to his hand. He snatched it from beneath my fingers, but I had already seen everything that would happen, felt the flames singeing my body as the city fell.

"How . . . ?" Siwang couldn't finish the sentence, his eyes flickering with shock and horror.

"You are going to kill all of them. Even your own people?"

"Fei . . . What did you see? You—" He grabbed my wrist. "What is this?"

The red string that Yexue had tied around my wrist, which I had forgotten to take off. "It's nothing."

Siwang's jaw went hard. "Tens of thousands of his army, both human and vampire, are inside Changchun right now. By burning the city to the ground, we will gain the upper hand again."

"There are twenty thousand of your own people in that city!"

"They are collateral damage," he murmured, turning away like a child who knew he had done something wrong but refused to admit it.

I laughed. It sounded more like choking. "You are just like Yexue. Like your father. Like every man who has tried to rule these lands!"

A pause as he slowly turned back to me, as if debating something.

"I should have done this a long time ago," he said. I waited for him to yell for his guards to take me away and lock me up, but he didn't. Instead, he set down a bronze token with his family seal. "Take this and go home, Fei. You don't belong here, and I never should have let you stay in harm's way for this long."

"No," I snapped. I wasn't going to let him or anyone else decide what I could and could not do anymore.

I didn't take his token. Instead, I grabbed the treaty and ran.

"Fei!" Siwang cried. "Catch her!"

I was out the door before his guards had time to react.

Outside, the camp was quiet; our numbers had dwindled in the time I'd been gone. There was no way these men could survive a battle with Yexue and his monsters. Even if Siwang's plan succeeded and he killed a portion of Yexue's vampires by setting fire to Changchun, it wouldn't matter. Yexue could always make more.

"Fei!" Siwang cried. I could hear the shuffle of his guards after me as I bolted for the campfires where most of the soldiers would be at this time.

"Siwang is lying to you!" I shouted when I was within earshot of the fires. "Lan has offered us a peace treaty, but Siwang won't take it! We have to stop! We are going to lose this war!"

A group of the soldiers turned to look at me with confused stares. "That's Little Li."

"I thought he had died . . ."

"Siwang is lying to you!" I bellowed as loudly as I could, holding the peace treaty as high as possible. "He is—"

Someone tackled me, knocking the air out of my lungs and sending me colliding against the field of mud and slush.

"Are you trying to cause hysteria in camp?" It took me a moment to realize that the person who had caught me was Caikun. He shoved my face into the mud until I couldn't breathe, his hand firm on my neck, choking me. "Traitor! My father died for rats like you! My brothers died for rats like you!"

"Caikun, stop!" Siwang shouted in the background, but his voice was muffled and distorted.

Caikun pulled me up and punched me across the jaw, then again, finding the edge of my cheek this time, then again, and again, but his fists were no longer finding my flesh. He was pounding the mud beside my head. "You should have died! Cowards like you are the reason we are losing this war!"

By the time someone pushed Caikun off me, black spots were already filling my vision. I tried to stand, but I only fell deeper into darkness.

"Get him out of here," I heard Siwang say in the background. "Li Fei has done enough for Rong. I hereby honorably discharge him. Send him home to his family."

52

"Someone . . . ," I croaked, my throat dry, "someone, save them. . . ."

53

In darkness, I dreamt of fire.

Of Changchun, a walled fortress stretching as far as eyes could see, half buried under sand, half drenched in blood.

In my dream, a symphony of screams melted into a roaring buzz, just like on the battlefields.

The city erupted into wild flames ignited by the fire powder strapped to the Rong soldiers who pretended to be defecting refugees seeking asylum in Lan's unsuspecting arms.

Under their cries for help, the world was painted scarlet by the inferno that grew redder and redder until it blinded my sight.

Against the violent light, shadows leaped from the city walls in their last attempts to flee. When their bodies crashed against the still winter-hardened soil, they sounded like limp cuts of meat hitting a butcher's slab.

I heard their bones break, shuddered when the force of the impact shattered their bodies into crimson puddles.

I smelled the stench of death in the air, felt its icy breath at my neck.

In my dreams, I screamed. Until my throat went hoarse, until my voice had been sanded to a husk.

—⚏—

My master told me once, a long time ago, that you are our best hope of a better tomorrow. Of peace. Your fate is the answer to everything. It will either bring the ruin of the continent, or save it.

Did I have to conscript myself to a life trapped behind palace walls for such a future to exist?

54

I woke in the back of a rattling carriage. Everything from my eyes to my limbs was heavy.

"You are awake?" a voice said beside me.

His face came into slow focus. It was Caikun, but he wasn't looking at me. "Here." He offered me a sheepskin of water. "You need to drink."

"Where are we?"

"Siwang told me to take you home."

A couple of months ago, I would have wanted nothing more than to go home, and stay as far from this war as possible. Not anymore. "How long have I been unconscious?"

"You have been out for two days, and we have been on the road for half of that," Caikun murmured. "I'm sorry. I didn't realize you were . . . Siwang didn't tell anyone. I can't believe I didn't recognize you. I thought you looked familiar, but I . . . I didn't know until Siwang finally told me. I never would have hit you if I had known you were Lifeng Fei, I—"

"Changchun. Has Siwang attacked Changchun?" I asked, finally taking the water from him. I didn't care if he knew who I was when he attacked me. I didn't even care that he'd attacked me. I just cared about the people of that city, the innocent civilians who were locked inside.

Yexue had told the truth. Those were damages inflicted by Siwang, not by Yexue and his men when they claimed the surrendered cities.

I should have believed him sooner.

"It happened last night."

No. "We have to turn back."

"It's already happened, there is nothing—"

"Yexue is going to attack in retaliation, and he is going to kill Siwang."

For the first time, Caikun looked at me, his eyes wide with disbelief.

I could tell him about the vision, but what was the point? I had cried out the truth in camp, and no one had batted an eye. I might see the future, but men would never choose my words over those of a prince. I could scream prophecies of warning from the rooftops, and they would not listen. "Yexue said he would kill Siwang himself if he didn't sign the treaty," I lied. "We have to go back and warn him."

"Why didn't you tell Siwang this?"

I wanted to laugh. "Do you think Siwang listens to me? Has anyone *ever* listened to me?"

This was the way of men. They heard what they wanted to hear and buried what they did not. My words of warning were useless unless they fell on willing ears.

I waited for Caikun to say something, but he just looked at the floor of the carriage in silence.

I sighed. "Stop the carriage! We need to turn back!" I cried.

To my surprise, the carriage stopped.

"Are you all right, Little Li?" Luyao asked from the driver's seat outside the carriage.

"Siwang wanted you to be with familiar faces when you woke up," Caikun explained. He did not tell Luyao to whip the horses back into motion. Instead, he just sat there, staring at nothing.

He was still wearing the bone-white clothes of mourning. My heart throbbed for him. Even if my face still ached, I couldn't blame him. Not after everything this war had put him through—after everything *Siwang* had put him through.

"I'm sorry for your loss," I whispered. "I don't remember much about your father, but I know he was a good man. Everyone from my father to the palace servants to the emperor knew this."

Caikun's eyes welled. "Thank you."

"Siwang is going to die if we don't go back," I said, my voice soft and luring. And I hated myself when I added, "Your father would want us to go back and save Siwang. If Siwang dies, we will *all* die. The emperor will kill every one of us who could have stopped Siwang from riding into battle against Yexue, but didn't."

I leaned a little closer, my eyes staring hard, willing him to look at me. "We both want what is the best for him, don't we?"

Caikun didn't turn my way. "I wish you had died in the mountains that day."

I flinched, my hand reaching for the blade that was no longer there. "What?"

"If you had died, then none of this would have happened," Caikun snapped. "Yexue wouldn't be waging this war, and my father would still be alive. All of this fighting is because of you! Because everyone wants the empress of all empresses. Everyone thinks that by having you, they will rule the continent."

Then Caikun did something I did not expect. He drew his dagger and pinned me to the wall. The force of it made the carriage rattle.

"Are you okay?" Luyao asked from outside.

"I am fine!" I croaked, even as Caikun pressed the tip of his blade against my throat, drawing blood.

How long had he been wanting to say this? And how many others blamed me?

"I'm sorry" was all I could say. "But killing me won't make Yexue spare Siwang. We have to go back, Caikun. We have to stop this battle from happening."

Caikun sheathed his dagger as quickly as he had drawn it.

Then he reached into his robe and handed me a folded piece of paper. "Siwang said he wanted me to give you this, in case he doesn't get to say it to you in person."

I took the letter from him but didn't read it. Nothing he could say would make me not hate him. "We need to go back, Caikun. You know loss, and you know death. This war isn't worth it. We have to convince Siwang to sign that treaty and end this once and for all."

"But Lan Yexue needs to pay for his crimes. He is a killer. He has killed thousands of Rong's soldiers. He killed my . . ."

"I know you are in mourning, but hating someone is not enough reason to send thousands of men to their deaths," I said. "Think of what your father would want you to do."

Caikun finally looked at me—really looked at me. "My father would want to fight the Lans. But he wouldn't want to watch Siwang die."

I swallowed. "留着青山在, 不怕没柴烧. *As long as we have the rolling green mountains, we don't have to worry about not having firewood to burn.* As long as Rong is still an empire and we are all alive, we can avenge those we have lost and fight Lan another day. But not right now. We are not strong enough to win this fight."

"留着青山在 不怕没柴烧...," Caikun echoed. He looked at me in silence for a moment. "If I defy Siwang's orders, it will be treason."

"If you save his life, and the life of every man in the Third Army, you will be a hero," I countered.

A deep breath, then: "Turn the carriage around!"

"There is no time." I tilted the sheepskin back and took several large gulps of water, then climbed out of the carriage. "Untie the horses, Luyao. We need to ride on horseback!"

When I jumped out of the carriage I realized Luyao and Da'sha were the ones behind the horses. Though I was the one giving the order, they both looked at Caikun, who climbed out of the carriage after me.

"Do as Little Li says," Caikun said.

I counted the horses. Four horses for four riders. "I hope you have spare weapons, because we are going to need them."

Caikun smiled and reached under the carriage to present me with my silver-tipped bow. "Of course we came prepared—Siwang wasn't going to send you into these war-torn lands without protection."

—⟋⟍—

As Luyao and Da'sha untied the horses, I read the letter from Siwang.

Fei,

When you left the capital, you promised that you would write to me, and you never did. So I guess that as always, I will have to make the first move.

When you read this, I hope you will be far from the front lines, and I hope I will be alive and victorious. But in case I am not, I am sorry we did not get more time, and I am sorry that I can't say this to you in person.

A year ago, you said the way to win your heart was by giving you a choice, by letting you choose me so that we could be equals. When the stars brought you back to me, I thought you had chosen me, and this was all that I had ever wanted. To be chosen by you. To be loved by you. It was never about the throne or the prophecy. It was always about you. My Fei. My beloved. You are destined for greatness; the stars have said so themselves. So to be worthy of you, I must be great, too. This is why I worked so hard. From scholarly scrolls to martial arts, I practiced and practiced so that I could be worthy of you.

I thought that as long as I tried my best, it would be enough. I thought if I loved you, and you loved me, the gods would protect us. But you are the fallen goddess promised by the stars, destined to be the empress of all empresses. And the only man who would ever be worthy of you is the most powerful man to walk this continent. This is why I cannot surrender to Yexue, why I must fight.

For you. My beloved, everything I do, I do it for you. I hope one day you will understand. I hope one day I get to explain all of this to you, in person, in the flesh. If not, then I will wait for you in the afterlife.

—And I'm sorry I took your choice by sending you away. I would die for you, but I cannot let you die for me.

Your Siwang

When I was done reading, I almost crumpled the paper up and threw it.

"You don't get to blame this war on me," I whispered. "None of you get to blame this on me."

When the horses were untied and saddled, I took a sword and a dagger from Luyao—hidden in the under-compartments of the carriage, in case we were attacked.

—m—

I rode as hard as I could. When Caikun punched me, he had knocked me out and left a bruised cheek, which throbbed with pain with every leap and gallop of the stallions, like I was getting punched all over again. I bit down the pain. I bit down everything.

You will not blame this war on me, Rong Siwang. You will not blame your selfish wants on me.

55

Please let us reach camp in time, I thought as the sun rose higher and higher like it had in my vision. *Please let the vision be tomorrow, or tomorrow's tomorrow. Let it be another day, be another dawn.*

But as we neared camp, it was clear the battle would not occur another day.

Because war drums were beating.

I kicked the horse into a gallop.

"Slow down!" Caikun cried. "This is no place for you! Get back to camp, Fei! I will pass the message to Siwang!"

"He won't listen to you!" I cried. Though Siwang didn't listen to me, either, I could make him listen. I would make both him and Yexue listen.

I rode into the field where the armies were gathered just as Siwang raised his hands in the horizon, a motion for his armies to attack.

"No!" My voice carried through the silence before the storm. "Stop!"

"Fei!" Despite the distance, Yexue heard me, and his hand paused on his sword.

"Stop!" I cried again. *Please, don't kill him.* I had seen this moment before; I knew what Yexue intended to do with that sword.

"You traitor!" someone cried as I rode toward the rear formation of Lan soldiers, kicking my horse harder, hoping to reach Yexue before—

Someone jumped out in front of my horse, scaring it to a stop. As it reared onto its hind legs, I grabbed tight to the reins to keep myself from falling.

"Little Li is a spy working for the Lans! Arrest him!" Someone ran up and tried to pull me from my horse.

"Stop!" Luyao cried, drawing his blade. "Li is not the enemy!"

In the background, a violent tempest of galloping hooves and clashing swords sounded.

Siwang. I need to protect Siwang.

I tried to turn and look for him, but all I saw was chaos. Flashes of crimson and deep blue, and earsplitting screams.

"Get back to camp!" Luyao hissed from behind me; our own comrades had us encircled now. "Caikun will tell Siwang to surrender, but you need to get back to camp! It is not safe here—"

Luyao never got to finish. Because the next thing I heard was his limp body hitting the ground.

Something sticky and hot sprayed the back of my neck, then my cheeks, then my eyes.

No.

"Luyao?" I turned to see Luyao clutching his throat where a blue-feathered arrow had lodged itself and blood was pouring out in thick, heavy torrents. *"Luyao!"*

Running over to us was a group of blue-uniformed soldiers. I recognized one of them as a guard who had accompanied Yexue and me to Xiangxi.

"Come with us!" he cried, and tried to grab me.

"Get off me!" I pushed him away and fell to my knees, pressing my hand where the arrow had struck Luyao.

Pressure. I need to apply pressure. I ripped a piece of my robe and pressed it against his throat, but the blood wasn't slowing.

"Fei," came Yexue's voice from beside me as his hand touched my cheek, where Caikun had hit me. "Who did this to you?"

It took all my will not to drive another dagger through his chest.

The shuffle of footsteps. His men quickly surrounded us, keeping us safe from Siwang's advancing soldiers.

Swords clashing.

Bodies falling.

"Let's go," Yexue repeated.

I didn't take his hand. I didn't even look at him. The only thing I could do was cry.

"Luyao . . ." On my knees, I clung to my friend. "Don't die. Please, don't die. . . ."

"Tell Zhangxi that I love her," Luyao choked through the blood. "Tell my son that his father died protecting him. Tell my Zhangxi that I hope our baby meets me through her stories, that our baby grows up knowing his father loved him. From the moment she told me the news, I've loved him. Please . . . Tell him . . ."

His words came to a stop.

"Luyao!" I cried, shaking him. "Please, Luyao, wake up. Wake—"

I flinched when I felt a hand touch my shoulder again, as if to comfort me.

Yexue.

"Save him," I begged, grabbing him by the hand, pulling closer to Luyao's limp body as if the mere presence of him was enough to change what had already been done. "Save him like you've saved me. He's a good man. He's kind. He has a wife and a child, and his baby needs to meet his father and know how good a man he is. He doesn't deserve to die. If *anyone* here deserves to live, it's him."

Yexue gave one fleeting glance down at Luyao, then shook his head. "He's dead."

Two words, plain and simple. "But I've seen you save others. You saved that boy!"

"Men die all the time, Fei." Yexue knelt until we were face to face, his lips thin as if it pained him to tell me this. But if Yexue wanted to save Luyao, he could. Right? "I can't bring the already dead back to life. Not even for you."

I held Luyao tighter. "You are lying."

"Even my magic has its limits. I can heal someone, or steal them from Death's arms. But once someone is gone, they are gone for good. Believe me, I've tried before."

Though his voice held a somber weight, there was no remorse or guilt in his eyes, as if he felt nothing over the death of a man. I wondered how many men he had killed in the past year, and whether he felt remorse for any of them. It wasn't fair, how he and Siwang got to remain high and mighty in their palaces while men like Luyao died.

Enough.

"Everything stops here. Today," I said.

"Take your hands off her!" Rong's soldiers broke through the circle of blue-uniformed men who had surrounded us, a man in black armor leading the way.

Siwang charged for Yexue, a silver sword in hand.

"Fei, we have to go," Yexue said, his eyes still lingering on me.

Which gave Siwang the chance to cut a path through the clashing soldiers and thrust his silver blade into Yexue's abdomen.

Yexue moved out of the way just in time to avoid the brunt of the impact, but not quickly enough to miss the blade entirely. A slash of crimson at his side, staining his impeccable white robes.

The Prince of Lan grimaced. "I hate it when my clothes get dirty."

Siwang laughed. "You are not immortal after all."

Yexue's lips rippled into a snarl. "I really didn't want to do this in front of Fei."

Just as Siwang raised his sword again, Yexue caught Siwang with inhuman speed and twisted his hand until Siwang fell to his knees, screaming. Yexue's wound was already healed under his silk robe; the only shades of red that remained were the blood clinging to his clothes.

Then, the crack of bones.

Siwang's hand bent at an unnatural angle.

I gasped.

Yexue seized the fallen sword and drove it deep into the folds of Siwang's armor, straight into his rib cage.

"An eye for an eye, a killing blow for a killing blow," Yexue whispered. "You are lucky that I am merciful. I will grant you a slower death than you intended for me."

Siwang let out an inhuman groan; his breathing became short and shallow in an instant.

Yexue threw down the blade and took Siwang by the throat, teeth bared like a tiger ready to devour prey. "My blood is a very precious thing, you know. If you spill even a drop, you have to pay the price."

"Stop!" I cried before Yexue could follow through with the threat by breaking either Siwang's neck or his other hand. I grabbed the fallen blade and thrust it up to Yexue's throat, close enough for the silver to press against his flesh, though not hard enough to draw blood.

On the other side of the blade, Yexue met my eyes. "You said he's not your prince anymore, Fei."

"Don't you think you've killed enough people today?" I choked, looking at Luyao's still body and the soldiers falling all around us as blades continued to clash. Red against blue, Rong against Lan, mortals against mortals. All divided by the idea of nations and borders and enemies and foes.

"Two lives will hardly matter on my tally," Yexue said quietly, his voice so nonchalant it made me shiver.

"You told me we should not feel responsible for the crimes of others, but that doesn't apply to men who are killing others under *your* orders."

Yexue's lips twitched. But it wasn't a smile. He tightened his grip around Siwang's throat, and Siwang let out another croak of pain. "The more you beg for his life, the more I want him dead, Fei. What's so great about him? A useless man like him does not deserve you begging like this. He wasn't worthy of you a year ago, and he surely isn't worthy now."

"I am not begging." I pressed the blade even harder against his throat. "I am negotiating. Let Siwang go; he will sign the treaty and end this war. Isn't this what you want?"

"I'm . . . not . . ." Siwang choked.

I swung the sword till it was pointing at Siwang this time, though not close enough to touch. "*You* are in no position to make demands," I snapped.

Yexue's lip fluttered at the edges, and his grip on Siwang loosened, just a little. "Too little, too late, empress-to-be. I've changed my mind. I don't want peace. I want his *blood.*"

"Fei . . . ," Siwang choked, my name a broken sound from his lips that only made Yexue tighten his grip. Siwang's face was already going red, his veins bulging.

"Yexue, you said that you want to be a good emperor." I swung the sword back in Yexue's direction until its tip bit where his jugular ticked.

The blade trembled in my hand as I looked up at Yexue's dark eyes. The eyes of a predator. But that man who had laughed and made jokes with me in the carriage had to be in there, somewhere.

But what would happen if I inched forward, just a little, and drew blood? Siwang had told me that one of the only ways to kill a vampire was by ripping out their heart or severing their head from this body. What if I tried to do that now, cut Yexue's head from his body . . . ? Would it work? Would it be the end of this war, the end of Yexue? Or would Yexue's patience run out before I could try? He was faster, and stronger. If he wanted me dead, it would be so easy.

"Your beloved prince burned Changchun and everyone inside to ashes without hesitation and without mercy," Yexue said. "Why shouldn't I do the same to avenge all the lives that were lost?"

"Because if you stoop to his level, then you will be as rotten as him. A good emperor doesn't rule with rage and petty grievances."

"Is that what you want, a man who rules with benevolence and understanding?" he asked, his eyes so soft when he looked at me, so fragile and breakable.

"Yes."

With reluctance, Yexue loosened his grip and let Siwang fall to the ground, gasping for air, blood marring the robes under his armor.

"Both of you, tell your men to back off and stop fighting," I snapped.

Yexue held his hand high, and like magic, his men stopped.

Siwang did the same, still choking, gulping for air, clutching his wound. I didn't like the way his breathing sounded: raspy, hollow.

"You need a doctor, now," I told Siwang.

He didn't answer me, didn't even look at me; all his attention was on his broken hand and its mangled bones. Bent at such angles that I didn't need to be a physician to know it would never heal to its former self. Siwang would never hold the reins of a horse, pick up a brush, sword, or bow ever again.

All the things he'd loved. All the things he took pride in, that his father praised him for, because these were the things that were expected of him.

"Can you breathe?" I asked, and I heard my voice waver. Had the knife punctured his lungs?

Siwang wasn't listening to me. He was crying and laughing all at once as he fell on his back, gasping for shallow breaths. "I am not going to sign that treaty. I am not going to give away my land and my people to a *demon*!"

"Watch your mouth," Yexue hissed, hands tightening back into fists. Before Yexue could do anything, I drew my hand back and slapped Siwang.

Blood pounded in my ears. He looked as stunned as I was. "You will sign the treaty," I said simply. "Or watch your people die senselessly for your pride. What happened to all those books you read? Why are you so set on sabotaging your one chance at surviving this war?"

His lips quivered, eyes watering.

I turned away. I didn't want to watch him cry. I would rather shed those tears and bear the burden of his sorrows myself than watch Siwang, my perfect and beloved Siwang, break down like this. Though he might have already shattered before my eyes.

"I'm sorry," Siwang whispered. "I—"

"死罪可免活罪难逃," Yexue interjected. *The punishment of death can be spared, but punishment itself will not.* "Even if he agrees to sign the treaty, he must pay for his crimes. He has spilled the blood of Lan. His sins must be atoned for." A wave of Yexue's hands, and a shuffle of soldiers came forth.

"No!" I gasped.

"Lan Yexue, don't push your luck," Caikun hissed from somewhere behind Siwang, raising his blade.

"Everyone . . . stand down," Siwang wheezed. "Lan Yexue is right . . . I need to . . . atone for my sins. . . ."

"No, you can't," I said to Yexue. "There will be no peace if you take Siwang as hostage. The emperor will never let this stand, and he will exhaust every resource to get Siwang back."

"I'd like to see him try," Yexue grumbled. "My mercy comes at a price, and if he does not take this last shred of kindness with grace, then I will conquer Rong the same way he tried to conquer Lan all those years ago."

"What if I am willing to bargain for your mercy?" I said, meeting the full weight of his gaze. "Let's play a game. Whoever loses will grant the winner one wish. Whatever they want. If I win, you will let Siwang go on the condition that he signs the treaty."

I looked over at Siwang to make sure he was listening. He didn't object, which was enough of a win, I guessed.

Yexue grimaced. "Why is it always him? Why do you always choose *him*?"

Because he's Siwang. Because he's my friend. Because . . . "Because I don't want anyone else to die," I said, a half lie.

"And if I win? Then I get to ask you for *whatever* I want?"

"Whatever you want." I looked down at a stray arrow not too far from us. "The imperial hunt wasn't where we first met, but it was how our fates became tangled. It'll be poetic, letting a hunt determine everything."

Yexue laughed. "Do you think I was born yesterday? We both know you have too much of an advantage on that front."

"What do you propose, then?"

Yexue looked around the battlefield as my insides twisted. If he turned down this bargain, it would be over for Rong. And if the Rong dynasty fell, what would happen to Siwang, who was raised to do one thing and one thing alone?

Then, almost begrudgingly, Yexue nodded. "I will pick the game, and choose the location. We meet in my camp in one hour. All you have to do is bring yourself."

"Your camp?"

He looked at me sharply. "Are you scared?"

"No," I lied.

"Good." He straightened. "I am not a ward of Rong anymore. I don't have to accede to any of your demands or bargains. If you want to play, then we are going to play by my rules."

I nodded. Yexue was right. He had the power, the leverage, and he had no reason to show us grace. Especially not after Siwang's attacks.

He was doing this for me. Whatever Yexue felt for me, it was real, and I meant to take advantage of it.

I glanced at Siwang on the ground, his breath still running short. "Let your doctors tend to Siwang first," I said.

"Or I can watch him suffer."

"He can't sign the treaty if he is dead, and if he dies, the Emperor of Rong will stop at nothing to kill you."

"I'd like to see him try."

I shot Yexue a sharp look, and he shook his head. Begrudgingly, Yexue bit his finger and placed a single droplet of blood in my hand. "This will last him until the end of the day. I don't want you to think about him when you are with me."

56

Yexue met me in an archery field, west of their camp.

I swung Siwang's silver-tipped bow from my back and stepped into one of the lanes. "What are the rules? Best out of three?"

"You are impatient."

Siwang doesn't have the time to waste.

Yexue took a step forward and touched my brow, where my face still ached with bruises. "Did he do this to you?"

I pulled away. "No, he did not. It was another soldier, who thought I was a traitor. . . ."

"Tell me who it is, and I will kill him for you."

I laughed. "If I wanted him dead, I can kill him myself." Yexue opened his mouth as if to say something, then turned away. "Best out of three."

I nocked my arrow and got into position. Instead of following my lead, Yexue sneered. "I didn't say we could start yet." He came to my side and placed a finger over my hand, motioning to me to lower the weapon. "What would you say if I asked you to marry me?"

I stumbled back at the suddenness of this question. "Is that your wish?"

He shrugged. "What would you say?"

"If you asked me to marry you right here and now, no strings attached, I'd reject you."

His jaw tightened, ever so slightly. "What if there were strings attached? I hold the life of your prince and the entirety of Rong as leverage. What do you have?"

My breath hitched. "*Nothing.* I have nothing." A truth that I hated. "I hold no power and no status. I am a country girl born with a prophecy I never asked for, and a magic I can't control. But that doesn't mean I am powerless." I held the silver tip of my bow to his chest. "I am not your toy, Lan Yexue. You might be a prince, but you cannot force your will upon me, not if you don't want a fight to the death."

Yexue smiled, and his dimples dipped into existence. "The girl from the mountains is still here after all."

He pulled my chin toward him, and I forgot how to breathe.

"Look at me," he whispered. My breathing was too fast, my heart was beating too hard. "Am I so repulsive, Fei?" He leaned a little closer, his lips brushing my jaw, my neck. I felt him smile against my skin as he placed a tender kiss over a vein. "I'll be good to you," he whispered, his teeth grazing my throat.

I felt like I was burning.

It took every ounce of dignity in me not to lean into his touch, pull him close until there was no space left between us. My head was light. The heat between my legs pulsed. I wanted him closer. I wanted to feel him kiss more of me, feel his hand on my skin.

I wanted and wanted and wanted until my legs were weak, until I could barely stand by myself.

Something inside me called to him. I could practically feel my blood vibrate for him.

My mouth was so dry, and the only thing I could think of was his blood. His sweet, nectar-like blood that filled my mouth and poured down my throat and made my body come alive in ways I didn't know were possible.

Gods. I was melting in his hands, and he knew it. *Touch me,* I desperately wanted to tell him. *Touch me. Touch me. Touch me. . . .*

"You and I, we are the same. I have known this since that night in the cave. Since the moment you drank my blood and I felt the power in you, so much like my own. In this life, you'll never find any equal but me."

With that, he bit me gently, teeth pulling and sucking at flesh. Not enough to draw blood, but enough to send my body into a burning torrent of wildfire. The sound I made was something caught between a cry and a whimper.

He chuckled. "It's incredible how easily your body reacts to mine. You can hate me, despise me to your very bones, but your blood will always heed my call. You will always burn for me when I command you to."

"You—" I gasped, pushed him away with all my strength, lost for words by what he was doing to me.

Like a veil slipping from my eyes, the glimmer of everything he'd made me feel slipped away like icy silk.

The fevered hum turned spine-chilling.

"Is that why you gave me your blood to drink, why you saved my life so many times?"

"You always assume the worst of me." He laughed, a hypnotizing sound. I knew that what I'd just felt was not real, but the shimmer of it all lingered on my skin like dusted sugar, glittering and entrancingly sweet. "Both times I gave you my blood, it was to save your life. *This* was an unexpected bonus. I didn't know it was something I was capable of until recently. Most people whom I give my blood to, well . . . They don't exactly *stay* human. Or alive."

My mind was reeling. When he said he could command me, he couldn't mean . . . "You have no right to make me feel those things! I'm not a puppet for you to play with!"

He clicked his tongue, shaking his head. "Those feelings were always there. I can't coax a fire without some sparks. And if you want me to touch you, all you have to do is ask."

I went cold. "You can hear my thoughts as well?"

"No. I *feel* them. I feel a lot of your emotions, actually. It doesn't matter where you are; my blood inside you calls to me. But when you are close enough, I feel everything you feel."

I picked up my bow, abandoned when he began to touch me. "I should kill you for this."

The sound of his laughter was more beautiful than anything had the right to be. "I'd like to see you try."

I raised the bow, nocked an arrow, and pointed it right at Yexue's heart. Even this wasn't enough to wipe that infuriating smile off his face.

"You are not going to waste an arrow on me, are you?" he said. "Even if you strike me in the heart, it will be an immediate forfeit. No points unless your arrow lands on that sheet."

I remembered how my knife had bounced right off him the last time I had tried this. But Siwang's silver knife had cut him. The tip of the bow would be a perfect weapon, but did I actually want to stab the Prince Regent of Lan?

I turned, directed the arrow toward the target, and caught a glimpse of gold before firing.

Bull's-eye.

"You are not my equal, Lan Yexue."

"We'll see about that."

Yexue picked up his own bow and arrow and fired.

Bull's-eye, slightly tilting left, but he hit the center without question. He was good. Vexingly so.

I picked up another arrow.

"Are you really choosing Siwang?" Yexue asked just as I drew the bow. "You know his heart is rotten; you just don't want to admit it."

I swallowed the lump in my throat. I thought of Siwang's feral eyes when he'd tried to justify his decision to burn Changchun just to weaken Yexue.

But I also thought of all the times when Siwang had held me when my heart was heavy with fear of the future and hate for the towering red walls that kept me prisoner.

All the times he'd broken his father's rules and snuck me out to see my family because he knew how much I longed for them. All the times he'd held my hand and wandered the night markets with me, ate sugared candies until our teeth ached when he didn't even like sweet things.

When I thought of my childhood, I thought of the palace, I thought of loneliness and fear and rage and sorrow . . . and I thought of Siwang. My single ray of light. A boy who'd do anything to make me happy. A boy who loved me so much it used to terrify me to no end, because what if he didn't love *me,* but the prophecy?

If this was the fate that awaited me, then I'd rather not have it at all. If I was to give myself over to love only to have my heart broken, then I'd rather not love at all.

"Neither of you is worthy of my hand in marriage," I said, my voice trembling. I swallowed and let the arrow go a moment too early.

It hit the mark, but not the center ring. I blinked away the tears in my eyes.

"Not bad," Yexue said, though that smirk said otherwise. I wanted to slash a knife across his perfect face.

"You did that on purpose," I accused through clenched teeth. He had felt everything I had just felt. He knew the effect those words would have on me.

"You have your advantages, and I have mine."

I laughed.

"When will I be worthy of you, then?" Yexue asked while he toyed with the arrows in his quiver. "What do I have to do for you to just *look* at me, give me the chance Siwang has never earned? Do I have to kill him to make you forget him? Because if so, I'll do just that. Whatever it takes for you to care about me just half as much as you do him."

With that, Yexue nocked an arrow and fired.

Bull's-eye. I was officially losing.

"I've only ever wanted three things in life, Fei." Yexue kept talking as he moved closer; my pulse grew faster.

Focus.

I nocked the next arrow and forced my heart to calm. I would not make the same mistake twice. I would not let what he said get to me. I'd already had one misfire. I couldn't afford another. If I hit the bull's-eye this round and got him to make a mistake next round, I could still win this.

I would win.

I had to.

For Luyao. For all the soldiers on both sides of this war. All the inno-cent lives that had yet to be ruined. For my family, our little village, which was currently too close to the front lines for comfort. And most of all . . .

For Siwang.

I won't let you die.

"My mother's love, my father's acceptance, and to live as bravely as you. These were the three things that I wanted," Yexue continued. "I never got the first two, but I've been reaching for the third since that night in the cave. I want to be worthy of you, Fei. Be it by earning it, by trickery, or whatever else. I'm not going to give up."

He leaned in once more, and I felt the coldness of his breath fan-ning my cheek, my neck.

Focus, Fei.

"Maybe I'll use my wish on you after all. Because if I can't have you, neither can Siwang."

"If you use your wish to chain me to you, then you're more despi-cable than I first thought," I hissed, setting the bow and arrow down. "If you won't give me peace and quiet to finish the game, then what's the point of playing?"

Yexue's face darkened. "The next time you jump in front of a blade to protect him, or beg me to save the life of another man, I'll show you how despicable I can be. He'll sacrifice you for power, Fei. You get only one wish if you win. Will you use it to save Siwang, or have me sign the peace treaty?"

My heart went still. "If he dies because of the injuries you gave him, that treaty will be meaningless."

"*Choose one.* Peace, or him?"

Perhaps Siwang was right, that Yexue really was a monster after all. Still, I said, "I would choose the treaty."

Yexue drew a sharp breath, taking a step back to give me more space.

I picked up the bow and arrow and turned my attention toward the target across the field. The quicker we finished the game, the quicker I could leave.

A deep breath. I waited for the glimmer of gold to guide me. I had to hit the bull's-eye this one. I couldn't afford another mistake. I drew the bow at the same time that Yexue leaned a little too close and whispered, "I love you, Fei."

I stopped breathing.

The arrow veered off course, missing the target completely.

Yexue was grinning like a boy who'd just won his new favorite toy at the night fair. "You've lost."

For a moment, I had half a mind to drive the silver point of my bow straight through his heart. "That was cheating!"

"I didn't touch you." He flashed that torrid smile again.

"I want to kill you." Maybe if I killed him, this bargain would be void, no more wishes. Only blood.

If Yexue was dead, wouldn't the war between Lan and Rong automatically end? It wouldn't be the most noble way of accomplishing peace, but peace was peace. If Yexue's death was what it took to save—

"I'll sign the treaty," he said, and everything stopped. "And I'll save that pitiful prince of yours."

I stared at him. "Really?"

"This is what you wanted, right? Peace for the land, and your prince safe and sound."

I stared at him. "Were you going to save Siwang and sign the treaty all along?"

"Of course."

"So all of this was pointless?"

He leveled a stare at me, his face serious. "I've been ready to stop fighting for a long time. As long as you are loyal to Rong, as long as your family lives in Rong, I won't touch these lands. There are plenty of other kingdoms for me to conquer . . . but not this one. Not your home."

Yexue watched me, a small smile on his face. Perhaps he wanted me to cry or jump for joy and thank him for his kindness. . . .

I laughed. "Do you know what I hate the most about people like you and Siwang?" The words were out of my mouth before I could stop myself, and Yexue's smile vanished. "I hate that the two of you are always in control of everything. It has not escaped me that in all of this"—I gestured at the shooting range around us—"I am a mere pawn. You took me to Longyan because you could. Siwang sent me away because he could. And now you are saving him because . . . you can. Every decision is made by the two of you, by the men who think so highly of themselves, never me."

"I thought you would be happy that I am saving Siwang."

"I am. But I hate that the power is never in my hands. They say I am destined to be the empress of all empresses, but what use is an empress if she has to wait on the whims of her emperor?"

He softened. "I would never ask you to wait on me, Fei."

"That is not the point. And I don't expect you to understand. You are a prince who can bring people back from the arms of Death and raise an army of supernatural soldiers. You and I, we are not the same. Even if we are both cursed by prophecies we do not want, and magic we do not know how to wield. Perhaps one day when you understand what it feels like to be this powerless, I might finally fall for you."

His lips thinned. "In that case, I've changed my mind; I want something in return for my mercy."

There it was. I should have known this was too good to be true. I braced myself. "What is it that you want?"

"I will honor this agreement only if you are patrolling these borders."

I frowned and was about to ask why when I realized . . . "If you can't have me, then you won't let Siwang have me, either?" I raised an eyebrow. "Perhaps this is for the best, for me to be thousands of miles from both of you."

"Do you always have to think so little of me?"

"I will stop thinking so little of you when you do something to prove that you are not that little."

He rolled his eyes. "I am giving you exactly what you want, Fei: I am giving you power. Tell your emperor that this treaty is valid only if you are here governing these borderlands. Here you will have power. You can raise an army of your own and be the person you want to be, not the girl the gods demand that you be."

I paused. "You . . . are going to ask the emperor to let me govern these lands?"

"And keep an army of your own, so that you will never be powerless again."

My heart stopped. "Is this your wish?"

"No. That's the price of my kindness. I am not doing this for myself, Fei. Will you accept this as the price of peace?"

"I'll do it." It was the easiest decision of my life. "I'll patrol these lands until my last breath."

"Good." His smile deepened until his dimples flashed and my heart leaped.

Despite everything that frightened me about him, there was kindness in Yexue.

"And I'll keep the wish, decide what I want from you when I'm ready. Or . . . when you are ready to give me what I want."

57

North of Yong'An, sunset stained the palace's tiles the same red as a battlefield soaked in blood. Crimson lanterns illuminated the opulent halls where Siwang held the celebration of the year.

Wine poured like rushing streams into the mouths of drunken men, their hazy eyes trailing the dancing courtesans. Everybody cheered and toasted and swayed to music as the sky deepened toward midnight.

A lavish party for all the high-ranked soldiers and commanders who had fought at Siwang's side. To celebrate those who had survived, and those who had died. Tonight marked the end of a blurred week of toasting the peace treaty that would make Lan and Rong allies for decades to come.

For his part in negotiating the treaty, Siwang was appointed grand general, a position that officially put him in charge of all the empire's military forces.

Before the entire court, the emperor kissed Siwang's head and declared his merits and sacrifices. "My brilliant son," he hailed him, and everyone in the imperial halls cheered.

In the days afterward, all anyone could talk about was Siwang's vigor, how he had tirelessly fought for Rong. No one spoke of Chang-chun, those who had died. Or how this war could have ended seasons ago if it hadn't been for Siwang's vanity.

No one spoke of me, Lifeng Fei, or even Li Fei.

This is for the better, I told myself. At least the emperor showed mercy by not beheading me for treason because I'd disguised myself as a man to serve in my father's place.

To the emperor's credit, he did reward me. At Siwang's plea, the emperor agreed to let my father return to court as Siwang's advisor, thus lifting my family's exile.

But my banishment was still in place. Though it now applied only to Lifeng Fei, not Li Fei, or Little Li, as my soldiers continued to call me.

However, it still stung that my hard work was being claimed by Siwang. While the historians celebrated him, I would be forgotten because the emperor didn't deem a girl worthy of their applause.

It doesn't matter. Again, I told myself. Honor was nothing against the blissful years I had obtained for the people of our borderlands.

I hoped only that in time, their broken hearts would heal, and their hate for Lan would fade.

Or maybe not. In the corner, Caikun drank alone. A jar of wine at his lips, still clad in the bone-white robes of mourning, he softly wept with every gulp.

Across the land, thousands were crying for their fathers, brothers, sons, and grandsons.

I thought of Luyao's child . . . a baby boy, just as he'd imagined, born a month before his death. Luyao never got to hear of the safe arrival of his first and only child, because Zhangxi had no way of getting the news to him.

I blinked away the tears that always seemed to prick at my eyes when I thought about these things.

A deep breath, then I emptied my cup.

That single drop of Yexue's blood had helped Siwang make a complete recovery in a single moon. His hand was still injured. He could still write and hold a teacup, but the doctors warned him against ever holding a sword again.

Siwang didn't let this deter him. If he couldn't hold a sword with his right hand, then he would hold it with his left.

A general who can't hold a sword will never keep the respect of his men. And Siwang would die before he lost the respect of his men.

When our eyes met across the room, he smiled.

It was time for me to slip away.

After tonight, Siwang would continue his life as the crown prince and grand general, and I would return to the border as a third-ranked commander of a small battalion. We had nothing to talk about. I would keep my promise to Yexue. I would be where he could see me, far from Siwang and the glimmering capital.

Far from everything.

Where I could train my army and amass the kind of power this empire would never allow a girl to have.

Siwang claimed he wanted to honor his men, but none of my comrades were invited to the feast.

The only people he wanted to honor were those with power and status who wished for an excuse to get drunk and boast for all to hear, while the soldiers who had risked their lives were forgotten and erased.

As I headed for the exit, someone touched my elbow at the darkened corner of the banquet hall, far from the dancing girls and cheering men.

I half expected to see Siwang flushed with alcohol, but instead saw my father's face.

I gasped. *"Baba?"*

"Child," my father whispered, tears already welling in his eyes.

I threw my arms around him and hugged him with all my might, relishing his familiar scent of pinewood and green tea.

"The crown prince said he's lifted our exile and wants me as his advisor. He also told me what you did in the war, Fei. How all of this was your doing. You saved Rong, my brilliant girl. You are a hero."

Hero. "This is the first time someone has called me that."

"It is what you are, Fei." He kissed my cheek, and I cried, too. "The crown prince told me to hurry. He said tonight is my last chance of seeing you before you return to the border?"

I nodded. "I'm supposed to be in the capital for only a few days, to face the emperor and receive my fate. I made a promise to Lan Yexue that I would be back as soon as possible."

Father nodded, didn't ask further questions. "Your mother and Fangyun are so proud."

At this, I perked up. "Mama? Fangyun? Are they—"

"Your mother is on her way. Fangyun hasn't decided whether she wants to come back to the capital yet."

I smiled. When Fangyun talked about how much she preferred life outside the capital, I'd always thought she said it to comfort me. It seemed she might have been honest after all. "And you are happy? Coming back to the capital?"

My father's smile was all the answer I needed.

I might never forgive Siwang for his mistakes, but he had done the right thing by calling my father back to court. The country life wasn't for him or Mother. Father didn't read all those scriptures just to let his wisdom waste away in a bamboo shack. Besides, Siwang needed good men like him in times like these.

Perhaps if my father had been at his side before the massacre of Changchun, he could have steered Siwang back to a more moral path?

Father's hand clutched mine. "Do you have to go back to the border? The crown prince told me about your deal with Lan's prince regent. I don't think a girl should—"

"I'll be okay, Father. I have survived the war. I can survive this."

"Prince Siwang—he loves you, Fei. He really does love you. Will you ever—"

"I made my choice a year ago." I interrupted him before he could wander down a path I didn't want to revisit. "And I have never regretted it for a single day. As for life at the border? Though I will not quite live life on my own terms, I'll be free, at least. I'll visit when I can, I promise."

This was for the best.

Father, Mother, and Fangyun all belonged here, no matter how much they tried to pretend otherwise for my sake.

In the south, free of courtly expectations, I'd had plenty of time to find out where I belonged. "I'm sorry."

He frowned. "What for?"

"For forcing you and Mama and Fangyun into exile, for acting so recklessly without stopping to think how my actions could affect my family." The words poured out as tears continued to sting and well and roll down my face. "I don't regret what I did a year ago. I don't regret breaking Siwang's heart. But I do regret how it punished the three of you. . . ."

Father pulled me into a tight hug. "We don't blame you. In fact, we are *so* proud of you. The courage it took to break your betrothal, and the selfless filiality when you enlisted in my place. You are everything your name prophesized you to be. An extraordinary woman full of courage to defy the world's expectations and stand for the things you believe in. Fei, I am so proud of you. We all are. I've said this before: if I wanted you to obey and be ordinary, I never would have named you *Fei*."

"I love you, Father."

"I love you, too, child." He sighed. "I just wish the world knew it was you who brought peace to our empire. That a girl was the real hero of this war, not the prince whose name they've already etched into history."

I smiled. However, the water clock in the corner was close to midnight. "I have to go, Father. Before the gates close."

The peace between Rong and Lan was conditioned on my presence at the border at all times. Though Yexue allowed me to leave from time to time, his kindness had its limits.

With a heavy breath, my father nodded, placed one last kiss on my forehead. "Be safe."

"You, too."

We didn't say goodbye.

I didn't turn back to look at him when I walked away, afraid that if I saw tears in his eyes, I wouldn't be able to bring myself to take another step.

The border was far from the capital. With this parting, I had no idea when I'd see Father or the rest of my family again. I had no idea when I'd see Siwang again.

If ever.

Be safe, I thought to the star-strewn sky. *Be happy.*

58

In the stables, the music quieted to a hum. I took Beifeng from his stall. Siwang would miss his favorite steed, but Beifeng would enjoy a life running free in the southern fields.

One last act of defiance. And something to remember him by.

The prince trapped behind palace walls, groomed to become the emperor of all emperors. And me, bound to the borders by the treaty of my choosing.

Maybe this was the best ending for both of us. Maybe the two of us were never meant to be.

I'd always love him. And I hoped that when his harem was filled with beautiful faces from across the land, he would remember the girl he'd once promised to make not his empress, but his wife.

Maybe in another life, another story, one where my hands weren't tied by my stubborn will and he wasn't drunk on ambition and greed.

"Are you stealing my horse?" His sudden voice from the entrance startled a gasp from me. "Are you going to leave without saying good-bye, again?"

I swallowed. "I am."

He knew.

I knew.

There was no point in lying.

"Because of what I did to Changchun?"

"Because of what you did and how you tried to justify it." My voice grew harder with each word, anger straining.

I felt his warmth coming up behind me. His hand grazed my arm, and I should have pushed him away. . . .

I didn't.

"You have the right to be angry," he said.

"I'm not angry. I'm *furious.* And I'm disappointed in you."

Gently, he turned me to face him. In the moonlight, his face was flushed and beautiful, his lips lush like petals. My pulse quickened as I remembered how they had caressed my skin all those months ago in his tent.

Our single night together.

"The Siwang you knew as a child is not who I am today," he murmured. "No matter how much we both wish otherwise. Maybe that Siwang died the day you left the capital." A soft flutter of a laugh. "After you left, winning the war became my only purpose. I didn't want to disappoint my father, or the ministers always looking for a reason to criticize me, taunt my father with how I shouldn't have been chosen as heir. They wanted to bring some of my older half brothers back to the palace. They wanted my father to reconsider. And for a second there, I thought they swayed my father. This is why I couldn't sign that treaty, Fei. I had to prove I was worthy."

I stiffened. "Worthy of what? Of being a tyrant?"

He flinched. "My teachers said that in life and war, victories come with sacrifices. I thought Changchun . . ." He paused and looked down. For the first time in years, he looked more like the boy I'd once known than the man he'd become.

"I still have nightmares. I hear their screams, smell the stench of their burning flesh in the wind. I should have listened to you, Fei. I'm sorry."

Words I had rarely heard from Siwang. If this had been about anything else, it would have been enough to make me forgive him.

"It's not my forgiveness you should be seeking, Siwang." Beifeng's reins in hand, I turned to leave.

"Wait." He stepped into my path, and when he looked at me, his eyes were red with tears. "I . . . I'll find a way to break your promise to Lan Yexue. You don't have to stay at the border for long."

And that was when I knew. The man Siwang had become . . . had no idea what I wanted.

I offered Siwang a small smile. "I heard Changchun is beautiful in the summer. When they finish rebuilding the city, I'm sure that will be true once more."

59

Beifeng lived up to his name. He was truly as fast as the northern wind. The journey from the capital passed in serene solitude. I arrived as the sun set against a silhouette of Changchun. The ghost city that now marked Lan's and Rong's borders.

Where the forest broke into a clearing of camps and half-constructed barracks, a shadow was waiting for me.

"Welcome home, deserter," he murmured when I approached.

"You shouldn't be here. Isn't this a breach of the peace treaty?" I asked as I dismounted.

Though he had been waiting for me, Yexue was not looking at me. "It would only be a breach if I brought an army with me," he replied, his voice deep.

I laughed. "Did you think I was going to break *my* promise?"

Yexue shrugged, still turned away from me. "I don't know. You are a hero of Rong now. You might deem yourself too good for border patrol."

I couldn't tell if he was mocking me. "I'm not a hero. You won our competition and essentially handed the victory to me."

"You did do something," he replied, his tone no longer so haughty. "Over a year ago, you saved my life when you didn't have to. You made me believe that good does exist in this world. Every time I see you, a part of me wants to be better. The type of man my mother would have been proud of if she were still alive."

"Is that why you've now waged war west against Yan, your neighbor?"

"I said I wanted to be kind. I never said I wanted to be a saint," he grumbled, turning to face me for the first time. "The stars and the gods gave me the power to create these extraordinary creatures for a reason, and I want to know why." He stepped forward, took my un-offered hand, and cradled it in his. "And the more power I amass, the more likely I'll find someone who knows why we were born with these abilities. Someone out there must have the answers we are seeking."

And someone must know where my stargazer is hiding. "But what if the answer isn't what we want to hear?"

"Then I will find another answer, then another, until I am satisfied."

I smiled. "In that case, let's find the answer together."

EPILOGUE

All my life, I saw the future but could not control it.
Perhaps it was time to change that.

ACKNOWLEDGMENTS

To Tricia Lin. I don't know how to put my gratitude into words. You worked tirelessly to help me make this book into the best version it could possibly be. So many late nights and weekends dedicated to editing this book—sorry for missing my deadline so many times. I promise things will be less hectic for book two . . . but don't hold me to that, haha!

To Suzie Townsend, who opened the door for me all those years ago, then picked me up off the ground and helped me steer the ship when I needed it the most. Thank you for your kindness and your friendship. Your wisdom makes me a better writer, and your guidance makes me a better author. I wouldn't be here without you.

To the entire Random House team: Lauren Stewart, Caroline Abbey, Mallory Loehr, Liz Dresner, Casey Moses, Ken Crossland, Rebecca Vitkus, Clare Perret, Natalia Dextre, Josh Redlich, Cynthia Lliguichuzhca, Stephania Villar, Gabriella Murdoch, and Michelle Campbell.

To the entire Gollancz team: Bethan Morgan, Zakirah Alam, and Jenna Petts.

Thank you to the entire New Leaf team, especially Sophia Ramos, Olivia Coleman, Kiefer Ludwig, Joanna Volpe, and Tracy Williams. Fingers crossed there will only be happy tears from now on!

To the friends who held my hands and gave me endless guidance and made me laugh each time I wanted to cry. You know who you are ♥. To Taylor Swift for the amazing music. I wrote *The Nightblood Prince* before you wrote "Cassandra" and "The Prophecy," and I like to think you wrote these songs specifically for Fei. To One Direction, for the songs that carried me through my teenage years. For writing "A.M," which I played on repeat while daydreaming about Siwang and Fei in my college dorm. To Liam Payne: I'm writing this on October 18, 2024, and it still doesn't feel real. Wherever you are, I hope you are at peace now. You, Louis, Niall, Zayn, and Harry helped me make so many lifelong friends, and those video diaries still feel like a comfort blanket on bad days. To Namjoon, Jin, Suga, Hobi, Taehyung, Jimin, and Jungkook, for getting me through 2020. To the amazing authors who read early versions of this book and offered such kind blurbs. To the booksellers for the endless support. To my foreign publishers for helping me meet so many wonderful readers from all over the world. To every author who helped me escape over the years. Especially to Stephenie Meyer, Cassandra Clare, Philip Pullman, and Rick Riordan, whose books helped me learn English all those years ago. To Sabaa Tahir, whose books make me believe that someone like me can be an author, too. Special thanks to Xiran Jay Zhao and Thea Guanzon for reading early drafts of this book and giving me the invaluable feed-back, even if it's just incoherent voice notes about which love interest you like the most, hahaha.

And most importantly, to you, my dear reader. When I wrote *The Nightblood Prince,* I had intended it as a last hurrah before I gave up writing for good. As a child, books were an escape, and I wrote *The Nightblood Prince* with all the love in my heart so that it can help someone out there escape the same way. I hope you enjoyed Fei's journey, and I can't wait for the drama to continue in book two!